THE WOLF'S MOON

Patrick Jones

To Sue
Hope you Enjoy the Book
Best wishes
[signature]
9 June 2012

Cover Design and Photography
By
Sandra L. Jones, B.S. H(ASCP)

Printed in the USA

Copyright Information

Author's Note

A big, bad wolf? Not really, as wolves in the wild are doing just what they do best – being a wolf.

Wolves are beautifully majestic animals that do only the things they need to in order to survive. Seeing a wolf in the wild must be a breathtaking experience, but alas, there are few left in the wild anymore.

The wonderful Endangered Wolf Center in Eureka, Missouri (just a fifteen minute or so drive west on Interstate 44 from St. Louis, MO) is about as close that most will ever get, and that includes myself.

This story is about animals that are twice the size of a Grey Wolf, doing what their instinct says to do – hunt to survive. These animals DID exist, although they have been extinct (in some areas) only a few thousand years. Nevertheless, they are all gone now. It is known that the bones found in the La Brea Tar Pits (or Rancho La Brea Tar Pits) in Los Angeles, California, speak volumes about what can be deduced and what still remains unknown. One more thing: Wolves are wild animals and NOT suited for pets. I have never recommended it for a minute. Go to your local animal shelter and adopt a dog.

PJ

Dedication Page

This book is first and foremost for my wife who believed in me and the toughest editor I've ever met. Next is for my son and daughter and their spouses and all my grandchildren...none of whom will be allowed to read this work until they have graduated college. I love you all.

This is also dedicated to all Veterans, active duty regardless of branch, but especially to the branch of service that is just now getting recognition; their families. They are just as dedicated and as tough as SEALS.

For all of the above: OOOYEAH and thank you.

Table of Contents

Prologue

The sweet melody of Claire de Lune drifted throughout the room weaving warm gentle tones to extend a caressing peace, much like the soothing sound of waves rolling up to a beach on a star filled night. The harp's delicate hypnotic meter lingered long after ending, leaving only a memory of enchantment.

Mark Lansdowne was reading an old well-worn copy of Dante's Divine Comedy that he found in a small, out of the way, antique store some weeks earlier. It was a warm Saturday morning in mid-September, seemingly much too warm yet for that time of year, when he first saw the white building with blue trim. Affixed to the front door of the shop was a sign reading Granny Barton's Antiques. The structure looked more like a large shed with a front porch that someone hastily threw paint on, than an antique shop.

Still, Lansdowne was intrigued enough to stop his pickup truck in order to see what treasures of the past were being offered by Granny Barton, if there was a Granny Barton. The wood planks of the porch protested their age by making cracking sounds as he stepped on them. Four by four posts which supported the sagging porch roof offered to extend little confidence, yet they stood fast. As he pushed with some effort, the slightly sticking door opened to reveal that there was, indeed, a Granny Barton.

A bell at the top of the door, along with the sound of it being forced open, alerted Granny that she had a possible customer. Granny was dusting the items on a shelf when he first saw her. She greeted him with a large sincere smile. Billowing clouds of thinning white hair framed the clear wide-set blue eyes. She wore an ankle length yellow dress with a white apron over it on her short, robust body. She indeed was someone's Granny – maybe for several generations she played the part.

The building was deeper on the inside than it first appeared. He wandered through rows of true antiques, much like Granny Barton. Lansdowne, in truth, neither wanted nor needed anything more than a diversion from the emptiness he was feeling.

On the top of a cherry wood three-legged hall table was sitting an old green cloth covered book, stained by years of fingers opening and closing the cover. The edges of the pages appeared to have been gilded in gold, but they too were worn away. On the fly leaf was an inscription written in fountain pen, which was no longer legible. A small string tag taped to the book announced the price set at five dollars. What prompted him to purchase the book he could not have said except it was possibly because he thought Granny needed the money.

After handing her a five dollar bill, she placed it in an old cigar box, adding she did not collect sales tax. The government got enough of an old person's money, so she never told them about her store. Anyway, what could they do if they caught her? If they put her in jail she would be warm, have a place to sleep, three meals a day and, at her age, no one would sexually molest her. (Her grin was a bit sheepish as she made the last of her statements!)

Lansdowne smiled at the gutsy old lady, and wished if he had a grandmother that she was like Granny Barton. He thanked her and left before she went on another tirade or flirted with him anymore. As he was walking through the door he stopped, turned toward Granny Barton and winked at her. Closing the door, he heard her say something about being old was hell.

From nearly sleeping fingers, the book slipped into his lap. All the light in the room came from the table lamp next to his leather chair in which he sat reading. The light from the lamp reflected off of the polished walnut ceiling and wall panels, which Lansdowne made and hung, giving the room a rich warm glow.

He hated the lamp from the moment he saw it. He referred to it as "butt-ugly" and often threatened to put it in the trash, but his wife Glenna would tell him to shut-up and move on. The lamp was originally white plaster and after so many years of hearing Lansdowne's verbal abuse directed towards it, she decided to antique it in brown with black highlights. Glenna was so proud of her labors with the lamp that she did the same thing to two old end tables. Still, Lansdowne hated the lamp, though he never admitted it was not quite as much. He felt Glenna had bought the lamp as a retribution for one of his misdeeds. There were so many, that he was never sure as to which one. His feeling about the lamp changed after Glenna passed away a year earlier. Lansdowne, now, would never part with the lamp.

Lansdowne was lost in the dreamless twilight that comes between almost asleep and sleep. For many years he had not slept deeply. A deep slumber would mean dreams. There were far too many ghosts from the past who would invade his sleep. Many times he attempted to apologize and tried to make friends, but all refused him. Lansdowne, at those times, would force himself awake only to find himself in chilled sweats and shaking so hard that his teeth would sometimes chatter. He thought the ghosts were letting him feel the cold of the grave. During those times, Glenna would hold him close and speak in soothing tones, until the shaking stopped and he was once again warm with life. Glenna, with her slight body, was no longer there to warm him and gone was the angelic voice that chased the ghosts away. He wanted only dreams of her, but the ghosts held her at bay never allowing her entry. Lansdowne doubted they ever would.

As he sat dozing, Moe (one of his three large dogs) emitted a low throaty growl causing him to crack his eyes into slits. He knew Moe's growl signified danger. The dog was staring at the french doors which led to the patio, pond and the field of neatly cut grass beyond to the woods. Larry and Curly stared at the double doors as well. The hairs of alarm stood on end about the necks and down the backs of the three. Never moving, the three animals stayed on alert.

He listened intensely attempting to hear something that was only within the dog's range and Moe's was especially acute. Lansdowne knew from the growl and the posture of the group, that someone or something was outside the doors. Lansdowne did live in a very rural area where wildlife was abundant. A deer drinking at the pond was a possibility, but then Moe would never growl at a drinking deer. The growl was of a very real perceived danger. Moe was never wrong about these matters.

Setting the book aside on the table next to his chair, Lansdowne reached up and turned off the lamp in order for his eyes to adjust to the dark. After the pupils of his eyes dilated enough for sight, he rose from his seat and walked across the room to his desk. Opening the top left drawer, Lansdowne reached in and found the loaded .357 magnum Smith and Wesson which he kept there. Feeling the grip of the weapon, to Lansdowne, was much like shaking the hand of an old friend; familiar and reassuring.

Looking through the glass panes of the doors, a full October moon lighted the area of the pond and the field to the forest tree line. He could see nothing amiss, but Moe was never wrong. Never...

The dogs stood at the door awaiting the command to action from their master. Instead, Lansdowne spoke in low calming tones and then commanded that they stand down.

He knew by stepping through the door, because of the light from the full moon, he would be a clear target. In order to investigate he had no choice. Even though the house was painted a dark brown, he would still be somewhat silhouetted because of the moon.

Turning the handle, he opened the door and stepped into the outside night. Lansdowne left the door cracked slightly open so should he need the dogs, they could get out of the house to assist him. Otherwise they would stand fast waiting on his word.

The night was completely silent. It was devoid of all of the sounds which should have been in the night. There were neither crickets chirping nor tree frogs singing their chorus of mating songs. There were no sounds of dried leaves rustling coming from the woods, made by creatures in search of full bellies. There was total and absolute silence.

However a slight breeze stirred and carried with it an odor so foul that the hairs on Lansdowne's neck bristled as the dogs hair had done. The smell was immediately recognized by Lansdowne as old blood and rotting meat. It was more than faint and coming from the direction of the woods. Standing immobile and silent, Lansdowne strained all senses. He knew something was at the edge of the woods but it was just out of sight. He waited for whatever it was to move. Minutes turned into tens and then into twenties, as he stood silently waiting. His vigilance was rewarded by a flash of two huge red eyes, withdrawing back into the woods. The smell receded with the eyes, as the leaves and dried brush crackled under the weight of whatever it was, returning to the dark of the forest. There had been no shot possible. The distance was simply too far for an accurate hit, but Lansdowne would not have ventured an attempt. His safety was not threatened. He felt that all was clear. The tree frogs agreed with his assessment by again starting their songs of passion.

Entering the house, he was greeted by the dogs and three wagging tails. Patting each one, Lansdowne told them to lie down when he finished.

They had individual favorite places and went to them. Moe was on the couch, Larry in front of the patio doors and Curly was next to the door that led to the deck and walk to the driveway. Lansdowne replaced the firearm in the drawer and closed it, feeling there was no further need. He turned on the switch of the "butt-ugly" lamp again lighting the room. Noting the book on the table, he decided that it was no longer of interest at that time, but a cup of green jasmine tea would be nice.

Turning on a light in the kitchen, he took the tea kettle, filled it with water and placed it on the stove to boil. The clock in the stove stated to him it was twelve forty-three.

Soon the water finished boiling and the tea leaves were steeped. Settling into his chair, he lit what was to be his last cigarette of the day. After exhaling a cloud of smoke he lifted the tea cup to his lips. A small smile pulled at the corners of his mouth. Glenna taught him the proper way to make a cup of tea, but she would be furious to know he now smoked in the house.

A chuckle was leaving his throat when a series of screams thundered through the valley into the room. The last was cut-off midway through.

It was not the scream from an animal; it sounded human. Sound carried far out in the country. He could not guess how far it traveled, but had something of an idea of direction. Even with the moon, it would be too dark for investigation. Calling the Sheriff would be of little or no use. All he could say was that he heard a scream. There were still many hours until the dawn. Nothing could be done until then, he thought, as he took another pull from the cigarette.

The tree frogs agreed. They sang no more that night.

October

Chapter 1

Fall came late that year. At least to mid-Missouri, fall seemed to take all the time it wanted.

Usually, from the middle of October to the first week or so of November, the wondrous colors of yellows, brilliant reds and oranges blanket the landscapes throughout the state. The Ozark region with its hills and mountains (which are not really mountains in the sense of the Smokey's or the Rocky's, unless you are attempting to walk up one of them) are just incredibly beautiful.

New England is known for dazzling fall colors and perfect weather for viewing nature at its best. Truly, the northeastern United States is one of the loveliest areas on planet Earth. But it is no more so than the Ozark Mountain Region, which is every bit as picturesque. In less than an hour's ride by automobile from St. Louis, eyes are treated to colors from fairy tales.

For only a few Sunday afternoons can people drive the interstate freeways to see the colors and have lunch in the small towns along the way. The best places to eat are the establishments that have pick-up trucks and ten year old cars in the parking lots. The local residents know where the food is best and the atmosphere is friendliest.

Missouri has a great many wineries which have won awards that profess the quality of their beverages. None are better than the one in St. James, Missouri. Wines are made from locally grown grapes and people are touted to stop and taste. The late harvest Vignoles is one of the best anywhere.

Charter buses filled with people returning from Branson, Missouri after witnessing Las Vegas class shows and reasonable gift shopping, still wish to stop at the winery in St. James.

Many, who have spent their time boating or fishing one of the many lakes or rivers, stop as well to get that bottle which will put the top on a wonderful weekend.

Whether they lived in-state or out-of-state, all are generally entertained with the colors of fall, proving that God is truly the master of all artists.

Usually that is the case, but not that fall. God seemed to be vacationing elsewhere.

By the end of October that year, fall had failed to make much of an appearance. Everything was still far too green. Oak trees had leaves starting to turn brown and flutter to the ground, but that was about all. Flowers in gardens were still blooming and no one was yet wearing a jacket. There were no little children jumping and rolling in leaves that had been raked into neat piles. No one had many leaves to rake. Halloween is the time for kids to run door to door making excited sounds, telling bad one-line jokes, in order to load grocery bags full of goodies and crush brown leaves underfoot.

The last day of October that year was when the occurrences were noticed for the first time around the community of Maple Hills, Missouri.

Small towns dot the countryside as they do in many states. For the most part, all are great places to live and raise a family. Most people who live in small towns are good people. They go to the church of their belief on Sundays and instill family values in their children. People spend time raising their children. School buses drive the gravel roads picking school children up in the mornings and taking them home afterward, making sure a parent is meeting them.

Maple Hills is not the exception, it is the norm. With a population of twelve hundred or so residents of the town, Maple Hills has most everything to offer; although there is no hospital or movie theater (there is one of each eight miles away in Sullivan).

Being part of Maple Hills is not restricted to people living in town. There are cattle farms and a few horse ranches which surround the town. The people who work these are as much a part of the town as those inside. Most have lived in the area for generations. Everyone knows everyone and many are related by a marriage that took place at one time or another. No secret can be kept, at least not for long.

People around Maple Hills believe the statement made about "God and Guns" clearly defines who they are, and it is a good thing.

Everyone has a favorite place to eat out, gather with others of like mind and discuss events that involved their everyday lives. Barkers' was one of those places. Owned by the town pharmacist, Tim Carter, and his brother Robert, Barkers had the best steaks within twenty miles of Maple Hills. The steaks were cut from beef grown and processed in the area. They were always tasty and large and cooked to perfection. That might be the reason most of the cattlemen and their families ate there. Barkers became a town favorite in a short time after the grand opening. The name of the place came from a dog that Tim and Robert owned as kids. As a puppy the animal never shut-up, barking at absolutely everything. So naming the dog was easy. The dog Barker was long dead except in the memory of the two men, who as boys really loved the dog. Over the bar on the smoking side is a large portrait of Barker.

Most who ate there were happy that there was a non-smoking room separate from the smoking. Yet after a leisurely meal with family members, the cattlemen would drift over by the bar to have conversation and a cold beer.

Any evening, Janey Malone was seen shuttling between tables taking food or drink orders, or delivering one. She always wore a smile and had kind words for everyone. No matter how busy she would be she had time to say hello, or in some cases, a hug. Janey was an attractive woman. Long dark hair and doe-like eyes made her stand out in a crowd. She sported a natural tan all year round. Her husband, Dave, was the cook at Barkers and a fine one at that.

Dave Malone was of true Irish decent. He was fair skinned with reddish blond hair, which helped to leave little doubt as to his ancestry. He and Janey were totally devoted to each other. They were one of a handful of married couples who could not only live together, but work together as well.

As the evening wore on, Janey would deliver fewer food orders and more drinks. She would hear the conversations that would always turn to the main topic: Cattle.

The previous year was a hard one for ranchers to make a living. It was one of the worst that anyone could remember. There was a small drought for a few years prior, but the last year was terrible. It was so bad that the grass the cattle would normally graze just could not grow. Hay cuttings were scarce for winter feed. Corn prices soared and became unaffordable to many. Then winter came and it was as bad as summer. It was colder than usual with record setting snowfalls. The deep snow froze so solid it was like cement. The cattle could not dig through the snow to get at what grass might have been under it. The beef was either freezing or starving to death at record rates. Many ranchers sold off a large part of their herds at below market prices as to have enough money to feed what was left – as well as themselves.

It was said only the coyotes had made out with full bellies.

But that year had been different.

Spring arrived early that year, snow melted and sunk into the ground with the thaw. Rain had been plentiful as well and the cattle ponds full. Corn prices were still high but had leveled out. Grass grew well. Some ranchers had three cuttings. There was a surplus of hay. It seemed no cattle would starve that coming winter.

The biggest problems were rustlers and coyotes. Ranchers north and west of town were losing cattle. They would find the bodies of cows in the fields, killed and eaten on the spot. Some found nothing more than huge puddles of blood and no carcass. Others had the head count of cattle shorter each week.

The County Sheriff had been notified, as well as the Department of Conservation, by the Cattleman's Association after all of the complaints.

Everyone knew the Sheriff would find and arrest the rustlers, and as for the coyotes, they would shoot them and be done with it.

All the ranchers felt more secure for the future.

While they drank their glasses of beer and talked, they had no idea, that no matter how much corn and hay were stored away; cattle starvation was the least of their worries.

Eventually the conversation turned from ranching to the upcoming rifle season for deer hunting. Halloween was Friday, so in two weeks they would be hunting. Bow season was already open for hunting, but so far no one had as much as seen a deer. That in itself seemed strange considering all of the abundant food for the deer.

Dora Cox, the bartender, made sure the conversations continued by keeping beer mugs full. If there was a lull in the conversation she would draw someone a beer and ask a question to get them talking again. The more they talked the more beer some drank and she knew that fact. In all the years of working a bar she made but one mistake mixing a drink, she rimmed a glass of Strawberry Margarita with salt instead of sugar. Dora was so embarrassed that if she had a sword she would have given thought to falling on it. Luckily, there are few swords in Maple Hills.

Over the years, Dora heard most of the exploits of hunting the trophy deer. Each deer season she would listen to the men speak of their time in the woods, as if she was hearing the stories for the first time. Dora would smile and nod her head, while she poured another brew.

Ben Ferguson talked about the trophy buck he shot at and missed. It was the same story each year. Truth be told, Ben was seventeen when he missed that buck. On his last birthday he was sixty-three. All Dora would say as she shook her head was, "Damn shame Benny," and pour another beer.

Dora once told Robert after having listened for hours about deer hunting, that she thought hunters were almost as big a liar as what most fishermen are, (speaking about the one that got away). Fishermen just have a longer season.

By eleven o'clock few were still in the bar drinking and those that were would leave shortly. Still, Dora yelled out that it was the last call for drinks.

Dave Malone had the kitchen broke down and spotlessly cleaned by eleven o'clock. He sat at the bar and drank a beer while waiting on his wife to finish her tables. Dave would have helped her clean up, but she would not hear of it. Janey told him he was paid to cook and she was paid to wait tables. Sometimes if Robert was busy, Dave helped fill the beer boxes for the next day's business.

Even if Dave and Janey left earlier than the midnight closing, Robert paid them until twelve o'clock. Money was tight for them. Dave was a very good mechanic and picked up jobs working on farm machines or cars. Janey had several homes she cleaned each week. They had no children at home so the money they made was enough to make ends meet. Since they only lived three or four miles from town, Dave and Janey would walk home. Only in the worst of weather would they drive the car. Gas was expensive and they needed it in order to get to the other jobs. They could be seen walking over moonlit country roads holding hands like newlyweds. After twenty years of marriage they were still deeply in love.

The door to Barkers was locked at midnight and all left for their homes.

Not all would get home that night.

Chapter 2

Mark Lansdowne sat in his chair all night watching the field, the pond and beyond. Looking through the panes of glass in the patio doors, he saw the moon pass behind the trees. He saw the dawn rise in the eastern sky. The sun caused the sky to turn a rose color, making him think what the Greek poet Homer called, "the rosy fingered dawn".

He had not slept, only sat and watched. There was no further movement outside all night. All was quiet.

Coffee sounded good to Lansdowne. He went into the kitchen, filled the coffee brewer with water and coffee, and then went to shower while it cooked.

Water in the shower felt extra hot and he thought that it felt good as he was toweling off. Taking a dry hand towel he wiped the steam from the mirror. Pale green eyes looked back at him while he examined his face. He decided again not to shave that day. It was several weeks since he shaved. His beard, not long before, had been dark but was now streaked with grey. Maybe too much so, still he was not about to shave. He did make a mental note to call Amie to get his hair cut. She cut Glenna's and his hair for many years.

Lansdowne was always glad to see Amie. She pampered him with what she called "manscaping" (styling his hair after washing it). Amie may have pampered him a bit more after Glenna died but it was only out of kindness. Lansdowne could talk to her as a friend. She had the two B's, brains and beauty, as well as a wonderful personality. She smiled, not only with her mouth but with her wondrous hazel colored eyes, making him feel that it was for him but knowing it was for everyone. Even to those difficult clients that she would have loved to take the electric clippers down the middle of their hair. Nonetheless, she was patient and kind to all.

Lansdowne would never love her as anything more than a friend, who he deeply respected. There were few of those in his life, far too few.

That morning he dressed as he did most days, blue jeans, sweatshirt and boots. The house was filled with the aroma of fresh brewed coffee and he was eager to drink a cup or two. He had a problem. No clean cups were to be found. He went to the dishwasher and withdrew the least dirty, rinsed it out and poured a cup of the hot black liquid.

As he looked around, he realized the house needed cleaning. He just used his last clean towel and was drinking his morning coffee, out of a not quite completely dirty cup. He would call Janey Malone later, he thought. She never minded how much it was a mess. If he did not call her, it was eat out or paper plates at dinner. He would call her.

The coffee cooled enough to drink. It tasted strong as he sipped it.

All of the dogs were dancing in circles wanting out. Knowing that there was a short period of time before he would be subject to a very unpleasant clean up, Lansdowne opened the door. The three large dogs very nearly knocked him down, each attempting to be the first outside. Lansdowne followed.

The morning air was cooler than what it had been lately. It felt as though fall had finally arrived. Dew drops glistened in the soft warm sunlight.

Lansdowne watched as the three dogs set to their morning task of marking each tree along the forest border. They marked a perimeter of territory as they urinated on anything in their path, until reaching the location where Lansdowne had seen the glowing eyes. There, they were curious about the scent that was left. All the dogs sniffed the ground and then turned to look at him. They looked into the woods wanting to follow whatever had left the vile odor. They stood waiting on a command each hoped would be given.

Lansdowne lifted his cup for another drink and found it empty. As he crushed out the cigarette in an ashtray on the patio he decided two things. The first was to have another cup of coffee and the second was to investigate the woods.

After pouring the coffee and before going outside again, he slipped the revolver into the small of his back. Having the weapon was nothing more than a precaution in his mind.

Standing by the patio table drinking his coffee, he breathed the morning air deep into his lungs and then exhaled through his nose. That would help to clear his sinuses of the cigarette smoke.

It did not matter. The wind changed direction and the stench, although not as prominent as the night before, was certainly discernible to him. Setting the cup on the table, he first headed to the pond.

Wildlife of all types would come to drink from the pond. It was not overly large, being about a quarter of an acre round but fifteen feet deep at the middle. Lansdowne placed several corn feeders by the water so wildlife could eat as well as drink. He did so at Glenna's urging and then after a while, her insistence. The feeders provided many hours of enjoyment for he and Glenna. Many evenings they watched the deer run from the pond after noticing the humans. After some time the deer, as well as other wildlife, came to know that no harm was intended. Still being vigil, the animals ate and drank at the pond.

When asked once by a neighbor if he was deer hunting that season, Lansdowne smiled and shook his head saying, since discovering grocery stores he no longer needed to hunt for suppers.

He had no problem with those who did hunt. Being the cause of so much death before he met his wife, Lansdowne simply did not wish to cause any more harm to man or animal.

On the bank around the pond were imprints of paws from many animals. The only fresh tracks were from his dogs. All the rest were barely discernible. No other animals were at the pond for some time. He checked that the feeders were still full of corn, even though several weeks before he filled them. Acorns from the oaks were falling but not to the degree that the corn had not been touched. It seemed that the squirrels did not stop by for a snack either.

Lansdowne continued to walk the perimeter of the pond seeking any type of fresh paw prints. On the side of the pond that faced the woods he found some new ones, as well as the smell from before.

The prints were huge, bigger than what Curly's, with his one hundred and twenty-five pounds of Rott-Sharpei mix, would make. The prints looked to be twice as big and twice as deep. His dogs did not make these. He was able to see that the tracks led to the woods where he had seen the eyes and the "guys" stood waiting for him. Distance from the front paw to the rear looked to be four to four and a half feet.

Lansdowne shook his head. That estimate could not be correct, yet there was the proof. Something else that he noticed was that there were no nail marks left. Dogs leave nail marks from their paws. Maybe a Mastiff or a St. Bernard could have left the tracks. A dog of that size certainly could. People dumped dogs all the time out in the country. He had once found a female Doberman, who appeared to have just had a litter of pups not long before, dead on the road. Someone dumped the body.

It was not impossible that it was a wild dog.

All the years of training did not include animal identification from tracks, after all he was a city boy.

"Time to find out who our mystery guest is," he said to himself out loud. He chuckled. He was talking to himself more lately. Maybe if he got out more around other people?

Lansdowne thought if he was going looking for something of the size he suspected, bigger firepower may be in order.

Returning to the house, he picked up the coffee cup and placed it in the dishwasher, placed soap in the dispenser and turned the machine on. That would help Janey Malone when she came to clean the house. He still needed to call her and Amie. When he returned later he would do so, he thought.

Walking into the guest room, he opened the closet. He moved all of Glenna's clothes into it from their bedroom. He meant to donate them to a charity, but was just not ready mentally to part with any of them. Pushing them aside, he unlocked an inner closet. Reaching in, he withdrew a Remington pump shotgun. The barrel was twenty-eight inches long and it had a modified choke, so that it could fire slugs. The block was removed as to accept five rounds of ammunition. Setting the safety, he loaded the weapon with slugs and then placed it on the guest room bed. Lansdowne donned an old camo blouse over his sweatshirt. In the hip pocket he put more ammunition. With the revolver still in his back and picking up the shotgun, he left on his expedition into the woods.

Whatever he was trailing would be easy enough, he decided. Even if he could not find any tracks or if it used game trails, all he had to do was follow the stink that was still there. The dogs and Lansdowne entered the woods and disappeared from sight.

Chapter 3

Mark Lansdowne did not have to go far into the woods before he found visible sign. At the edge of the field where it met the tree line, grass was matted down. Something had laid there. That something was what he saw the prior night. The smell was still strong and led away into the forest.

Sunlight slipped through breaks of the canopy of leaves yet holding on the trees, lighting the forest. Birds sang their morning songs, only to stop when the group slowly walked past. The squirrels ran along the branches searching for nuts and acorns which should have littered the forest floor but as of yet had not fallen.

Lansdowne could not help but notice that they were not directly above him. Whether it was because of him and the dogs or the odor which rose from the ground when the breeze would stir, or even something else altogether, he could not say. The game trail he walked was old and it seemed not to have been used for quite some time, yet the odor was leading the way. Brush and grass was thick to either side of the path. Scrub trees along the way showed no signs of use by deer, who would rub the itching velvet from new grown antlers. The few rubs that were visible had been caused seasons long ago, demonstrated by the healing of the bark on the trees.

Larry, who was the largest of the three dogs in height and who weighed well over one hundred pounds, led the way. Moe had the best hearing; Larry's nose was the best. Once given a scent, Larry could find anything. That day Lansdowne did not need Larry for tracking. His own nose did just fine.

Along the path, Lansdowne would stop to examine an imprint in the ground. The ones he saw were fresh and from the size, were made by his dogs. What struck him as strange about the paw prints was that there were no nail marks like what his dog left on the dirt; the prints of pads but no claw or nail impressions.

The scent was becoming more pronounced with every step. It may have been stronger because the game trail ran between two hills, with the distance between them narrowing. Here the brambles and brown dried grass were almost as tall as Lansdowne, who stood almost six foot tall. It reminded him of times and places from before.

The hill to the left of Lansdowne had a rock face that buttressed it to nearly the top. Wind blowing through the narrow caused the smell to become sickening. Lansdowne had not smelled the odor that strong for many years. The smell of meat left rotting in the sun for many days. As he forced himself forward, not only could he smell it, he could taste it as the stench attacked his sinuses.

Moe and Larry would go no further. Curly was nowhere to be seen. The two dogs were on alert much like the night before, as they stood where the game trail narrowed leading to the rock face. Lansdowne tried to quiet the dogs, with little success. They were trained to protect and that was exactly what they were doing. With a much more stern but quiet voice, he commanded the two dogs to stand down. The animals stopped growling, but were ready for action should the need arise.

Curly's Rottweiler body broke through the brush. In his mouth was a bone. Lansdowne told Curly to drop the bone. He was reluctant to do so but the tone of Lansdowne's voice indicated it was a wise idea, so he did.

Examining the bone, or what was left of it, he saw it had been gnawed by massive molars. The socket ball was intact and still had the tendons attached. It was long but light in size. Where the bone was broken he noticed something shiny. Wiping the dirt away, he saw it was a screw. He held, what Lansdowne believed to be, a human femur. A sick feeling came over him as he put the bone fragment into his left blouse pocket.

He was fairly certain that there was no other animal in the immediate area or Curly would not have made off with the bone fragment so easily. Still, caution seemed reasonable. Unshouldering the shotgun, he pumped a round into the chamber and released the safety with his index finger. Placing his finger alongside the trigger guard, he commanded the dogs to stay, not wanting to shoot one by accident.

There was a small amount of tension in his neck and shoulders as he walked forward through the high grass. Lansdowne had no idea what he would find, nor was he anxious to see. He had placed himself in the position that turning back was not an option. Most probably, he would not have turned back if there had been the opportunity. His curiosity was far too high, as was his adrenalin.

The tall grass gave way to a clearing under the rock face. At the bottom, there seemed to be a possible cave opening. Throughout the clearing bones littered the ground. Before him, bones that he could identify as bovine and deer lay white and shining in the sunlight. Stepping forward and attempting not to step on any of the bones, he studied the area. Something which left large paw prints had been feeding there for a long time, a very long time.

Walking lightly, he would toe a bone out of his path as he advanced toward the mouth of the cave. The circumference of the clearing, as best Lansdowne could judge, was twenty feet. To his right was another opening from the outside into the clearing. Wary of a possible attack from there, he turned and faced the trail while still heading toward the cave. The dogs were covering his back, so he had no fear of a rear attack, should whatever the animal was return.

The smell was concentrated in the cave. Lansdowne, to avoid the stench, was breathing through his mouth, closing his sinus passages. Otherwise, he would not have been able to tolerate the overwhelming odor.

On the ground, a yard or so inside of the cave, the other part of the femur lay. He was sure it was the mate to the piece in his pocket. It had two screws in it as well but it was still attached to the rest of the leg, which was in what was left of designer jeans. The foot had a tennis shoe yet on it. The torso was on its back and the meat on the front as well as most of the internal organs, were gone. Part of the right breast was there. Looking up the body farther was long brown hair matted in blood with leaves mixed in.

There was one brown eye staring at him. Flies were coming and going from where the other had been, as well as from the mouth. The mask of absolute terror was still on the dead face of Janey Malone, whose head was barely attached to her neck.

Chapter 4

As on most nights after closing and locking the door to Barkers, Dora Cox and Robert Carter would offer Dave and Janey a ride home. And as most nights they would thank them, but refuse unless Janey's leg was causing her more pain than was usual. The right one she broke shortly after being wed to Dave and it needed four screws in order for it to mend.

Dora and Robert did not live together. They were neighbors but both knew one day that would change, just not yet.

Dora still needed time. She divorced her ex, Myron Cox, only the year before. What could have been a messy termination of marriage actually went very smoothly, after Dora was found not guilty of shooting Myron in both legs, blowing his kneecap out. The incident was clearly self-defense.

Myron Cox was a wealthy, mean drunk, and he was drunk most days. His mouth would overload his ass to someone bigger or tougher, while drinking. He would end up getting the snot beat out of himself. So when he got home he would beat Dora. For several years she explained the black eyes and bruises coming from her own carelessness, as do so many other abused women. When he did not punch on her, the verbal abuse was almost as bad. Dora lost self-esteem and self-confidence.

That is, until the night he picked up the fireplace poker to hit her. She ran to the gun case and took out the shotgun, pointing it at him. Laughing as he raised the poker to strike, she pulled the trigger blowing his leg out from under him. Even though there had only been one shell in the twelve-gauge, she continued to rack the pump-action and pull the trigger.

At that moment she hated him so much and wanted him dead to end the abuse from which she had suffered for so long.

Once the rage had passed, Dora called the Sheriff stating she had shot Myron. The 911 operator could hear his screams and sent an ambulance and deputy. Dora went to the kitchen and poured a cup of coffee, lit a cigarette and waited for the Sheriff, as Myron screamed in pain.

The investigation proved Dora had acted in self-defense and should have been the end of the matter. Should have been, but was not.

Myron Cox had two very rich parents that refused to believe that their son was capable of doing the things Dora claimed. They lived in the wealthier suburbs of St. Louis and had only occasional contact with Dora and Myron. They felt it was that "crazy country bitch" that was at fault.

After several months and a great deal of money and favors spent by Myron's parents, Dora was charged with assault in the first degree. The trial took one day and the jury less than a half an hour to return a not guilty decision. Myron Cox and his parents really pissed off the trial judge over the matter, so it went quick with the divorce.

Dora ended up a very wealthy young lady, getting half of the value of the fifteen hundred acre ranch, livestock and home. She also got the forty-five acre and home piece of property that was jointly owned.

The property joined Robert Carter's place, rather his parents land. He bought a few acres from them and put a modular home on it. From where Robert lived he was able to see Dora's house. That is how they met one morning.

Dora's house, though structurally sound, needed a great deal of attention. Robert went to Dora's and introduced himself. They spent an hour talking about the house. She told him she could clean and paint but that the electric needed to be looked at, and that her only water was from the hand pump. She cooked on a white gas camping stove until she could get propane delivered and lighted the house with candles.

Robert volunteered to work on the electric and water. She was hesitant at first, but remembering she would once again have to wash at the kitchen sink after dragging a couple of gallons of water from the pump, she relented. She would pay him for his work. Robert went home, got some tools, and immediately on returning started checking the electric. The wiring and outlets were good. He opened the breaker box, pulled the main, and checked the breakers for corrosion. All he found wrong was that a mouse had made a nest, which he promptly cleaned out. Dora called the electric co-op to get the power turned on. Later that afternoon she had power. Robert opened all the faucets, crossed his fingers, and threw the breaker for the water pump. Immediately the faucets all spit water as air was pushed from the pipes.

Dora was thrilled. She looked a Robert with a "my hero" face. That evening he took her to dinner at Barkers. She attempted to pay for dinner but could not get a check from Janey Malone. Robert told her that dinner was on him, that he could not bear to think of her cooking on a camp stove. Anyway he owned the place, or half of it. Dora started working behind the bar a week later.

For the next several weeks when Robert was not tending to cattle or working at Barkers, he was working at Dora's house. Sometimes they would just sit and talk. Dora did most of the talking now that there was someone who listened and seemed honestly interested. Robert by nature was quiet, but he really liked the sound of Dora's voice.

Late one afternoon, Myron Cox drove up the white gravel driveway to the front of Dora's house. Getting out of the older white Cadillac, which now looked beige because of road dust, was a chore. His right kneecap was gone from the shotgun blast along with a good part of his left thigh. Being more drunk than usual made the task that much more difficult. He used a cane now and cursed Dora, especially when the weather changes caused him pain. He blamed her for his lack of mobility.

Myron was far too drunk for an attempt up the steps to the porch so he stood at the bottom yelling drunken slurs, as he beat the cane on the steps. He demanded she come out of the house. His whisky soaked plan was to beat her to death with his cane.

Hearing his voice, Dora started to shake. Her stomach did flip-flops up to her throat. Tears filled her eyes as past memories flooded through her brain.

Myron continued to curse her while beating the steps and porch with his cane. The longer he had to wait, the angrier and meaner he became. His yelling at the door kept getting louder because she would not meet his demands.

Robert, who was working at the rear of the house, heard the commotion and walked to the front and confronted Myron Cox. Carter was a head taller than Cox. He in the past handled a drunk or two at Barkers. Ordinarily most, after seeing his piercing stare, left quietly. Those that did not, still left. Some people compared Robert to a rattlesnake. He would give a warning, then strike.

"You're Carter, aren't you?"

Robert nodded and then said, "Time for you to go."

"You her boyfriend or just screwing her?"

"That was disrespectful. No to both questions. Like I said, time to go. Now!" Robert's voice was just a bit louder than a whisper.

Myron Cox was also a stupid drunk. Taking his cane, he swung it at Robert's head trying for a "Babe Ruth". Carter stepped out of the way as the cane swooshed the air in front of his face. The momentum of the swing carried Cox around causing the cane to fly from his hands. Two disabled legs, along with too much Jack Daniels, helped Cox fly several feet from where he had stood, landing face down in the grass hitting hard.

Robert picked the cane up from the ground. Gripping Myron by the back of his hair and collar, he dragged him to the car. Opening the door of the Caddy, Robert threw the cane on the backseat and

Myron on the front, where he commenced to puking on the passenger's side of the floor. When he finished getting sick, he pulled his legs into the car after righting himself behind the wheel and drove off. He stopped long enough to scream from a puke and tear covered face, that he would be back to kill them both.

Shaking his head and smiling, Robert rather doubted it.

Dora watched and heard everything from the front window. Seeing Myron Cox leave her property was a relief for her. She was still shaking and crying when she pulled open the door and ran down the steps into Robert's arms. He held her close saying nothing, while she sobbed.

Once she settled down enough to compose herself, Dora told Robert, "He will be back."

Robert gently pushed her back enough to kiss her on the cheek. Smiling at her, he told her that if Myron did return it was okay. He was not going anywhere for long. He would stay close.

Through tear filled sky blue eyes, she smiled at Robert. For the first time in a very long time, Dora Cox felt safe.

Later than night, Dora's feelings about her safety and security changed.

Robert had to go to work at Barkers that night. He wanted Dora to go with him but she refused, saying she had things to do around the house. Promising to lock all the doors and first floor windows, Robert reluctantly left for work. He was due by six o'clock. Dave and Janey Malone should already be there working.

Robert understood Dora did not wish to be around people who would ask why her eyes were so red. Everyone would have asked. Robert Carter arrived at Barkers to find Dave and Janey were not there working. Ann Marie, the day manager, said she called several times since five o'clock with no answer at their house, or on either cell phone. She agreed to stay and wait tables and Robert would work the bar as planned. He asked the part-time cook to stay until Dave arrived. Robert could not imagine where the Malone's were. They had never missed a day of work. Even if they would be a few minutes late, they would call to let someone know.

Dora needed to keep busy. There was laundry to be washed and dried. She turned on the television, more for noise than for entertainment. Being alone may not have been such a good idea, she thought. Robert would probably stop by to check on her after he closed. That thought alone, that Robert would see to her safety, made her feel better.

After finishing the laundry and eating a late supper, she drifted off to sleep while waiting for Robert.

She awoke to the sound of a car coming up her driveway. A car door opened and then closed. Dora glanced at the clock. It was eleven-twenty, too early for Robert. Dora thought he would not be there for another hour.

Looking out the blinds that covered the front windows, she saw the white Cadillac. Myron Cox was screaming obscenities while attempting to climb the steps, taking one up and then resting before trying the next. He was no longer as drunk and he was sure Robert was not in Dora's home.

After leaving earlier, Myron went home and fell asleep. Upon waking, he sat and stewed over what he believed Robert had done to him. The longer he thought, the angrier he became. When he had a few more drinks inside of himself, he decided it was payback time. Grabbing the oak cane with the heavy brass handle and a bottle of whiskey, he headed to Dora's. She was going to pay for the embarrassment imposed upon him by Robert. He would beat her like a red-headed stepchild. She was going to hurt as bad as he did every minute of every day. In his whiskey-soaked brain, he never gave a thought as to how long it would take him to get up the stairs onto the porch, or how he could get through a locked door. Standing on the steps, all he thought of was beating her, busting her up to a bloody pulp.

Seeing Myron, Dora ran to the phone and called Robert. He could be to her house in ten minutes if he hurried. The phone at Barkers rang and rang. She hung up and redialed the phone number. Still it only rang, with yet no answer.

Myron was up the steps, still yelling for her to open the door. He beat the door with the brass handle of the cane. Each time he struck there was a solid "thud" which shook the door.

Dora kept calling Robert. There were only four deputies working for the Sheriff's department and they had the entire county to patrol. She did not feel they could arrive before Myron could get inside the house.

Finally, Robert answered the phone. Dora said that Myron was beating down the door. He said that he would return to kill her and now he was there.

He told her that he was on the way. Robert, in a hurry, told Ann Marie to lock up as he ran to the office and got the 9 mm handgun kept there. Running out of Barkers, he jumped into his car and headed toward Dora's home.

Myron's beating on the front door slowed up. He had used all of what drunken strength he had. Now he leaned against the door yelling to let him inside, saying he only wanted to talk.

Dora stayed back from the door sitting as a huddled mass, her arms folded around her legs. She rocked back and forth, shaking and crying. She was more scared than the night she shot him.

Myron started beating the door again, this time though with his fists, not the cane. He screamed for her to let him into the house. His screams were not of rage, but of fear. In Dora's mind, she could not tell the difference.

"Let me in! Please! It will kill me! Please Dora, Please!"

Dora heard a scream from Myron much like the one he screamed the night of the shooting, but this one was cut-off midway through.

Still, she sat on the couch rocking. She was not moving from the spot. Moments later, headlights of a car shined through the blinds. She heard a car engine. The car stopped in front, then moved around to the rear of the house and the engine cut off. Dora's phone rang. Quickly she picked it up. It was Robert. He was at the back door and wanted inside.

With the phone yet at her ear, she ran to the door and unlocked it. Robert practically pushed her out of the way as he entered the house with the pistol in his hand. He went room to room checking windows. Myron was not seen by Robert in the front nor the back of the house, or on the side as he drove past. He told Dora maybe Myron saw his car and was hiding around the outside of the house. He would look to see if that was the case.

Flipping the switch for the front porch light, Robert opened the door. As Robert started to step through the door, he heard Dora stifle a scream. He stopped and turned his head to look at Dora. With wide eyes and an opened mouth, she stared at the outside of the door. He turned his head to see what Dora was looking at. A good amount of red splatter covered the outside of the door. At the threshold was a pool of the same red, which trailed to the end of the porch.

Myron's cane was there on the porch.

Myron's car was in the driveway.

Myron was not.

Chapter 5

Mark Lansdowne saw enough, maybe too much. His stomach was turning, not just from what he saw but from the revolting putrid smell. Closing off his nose no longer was much of a help. As he backed out of the cave into the clearing, he avoided looking into Janey Malone's dead face. He did not want to see her like that again.

It was easy to like her. She had a wonderful smile, worked hard and was easy to look at, especially in the summer when she cleaned his house in shorts and a halter top. Janey thought nothing of dressing like that. She and Dave knew Lansdowne only wanted his house cleaned and dusted and he paid more than the others she cleaned. The only drawback with her, to Lansdowne, was she talked the entire time while cleaning. It was such a small thing and in time he came to like the sound of another woman's voice in the house. He so missed Glenna's voice that no matter what she said, Lansdowne listened to Janey.

He thought that there were more human remains in the cave, but without a flashlight he could not be sure. There was not enough sunlight for visibility nor was he sure how deep the cave went back. Janey had been fed on near the mouth of the cave and with the midmorning sun he was able to see her body.

The one thing that he thought not only possible, but probable, was whatever had killed Janey would return. That area was a feeding ground.

He could sit and wait for it to come back and kill it. Looking over the sheer size and scope of the area, it did not seem any one creature could have committed such havoc. Lansdowne was not a trained animal tracker and could not say if all the tracks made in the ground of the clearing were from multiple animals. He guessed it would have had to have been more than one. Several, he thought.

It was time to go. He was not Dana Brown and big game hunting was not his thing. Lansdowne was more than angered over what had befallen Janey. He was downright pissed but he knew that this was more than what he could handle alone. It was a problem for the Sheriff or the Department of Conservation. The Department of Conservation had good people working for it. Maybe one of them was a Dana Brown.

He stood listening for movement toward his location. Hearing none, he eased from the clearing to the trail where the dogs were waiting for him. Lansdowne safetied the shotgun but kept it at the ready.

Moving back onto the trail, he set his jaw in anger and disgust. Knowing that there was nothing more he could do was of little consolation. It went against his grain not to avenge Janey.

Lansdowne did not bring his cell phone, not that he would have had a signal. He was too deep into the forest. Even if he brought the phone and had a signal, there was no way to explain where the clearing was located. Knowing that after the proper authorities were notified he would still have to lead them back to where Janey was, angered him still more. Having no choice but to leave her did nothing to make his disposition any sunnier.

The pace back was quicker, as he now knew the way and did not need to stop and look for tracks. The dogs had a harder time moving through the dense brush than did Lansdowne, who used his body like a bulldozer seemingly mowing down everything he encountered.

Breaking through the last of the scrub trees and brush into the field, he could see his pond and the house just beyond. He ran at a pace only the dogs could keep. They stopped at the pond for a drink while he continued to the house.

After unloading the weapon he entered the house, going directly to the liquor cabinet. Taking out a glass, he poured himself three fingers of vodka and drank it down in a single swallow. Wanting another, he decided against it, at least not until he notified the Sheriff's department.

The 911 operator who answered his call sounded a bit bored and possibly a tad irritated at being disturbed. The operator, who identified herself as Jenkins, asked what type of emergency. Lansdowne said he had found a dead person in the woods by his house. Asked if he was certain the person was dead, he responded that he was "quite certain". He gave his name and address, saying he would meet and direct the officer upon his arrival.

After ringing off from the police, Lansdowne poured himself another glass of Vodka from the almost empty Smirnoff bottle. This one he took into his kitchen and added ice from the freezer.

Taking his drink, he went to the front deck to await the Sheriff. He did not want to return to the horrific scene he had earlier encountered, but he would have to lead the Sheriff's deputy to it.

Lighting another cigarette and having another sip of the cold vodka, he thought about the events of the morning. He tried to make sense of it. Finally, he decided it was simply that "something" killed and ate Janey Malone. Furthermore, it was just not his problem or responsibility. Yes he liked Dave and Janey, but the situation now belonged to the authorities.

Dave Malone. Just where was he? Lansdowne could not imagine just where he could be, or how something could have killed Janey.

He was going to have to find someone else to clean the house. Lansdowne shook that thought from his mind. It was completely out of line and totally disrespectful toward Janey. Still, he would have to look for someone else but that was another day. As for then, he would wait for the Sheriff.

Crawford County Sheriff's Department does not have the number of deputies that the Sheriff, Ralph Benson, would have liked. As with so many other Police Departments, there was just no budget for more officers. The officers he did have were good, truly professional men and women. Benson was proud of the department and the people, both civilian and commissioned. He just wished the budget could allow for more personnel, but more people were something that was just not going to happen.

When it got busy and the Sheriff did not have the manpower, the towns that are closest or the Highway Patrol could be counted on to assist with incidents.

Benson would make himself available to take radio calls when he was on the road. He felt just because he carried the title of County Sheriff did not remove duties of a policeman. That is what he was, first and foremost, a policeman.

Sheriff Benson took the call of a man down and responded to Mark Lansdowne's residence. Morrison, one of the deputies, was on call at Dora Cox's home and several others were working a fatal accident over on Highway L. They would be tied up until relief time with that, and the Highway Patrol out of Rolla, Missouri was assisting them. That was where Benson was heading when he took the man down call.

He had met Lansdowne a few times at different social events that commanded his presence, when he would have rather have been doing something else. Those things were part of the job and he did want to be re-elected. The conversations between Lansdowne and himself had been for the most part, brief but interesting. Benson prided himself as a decent judge of character and felt Lansdowne would not give in to call rashly. If he called, there was something to it.

Recalling the last time he spoke to Lansdowne, his wife Glenna was alive. That was at the annual chili cook-off where he and Lansdowne were judges. He and Lansdowne, after the judging, ate a half of a bottle of Rolaids each, and drank several bottles of beer in order to put out the fire in their stomachs and throats. Neither of the men wanted the job of judging, but their wives nominated them. Benson really liked Lansdowne and his wife. She always smiled. They were a great looking couple and were very much in love with each other. It was a damn shame she passed away so early in life. He could not remember exactly what she died from, but he thought it was the flu or something like it.

Since her passing Lansdowne stayed to himself, he thought, as he turned the patrol car onto the white gravel driveway. Benson saw Lansdowne sitting on the deck as he stopped the car and radioed the dispatcher of his arrival.

Lansdowne met him as Benson was opening the car door, and replaced the radio microphone on the stand. After stepping out of the car, he shook the hand Lansdowne extended.

Benson told Lansdowne he was sorry when he heard about his wife. Lansdowne could only bow his head and nod his thanks. He was not prepared for Benson to bring up Glenna's death.

Lansdowne composed himself and then explained the reason for the call. He related the events of the previous night, leaving out seeing the eyes that looked back at him. He went on to explain about his morning excursion into the woods and as to what he had found.

Benson listened to every word trying to fully digest the possible implications. Over the miniature police radio that the Sheriff wore on his gun belt, he heard Deputy Morrison receive an assignment to meet an officer on Lone Creek Road. That was a few miles north of Benson's present location.

A look of astonishment washed over Ralph Benson's face, one that from most anyone else telling the tale would have looked more like disbelief. He knew from conversations he had held with Lansdowne in the past that every word spoken was truth, but he also knew Lansdowne was holding some information back.

The police radio crackled again and Benson heard Morrison ask for the Sheriff's location. Benson raised a finger for Lansdowne to wait. He answered Morrison telling him he was at Lansdowne's residence. The deputy asked for Benson to meet him on channel two of the police radio. That is the frequency that is scrambled to scanners. Channel two is only used when something is about to be said that needs to be shielded from the listening public, or more importantly the media.

Lansdowne nodded to the Sheriff that he would wait and stepped a few feet away so Benson could listen and speak with a degree of privacy.

Morrison related how he received a call to meet an officer. It was from Christine McKay from the Department of Conservation. She was on her way to a report of a deer struck by a car, when she noticed someone in the ditch on the side of the road. Stopping to see if she could help the person, she found Dave Morrison dead. Benson asked if he had been struck by a car, to which Ron Morrison replied, "I don't think so, boss. You really need to come and see this for yourself. Dave is dead."

Lansdowne could not help but to have overheard the conversation. Taking the bone fragment from his pocket, he handed it to Benson, who was wide-eyed as he saw the chew marks which were readily evident. "Do you remember when Janey Malone broke her leg on the ice? She fell down the hill by her pond." Benson shook his head. He had not known about the accident.

"She was going to fill the corn feeders and slipped. Janey was wedged between the trunks of two trees. Dave found her after an hour of her yelling for him. Janey needed screws placed in her leg."

Benson examined the bone closer and saw the screws.

"I know where Janey is at. She's dead too."

Benson now knew what information Lansdowne was holding back from him.

Chapter 6

Sheriff Ralph Benson's wide-set eyes narrowed as he studied the bone fragment Lansdowne handed to him. Grooves in the bone appeared to have been made by massive teeth, although Benson could not have said what type of animal made them. The bone looked fresh. Blood on the fragment had dried brown but enough red still existed to announce age. The ball socket was chewed on, cracked open just enough for the marrow inside to be evident. Strands of tendons that were attached to the underside of the ball and heel were almost completely gnawed away.

Lifting his gaze from the bone, he looked directly into Lansdowne's green eyes and face. His face was granite, as if chiseled by a stone mason, and belied nothing as to Lansdowne's thoughts and feelings.

"And you think this belongs to Janey Malone?"

"It does," Lansdowne said matter-of-factly. "I found the rest of her in much the same condition. She's in a cave about a five klic walk through the woods…or she was there an hour or so ago. Whatever animal that killed her will probably be back to finish it's feeding.

"You think?"

"Yeah, pretty sure anyway. There was a lot of her left; rather there was an hour ago. There wasn't anything around then or Curly could not have snaked the bone and I would not have been able to go in or leave."

"Who's Curly?"

"I'm sorry, my Rott. I took the dogs with me, strength in numbers. Perhaps you may want to see Dave first and then come back? I'm only guessing, but I'd bet the two incidents are related."

"Good bet," said Benson as he walked to the rear of his patrol car. Opening the trunk, he took out a clear plastic evidence bag and placed the bone fragment into it. With the pen from his shirt pocket, he wrote the date and time on the bag, then placed it in the trunk and closed the lid. As Benson got into the car and started the engine, he told Lansdowne he would be back as soon as possible.

Lansdowne only nodded his head and watched Benson head to Lone Creek Road and Dave Malone.

The drive to Lone Creek Road was a short one for Benson, using red lights and siren. During the drive, his mind raced through the events of the morning so far and Benson wondered as to what he was going to encounter.

Turning the car off the state highway and onto the brown gravel road, Benson could make out the flashing lights of Deputy Morrison's patrol car and the ambulance. Both emergency vehicles were parked behind a green Department of Conservation pickup truck.

Ron Morrison was an up and coming deputy on the Sheriff's Department. Although one of the youngest on the job, he was one of Benson's best, with eyes that saw everything and a quick mind to analyze it. Benson, upon arrival, noted Morrison had taped off the crime scene and was photographing the area. One day, Benson thought, that kid will be Sheriff.

Morrison stopped his photography and walked to meet Benson. The deputy explained he was on a call at Dora Cox's home and had just finished when he got the call to meet an officer. The County Conservation agent, Christine McKay, had found Malone. After seeing the body, thinking he was a victim of a car accident, she called it into the dispatcher.

"Boss, I'm letting her continue to think it was a car accident but I don't believe it," said Morrison to Benson.

"Why's that?"

"One look and you'll know that no car did that to him. I've got the Coroner on the way out and the crime scene unit is still at Dora's home. That's a mess. Myron was there last night. His car is still there for now. There is blood all over the place but no Myron. The detectives have been notified but I think we'll need them here as well. The paramedics never got close to the body. One look was enough for them. They stayed for Christine. She was upset but has settled down. She never saw anything like this. As far as that goes, neither have I."

Benson nodded, as he walked up the road to view Malone's body with the deputy in tow. Christine McKay, sitting sideways on the pickup's seat, was flanked by a paramedic to either side and looked up as Benson passed her. She forced a half-smile from her lips on her small impish face. Her eyes were red from crying.

Viewing the area where Malone's body lay was just to the left of the road. It was half in the tall grass, half in the culvert ditch that ran alongside. Benson stooped next to the body for a closer look. Leaves stuck to the body as the rivers of blood had flowed. The left arm was several feet away in the grass. Clenched in his fist was grey hair that had been ripped out. Dave Malone's throat was gone. The bite marks of huge canines were visible in the flesh that was left of the neck. The index finger of the still attached right arm, pointed to the woods. Not far away, a pocket knife covered in blood lay with the blade open. Intestines had been dragged out of the body and were in an equally straight line with the pointing finger.

Dave Malone had fought hard, very hard. Benson quietly said to ears, which no longer could hear, "Proud of you son, it just wasn't enough. Sorry." The Sheriff placed his hand over his eyes as if in prayer, but actually hiding his tear-filled eyes. A few very long minutes later, Benson stood, composed himself and turned to his deputy stating, "You were right to maintain this as an accident. Keep it that way for now."

Morrison nodded, asking if the Sheriff would make notification to Janey Malone about Dave. Benson had no actual knowledge Janey was dead, just a piece of human bone as evidence.

"Yeah, I'll take care of that. Get an ETA on the Coroner. I want to talk to Christine. Have the detective crew, when they're done at Cox's house, finish this up – as a leaving the scene of an auto accident. Give them your camera for the report.

Once everything is cleared out here, go to the Carr place and see if the old man heard anything. He's the only one around here for a few miles."

"Dave just lived a half a mile up the road. Maybe his wife heard something, boss," the deputy stated.

"Maybe. I'll take care of it later when I notify her. For now get the Coroner here," he ordered, turning to talk to Christine McKay.

She was a small woman standing no more than five feet three inches. McKay's usually cheerful attitude was now a tearful, more somber one. Her light complexion was flushed red. Breasts, big enough to feed a Third World nation, no longer strained the material of her brown uniform shirt from heavy breaths she took while crying. Christine had calmed down enough for Benson to speak with her.

Benson checked with the medics about her condition. They told him that it seemed she was emotionally traumatized at first but she was better. Just take it easy with her. She wasn't far from shock, but there was nothing more they could do for her just then.

Pulling the paramedics aside, he requested that their report reflect simply that they responded to a fatal car accident and nothing more. That was how the Sheriff's Department was treating the incident, and to please talk to no one. Until the Coroner said differently, it was probably just scavengers feeding.

Both men said that was what the report would say, as they loaded the equipment back into the ambulance. Benson thanked them and then turned to speak with McKay.

Conservation Agent Christine McKay was a lifelong resident of Crawford County living in Maple Hills, leaving only for college, a bad marriage and divorce. She knew everyone and everyone knew and liked her. Being a kind and generous person sometimes got her into trouble, usually with men, but nothing she could not handle. They wanted to fall in love and she did not. Rather, they wanted sex and more often than not, she didn't. Christine belonged to a group of gal pals who met once a week at a different local bar for beer, music and talking bad about men in general. It really did not matter if they were ex-husbands or ex-boyfriends, all were worse than toad slime, at least until they met the next one who could rock their world. All except Christine. She hated her ex-husband, who she referred to as "the pedophile who liked little girls". Still, she strove to remember the few good things about their relationship. McKay let few men enter her private life. Those few she considered trusted friends.

Benson knew McKay most of her life. He knew her family. Her uncle had been the Sheriff when he was a kid and was a big influence in his decision to go into law enforcement. Like Christine, her uncle was a great person, who was shot and killed answering a call for a dog barking. Everyone in the county, except the guy who shot him, went to the funeral. Benson remembered how hard Christine had taken his death. She looked much the same that day as when her uncle was put to rest.

Asking if she was okay enough to answer a few questions, she responded, "Sure."

"Can you tell me what happened?"

"No. I didn't see anything. Like I told Ronny, I was headed over to Vance Road for a deer struck by a car. I cut over Lone Creek from the state highway to get there. As I passed by, I thought someone was in the ditch hurt, so I stopped and found Davey. Oh God, Ralph…"

Christine started crying again. Benson put an arm around her shoulders and waited long enough for her to finish crying. He always truly hated this part of the job. Sheriff Benson could sometimes be too empathetic with victims and he considered McKay almost as much a victim as Dave Malone.

"Ralph, who's going to tell Janey, it'll kill her!"

If Lansdowne was right she's already dead, the Sheriff thought. They are already together, if there is a God in Heaven.

"I'll be the one to tell her. Are you okay enough to drive?"

"Yeah, Ralph. I'm fine. There's one more thing."

"What's that, Chrissy?"

"Dave wasn't killed by a car and wasn't eaten by scavengers."

"I know, but for now keep this to yourself until we sort things out."

Chapter 7

Benson watched Christine McKay drive away, as an unmarked Sheriff's Department car with two detectives inside pulled up on the scene. Both were retired St. Louis City Police Detectives who were hired because of their extensive background. Neither man was much over forty years of age.

Nodding a greeting to the Sheriff, they asked what they had. Benson explained the situation and told them how to handle it until he knew more. Then he asked what went on at Dora Cox's place. They pretty much said all that Morrison had. There was a lot of blood but no body. The only information added was when one of the detectives told him about the paw prints in the blood. The prints looked as though the animal was backing up, dragging something through the blood. The blood trail went off the side of the front porch into the grass and then disappeared. After last summer with the two girls who disappeared while floating, they were not calling for tracking dogs. They followed the blood into the woods and lost it a few feet in. Something smelled dead. Like it had died some time ago and was rotting.

Benson noticed the same smell by Dave Malone's body but just faintly. Lansdowne said he smelled something as well, like rotting meat. The grass by where Malone lay was too thick for prints and nothing appeared to have been dragged. McKay might have helped with that but it was doubtful considering her state of mind.

The two detectives were busy making sketches and taking measurements while Morrison was leaving for the Carr place.

All that was left for the Sheriff was to return to Lansdowne's place. He mentioned to the detectives that they may still have another call to process today. Oh, and the Coroner is supposed to be on the way. The two plain clothes officers returned to their work after the Sheriff drove back down Lone Creek Road. The younger of the two asked, "Have you ever seen anything like this?"

The other stated he had. "When I was a young officer in the Fifth District, we had a missing kid. We found him the next day, dead on the other side of the flood wall. Most of him was gone, eaten by a pack of dogs. I puked for a week after every time I thought of it. I still don't sleep well."

Benson, leaving to meet Deputy Morrison, left nothing more for Lansdowne to do but to wait for the Sheriff's return. He got himself another cup of coffee and returned to his seat on the deck. Most days Lansdowne would work refinishing antique furniture for one of the many stores in the area, but only real antiques. Not the stuff from the 60's or the 70's, mostly from 1945 back. Everyone knew not to get into a hurry for their piece to be completed. Since Glenna's death Lansdowne was doing much less work. It was something of little interest now. If he started refinishing something he would finish it but he was not taking much more work. Usually just for the nice couple who ran the store in Cuba, Missouri.

Lansdowne sat sipping the hot cup of coffee and staring at the white gravel road. Glenna had convinced him to move to the country. She loved the gravel roads. Why she did, he never really knew. He suspected it was just the total country thing and gravel roads were a part of it.

Crawford County road crews, in Lansdowne's opinion, did an excellent job maintaining the gravel roads. Summertime, the roads were graded and new gravel placed. Winter time, as soon as the snows stopped, they were clearing it away. Residents would have to clear it from in front of their driveways but that was a small price to pay for a clean as possible gravel road. Rains would cause the roads to wave like old fashioned washboards. Road crews responded and straightened it out. Some residents wanted the chip and sealed asphalt roads. That type of road was just too costly and always needing repair because of farm equipment moving over them. Money just wasn't in the county's budget for constant repairs.

After seeing the house, Glenna told him regardless of his thoughts, she at least was buying it. Together they had looked at a good many houses but none that both could agree upon, only this one. He smiled at her after she made that statement and kissed her saying that it was perfect for them.

St. Louis held conveniences such as "The Hill", the Italian section of town. True Italian sausage was impossible to buy in the country. Country sausage - yes, salsiccia - no. There was a bakery in Cuba, Missouri but no cannoli; that cheese filled pastry which Mark Lansdowne loved almost as much as his wife.

There was no Soulard market (Soulard was a market established for farmers since 1789, or so the sign said), for fresh fruits and vegetables. People would sell the produce in road side stands in southern Missouri and Arkansas. One just never knew when they would have it or where they would be located.

Such small things like those were cured with an hour's drive and a day's outing together. Before returning to their new home, they would stop somewhere for dinner and drinks (usually the Mexican place in Cuba Missouri). Glenna loved chips and salsa. Lansdowne himself, did not care for Mexican food.

Mark Lansdowne was over indulgent to his wife and would give in to most any of her whims. Not all, but most. Glenna told him once that he spoiled her far too much, to which he responded that he would continue to do so the rest of her life.

That was not to be much longer.

Early in the spring of that year Lansdowne tore down and replaced the deck. It had been the only bad thing about the house. Then he went to work digging the flower garden which surrounded it. He dug as Glenna planted the flowers. Together, and several thousands of dollars later, the deck and garden were finished. Glenna had developed a cough and he thought it had to do with the flowers or the spring pollen.

Lansdowne poured the concrete below the deck for the patio and then went to work digging the pond. Rather, he hired a man with a back-hoe and let him do it. The springtime rains were too few to fill the pond; it was too deep…so Lansdowne helped it with a hose from the well.

A week later he had to have the well pump replaced and nearly had a coronary when he saw the electric bill for helping to fill the hole with water.

She was busy painting the inside of the house while he built deer feeders for her. When they finished, they took what was a great place to live and turned it into a wonderland that Walt Disney would have loved.

Glenna's cough got worse and she was fatigued easily. The doctor ran some tests but found nothing really wrong. He told her to slow up a bit and to rest more. She was probably just tired.

Lansdowne felt the place was perfect but Glenna said it lacked something, "What is a country home without a dog?"

On one of the trips to St. Louis, the two ended up at the Animal Control Center's Shelter on Gasconade Street. Animal Control for St. Louis City picks up strays and takes in unwanted animals. The animals are given the best care possible, for a government agency. Feed is supplied daily. Some is bought with the limited funds and some is donated by companies. Cages are cleaned daily and the dogs are exercised outside as often as possible. Most of the dogs and cats never find a home, the few that do seem to be grateful. Somehow they knew the fate that awaited them and showed thanks to the people who had adopted them. They had something that previously had been unknown – a home.

Seemingly, most had a high degree of intelligence. Possibly it was genes or maybe it was from time on the streets, where in order to eat they had to be smart and learn quickly.

Glenna would have taken all of the dogs. She was a sucker for a pitiful face. For her, deciding on one dog was slow in happening. Soon though, they had decided between three. Moe was definitely a street mutt, but friendly. Brown with ears tipped in black and the biggest eyes. Glenna said it looked as though he used eyeliner to accentuate them. He was young, but big. Still having puppy teeth, he weighed sixty pounds.

Larry was a different story in a way. He was young and friendly as well, but much bigger. Nearly thirty pounds more and a third taller with a tail that would, in the future, clear any end table completely of its contents.

Curly was…well, Curly. He outweighed both. With a Rottweiler's body and a face of a Sharpei, only Glenna could love him and she immediately did. It was love at first sight for both. Curly was big enough to tackle a bear but when they walked in the exercise pen he was gentle, not dragging her. He did not seem to care about Lansdowne as did the other two dogs but somehow knew it was a package deal. It was him and her, or it was back to the pen and who knew to what end. So he feigned a half-heart felt wag of the nub of a tail towards Lansdowne, hoping it was enough.

Glenna and Mark Lansdowne could not completely agree on any one of the three. Glenna looked deeply into Mark's eyes and said she really wanted Curly. He knew that no matter the reason he could come up with, the dog was going home with them. He would deny her nothing. Still, he liked the other two and could not make up his mind if two dogs would work. She made the decision and told the Animal Control Agent at the front desk they would take all three dogs. She filled out the questionnaires while he paid the neutering fees. The Animal Control Agent was at first skeptical that they would be allowed to adopt three dogs, but upon hearing how much land they had for the dogs to run, she said she would pass it through.

Within a week the stooges had a new home and forty-five of their own acres to run, as well as the woods of the State Park which abutted the property. Strangely enough, all three seemed housebroken. There was never an accident. All were loyal and protective (Curly especially toward Glenna), but not junkyard dogs. They even tolerated Warren Skruggs, Lansdowne's lifelong friend.

As time passed, Glenna's cough and fatigue worsened. She either rested in bed or on the family room couch, or sat on the deck or patio watching the deer eat from the corn feeders or drink from the pond.

The doctor had no answer. By the time she would allow herself to be hospitalized, it was nearly Christmas. Doctors sent her blood to the Center for Disease Control. It was a flu virus but not one they had ever seen before. Nothing was known about it. There were no other cases from which to draw information. No one seemed to have a method for treatment, except different antivirals and antibiotics to keep her from catching lower lobe pneumonia.

Breathing therapy seemed to help at first, then no longer. Glenna was of Scottish descent and never really tanned, instead turned a pale red. Now she was an almost ghostly white.

Christmas, New Years and Valentine's Day all came and went. Mark Lansdowne was helpless and did not at all like it. This was an uncommon enemy that he could not stand and fight. A damn bug! Something one could not see without a microscope, much less one that no one had ever before seen, or knew how to treat.

March came and for no apparent reason Glenna started getting better. Her color came back and her grey eyes were clear, no longer a watery-cloud color. The blood work was returning to within normal ranges. The virus was still present but was failing in scope. Something was working for her but still no one could account as to why. Soon she was moved from the high-tech isolation room where she had been for so long, to a more cheerful private room. Nurses came in without gowns, masks or rubber gloves and would say more in the way of a conversation than, "How are we today?" The doctors, who for so long had struggled seeking an answer on how and what to do for her, no longer had a grim look on their faces, they smiled and were happy with her recovery. Privately they patted themselves on the back, they just did not know what they had done but surely it was working.

Mark Lansdowne had almost a sigh of relief when the virus made its last stand and won.

Within a matter of hours as Lansdowne watched the futile efforts, it seemed like minutes of slow motion before Glenna passed away. Mark Lansdowne no longer stood out of the way of the throng of doctors and nurses. He pushed past them all and took her hand. She smiled and blew him a kiss, then died. He then did something he could never remember doing in his life, he cried. Everyone left him alone in the room with her. There was nothing that could be done for her and he was not the type of man to be comforted right now.

He picked her up into his arms and held her while he cried. She was all he had ever loved in his life. He never had a life, only an existence, until her. Lansdowne was an orphan and raised himself. There had never been a personal purpose in his life until Glenna. She was all he ever deeply loved. He did not know he could love, or even what it felt like to love or be loved before her. The closest thing to family was Warren Skruggs and his wife, Lona.

As he laid her back down, he thought of all the things that he could have done to have proved his love for her. All the things he would never get to do or say ran through his mind.

Someone brave, stupid, or just unknowing entered the room and told him they had to take her away. Lansdowne never saw the person but knew it was a man's voice. While trying to arrange her hair, Lansdowne, not turning, said, "Try to touch her before I'm ready and it's over for you. Two bodies will leave here tonight." He heard the door close as footsteps moved quickly down the hall from the room.

Glenna's mother and father died before he met her. There were no siblings to notify. Now there was only him. He had been alone before but not like that. He was totally empty and immediately lonely. He was nothing more than a shell again. The only reason to live was gone from him. She was for him, the true meaning of life.

Finally leaving the room, he walked what seemed a mile to the nurse's station. Without turning to face anyone he said, "You may take her now. For everyone's sake, use due diligence and respect." All who heard his words knew it was not a request.

He, himself, buried her ashes in the garden under the weeping cherry tree she so loved. It was March 17th, St. Patrick's Day. The only people present were Skruggs and his wife Lona.

Curly lay in front of the tree for days. Even in death, she was his only master.

He moved his gaze from the road to the garden. He neglected most of it. Around the redbud where Glenna's ashes rested looked good, but the rest he let go. He was by no means a botanist, but he was sure the green "something's" that were popping up through the mulch, were weeds. Maybe tomorrow he thought, he would pull them out. They had worked so hard to make the gardens something the Missouri Botanical Gardens would envy, and now it was a disgrace. He vowed to himself, that the following spring he would again make it look like she had.

Lifting the cup to his lips, he found the cup empty. Lansdowne sat waiting for the Sheriff to return longer than he had anticipated. Shaking the pack of cigarettes, he found it empty as well. There had been five in the pack when he first sat down.

Damn it, a year she's been gone, soon it will be two.

Lansdowne knew he needed to move on, he just did not know how or even if he could. He also knew Glenna would not like him mourning for so long. She would tell him to, "Cowboy the hell up! You've had ample time feeling sorry for yourself. Enough is enough."

He chuckled as he heard her voice making that statement to him.

Maybe it was time to move on. He needed to call Amie and make an appointment to cut his hair. She might like to have dinner with him afterward. She was a friend, nothing more. They always laughed while she cut his hair, especially when she trimmed his mustache. The clippers would tickle his upper lip. It took as long to trim the hair under his nose as it did to cut his hair. He wondered if she would like the beard. She may be seeing someone. Amie is young and beautiful. She probably was seeing someone, and he did not know if he would be able to ask her to dinner. Anyway, if she accepted, she was a person who did not play games. She was as real as a person could be. If he asked her out she would say yes or no, as simple as that.

He left the deck and returned to the house for another pack of butts and cup of coffee. The little red light on the coffee maker was no longer glowing. The coffee was cold. Pouring a full cup, he placed it in the microwave and nuked it hot. While waiting for the microwave, he went to the right drawer of his desk and took a new pack of cigarettes from the carton. There were eight packs left which was enough for two weeks, usually. The events of the previous night and that day had caused him to smoke three days' worth in just several hours. The microwave beeped to let Lansdowne know his cup of coffee was hot.

Opening the door of the microwave to get his cup, he noticed the calendar over it. It was Friday October 31st, more commonly known as Halloween. He smiled, thinking of the irony of the events of the day. Later that night children would be running from house to house to collect bags of goodies from residents of Maple Hills. All of them dressed as a terrifying monster.

If they only knew about the monster that was out there.

If.

Chapter 8

As Ralph Benson drove the patrol car the few miles from the location where Dave Malone's body was found to Lansdowne's home, he ran everything over in his mind. He thought about what Lansdowne told him, about what Deputy Morrison reported about the incident at Dora Cox's place, and what he saw that was left of Dave Malone. He never saw the few oncoming cars or the expanse of pastures and the cattle feeding in them. So lost in thought was he that he almost missed the turn onto the road that led to Lansdowne's house.

Most of what he thought about was questions, although there were more questions than answers. Were the two incidents tied together? Probably. What was killing these people? What sort of animal? A bear? The Maple Hills Police chased a black bear off the interstate back into the woods just a couple of years ago. There was a report of a mountain lion somewhere in Franklin County, but that too was a couple of years past. Feral dogs? Maybe. That was not unheard of either. Wait, wasn't the mountain lion thing discredited? He could not remember. It did not matter. Something was killing people, one for sure. Whatever it was, it had to be stopped. Conservation was going to have to be notified. Christine McKay may have already done so.

The drive down the gravel road seemed to take forever. Benson's stomach was becoming upset and he was well on his way to having a whopper of a headache. Tension like this was causing his hair to fall out. It had nothing to do with genes or years of wearing a uniform cap. It was tension on the job. He wondered if hair replacement therapy was covered under workers compensation. Most likely not, and there was no way to work it into his meager budget.

Hearing the dogs barking and the crunching sound of the white gravel, Lansdowne knew the Sheriff had returned. He left his thoughts, and a cup of coffee, to meet Benson at the door.

The Sheriff stopped as he traversed the path of sandstone flags surrounded by gravel. His gait seemed heavier than when he left. It was as if what he just viewed set a terrible weight upon him. Lansdowne could only guess at the scene of Dave Malone, but he knew it was only going to get worse for Benson.

Yelling at the dogs to quiet and stand down, he opened the door to allow the Sheriff entry into the house.

The Sheriff's complexion had gone from tan to noticeably pale, and his breathing was labored a bit. He was offered a glass of water or shot of liquor, by Lansdowne. Both were refused although the alcohol did sound good, but then so did his Mylanta that was miles away in his desk. Benson said he just wanted to get moving.

Shrugging his shoulders, Lansdowne turned his back to the Sheriff and reloaded the shotgun. Benson saw the outline of the revolver under Lansdowne's shirt. Asking if he always carried the weapon, Lansdowne told him it was only for balance when he walked.

"And the heavy rounds in the shotgun?"

"Yes, well, they are for close encounters of the final kind."

"Kinda' over kill, isn't it?"

Turning his head and looking deep into the Sheriff's eyes, "I do truly hope so," he said. Then, "Let's go."

Exiting the house by way of the patio doors, the two men headed for the pond. As the dogs started to follow, they were ordered to stay put. Upon reaching the pond, Lansdowne pointed out the prints that the dogs had not obscured. Even though Lansdowne's dogs were big, the prints in the dirt were made by something much larger, much heavier. Benson went down to one knee and examined them. The prints were deep into the moist soil that surrounded the pond. They looked like prints from a dog, yet they were different. Benson said as much and Lansdowne agreed. Lansdowne said there were no nails in the soil in front of the pads. It was evident; the unknown animal had drunk from the pond and then turned to the woods, which was the direction the two headed.

Benson looked at the ground as he walked, looking for anything that could further the information he had attained so far.

Approaching the edge of the forest, Benson was able to smell the same odor that had surrounded Dave Malone. This was stronger, not the faint scent he experienced earlier. He started to gag but pushed it back. Lansdowne offered to go back and get some Vick's Vaporub from his house. Shaking his head, Benson said, "No, I'm good."

"Sure you are. Breathe through your mouth."

Lansdowne moved through the brush along the game trail at a quick and certain pace while Benson struggled to keep up with Mark. The brush was thick, and Benson was not dressed to travel through it at the rate Lansdowne set. He was wearing shoes rather than boots. Fallen sticks, branches from the scrub trees and thorny brush were cutting him from ankle to thigh.

As they went, Lansdowne would point out a broken branch or hair in the thorn bushes by pointing and never speaking. Benson, several feet behind, would look at whatever Mark pointed at, making a mental note of its location. It may be evidence and he would need to remember where for collection.

Just as quickly as he moved through the woods, Lansdowne came to a complete halt. Half-turning, he signaled for Benson to stop as well. Moving only his eyes with a gaze to detect the slightest movement, Lansdowne stood completely motionless. Ever so slightly, he cocked his head to one side listening.

The Sheriff watched as Lansdowne pushed the safety on the shotgun to the firing position and set his index finger along the trigger guard. He drew his weapon from his holster as well. Although he did not know what Lansdowne was looking to see or listening to hear, he knew by his composure it was not the first time he led a hunt. Benson had to trust Mark's instincts and, what seemed to be, experience.

After a few more minutes, Benson could no longer keep quiet. Whispering, he said he heard or saw nothing.

Lansdowne nodded. Still scanning the area he said, "You're right. No birds, no squirrels. The odor is stronger and more recent." Then he pointed to the ground. Benson saw a paw print that was again a third bigger than the ones by the pond.

"That wasn't there before. Stay frosty. We need to move. Now!"

As abruptly as he had stopped, Lansdowne moved down the trail with Benson keeping up with his speed, avoiding the low hanging branches and no longer caring how badly his ankles bled.

Not sure how far they had traveled, Benson asked how much farther they needed to go. In a barely audible voice, Lansdowne told him maybe a quarter of a mile more.

The sun dropped in the afternoon sky. No longer did it light the way through breaks in the trees towering above. It caused shadows to be thrown, making Benson apprehensive of trekking deeper, yet rationally knowing he must.

If Lansdowne had any fears, the Sheriff did not detect them. He saw only a single minded purpose in his steps. A trained and determined air was in every movement. A certainty of his abilities was absolute. Benson did not know him well, but was now sure that Lansdowne could be every bit as deadly as what was out there.

Approaching the place in the woods where the trees backed off giving way to tall grass in a hollow, the men stopped. Listening intensely for any sound of movement, they waited for a minute. Nothing was heard. Even though Benson was breathing through his mouth as to avoid the stench, so overwhelming was it that it no longer mattered how he breathed.

Calmly but quietly, Lansdowne said, "The trails go in there. You cover left. I got the right. The cave is across the clearing in the rock face. Once we've cleared the area, circle towards the cave facing the grass. I'll cover the other side until we meet at the cave."

Benson became irritated with him giving commands. He was, after all, the Sheriff.

"You know, I've done things like this before."

"Yeah, well, maybe, but not with me. I need to get back and make an appointment for a haircut – and I want my head still on my body."

Lansdowne's face was completely emotionless except for the set of his jaw. It was then that Benson realized he was looking at the face of a man who was not in the habit of taking orders, but giving them. He expected them to be carried out with no questions or excuses.

Without further conversation or even looking at Benson, he stepped forward through the high gold-colored grass into the clearing, soundlessly, with Benson following.

Chapter 9

Circling the hollow was without incident. By the time Benson finished his sweep, Lansdowne was already at the front of the cave facing out into the clearing, watching.

"I told you what's in there, but even so you're not going to be prepared for what you will see. I'll cover the area if you still want to go inside."

At that moment, Benson would rather have gotten an ass-kicking from an escaped, three-hundred pound mental patient than go into the cave. It was dark and smelled like a sewer treatment plant, yet it was his job. Goose-bumps popped up on his arms under the long sleeves of his uniform shirt. Hairs on his neck stood up. The instinctive fear, present inside every person from the time before man made his first stone tool until today, flared in the Sheriff's stomach. His shirt was stained from sweat at the armpits and glistened on his receding brow line.

"Ralph, I'll understand if you don't go, no one will ever know."

Benson shot a look at Lansdowne. There was something that resembled pity in his eyes for the Sheriff.

"Thanks pal, but I have to go."

"I know." The pity was in his voice as well.

Mustering all the courage he had in order to dispel the fears and anxiety, Benson stepped into the yawning mouth of darkness, belonging to the cave.

The sunlight no longer shed its rays into the cave. It was now below the tops of the trees. Benson took out of his pocket a small flashlight that looked like the larger one that was standard issue. The one from his pocket was far from being as powerful, but it lit the inside of the cave enough to see Jancy Malone looking at him. All he could think was for God to protect him.

Janey was no longer the beautiful young woman that flirted with him as she set his dinner on the table at Barkers. She was not much of anything now.

He could no longer look at what was left of her, as tears started to fill his eyes. Moving his head and redirecting the small flashlight, something caught his eye. Taking a half step, he saw a tennis shoe. It was blue with a white sole, or it had been. Now it was dirty and chewed.

Months before he saw the mate to it.

Benson's mind flashed the vivid memories of events that took place in late summer. They belonged to a college girl who was floating the river with her girlfriend. They both disappeared without a trace.

Around the town of Maple Hills are several rivers which are favorites of people from the city. The campgrounds, of which there are many, are clean. Many have showers so that after a long day of drinking beer, floating downriver in a rented canoe while getting lobster-red, people can wash the sand and river mud from their bodies. Some leave the city on Thursday night but most on Friday, staying as late as they possibly can on Sunday before taking the hour drive back.

Melissa Keene and Alice Sharpe, two beautiful young junior college students from St.

Louis, decided to float the river on a Wednesday. They were fairly sure they would have the river to themselves. Both were looking forward to one last long day of floating before returning to their studies.

The day was a beautiful one, with a cloudless blue sky and a warm temperature. The river was high enough that they would not have to drag the canoe over gravel bars, although the current was faster. Because it was faster, the girls opted for the seven mile float rather than the five.

The fifteen minute ride in the old school bus, that had been converted to carry canoes as well as passengers, was filled with small talk from the twenty year old kid who drove.

He was a hardworking young man, who spent his summers at the campground during the day and a fast-food place at night, trying to earn enough money to buy books and gas for school.

Arriving at the location where the girls would start their daylong adventure, they carried the cooler filled with sodas and sandwiches to the edge of the river, while the driver carried the canoe. Melissa and Alice stripped from tank tops and long shorts to reveal their two piece swimsuits. Both weaved their long hair through the back of their ball caps and set sunglasses on their noses. The driver handed them two lifejackets and two paddles and watched them make the middle of the river, until disappearing around the bend.

He had four to five hours to get the campground ready for the weekend crowd before he needed to pick the girls up seven miles downstream.

Six and a half hours later, there was no sign of the canoe or the girls. The driver radioed the campground that the canoe had not come in. He was told to return and get a motor boat to look for them.

The canoe was found forty-five minutes later, three miles upstream from the pick-up point. It was tied off to a tree. The cooler, lifejackets, and paddles were still in it. Thinking that the girls must have pulled over for a pee break, he followed the trail of the tennis shoes into the woods. A short distance in, he lost the trail. He called out to the girls and waited for a reply. There was none. If they went too far into the woods they could have become lost. Without the sounds of other floaters coming from the river, they might easily have walked the wrong way.

He walked further into the woods calling for them. Alongside of a downed tree, he saw the bottom of the swimsuit Alice was wearing. The tree was wet in that spot where she must have sat to relieve herself. He knew it did not take three years of college to figure out they were in serious trouble. As he ran back to the boat, he smelled a foul odor that was unfamiliar.

Radioing his boss, he was instructed to stay put and continue calling out until the Water Patrol arrived. Fifteen minutes later, he led the officer into the woods as far as he went and pointed out the swimsuit bottoms. The kid was really scared.

It would be dark in a few hours and these poor girls were out there lost and one half naked. The question was; what had caused Alice to leave the bottom of her swimsuit?

For two full weeks, the woods were searched. The river was dragged from side to side, a mile upstream and a couple of miles downstream. Divers spent many days combing the murky bottom of the river as well. There were no bodies caught in a submerged tree. Canine units from as far away as St. Louis in the east, and Military Canines from Fort Leonard Wood in the west, responded for the search.

The local newspapers printed the story. Shortly after, satellite trucks carrying twenty-five year old bleached blonde news anchors, dressed in jeans, (as if they were assisting in the search), arrived. They asked their questions and were polite enough to not get in the way.

A man who was fishing the day the girls went missing called the Sheriff after reading the newspaper. He saw the girls, if they were the same ones, around noon just by the Campbell Bridge. They seemed fine, asking if he caught anything. He told them, no, as the current took them farther downstream. The only reason he remembered them was that it was unusual for a canoe to be on the river in the middle of the week. He could not remember what they were wearing except that they both had ball caps and sunglasses on. They were both young and had pretty smiles.

Even as dense as the forest was, the Highway Patrol put up a helicopter to assist.

At the end of the second week, all that was found was the swimsuit bottoms, the urine on the tree which matched Alice's DNA, as well as a trail of human stool that led to one blue tennis shoe with a white sole. One of the girls was literally, scared shitless.

The job fell to Ralph Benson to tell the parents of their failure to find the girls. He cried with the parents as he told them.

Inside the cave, he counted what appeared to be the remains of at least three more people other than Janey. Benson knew who the two were; they were more than likely the floaters. The last he could not see as it was too far back, and he had pushed his courage beyond the limits. Anyway, the flashlight was dimming and it was an hour or so from sunset. Under no conditions did he want to be there in the dark.

Benson backed out of the cave being careful not to step on the bones that littered the floor. It reminded him briefly of the floor of his wife's car, with all the fast food wrappers.

Lansdowne told him they would leave the same way they came, into the hollow. Benson nodded that he understood. They made it out of the clearing and back to the game trail in half the time.

Benson was quite ready to get away from there, but Lansdowne stopped him by saying, "One of us must stay."

Benson's mouth dropped open.

Chapter 10

Bud Carr was a crusty-looking, tough, older man. At something a bit over six foot tall and weighing in at over two hundred pounds, for seventy-odd years old he still cut an imposing figure. He still had biceps that did not sag and no fat around the middle. The short white hair combed straight back, framed a face of furrows that some called age wrinkles. That was only partly true. Most came from over sixty years of working cattle in the sun, on the ranch which had been in his family since the end of the Civil War. His grandfather had fought for the North, and was rewarded with one hundred and sixty acres of newly acquired Indian land.

Three generations worked the land raising cattle. He was to be the last. He and his wife Carol had no children. There were two miscarriages and the doctor told them another could kill her, so there were no more attempts at a family.

Carol was discovered with breast cancer a few years back and was now in a nursing home. The doctors told him it was only a matter of time.

Bud drove the forty miles every day, regardless of the weather, to sit with her in the evenings. Whether they played cards, board games, or just watched television, they did not care - they were together. Anymore, he just sat and watched her sleep. She was getting weaker every day. It would not be long. Still, he read a chapter of a book to her before he would leave her. He did so ever since her eyesight failed months before.

He cried the entire drive home.

Deputy Ron Morrison drove from the state highway up the dirt road that ended at Bud Carr's front door. He knew Bud would not be in the house but in one of the outbuildings working. It was past lunchtime and Morrison knew Bud's routine of going to see his wife. Everyone in the county knew.

Carr heard the vehicle's engine shut off. He was in the tractor shed working. He wondered who could be coming to see him. Bud did not get many visitors these days, so one was a welcome novelty to his day.

The two men met halfway between the police car and the shed. Because of the sun in his eyes, Bud had trouble making out who was visiting him. Raising a strong, calloused paw over blue eyes to shade the sun, Bud recognized the deputy. A wide smile spread across his face, welcoming Morrison.

When Ron Morrison was in high school, Bud Carr gave him a job helping to work the cattle. Before school and after, weekends and holidays, Morrison worked with Carr. He had spent his entire summer working. Carr told him he should be at the swimming hole with his friends and his sweetie. He cut hay, moved cattle from one pasture to another, and even sat nights with a rifle when there was an invasion of hungry coyotes killing livestock.

Carr did not need the help, but the persistence of the kid asking for a job caused him to finally give in and hire Morrison. Bud was never sorry about the decision.

Over the past few years, while Morrison was in college, the two men saw little of each other. The deputy received a full academic scholarship at graduation from high school to a college in Illinois. Bud and Carol Carr were invited to his graduation and acted like excited grandparents. They were so proud and came to actually love him over the years.

Bud Carr stuck out a greasy, ham-sized hand for the deputy to shake. Morrison, not caring about the grime, shook hands. The old man's grip still felt like a vise crushing his hand. Carr, in his excitement, did not notice how dirty his hand was. He pulled a clean shop towel out from the back pocket of the old work jeans and handed it to Morrison, apologizing. The deputy shook his head, smiling at his old boss and mentor, saying there was no reason to apologize. He was working.

The boy still had manners, Carr thought. "How's Carol? I've thought to go see her a hundred times, I just…"

The smile on Carr's face faded a bit, relaxing the deep furrows that had been plowed by the years. His eyes clouded some with tears.

"No change really, son. Don't think it'll be much longer."

"I am so sorry, Bud."

The old man composed himself and asked Ron if he wanted a drink. He had some cold sweet tea in the refrigerator, saying he had to buy the gallon jugs now. He just could not make it like Carol.

Ron Morrison felt Bud's pain as he spoke about his wife. He wanted to sit on the porch, at the table that Carr had built for his wife and drink a glass of tea. He knew that he had neglected his old friend, but he also knew he could not spend the time that day.

"Wish I could Bud, but there's been some trouble down the road and wondered if you heard or saw anything last night?"

Carr shook his head. "I was with Carol until around ten. Got home about eleven, took out my hearing aids (yeah, a new addition) and went to bed. If I can ask, what happened?"

"Right now it looks like a hit and run. Dave Malone is dead."

"Aw, not Davey! He's such a good kid. How's Janey taking it?

Morrison said he did not know. The Sheriff said he would tell her. Right now the incident was under investigation.

Carr said it was a damn shame and Ron nodded his agreement, saying he was a hell of a mechanic, not to mention, a cook at Barkers. Christine McKay found him that morning.

"If there's anything I can do…"

"I'll be sure the Sheriff will tell Janey you're around. Bud, I hate to say I have to go, but I need to. If you hear anything, I'd appreciate it."

"Sure son, you'll be the first."

As the two men walked towards the police car, Bud said, "I've got a question. Maybe you know."

"Shoot."

"Has anyone else been missing calves? I'm down three, maybe four. Haven't been able to make a cattleman's meeting in months cause of Carol. Haven't seen anyone else to ask but Burt at the feed store, and he never knows anything."

Morrison opened the car door and leaned over the top, facing Bud.

"Yeah, Burt's certainly not the sharpest knife in the drawer, but in answer to your questions, no I haven't. You think its rustlers?"

"Ronny, I just don't know. No fences are down and no truck tracks around. They just seemed to disappear. I know it's not any of those UFO's. They just bleed 'em dry and take sex organs. I watch that cable channel."

Bud winked his right eye. Morrison smiled, saying that he would rotate to the night watch the following week and would try to pay attention to the area. Maybe he could arrest some aliens. The men again shook hands. Morrison got in his car, backed around and headed toward the state highway. Bud watched him until he turned out of sight.

He turned and walked back to the tractor shed thinking, "Yeah, aliens. Lots of new Mexicans in the area now," and he chuckled to himself.

Bud bent over the engine of the green painted tractor and picked up the ratchet again in his right hand to try and break loose the last bolt so he could replace the head seal. Dave could have helped him. Bud felt he was just too old. Maybe he could sell everything, retire and move closer to Carol.

He braced himself and gave a strong push on the ratchet. The triceps on the back of his arms bulged with the effort, but the bolt would not break loose. Again he tried. This time he pushed so hard the effort took his breath. As he relaxed his grip and took a big gulp of air through his nose, he noticed a smell which reminded him of the time his dog would crap in the kitchen when it was a puppy. This smell was much worse. As he looked toward the rear of the shed he saw a pile as big as what a horse would leave.

Bud Carr could not imagine not noticing the smell before Ron Morrison's visit. Walking toward the pile of crap, he took a square-end shovel from the wall where he kept all of the small gardening tools. He was not going to work with that stink in his shed. As he scooped up the pile, there was something long and white with a red tip, in the mess. He took the shovel full of dung out of the shed and dropped it in the rear. Taking the edge of the shovel, he pushed the heap open as to be able to see in the sunlight what the white thing might be. A glint of something bright caught his attention, something like when the sun bounces its light off of a dew drop. He picked up a stick nearby that was on the ground and dug through the mess, revealing the horrible sight of a diamond wedding ring still on a woman's finger, the nail painted bright red.

He might have screamed but could not, as what felt like two hot knives entered through the top of his head.

The pain was immense, but only for a moment.

Chapter 11

Benson started to protest. It was far too risky for one man to stay there by himself. It was risky enough, after the carnage he had just witnessed, for the two of them to stay there.

"You have to go back. Your people wouldn't listen to me and I don't know what equipment you'll need. I'll stay."

"We both need to go! You can't stay by yourself. Last thing I need is another body."

Lansdowne smiled slightly, as he said he had no intention of becoming a victim.

"You're burning what daylight is left, Ralph. Your radio will only break up in here and you need to bring your people in. I was thinking if you come in from the north-northwest, it should be all field. It may be a little longer, but faster."

"You can't stay! That's an order!"

"Arrest me when you get back."

"Dammit, why the hell won't you go?"

Lansdowne looked into the Sheriff's eyes. He showed no emotion when he said, "Something has fed on Janey enough. Whatever it may be is not going to get to finish its meal. It ate enough."

Benson knew that was about the most emotion he ever heard from Lansdowne. His jaw was set and Benson knew no amount of arguing, pleading or ordering was going to make him leave.

"Okay then, for reasons of evidence of a crime scene, consider yourself a deputy."

"Is there a paycheck, or just the plastic Junior Deputy badge?" Lansdowne quipped.

"Just the badge. I hope my paycheck clears from week to week."

"It's a bad idea Ralph. People find out, they want me to fix a ticket and the next thing, the mob is trying to buy me. Then we're both up on corruption charges. All things equal, I'd rather pass. Go get your people. I don't want to be here longer than I have to be. I may just have enough time to get a haircut appointment."

"You really want a haircut, don't you?"

"You've never seen Amie."

The Sheriff was more relaxed. Lansdowne had just helped relieve some of the tension. A little bit it seemed.

"I'll be back and bring in the troops."

"Just make sure it's not the 7th Calvary. They didn't fare too well on their last outing."

Benson took a moment and placed a hand on Lansdowne's shoulder as a sign of thanks and for luck and said, "I'll be back. Soon." He then took off, moving at a faster pace back down the trail than ten minutes prior what he would have thought possible.

He heard Lansdowne say, "Ooo-yeah," as he broke into more of a trot.

Light was fading fast and Benson really watched where he placed his steps. He could not afford to slip and fall. That would burn precious time. His heart pounded in his ears. The uniform shirt he wore was now wet with his sweat. Benson was glad he quit smoking. He would not have been able to run as well as he did if he had not done so.

No longer did he feel the pain from the numerous cuts and tears his ankles sustained when going in with Lansdowne. A low branch from a scrub tree tore the left leg of his pants, digging a deep gouge out of his thigh, leaving meat on it. Blood was warm as it ran down his leg, becoming sticky in his shoe. Benson wanted to stop and look at the injury, but instead kept running. He wanted to yell out in pain, yet did not. His single-minded purpose was to get his people and then get back to Lansdowne.

Breaths were coming in great gasps as he broke from the woods.

The three dogs saw him and ran to meet him. They ran alongside as if he were a friend who ran with them in the past.

Benson ran past the pond to the patio doors, where he stopped. He was completely out of breath and sat on one of the wrought iron padded chairs on the patio. Though it was less than a minute, it seemed an hour before he had enough wind and could speak.

Telling the dispatcher to go to the scrambled channel, he was able to bark orders as to what he wanted.

Every available man was to report to Lansdowne's residence. Call in the detectives and they were to bring all the crime scene gear. Use the four wheel drives, not the cars. Call the Highway Patrol to respond no matter what they were doing, and he wanted them there ten minutes ago.

He was breathing easier, but his heart was still pounding as if it would explode out of his chest, like that creature did in that movie. He wondered if that was what it felt like when you had a heart attack.

Benson took deep breaths and slowly released them from his lungs. In a minute or two, his heart slowed enough that he was no longer dizzy and no longer wanted an oxygen bottle to suck on. His left leg was now throbbing and still bleeding but not as bad as earlier. The pant leg was stuck to the wound helping it to clot.

Breathing for him was now regular and his heart was a rhythmic steady beat. He was thirsty. Getting out of the chair required an effort, one that Sampson from the Bible would have envied. Hobbling his way through the doors, he found the kitchen and a glass which he filled from the tap. He sipped the first few drinks of the cold well water. Once the water sat in his stomach and did not make him feel like he wanted to throw up, he drank deeply.

He had not noticed before but the dogs had followed him into the house. They still seemed friendly toward him. Taking his time, he closed the patio doors and then walked out of the front door to wait for his posse. The dogs were inside of the house. His people were safe…from them.

Before he could sit on the seat of his car, the first deputy arrived.

Ron Morrison was writing his report on Dora Cox's incident when the officer in need of aid call came out, all points. Dropping his pen, he ran for his vehicle as did everyone else. Denny Wade, a ten year veteran, cut off his run to his car, as he heard the use of four wheel drives was advised. He jumped behind the wheel of the closest one in the garage, while Morrison slid into the passenger side. Within two minutes, a convoy of police cars from every town in the area joined the cars from the Sheriff's Department to answer the aid call.

There is an unwritten rule that every policeman obeys. When an officer in need of aid call goes out over the air, you drop whatever it may be that you are doing and you respond. You respond just as quickly as possible, even if you hate the guy. One day it could be you needing the help. You would have the same feeling as you would have should you give a party and no one came. Cops only have other cops in the end. They are a family like no other.

Literally minutes after Benson cleared his radio call, the cars started to pull in the driveway. Soon Sheriff's cars, as well as Police Officers from Sullivan, Maple Hills, Cuba, and three available Highway Patrol units, were waiting for the Sheriff to speak.

Over a bullhorn, Benson briefly explained the situation. He told them Lansdowne was still out there with whatever monster had killed Janey and Dave Malone. The first and foremost order of business was to secure Lansdowne's safety. Everyone was to go in, no less than in groups of two. They were to cut over land through the Carter's fields, entering where Dora Cox now lived. That was the fastest way. Nothing was to go out over the radio. Cell phones only or channel two of the Sheriff's Department radio. Nothing over the air that could be picked up over a scanner.

The sky was not quite twilight but Benson knew they had less than fifteen or twenty minutes of light left.

Someone made a comment that he needed a medic unit. Benson agreed. Have one on standby at Dora's.

"Now, for you, you're a damn sight."

Benson gave a look at the officer that was icy-cold and said, "Later. We have a damn brave man we need to get."

The phalanx of red and blue lighted police cars sped the miles to the entry point of Robert Carter's home. There, upon their arrival, they were met by a four-wheel pickup truck driven by the two detectives. The bed was filled with generators, floodlights, fuel and more. Behind them was the Coroner.

Overhead, the whirling sound of blades slicing through the air from the Highway Patrol helicopter, were heard. A trooper on the ground told the Sheriff to take the lead. The bird would light the way with his floods. Benson was the only one who knew the location. He prayed he could find it, coming in this way. Sitting high in the four-wheeler helped him see over the uncut grass. Somewhere there was a wide wet weather creek, but he wasn't sure just where it was, exactly in relation to where he left Lansdowne.

He saw the tree line and drove slower as to see. Almost directly in front were the two hills and the rock face with the cave. Benson honked his horn, but Lansdowne failed to appear. He knew there was no way that the man he left standing guard could possibly fail to hear the cars or the helicopter.

All of the vehicles stopped at the edge of the woods. Headlights and floodlights lit the area bright as day. There was still no Lansdowne. Benson yelled for everyone to spread out and look. He had to be there. Oh God let him be there, Benson prayed. His belly was again doing the flip-flops. Benson was scared. He should never have allowed him to stay. He should have forced him to go back.

Benson screamed for his men to find Lansdowne, but the brief search availed nothing.

"Does anyone see him?" No one said a word. Only vacant stares met Benson's eyes.

Suddenly the roar of five shotgun blasts, were heard east of their present location.

"You two with the big flashlights, with me! Now goddammit, now!"

Chapter 12

Lansdowne watched Benson move back down the trail from the grotesque and appalling place, until he was out of sight. The Sheriff's breathing was labored earlier, during their walk into the woods. He hoped the man would pace himself back. There was no need for him to have a heart attack.

Scanning the landscape, he looked for a more defensible location. Where he then stood was a strategic mistake. He was open to attack on three sides. For just a moment, he felt like a Judas Goat. Just a piece of bait. Hoping to find a position that was not just defensible, but would offer an offensive one as well, he looked to the trees.

As most deer hunters know, an elevated position renders the best angle of vision, as well as prevents detection by the quarry.

Finding an oak tree that was manageable to climb and giving him a complete range of view, he set the safety on his weapon and shouldered it. He had to climb up the hill opposite the rock face to get to the tree he wanted. The clamber up the thirty or so degree grade was somewhat taxing, even for Lansdowne. He used scrub trees and thorn bushes to assist, grabbing them one by one, pulling himself up until reaching the base of the tree.

The tree was not a wide one but it offered him the ability for his ascent. The branch picked was twenty feet above the ground and still had an abundance of leaves for concealment. It rendered the best viewing on two sides. From his perch, he was able to see the mouth of the cave, though it was much too far for the firing range of his weapon. With the short barrel, he had a comfortable kill shot of thirty to thirty-five yards. Possibly up to forty-five yards, but it would have to be a standing target. The magnum revolver, sitting at the small of his back, would give him just a small degree of more distance, but less stopping power. If he encountered the thing that was killing people, he wanted it dead.

There was a slight breeze into his face. It was not enough to affect a shot, and as high up as he sat it would conceal his scent…or he hoped it would.

Unslinging his weapon and bracing his legs around the branch with his back to the trunk of the tree, all he had to do was wait, either for it to return or for Benson. He did not care which happened first.

The sun was behind him and daylight was waning. The blue sky was being filled with hues of reds, pinks and purples. Lansdowne could not see the beauty of the setting sun which was shedding the last of its golden beams, about to give way to a black starry night. Nor did he care.

He did not care how long it took Benson and his troops to arrive. His total concentration was on the area surrounding him. He watched and listened for any movement. On the ground, the breeze that gently touched his face was nonexistent. The tall grass was to his right. Anything moving through would part it, like waves to a beach. To his left was the game trail that it was traversing and the woods that gave it cover.

All he could now do was to wait. Wait for whatever was going to happen. That was not the first time that Lansdowne had sat perched in a tree, waiting to take just one shot. One kill shot.

You do not eat, urinate, sleep, or even think. No distractions from the purpose; just watch and wait. No matter how long...for just the one shot.

Lansdowne did not have to wait long at all.

To his right the grass was parting, with sounds of something putting forth the effort in dragging a heavy weight. Slowly, the unmistakable odor rose and swamped Lansdowne's nose. His target was below but still out of sight and range. Tugging sounds were interrupted with an occasional low throaty growl, seemingly to be from a mix of effort and frustration.

With every passing second it was getting closer. Lansdowne slowly and quietly leaned forward, resting on the branch. He snugged the butt of the shotgun tight into his shoulder, releasing the safety to the firing position. His breathing was even, as he moved the tip of his index finger to settle lightly, but firmly, on the trigger.

He hoped for a head shot. Everything dies when its brains are spread across a distance of ground. For a nanosecond, Janey Malone's face flashed through his mind causing him to force the thought out. He could have nothing to interrupt his shot. The only thing that mattered just then was the kill. Not the reasons for it. Thinking, thoughts, reasons, are for afterward...if even then.

Just as suddenly as he had heard the movement, it stopped. It was still at least twenty yards out and not in sight. There was no shot. The grass that was separating no longer did so. It sensed something wrong. Lansdowne could hear it sniffing the air. Surely it could not smell him. He was too high and the wind, which was even less than before, was with him. It must have picked up his and Benson's scent in the clearing. That could be the only explanation. He continued to wait until it was satisfied the way was safe to continue.

Two determined killers waiting for the other to make a mistake.

Steadily, one step at a time, it moved closer to the clearing. It would take a step and then sniff the air again. Lansdowne thought he could almost make out the top of the back of the creature, just not enough for a shot at it. He could make an educated guess, but if it was wrong there would be no trying again. No second chance. There was no other choice but continue to wait, as time seemed to stand still.

There was movement in the grass, not toward the clearing though, but back away from it. For whatever reason, if animals can reason, it decided against entering the clearing. Perhaps instinctually it felt being watched, or perhaps the smell of the two men permeated the clearing. Regardless, it was headed back through the grass in the direction from which it came. But it was not leaving alone. It was again dragging whatever it was with it.

Lansdowne felt fairly certain it must be a meal. Little else would cause an animal, feeling a possible impending danger, not to flee as fast as possible. Almost always hunger. And this one must be hungry enough not to want to lose it.

That was all the edge Lansdowne would need. Being greedy should slow it up…or so he hoped.

Coming out of the tree from his perch, Lansdowne was as quiet as a snake.

He formulated a quick plan. Calculating the pace which the animal was moving pulling its burden along, as well as the direction, he could cut it off. If he walked across the incline then down the hill to his right, he would meet the high grassy field. Then cutting up and around, with a small bit of luck, he should be able to get in front of it for a shot.

Lansdowne moved as quickly and silently as possible upon the litter of sticks and leaves blanketing the forest floor. Brambles intertwined into the scrubs could have made passing impossible had he not been intent with his prey. His eyes adjusted to what small amount of light remained, lessened by the forest thickness. There would be more light once in the field, but only a fraction, and he needed every sun ray. Once it was dark he would lose his edge to the animal. Evolution endowed beasts of the field with night vision, attained by man only with technology.

Once in the grass, stalking became no easier. He had to crouch low as he was taller than the grass. He could still hear the sound of the beast's labor. Continuing with his plan, he circled around attempting to get in front, taking steps several at a time and then stopping to listen. The breeze changed direction and not in his favor. Possibly it was too preoccupied and would only smell the blood of its victim.

The smell of the thing was all around him enveloping the area. It had to be very close but there was no sound at all. The quiet was deafening.

Slowly parting the grass with the barrel of the twelve-gauge, his whole being was on alert. The golden-brown strands separated enough to see a body of an old woman, wearing a torn and tattered blue dress. Cloud white hair had been replaced with hair covered in brown and red blood. Leaves, grass, and dirt covered her once delightful smiling face.

He dwelled looking too long. The only word entering his mind was, "Shit!" Lansdowne knew he had been outwitted. It was there. He could smell it like it had smelled him all the time. It left its food lay there in order to protect it. There was nothing more vicious than a wild animal, nor was there anything more moronic than for someone to try to take its food away.

He had figured on its hunger and greed. He was wrong, and it may now cost him his life. The idea of becoming a second entrée on the menu did not appeal to him. It was hunting him and it was a professional. That is what it did for a living. All Lansdowne could do was to let it attack and hope to counter.

As motionless as the body in front of him, he waited. Not only could he smell it, he could hear its breathing over the sound of his heart pounding. They were slow deep breaths an animal takes moments before a sure kill.

That is when it made its only mistake. Stepping on a dried leaf, causing a crunching sound that seemed to echo in Lansdowne's ears, signaled it was behind him. It too, heard the leaf crunch. As it did, it sprung through the air with a practiced attack.

Lansdowne did not hesitate propelling himself forward, turning to his side while in the air, and firing the weapon. The first round hit the beast squarely in its massive chest causing it to flip head over backwards. Amazingly, it found its feet again and started another charge. The mouth of the beast was a gaping chasm, with saliva mixed with its own blood running down the mouth to the neck. The canines were large thick daggers protruding from the top of its huge square muzzle. It took no notice that a good chunk of its innards had just been blown out its asshole, while it launched itself for an airborne attack.

The old lady was a fresh enough kill that blood still pooled an amount, enough so that when Lansdowne tried to right himself, he slipped in it and over the body. The second shot he fired hit nothing. He rolled and attempted to get his feet away from the body. Racking a third round, he was about to fire when the beast found him, sinking only one of its teeth into his left shoulder. The four inch canine was buried all the way in his body. He felt his collar bone break. The warm sticky blood spurted from the wound into his face and eyes. The animal turned and twisted trying to get the tooth out, causing Lansdowne to scream in pain very nearly dropping his only defense. If he had dropped the shotgun, there would have been no chance to get the magnum. Lansdowne felt that he knew he was going to die, but through the pain and blood was pissed, pissed beyond pissed. If he was going to die, so was that son of a bitch. With one huge twist the beast broke itself free, ripping the flesh and muscle in his chest, laying it open. Lansdowne screamed again from the horrendous pain, but got to his knees. His left arm was useless now. The monster threw its head back to bring down the death blow. As the head went back, Lansdowne fired hitting it under the throat. The round passed into, and out of the top of, the gigantic head. Lansdowne, throwing the weapon up, grabbed the pump action, racked another round and fired again hitting it in the head. What teeth and brains the last round missed, that one got. Using the stock of the weapon on the ground, Lansdowne pushed himself up to his feet. Once more, he racked the weapon and fired. If before he was pretty sure it was dead, he was then absolutely sure.

He turned and staggered over to the body of the old woman. Dropping the shotgun, he picked up her hand and held it. Tears ran from the corners of his eyes. Not for him but for her. He knelt next to her, crying.

Voices calling his name were followed by three men with flashlights.

"Mark, Mark, it's me, Ralph."

Looking up, he saw the Sheriff's face and half smiled saying, "Hi Ralph...best I...could do...was...get us even. I'm sorry."

Benson grabbed him as he fell forward, telling him he had him. He would be okay. Medics were on the way. Just hold on.

Lansdowne looked at him. He knew he was close to Benson's face but it was just a blur.

"Bullshit, Ralph."

Lansdowne's eyes closed.

November

Chapter 1

Light hurt his eyes under the strained attempt to open them. The effort seemed more trouble expending the energy to see than what it was worth. Relaxing momentarily before trying again, he tried listening for sounds to identify his environment. There was nothing he could discern. There was a machine humming softly and steadily. Then a click, click, click. Yes, it was a clock counting off the seconds.

Wondering if he could move, he raised the index finger of his right hand. It went up, then the middle finger. He was able to raise it as well. Wiggling all of the fingers on his right hand worked. As he sought to lift his arm he felt the wrist restraint. Hmmm, okay, the left he thought, but there was no feeling.

Fear gripped him. The injury was bad. He knew that. How bad? Had he lost his arm? He had to see. He must make his eyes open.

With all the mental concentration he could muster, the left eye opened. It was just a slit with little focus. Even as blurry as his sight may have been, the outline of his left hand was visible. His heart slowed down as he realized that if he had a left hand, it must still be attached to an arm.

Lansdowne felt a tube in his nose. Oxygen, he wondered? His throat was dry and sort of burned. It must be O_2. The thought flew through his morphine-saturated mind.

Women's voices, speaking softly, floated into his ears. The sounds they made were sweet and musical to hear. The clicking of the clock started irritating him. It seemed as though it kept getting louder. He tried to listen to the voices of the women. He concentrated hard, but the damn clock would not be silenced.

He was able to open the right eye. Steadily, but slowly, sight was returning. Objects in the room came into focus first. IV tubes ran to the back of both hands. There was one that had red fluid going into his right forearm. Blood. A machine with red number readouts was on one side and another to the other side. The second one had electrical leads from it to his chest. The other seemed to control the IV's.

Moving his head to the right, he saw the thick shock of short, grayish-looking hair that unmistakably belonged to Warren Skruggs. His chin rested on his chest as he sat in a hospital reclining chair. Skruggsy was sleeping soundly. A blanket covered his large frame up to his neck except for his right arm.

Lansdowne knew Skruggs was sitting watch. It must have been touch and go for him if Skruggs was there.

Venturing to turn his head to the left, he set off all the bells and whistles on the machines. From the corner of his eye he saw Skruggs get up and out of the chair. He was walking to his side wearing a wide, toothy grin.

"They've been taking odds on you, pal. You just won me a bunch of money."

One of the nurses rushed into the room shutting alarms off that sounded from the machines.

She was of medium height and slim, with hair the color of new copper wire, cut short, framing her creamy complexion.

Lansdowne wanted to say something, but could not. His throat was drier than the Sahara in summer.

After working with the machines, the nurse left the room briefly. When she returned there was a white Styrofoam cup in her delicate right hand. Taking a white plastic spoon, she retrieved a few ice chips and put them into Lansdowne's mouth. The frozen liquid soothed the burning and tasted better than the most expensive liquor that he had ever drank. She gave him a few more to melt in his mouth. Again, attempts at speaking were futile.

"Just a little more then that's all for now." Her voice sounded like she was singing rather than speaking.

She picked up the handle attached to the machine, with the plunger button on the end. Before the nurse could push the button, Lansdowne managed to get the word, "Wait," out. It was more of a mouthed whisper, but she heard it.

With his right index finger he indicated for her to come near, looking into her light brown eyes he could actually see. Her nose turned up slightly at the end like a pixie's. She leaned her ear close to his mouth as he said, "Tell him he owes me half the money, and you have a great ass." Her perfume smelled like flowers, light and delicate. It was perfect for her.

Blushing slightly with a bit of an impish smile, she looked at him and said, "Go back to sleep," and pressed the button.

He wanted to say no but it was too late, as waves of morphine washed over him.

The last thing he heard before drifting off was Skruggs saying, "Shut up and enjoy it. It's legal."

From what sounded like a voice over a great distance, barely audible, came to him. The tender loving voice he had not heard for such a very long time, spoke.

"Mike, Mike! Listen to me. Can you hear me?" It was her "I have another project for the list, but I want it done first," voice. It was more of a command than a request voice, which all married men have heard.

"Yes Glenna, I hear you. Where are you? I can't see you!"

"No you can't, but I'm right here with you. I only have a short time, so listen." Her voice faded in and out, like listening to a song you want to hear on a car radio from a distant station.

"You need to get better. Your wounds are terrible, but they will heal quickly. Mike, you have to stop it! You must!"

"I don't want to get better. I want you."

"You had me my love, now you have to move on."

"I just want us to be together again. Like before. Just you and me."

"No Mike, you have to go on. The stooges need you, especially Curly. He does love you."

"Only because I feed him."

"I have to go now. I love you." Her voice was again fading.

"Don't go yet! Will we talk again?"

"No."

"Don't go," he was pleading, begging.

"I still have your ugly lamp."

Her girlish giggle was fading into the distant realm from which it had come.

"I love you, Mike. Good-bye, my love."

"I love you too, my sweet Glenna."

A nurse working the night shift, checking the machines, saw the tears rolling down his sleeping cheeks. Thinking he must be in pain, she pushed the button.

Light caused pain, sending shocks to the back of his brain, bouncing around from each side to settle behind the eyes. He could see the blue painted walls. On one wall hung a picture of a landscape that was bad enough to keep him in intensive care. The front wall of the room, from ceiling to floor, was glass only interrupted by the doorway. Nurses spoke softly as they moved from room to room checking other patients, while others at the desk studied charts or made notations within them. The recliner was there against the wall to the right of his bed. The blanket, which had covered Skruggs during his vigil by Lansdowne's side, was neatly folded on the seat. Skruggs was gone...or at least, he was not in the room. The machines still gently hummed and the clock still clicked off the seconds.

He did not move any part of his body. The majority of his extremities had functioned well enough and moving would only set off the alarms.

Then again, he wondered if the redhead with the nice butt would enter the room and turn them off. He also wondered if she, in fact, did have as nice a butt, or if it was the morphine that made him think she did. If he set the alarms off it would only give him a headache. Instead of an aspirin they would just shoot him with more morphine. Since he was formulating clear thoughts, not having someone fill him with more dope was a good idea.

No more was his throat burning or dry. The oxygen tube to his nose was gone. So was the bag of blood that replaced what he lost during the brief, but nearly fatal, battle. Lansdowne may not have fared very well, but on the upside he was still alive. His adversary was not as lucky…as if being in a hospital bed with tubes and drugs inside his body, was lucky.

Lansdowne felt a pang of hunger. With having no knowledge of how long he laid in the hospital, the last meal he remembered was the evening before the incident. The memory was fuzzy as to what he ate. Really, it did not matter, he was hungry now. However, how to go about getting some food without causing a commotion eluded him. So he said, "What the hell," and made a half-hearted attempt of sitting upright, hoping to set off the alarms.

He did. Every alarm in the room exploded a warning to the nursing station that something was very wrong. Lansdowne was not laughing on the outside, but was roaring with laughter inside watching the nurses scramble into his room, including the redhead. She made the door first, followed by three more with concern painted upon their faces.

Shutting off the alarms and checking the readout of the machines with flashing numbers was performed by the other three nurses, while Red went to his side. Smiling, he winked at her and said, "Food." The pain emanating from his shoulder and chest gave him pause not to move like that again. The look on Red's face told him if the incident was repeated she would be sorely vexed with him. Her face was flushed red, but he could tell she was only mildly angry.

"You do that again and they may have to redo everything. Now be a good boy and lay there." Her tone was one that Lansdowne, in his condition, was smart enough not to challenge.

"Maybe I should have said, "Please!" He winked at her again. She smiled and told him she could raise the back of the bed if he would like.

"Please."

Pushing a control button, she raised the back halfway up and then set the control out of his reach. Without saying another word, she walked out of the room to the nurses' station. He could see them clearly, as his room was immediately in front of the nurses' station and his head no longer foggy. She was behind the desk, bent half over at the waist, looking at a computer monitor. Her face was expressionless as she turned and walked out of his viewing.

Awake only a small amount of time, he was bored with nothing to do but lie there and listen to the clock tick off time. The hands of the clock indicated the time at 10:30, but day or night? Not that it mattered. He was going nowhere. He could not even sit upright without assistance and he hoped Red was not too upset with him. She was all he had just then. He was not tired, but closed his eyes anyway.

Maybe if he listened to the clock tick long enough he would fall back to sleep. Concentrating as hard as he possibly could, the ticking just got louder. There was no way he was going to sleep again. No time soon.

Someone entered his room. He listened to the light footsteps approaching. Slowly opening his eyes, Red was standing next to his bed with a food tray. Setting the tray on the bedside table, she turned to lower the bedrail. No aroma came from the direction of the tray. He wondered if it was food. Her turn was more graceful than a ballet dancer as she moved the tray table into position. Red balanced the white plastic spoon in her fingers, much as a skilled surgeon would a scalpel. Her fingers were a little long and her fingernails were unpainted. On her left wrist she wore a black banded watch with a large face. Placing the spoon into a white plastic bowl, she picked up a chunk of the old staple of the hospital…green jello.

"Before you feed me, what is your name?"

"Cindy," she told him, without much expression on her face or in her voice.

"I do apologize for any word or action said or done by me, to cause you or anyone else a problem." He made his voice as sincere as he could. The green jello was not what he had in mind as an item on the menu.

"You did nothing wrong. Your trying to sit up could have torn everything loose. No one wants that. We're all amazed and happy at your recovery so far."

"Then I don't have to fall on my knees, bowing low before your feet, to get real food rather than a green something that you're about to feed me? For a steak, I would almost be willing to sacrifice my first-born son to you."

Cindy laughed at his words. She liked him. He had a sense of humor. That was different from the patients normally in her charge. They were sick people and concerned with what was going to happen to them. Most were as nice as they could be under the circumstances they were facing. Still, he made her laugh and more than once.

"Mr. Lansdowne…"

"Mark. Please, call me Mark."

"Okay, Mark, you have not had any food for a bit. We have to start slow. Your stomach won't take it. Right now, solid food would make you sick. You'd probably throw up. That would cause more problems than you want. Now, open up or I'll force feed you, buster!"

She was smiling. Lansdowne thought it was a wonderful smile. Her lips parted just enough to see very white teeth.

"I'll eat, but one other question?"

"As long as it has nothing to do with my anatomy," said Nurse Cindy.

"It doesn't. I'll ask those later. Is it day or night?"

"Day. Now shut up and eat."

"Yes ma'am."

Cindy placed the green jello into his mouth. He thought of baby birds being fed in the nest, with heads back chirping for more. He bet that was what he looked like just then. She took the time for each cube of the cold gelatin to melt in his mouth and run down his throat. She watched him closely for any signs of a problem, as he swallowed the lime-tasting fluid.

He turned his head for her to wait on the next spoonful. He asked how long he had been hospitalized. She told him the doctor would be in later and would talk to him. He nodded, and then asked what day it was? Friday, she told him. He knew he had been there at least a week. There was more than one way to get an answer. He knew it was almost 11:00 A.M. on a Friday, at least a week later. It was Friday on the day of the incident.

She gave him another lime chunk. There was a small tan line on her left hand's ring finger. Cindy was either not wearing her wedding ring because of the job, or was no longer married. Women, as a general rule, do not remove a wedding ring unless forced to do so. It was a question that was too soon, and maybe too personal, to ask. The question could wait to be asked later...if ever. Really, Lansdowne did not know how well he wanted to get to know her if she was to continue feeding him the green stuff. He could feel his wedding ring was still in place. Knowing items like jewelry were taken for safekeeping, he asked Nurse Cindy why he was allowed to keep wearing the plain gold band.

Not actually present in the emergency room at the time, she related what she heard. One of the male nurses attempted to remove the ring, but Lansdowne, even next to death, grabbed the man's wrist and almost broke it to prevent the removal. It took three large men to get him to break his grip on the man, but only after the doctor convinced Lansdowne it could stay.

Lansdowne told her that if she should see him, to tell him that he apologized for hurting him. She said the guy was a bit of a sissy and was off from work.

The nurse placed the last of the lime gelatin in his mouth and asked if he wanted more. He could have another bowl.

"I'd rather be waterboarded. Maybe later," he responded.

A smile that turned up the corners of her mouth and eyes came over her face. She did look like a pixie. "Okay, Mark. I'll be back later," she said, turning to leave the room.

He watched her leave the room with the tray, and smiled.

She does have a nice butt, he thought, letting sleep again ebb and flow over his body.

Chapter 2

Several more days passed after Lansdowne regained consciousness. As promised, the doctor was in everyday to see him as well as to give him a daily update. Lansdowne was healing at an unheard of rate. The wound in his neck and chest should still have been red, but instead were pink. The pain had diminished greatly, where no pain medications were ordered unless he asked for them.

Doctor Paul Kastor would not go into detail about the seriousness of the wounds or the extent of injury. He would enter the room, remove the dressing and check the sutures. When pressed by Lansdowne, he did say that the clavicle was nicked by the puncture, but the fang had otherwise missed anything vital. He had lost a good deal of blood and was worried about infection. That, as a matter of fact, was the largest concern. The combination of antibiotics he was receiving must be the reason Lansdowne was healing at such a rapid rate. The bandages were no longer a reddish color with blood and yellowish-green ooze. They came off without sticking to the wound.

For the four days since waking, the only things in the way of nutrition were soup and gelatin. He asked the doctor when he could have solid food and when his incarceration would be terminated. He felt well enough for both.

Kastor smiled. He could have a small amount of solid food that evening. The doctor also felt he could be moved from intensive care to a private room, but Lansdowne should consider being a guest a bit longer. It was possible he could be home by Saturday of that week, but to wait and see. One other thing, the Sheriff wanted to speak with him as soon as Lansdowne felt well enough. Tomorrow in his new room would be fine, but it would cost him two big hamburgers with fried onions, and a big cup of Coke.

It was the small things having been denied that he wanted most. Hamburgers were not his favorite food. They just sounded wonderful.

Kastor said he would pass it along.

Nurse Cindy had not been at work the past several days and Lansdowne missed talking to her. She was intelligent and witty but avoided questions about herself, even when he would ask the question again later rephrasing it. He heard of patients who fell in love with their nurses. She was probably avoiding that situation. He, in no way, wanted to fall in love for any reason. Once had been enough. Lansdowne needed no romantic interest in his life. He was just curious about her. Nurse Cindy did not know him or his feelings, and was just being protective for both.

He had found out that she worked three days, consisting of a twelve hour shift each day and then off for the next four days. That piece of information came from a nurse on nights. Most all of the nurses in ICU worked those hours.

Lansdowne was moved that evening into a private room. Most everything about the room was the same, except there was no glass wall; the room had a toilet with a shower and a television that worked. A window to the outside world decorated one wall. The view was mostly of the parking lot, but he could see the world. Shortly after arriving in his new room, he received a food tray brought into his room by a smiling, a bit overweight, grey-haired nurse named Emma. She placed it on the tray table, dropped the guard rail of the bed and swung the table across him. His right arm was free to use, no longer was there an IV in it. There was only the one in the left arm yet.

"You need some help?" Nurse Emma offered.

"Only if you'll help bust me out of here."

"Can't do that. Push the button if you need something. Otherwise I'll be back later to get your tray. I have sick people in here," she said, smiling at him as she left the room.

Taking the lid from the tray revealed his feast was meatloaf, green beans and mashed potatoes. It was the same evening meal occupants of jails get every day, he thought. Oh well! He took his time chewing his supper, relishing each bite.

Good to her word, Nurse Emma returned for his tray along with several pills in a small white cup. Popping the pills in his mouth and washing them down with a sip of water, he asked what they were. Something to help him sleep, he was told.

"Emma, sleeping is not the problem. It's dreaming."

"You won't, and if you do you won't remember. Goodnight son." She turned off the light to the room as she left. The television was still on.

Soon he slumbered. Not deeply, but without dreams.

Morning came, and with it the light of day and a breakfast tray consisting of scrambled eggs, bacon, unbuttered toast and lukewarm coffee. All in all, he was pleased with the meal.

Sometime during the night someone turned the TV off. He saw the time was 8:15 A.M., so he could catch the news with his favorite green-eyed news anchor and John what's-his-name on Channel 2. He did not get to see much of her, as Doctor Kastor came in his room followed dutifully by new interns. They surrounded his bed, seriously watching everything Kastor did and said. Kastor gave the group a brief history, saying he had been attacked by an animal.

A very pretty, young, soon to be doctor asked, "What kind of an animal could inflict such a wound?" As Kastor removed the bandage, she almost turned white and her large brown eyes got even larger looking at the wound.

"A very large pissed off one," Lansdowne told them, but directed it to her. "I felt like Goldilocks." There were a few chuckles from the male interns. The chuckling immediately stopped when Kastor set his gaze upon them.

"Doc, one way or another, I'm outta here Saturday. Okay?"

"Chances are good. Now, let's get that thread out."

Sheriff Ralph Benson and Deputy Ron Morrison appeared at the doorway of the hospital room near lunchtime. Benson carried a brown paper bag and the deputy had a two-liter bottle of soda. They both were smiling very happily; Lansdowne was alive and recovering. The men held great admiration for Lansdowne and for the deed accomplished. Few men could have lived.

Benson handed the bag to Lansdowne, who tore into it. Within a minute of opening one of the wrapped burgers, the room was blanketed with the smell of fried onions. It reminded Lansdowne of the greasy spoon where he ate so many meals as a kid, one of the few good childhood memories he still retained.

Lansdowne ate and the Sheriff spoke, telling him his dogs were being taken care of by Skruggs. After the incident the dogs would not let anyone into the house. Morrison remembered about the friendship between the two and told him what took place. Benson said he felt uneasy around Skruggs. He grinned too much.

"If he stops grinning at you, leave just as fast as you can...if you can," Lansdowne stated. "Otherwise you're fine around him. We've been friends since we were kids. He always grins." Lansdowne knew the deadly consequences when Skruggs stopped grinning.

The Sheriff and Morrison had pulled chairs next to the hospital bed, and waited for Lansdowne to finish the first burger before asking if he remembered much of what had happened.

Up until the time he passed out, he remembered everything clearly. Lansdowne gave his reasons for moving and what occurred thereafter until the Sheriff arrived. Damn shame about Granny

Barton. Benson nodded his agreement, saying that she thought she was getting over on the county not paying sales tax or getting permits. Most of the stuff in the place was her property. The county just considered it a yard sale. He doubted she ever made enough to buy groceries. When they went into her house they found three dresses in the closet; a yellow, a white, and a black dress. She was buried in the white.

Lansdowne had the second hamburger unwrapped, thinking of the old woman's smiling face, when he looked at Benson and asked, "How many? How many total?"

"We're not sure, but it may be as high as seven. You know about the three. There were two girls from earlier in the year; we're waiting on DNA to come back. Myron Cox has disappeared and Bud Carr was killed and fed on at his home. Bud's wife, Carol, passed away at the nursing home that evening. No one could find him so they called us to make the notification. Morrison, here, found him the next morning."

"Seven, huh?"

"Well, none of this is to leave this room, but Maple Hills has two missing kids. They were out trick-or-treating and never came home. In view of what happened, Maple Hill's P. D. turned it over to us. There's been an Amber Alert out, but…nothing so far. The searches have turned nothing up."

"How old were they?" asked Lansdowne, not touching the other sandwich.

"Nine and ten. A ten year old boy and his sister."

Rewrapping the second burger, Lansdowne, no longer with an appetite, placed it back into the bag. There was a long silence before he could find a voice.

"It was getting dark and everything happened in a New York minute, but what was that damn thing? It looked like a wolf...sort of. The face was too flat and the head was too wide. A feral dog?"

"We're waiting on DNA from that as well. I'll take your word on what the face looked like. A man spent two days recovering bone fragments. The canines measured three and three-quarter inches."

"Yeah, I know all about them, but mea culpa on blowing the head away. It just seemed like a good idea at the time."

Morrison piped up asking, "What kind of round did you use? There were lead fragments all through it."

"Hot load wad cutters."

"Why on earth would you have those?"

"Obviously, to kill big bad things trying to eat me, or most anything else wishing to cause my immediate demise. They seemed to do the job, but it did take all five. By the way Ralph, what did you do with my weapon?"

"We kept the shotgun for evidence. You'll get it back later. I promise. The revolver, I gave to your pal Skruggs."

"I'll never see it again. He's wanted it for years."

"Sorry."

"Don't be. I was going to give it to him for Christmas anyway."

Framed in the doorway was one of the most beautiful women either the Sheriff or his deputy had ever seen. Long platinum hair fell in waves crashing to her shoulders, while surrounding the smiling eyes and bright red lips, parted to reveal perfect white teeth. She wore a black blouse, opened to the crevasse between her breasts. The designer jeans fit perfectly, only indicating what would be beneath them. The heels she wore only accentuated her legs, making her just a little taller than she really was. A graceful walk carried her to the side of Lansdowne's bed. She completely ignored the two law officers sitting there, pushing past them. Then she set the gym bag on the floor, putting one of her arms around his waist ever so gently and the other behind his neck, kissing Lansdowne on the cheek. The kiss lasted just a bit longer than a moment.

"I am so glad you're alive Mike...er...Mark." She shot a glance at the Sheriff to see if he heard her slip. She saw no reaction other than his open mouth.

"Hear you need a haircut, darlin'. Ready?"

"Sure, Amie." Lansdowne said smiling. Turning his head toward Benson, "Now you understand."

Benson wore a wide grin. "Yeah, yeah I do."

"Before you leave, one other question: What was the sex of the animal I killed, if you know?"

"Female. Why?" asked Benson with a quizzical look.

"I was just wondering, that's all."

Chapter 3

After cutting his hair and manscaping his beard, Amie stayed another couple of hours talking to him. Lansdowne had no idea what her IQ tested out to be, but there was never any doubt it was high. Speaking to her and listening was always a treat. She was so gentle and caring, yet underneath all the intelligence and beauty she was tough as nails. After Glenna passed, Amie went and fixed her hair and applied her makeup. Glenna looked as she always looked when she slept. Amie always thought highly of Glenna, as did Glenna of her. Amie had cut their hair for years. Before Mark Lansdowne was Mark Lansdowne. She was one of the very few people he trusted almost completely. Amie knew that when she was around him she was safer than with God in church. Glenna knew that feeling everyday of her life.

Amie Beels was comfortable in the friendship with Glenna and Mark Lansdowne, knowing it was friendship. After Glenna died she was glad to know the friendship with Mark would stay the same. Lansdowne felt deeply about her, but never could feel about anyone as he did his wife, and she knew and respected that. She never wanted more. He knew that too.

As she got ready to leave, she kissed him again on the cheek never giving a thought to his lips. He told her he would send her a check when he got home. She smiled the warm smile she kept for those closest to her, as the light danced in her eyes, "It's on me, Darlin'. I don't want to come back here. You come see me in six weeks, okay?"

"Sure. Anything you say, kiddo."

Reaching the door she heard him say, "Thanks. Love ya, pal."

She turned and looked at him and smiling, blew him a kiss. "Love you too. Now get better." She left him for the hour drive back to St. Louis. She had appointments that evening with other clients.

After Amie left he had time to think. Not about her, but rather his conversation with the Sheriff and deputy.

There were possibly nine, maybe as many as eleven people dead or missing, and two of them not much more than babies. He did not know Myron Cox and from what he heard about him not many, if any, would very much miss him.

Still too many people died in one day. It did not make sense.

Dave and Janey were killed early in the morning of the 31st. Janey's body had been fed on. Later that day, Bud Carr died, but at what time? He killed the beast that killed Granny Barton and presumably Cox as well. It was just too many for one animal. Too much distance for one animal to cover and just too many kills. No one animal, even as big as the one he killed, could be that hungry. Or could it? He did not think it could be possible, yet the Sheriff did not mention any more people missing or dead since then.

He shook his head to clear the thoughts. It wasn't his problem. It just wasn't, not that night. Because he was pissed about Janey, he had made it his problem and it damn near cost him his life. Enough is enough. It was Benson's problem, not his, even if he felt bad about the babies. He had done too much as it was.

Lansdowne's thoughts were interrupted by Nurse Cindy walking into his room, except she was not dressed as a nurse for work. She was dazzlingly beautiful. More so than his stay in intensive care. Or maybe he had been too drugged as to really be able to notice. The light from overhead jumped from one place of her hair to the next, causing brilliantly shining copper colors to accentuate other patches with a dark red hue. Her lipstick almost matched the color of her hair. The sheepish smile slanted the corners of her eyes and mouth upward. A blue sweater fought to restrain her breasts and looked like it was losing the battle. The black dress slacks formed perfectly around her legs. He knew without seeing that the pants did the same for her butt. She was taller, as the three-inch heels raised her in height.

"After your friend left it didn't seem that you had any visitors. I thought you might like one," she said, in a low melodious voice. Taking his right hand into hers, she asked how he felt.

"You wouldn't believe me," thinking first of Amie, now her.

"Not that I care, but isn't this against some sort of hospital policy? I wouldn't want you to get in trouble with the powers here, or your husband."

"Ex-husband, and there's no policy I can think of as long as there's no sex involved. Anyway, you're wearing a wedding band. I just came in to check on you. Where's your wife anyway?"

"She died some time ago."

"I am so sorry to have even asked." She flushed again with embarrassment.

"No need. It has been over a year." He thought maybe he should change the subject, quickly. She looked as though she was about to cry.

"I don't even know your last name, if I may ask."

Her face brightened and she asked, "Married or maiden?"

"Why not both?"

"Married is Winters. Maiden is Roberts. My family is in Perryville. I moved here after we married. He is from here."

"Which do you go by?"

"Winters. It would cost too much to change it back."

"Why don't you tell me about yourself; becoming a nurse, where you went to school, things like that."

"Are you sure you want to know?" She was so happy that he was not upset about the wife crack she had made, that she started a monologue that went on for over an hour.

Lansdowne could tell it was nervous chatter but he did like the sound of her soft voice. He judged her to be in her mid-thirties just from things she spoke about, and she spoke about a good many things.

While she talked, his supper tray arrived. He told the young girl who was delivering the trays he did not care for it, but thank you for the effort. Cindy Winters told the girl to leave the tray. She told him he would eat it himself or she would force feed him. He protested, saying if he wanted prison food he could have asked the Sheriff to arrest him, and that he could eat at the expense of the County.

She looked at him startled for a moment then said, "You don't know, do you?"

"Know what?" Raising an eyebrow.

"You are here at the expense of the County. You were admitted as a Deputy. Then your friend showed the Sheriff his badge and I.D., and said you were a Federal agent, like him."

Lansdowne laughed out loud, "He did, did he?"

It was at that exact time the lanky, toothy-grinned Warren Skruggs entered the room. He was closely followed by the beautiful blonde-haired, blue-eyed woman, who he did not have the right to be in her company. Lonny Skruggs, Warren's wife of eight years.

Lansdowne made introductions all around. Skruggs piped out, "I remember you. You've got the great…"

Lansdowne, remembering what he had said, cut Skruggs off before he could finish.

"Yes, she does. Leave it alone, Skruggsy." Skruggs' smile got wider and Lonny looked confused. Cindy just turned a deep shade of red.

Lonny placed a bag on the tray table and took out a large Styrofoam to-go box, then opened it revealing what Lansdowne felt was the world's most wonderful steak. The Steak Tuscany from Aldo's made exclusively for Lansdowne by Aldo himself. Lonny put the steak on a dinner plate and said, "Al says to get better. Can you feed yourself or should I do it for you?"

Before Lansdowne could answer, Cindy Winters had cut a slice of the steak and set it into his mouth. Lansdowne was in heaven. It is best steak in the world. The best and only friend left in the world and two of the best looking women in the world willing to feed him, after having his hair cut by one of the most beautiful women on earth.

Lansdowne now wondered how long he could make his recovery last.

Chapter 4

Wolves have not existed in the State of Missouri since before the last century. On the rare occasion that one has been sighted, it is more often mistaken for a large coyote or a wild dog. This was the case in 1999 when a livestock owner thought a coyote was attacking his sheep. He shot and killed the animal. After examining the body, the farmer found a radio collar as well as an ear tag. He called Missouri Conservation and turned it over to them. They traced the animal to northern Michigan where it was collared, tagged, and released. It traveled all that distance and no one seemed to notice. Not even Michigan, for whatever reason (the one given, and probably the truth was that the collar stopped transmitting a signal). They had neither funds nor manpower to look for it.

That incident was the rare one, and the one most often referred to by Conservation agents in Missouri. Otherwise, "They just ain't here," as it was once said. But it was once said there were no black bears in Missouri. The Police Officers in Maple Hills chased one off the interstate into the woods several years ago. Up to then, "They just ain't here." Wild hogs, "Just ain't here," either.

In fairness to the wonderful hardworking men and women, who do their best to answer the public's questions after being fed misinformation, they can only guess at the truth. These people do the best possible job.

The local conservation agents, like Christine McKay, know a wolf sighting in the Ozark region is slim to none. They, from their experience, feel confident enough to truthfully say, "They just ain't here." Insofar as they know, that is the truth.

That was why the Conservation Department was a bit more than boggled over the carcass from Crawford County, as it resembled an extra-large grey wolf. By extra-large, it outweighed most adult male grey wolves by fifty pounds (once all the pieces were weighed). The beast was much wider and much longer than any known species. On the autopsy table, most of what the doctors had led them to want to say was that it was a hybrid. Some type of mix. Hybrids are not unheard of in the wild. But true professionals want facts, not guesses or assumptions.

DNA testing of the hair from the animal revealed an absolute fact. It was a wolf. Hair samples taken out of Dave Malone's dead fingers revealed they belonged to a wolf, as well as did samples from the cave. The problem was that the experts could not match the results with any type of wolf in the database. The decision was made to send samples to the U.S. Fish and Wildlife Service and have them tested. Their database was much more extensive. It was felt by the time they finished testing, the people in Missouri could have the skull reconstructed.

Doctor Paul Kastor was a man of his word and released Lansdowne the following Saturday. Kastor was more than pleased with his progress, and was completely amazed when Lansdowne was not only able to bend his left arm, but lift it over his head. He should have been weeks away from the ability to perform that feat. All the new young doctors were also so impressed that they applauded.

Skruggs brought him clothes for the trip home but Cindy Winters, who was working that day, took her lunch early and helped him dress.

Lansdowne found he liked the feel of her touching him. He could smell her hair as she buttoned his shirt. It was a floral smell possibly from her shampoo. Her nimble, delicate fingers reached each buttonhole pushing the button through, yet the air between them was as though Cindy would rather have unbuttoned them. The look in her eyes, as she slowly glanced up into his eyes looking for a reaction, was provocative. The hospital room was not the place for such a look but she could not help herself, nor did she want to. Cindy Winters wanted him to want her. If she had thought it out, she did not know why, only that she did.

After fastening the last button at the top of the shirt, she stopped and kept her hands there for a few seconds more. Skruggs saw Lansdowne was just a tad uncomfortable and asked her if his arm should be in a sling. There was a brief pause, and then she said it should have one. Winters had one ready and placed it on his neck, then assisted putting his arm in it slowly and carefully.

Warren Skruggs could take no more goo-goo eyes between them. Grabbing the bag that held all the items hospitals send home with the patients, he said he would pull the car to the front door of the hospital and left the room almost laughing out loud, thinking Lansdowne was about to enter into a world of women trouble and just did not know it yet.

Cindy said her lunch break was nearly up and she had to return to ICU. She would get one of the floor nurses to wheel him in a wheelchair to the doors. Heading for the door, she stopped and mustered the courage to ask if she could come to his house and check on his progress. Maybe tonight after she finished her shift. She'd bring dinner… Chinese take-out?

He said company that evening would be nice and yes, he liked Chinese food just fine. Skruggs had given him a couple of hundred dollars the day prior should he need to buy any incidentals. Reaching into the right pocket of his slacks, he handed her a fifty dollar bill which she refused. He said to her, "You fly, I'll buy. Now take the money. I wouldn't feel right if you bought and brought. I insist."

Reluctantly, she took the currency and said next time would be her treat. She smiled and said she would see him around eight o'clock. Cindy then walked from the room with a bounce in her step, feeling like a schoolgirl who was just asked to the prom.

Ten minutes later, Skruggs was driving Lansdowne home. Nothing was said between them until Skruggs burst out laughing.

"I know, I know. Just leave it alone. She's coming over tonight with Chinese."

"You are in trouble pal! And you know what they say about redheads! Yes, my man, you are about to enter a world of shit."

"Knock it off. It's just dinner," Lansdowne stated, becoming mildly irritated and embarrassed.

"Sure it is, for you maybe. She's in love. Hopefully lust, but not with those looks. You be in trouble, yes sirree. Big time!"

"Shut up asshole, or I'll tell Lonny you're still smoking."

"Not fair. Not fair at all. I'm not snitching you out."

"Lonny will know everything within five minutes after you get home. Give me a break."

"Speaking of cigarettes, there's a pack in the glove box. I'll take one too."

Opening the glove box, Lansdowne saw a pack of his Pall Mall Lights with over half gone. He turned his head toward Skruggs and said, "Thief! Out of my carton." He fired one up and handed it to Warren. Lighting one for himself, he drew the smoke deep into his chest then slowly exhaled. It tasted good. Better than good. That cigarette was the first he had in several weeks.

"Ya want to stop and get a cup of real coffee?" Skruggs asked then, "I'll buy. Oh, and after we do you may want to stop and get a carton of cigarettes? You're out at home."

Lansdowne laughed and shook his head. Lonny made Skruggs quit smoking (or thought he had a couple years before), but he had packs stashed everywhere; in the shed, in the barn, just anywhere and everywhere that Lonny would not go or look. He did not smoke many per day. Lansdowne most likely smoked more, but for Skruggs it was the idea he wasn't supposed to be smoking and that he was getting over on her. He had always been like that. Even as kids he liked to get over on people. Lansdowne was the only one he did not do it to. Even if he could he would not have tried. It would be like lying to him. They did not lie to each other.

"By the way, what was with the C. I. D. crap?"

"They wouldn't let me in to see you. They took care of you like one of their own. So I pulled rank."

"You still have that damn I.D.?"

"Yep, and the one from the CIA. I thought using that one was over the top. That nosey damn Sheriff checked me out. That's why I was gone for a few days. I was in DC explaining to the Skipper why I still had it and why I flashed it. After he reamed me a new asshole, he forgave me and took it back. It worked out okay."

"Bet you didn't tell him you had a couple of replacements."

"Nope, I may be crazy Mikey, but I'm not stupid."

"Mark. Remember, my name is Mark. Amie called me Mike in front of the Sheriff but I think he missed it."

"I'll never get used to Mark, but okay," as he pulled the jeep into the parking lot of the quaint coffee shop next to the cigarette store. Skruggs went and bought coffee in go cups while Lansdowne replaced the carton of cigarettes.

With both men back in the car, Lansdowne asked Skruggs if he needed to get home immediately. He said he did not, so Lansdowne suggested they drive to the river, park, and drink their coffee. Skruggs nodded okay.

The drive to the river did not take long. It was November and almost Thanksgiving, as well as the last weekend of firearms deer hunting, so they had the river to themselves. The clouds were billowing dark greys that were heavy with threatening snow. It was cold out, which made Lansdowne's shoulder hurt all the more. Kastor said it would. They were inside the car with the heater going but he felt the cold windy bite of the air. The river flowed past, at a fast clip, carrying debris down the river that was blown into the icy water. The scene should have depressed Lansdowne, but instead helped him think about everything again.

"I've been thinking about what's happened," he said, taking another sip of his coffee.

"Me too," Skruggs said. He was not grinning, which meant he was angry.

"About what?"

"How you didn't call me to cover your six. You left that to someone who had no idea how to do it. You didn't call me and almost came out of those woods dead. We are all we have left. Most everything we ever knew was taken from us, including your name, all because we didn't cover each other in the field. We watched the others go down because we trusted that others would cover us. They didn't, and you barely made it out alive. My way of thinking, Squid, this was no different and it almost cost you big time."

"Yeah, okay. You're right. I shouldn't have even been there. But I was there. So if you're finished chastising me, I've had almost three weeks to think about how stupid I was for staying out there."

Skruggs looked at his only friend and thought about the times they had saved each other's lives. He felt bad about upsetting Lansdowne but he had to say those things. He was scared of losing a pal. There was a bond between them since childhood. Immediate and everlasting was the bond when they first met, and stayed unbroken.

"I'm sorry, but I was worried about you. You've never been able to walk and chew gum without me there to cover your ass…or you to cover mine."

"You're such an asshole."

"Yep, that's me." They both smiled and drank some more of the coffee which was getting cold. Skruggs wrinkled his nose at the drink. He liked strong black coffee, hot. Once it cooled to a certain point he would toss it. Lansdowne did not pay attention that the brew had cooled.

"As I was about to say before your rude interruption…do you know how many people were killed?"

"A bunch, but number-wise, no. Does it matter?"

"It does, Skruggsy. Not so much the number in one sense, but where they were killed. Most were in a relatively small area and it all seemed to take place in a short period of time. No animal is that hungry. I killed a female, which should mean there is a male close around. And continuing on that train of thought…"

Skruggs looked at Lansdowne across the interior of the Jeep, and was also not smiling when he broke in with, "Young ones? There is more than one?"

Lansdowne pushed the button located in the center console, lowering his window and dumping the rest of his coffee from the cup onto the ground. Outside, the wind which had picked up touched the two men with its frigid fingers as it blew through the open window. Lansdowne closed it as Skruggs turned the speed up on the fan as to put out more heat. It was only one notch but it was effective in warming them.

"Yeah, more than one." He looked at his friend and said, "Not my problem. Take me home Skruggsy, I have a dinner date."

The thought of more than one of those terrors lingered in his mind during the drive.

Chapter 5

Hunting season that year was not a good one for the harvesting of bucks or does. Few animals moved around unless they were high in the trees and then it was not many during the daylight hours. Hunters sitting in tree stands saw no deer at all.

A good many things have to occur for a successful deer hunt. Plentiful, but not too much food, water in ponds should be full, and of course location. Deer will also tend to graze with cattle, mixing themselves in as to not be too visible. They especially like the corn feeders. All or most all of those things occurred that year. There should have been a record number of deer taken in the harvest. It just did not take place. Neighboring counties did not do badly. The official reason was deer migration. No one who lived in the county bought that story. Everyone knew something was happening in the woods, but there were no straight answers from the officials of any department or agency.

Agent Christine McKay suspected what was happening, but she gave the official statement when interviewed by local news media. McKay had no actual proof to offer, and after all, she needed her job. She was informed that Lansdowne was attacked by a feral dog, a large feral dog, but nothing more. Maybe he was, but whatever attacked and killed Dave Malone was not a dog, wild or otherwise. Still, she had no proof. She had been left out of the loop and all information purposely withheld from her; plausible deniability. All of her inquiries had met with closed-door answers. Wagons were being circled and McKay had no reasons as to why. It was only her suspicions, albeit well educated, but nothing more. She did, after all, need her job.

The day that Lansdowne was released from the hospital was the last day of hunting season for deer. Ordinarily, the small arms fire was heavy enough that he thought maybe the deer were shooting back! That day, he never gave a thought that it was the last day for firearms hunting. He had not heard a single round fired after getting home. Had he known, he would have been even more thankful for the peace and quiet. The dogs met him at the door with tails wagging and tongues panting. They all wanted to be petted by him. Even Curly, who usually shied away from Lansdowne's touch, wanted pets from him. Other than when Glenna was sick in the hospital, this was the longest period he had been away from them. All three vied for first pets by nudging each other away. After a few minutes, Skruggs opened the door and they ran out happy that their master was home.

Skruggs kicked a fire up in the stove, as the temperature in the room was borderline between chilly and cold. Lansdowne, meanwhile, took out the best bottle of Brandy and poured two glasses, one for each man. Handing one to his friend, they touched the glasses together causing a barely audible clink as they toasted in silence to the fact that Lansdowne was still alive, that he had once again beat the odds. Beating the odds was a thing both men had a knack for doing. They both knew that one day their luck would run out.

"We're getting too old for this crap," stated Skruggs, while placing his empty glass in the kitchen sink.

"Yeah, we are. Maybe it's enough is enough.

"What time is your girlfriend coming by?"

"Seven-thirty or so, whenever she gets the carryout...and she is not my girlfriend."

"Maybe you better let her know that. Me, I don't care." The grin on Skruggs' face went from ear to ear.

"Go home and harass your wife. I want to rest for a while."

"Okay, pal. If you need something, call. Otherwise I'll see you tomorrow." Skruggs put his hand on the doorknob but before he left asked, "Lonny wants to know what you are doing for Thanksgiving?"

"I don't know - when is it?"

"This Thursday."

"Talk to me later."

"Okay, well think about it."

Lansdowne nodded he would as Skruggs left. He turned on the stereo, poured another brandy and sat in his chair. The dogs were at the door wanting to be let inside. He got up and opened the door to let them into the warmth of the house. The sky was a gunmetal color but the wind had slowed in its intensity. Wind or not, it was cold. Nature was letting people know that she was showing winter this way, and that he would be staying a long while once he arrived. He closed the door and returned to his chair and glass of brandy. The dogs were all in their customary spots. Two were on the big couch, one on the small couch and one on the floor by the fire.

That is when it struck him; one by the fire on the floor. That made four dogs. The one by the fire looked like Moe, but was much bigger. He guessed twenty-five or more pounds bigger, not fat but bigger. Lansdowne snapped his fingers to get the new dog's attention. He raised his head and looked at Lansdowne, all the while scooting closer to the fire. Lansdowne, in his soothing voice, called the animal to him. Although he did not want to leave his warm spot by the fire, the dog got up and walked the few feet to Lansdowne and then promptly sat down. The dog was big, brown and covered with many scars from nose to rump. One of his ears had been torn away from the tip, halfway down. His face had scars. Some had been deep wounds. A few looked as if they were treated by a vet, but most looked as if they healed by themselves. The dog sat his head in Lansdowne's lap. He petted the new dog gently, continuing to speak to him in low reassuring tones. There was no collar or marking on the ears. Lansdowne told the dog to go back by the fire, pointing to it. The new dog licked his wrist several times and then returned to his place in front of the fire.

His paws were big, but smaller than the prints left on the dirt, and looked nothing like what he had killed. As for now, the dog could stay. He got along with the stooges well enough, and they with him.

Lansdowne's eyes were getting heavy and Cindy would be over later. He closed his eyes for a nap.

Chapter 6

Having a nap of several hours, Lansdowne awoke much refreshed and ready for an evening of dinner and conversation. He started to stretch, completely forgetting his injury. Halfway through the attempt, his shoulder reminded him with a large dose of pain that sent shocks down his back into his left butt cheek. More so was the pain from his chest into his groin. After letting out a yell his neighbors could hear (if he had any neighbors), Lansdowne decided not to do that again. The four dogs perked up at the scream and after seeing nothing amiss, settled back into a restful state alongside him. Raising his arm above his shoulder should be done in measured attempts over a period of recuperative time. He should, under no circumstances, try to hurry it along.

His mouth tasted like the bottom of a bird cage, so he went first to brush his teeth. He felt good to be back in his own home with all the familiar things, and the proper places for them. The sling was becoming a nuisance. He was able to undress, but it took longer than he thought. Showering was a problem when it came to soaping his right side, but he managed. Toweling was a different thing altogether. After thinking it out, it too proved manageable. Dressing was not hard once he thought about it. He opted for loafers without socks for the evening. The sling went back on. It did take pressure off his shoulder. Running a comb through his semi-wet hair was the last action to finish his task. Looking in the mirror, he decided it was not the best he had ever looked but for tonight it would work. Flipping out the light in the bathroom, he went to the kitchen and made coffee.

It took about ten minutes for the aroma of coffee to fill the house. While waiting for the coffee to finish brewing, he filled the dog's bowls with food. Having only three bowls, he took the old green plastic salad bowl and filled it for dog number four. He called the dogs to eat. Dog four did not seem as though he knew what to do, after watching the other three nearly knock Lansdowne from his feet in order to get to their food bowls.

He called him to his food. Getting his massive bulk onto his feet, the new dog walked to the kitchen and joined the others. It seemed to Lansdowne that the dog acted as though receiving food was a foreign action, one he not often saw. Lansdowne urged him into eating by telling him it was alright. That was his bowl. Finally, the dog did eat.

After pouring a cup of coffee and all of the dogs had finished eating, he opened the door and let them out. As he was about to sit in his chair and enjoy his cup of the fresh black brew, he saw headlights flash into the room and the sound of a car coming down the driveway. The car stopped and parked next to his pickup truck. The driver's side door opened, and from the interior lights he saw Cindy Winters carrying a large grocery bag. She was fumbling with it and her purse while getting out of her car. Bumping the car door closed with her hip, she walked across the gravel drive with grace, while in three-inch heels.

He opened the door for her, and for his efforts she gave him a large smile. Taking the large bag from her directly to the dining room table, he could smell the food. It smelled wonderful and he realized he had not eaten all day. He directed her to place her long camel hair coat and her purse on the bed in the guest room, while he took plates from the cupboard.

Cindy Winters emerged from the bedroom looking stunningly beautiful, more so than Lansdowne could have ever imagined. She wore an aqua-marine colored sweater with a plunging neckline that revealed the whiteness of her breasts. The sweater fought hard to retain the braless bosom within its confines, but nonetheless losing the battle. The heels she wore accentuated her legs in the designer jeans. Light bounced from hair to hair, the red lipstick made her lips full. Her face flushed again, but only slightly as she smiled. She had a dimple on the right side which he had not noticed before. At that moment, Cindy Winters could make a Greek goddess fill with envy. When he finished setting the table he took a bottle of wine from the refrigerator and, after a small amount of trouble with the corkscrew, opened it. Lansdowne apologized for the semisweet red wine but said he was not sure what type of wine went with Chinese food.

She picked up her glass and toasted, "To our first dinner together."

That statement made him feel a tad uncomfortable. He hid the feeling of guilt, almost as though he was cheating on his wife. He had mixed feelings about Winters. What the hell, it was only dinner he thought, as he raised his glass.

She divided the food from the boxes onto the plates and they ate and talked. He really did like her voice. It was soft and mellow. Her words sat floating in the air to his ears. She spoke about her work, about her ex-husband and about her family. He did not care, but he listened to her voice enjoying each sound, each word, between bites of her food. He said little except to direct the conversation.

Dinner was finished and it was time to open the fortune cookies. Cindy Winters was part of the way through her third glass of wine when she told Lansdowne of a game she and her friends played in school, with the fortunes from the cookies.

"Whatever it says, you have to add the words "in bed" to the end of it. Some are really very funny. Let's try it."

"Okay," he said, "Yours first."

Breaking open the sweet egg wrap revealing her fortune she read, "You will enjoy making a new friend...in bed." Her face was red as her voice trailed off to a whisper. She looked up from the piece of paper to see his reaction. He sat with a slight smile pulling at the corners of his mouth. She could read nothing in his face.

Very softly and impishly she said, "Your turn."

He broke open the cookie, read it to himself and threw it onto the empty plate.

"What did it say?"

"Nothing that made sense, anyway it wasn't funny. I liked yours better. Excuse me a minute."

He pushed his chair back and walked down the hall to the bathroom. After hearing the door close, she reached over and took the paper from the plate. It read, "No man is without enemies." She sat stunned and looked down the hall at the closed door. No wonder he did not want to read it. No matter what was added to the end it would not be funny. The door opened and she placed it back on his plate.

He asked if she would like a cup of coffee. She said she would, and black with no sugar. He liked that. It was rare a woman drank coffee, much less black coffee.

She had already left the table to the rec room. When he entered he found her sitting in his chair, barefoot with her legs folded beneath her. Her toenails were painted bright red, like her lipstick. She was making herself comfortable and in fact felt very much so. For whatever reason, she felt safe with him, safer than she had ever felt in her life. Maybe it was the wine, but she did not think so. It was him. He made her comfortable.

Setting the coffee down on the table, he walked to his desk and picked up a pack of cigarettes. He took one out and fired it up with his Zippo. He took a deep drag and as he exhaled, turned to see Cindy Winters with a look of disbelief on her face.

"You smoke?" It was more of an exclamation than a question.

"Obviously, cigarettes are one of the few vices that I have left. I don't get drunk. I don't chase nasty women."

"They will kill you."

His mind drifted back to the events of the recent past and quietly said, "There are a great many things that could kill me." Shaking the thought from his mind he added, "Everyone dies…sooner or later." Anyway, I smoke in the house, the truck or on the deck. It's my house, my rules. End of story. Okay?"

"Yeah, okay. I'm sorry." She looked down.

"There's nothing to be sorry about. Next subject."

She smiled that she had not offended or angered him. Still, she did not like him smoking.

"Was that our first fight?"

"Nope. I am who I am and I don't want to change unless I want the change. Just letting you know up front."

"Okay." She blew him a kiss. He winked at her.

For the next hour they talked about many subjects, but none of any importance.

It was getting late and Cindy Winters decided it was time for her to go home. She cleared the dishes from the table, rinsed them off and opened the dishwasher. It was full. It was full the day he found Janey Malone. The dishwasher was still full with the same dishes. Cindy found the soap under the sink and started the machine cleaning. He let the dogs inside, before he said that he had washed those weeks earlier. All the dogs ran to her, each taking a turn sniffing her crotch and butt. They returned to the rec room, except for Curly who followed her wherever she went. His tail was wagging. Lansdowne had not seen him that happy since the very last time Glenna was home. Cindy liked him too.

She went to the bedroom, retrieved her coat and bag readying herself to leave. She was happy and content. It had been a good evening and Lansdowne hoped this was the first of many, as she slipped into her shoes.

Moe, who was on the couch, started his low growl. Lansdowne, standing by the door to walk her to the car, stopped and watched the dog. Moe was hearing something outside. Lansdowne told Cindy to wait, not to go outside just yet. He could see nothing looking through the blinds in the door. Something was out there. Moe was NEVER wrong. He walked to the desk, opened the top left drawer and saw Skruggs had put his revolver back.

Then he heard the loud, strong, unmistakable howl of a wolf. It was answered, and by another still. He looked out of the blinds again and saw two huge red eyes looking at the house from the edge of the woods.

His stomach made a growling sound. His jaw went tight. Cindy Winters had a bewildered look when she heard the howls.

Lansdowne took the weapon from the drawer, opened the cylinder checking to see if it was loaded. It was. Closing the weapon, he put it into his sling.

"Take off your coat. You're staying the night."

Chapter 7

Sometime during the night, snow started to fall. At first, fine flakes looking as winking stars, floated down gently settling on the earth. As time passed, the flakes became large and wet sticking to everything they touched. The snow piled on tree branches and on the ground, transformed the landscape to a fantasy land. Soon dawn would arrive and attempt to light the sky, but she would have her work cut out for her. The clouds were still heavy with new snow to fall. Anything outside that was not yet covered, would be soon.

Cindy Winters was snuggled in on the couch, asleep. She had finally fallen to sleep after midnight and was not yet aware of the snow. Lansdowne looked at her sleeping and thought how much she looked like a porcelain doll.

She heard the howling, but had no idea what it meant…until Lansdowne told her. He explained some of what occurred in the woods. Maybe it was a feral dog, but he did not think so. He was not sure exactly what type of animal, but it no longer mattered. There was more than one, and they were close. Too close for her to chance leaving. She would stay until morning. Cindy Winters agreed it would be prudent to stay. They sat on the couch talking and drinking hot tea, which they switched to from the coffee. As her eyes got heavy, she pulled her legs under her and put her head on his shoulder. Easing his right arm around her shoulders, he drew her body clo   e smelled the floral fragrance in her hair. It was light, sweet and intoxicating. Soon after, she was asleep. Ever so slowly, he lowered her to a lying position, gave her a pillow and covered her with a blue afghan. He moved to his chair where he could better see both outside doors and watch.

Two of the dogs, Larry and Moe, guarded the patio doors. The new, not yet named, dog was at the front door. Curly was in front of the couch at Cindy's side. He had taken to her immediately, which for Curly was unusual. He was by nature aloof, but even more so since Glenna died. The other dogs were his only friends. People were, well, just people. Curly, it could be said, had no prejudice. He disliked everyone. Warren and Lonny, even Lansdowne, were tolerated by Curly, no one else...until Cindy Winters that night.

Lansdowne sat in his chair catnapping through the night. They were out there somewhere. For reasons unknown to him, they were watching him. He saw the eyes reflecting from the light. Big, red and bold were the eyes that watched that night. Later in the day he would let Benson know, otherwise there was nothing to do. Less than a month prior, it was the same with one exception. He wasn't going looking. He could not go if he wanted to, but he did not want to go. The problem belonged to someone other than him. His problem was the pain in his chest and arm caused by the damn thing.

He watched the snow falling and remembered how much Glenna loved the snow.

Outside, the sky was getting lighter and the heavy flakes were giving way to smaller ones falling more sparsely. The clouds remained heavy, battleship grey pillows, stagnant in the sky. No upper winds moved them along. They sat low to the earth looking menacing and daring nature to make an attempt to oust them, saying that for today at least, they were not leaving.

Lansdowne glanced at the statuesque figure asleep on his couch guarded by a Cerberus-like dog. He would let her sleep. Later he would make breakfast for them both. When she was ready to leave, he could help her dig out or take his truck. His four-wheeled Chevy could go anywhere.

Larry and Moe stood up, looked at Lansdowne, and started doing their "I need out" dance. They were joined by the new guy. Mark got up and opened the patio door for them. The three filed out the door. Curly did not move, but instead whined with indecision. He wanted to go but did not want to leave his self-imposed post by Cindy Winters side.

Lansdowne told him to go ahead out. He would guard her. Curly looked at him, turned his head and looked at her, then bolted from the room to join the others.

The cold entered the room before he could close the door and touched Cindy Winters' sleeping face. It was enough that she slowly opened her eyes and greeted him with a sleepy smile and asked the time. He said the time was nearly a quarter past eight. The small clock in the great room chimed its agreement. Winters quickly sat upright and said she needed to go, as she was late for work. Returning her smile, he informed her of the snow overnight and that it was still coming down. She might get out of the driveway, but the roads would be too deep for her Mustang to transverse. She could call in sick.

Through a groggy-mind, she knew the patient load in the hospital was light. At holiday time it always dropped. No one wanted to be in a hospital from Thanksgiving until after New Year's. She had no sick days for several years and still had vacation time on the books. Winters told him she could call into work but needed clean clothes, a toothbrush and a shower.

He listened while making a new pot of coffee. When she finished with her reasons to leave, he told her there was everything she needed. Cindy was close to Glenna's size and the closet was full, as well as the dresser. She could wear what she liked. He was going to fix breakfast while she showered.

Looking out the door at the snow as it fell, she saw her car covered. It was too cold and snowy out and it was warm and cozy inside. She thought it might be fun to spend a Sunday stranded with this handsome man. It had been a long time for her as well, being alone with someone. Dates were one thing, this was something more. Finding her purse, she called the head nurse on her cell phone saying she was snowbound and could not get into work. A brief conversation later, Winters walked into the kitchen and asked Lansdowne, "Where's the shower?" There was a big smile on her mouth.

He pointed down the hallway and told her where to find the things she would want. She heard the rustling of pans as she closed the door to the bathroom.

For breakfast he made sausage links, cheese scrambled eggs and toast. The juice and milk had been in the refrigerator for a week before his hospital stay. He did not even give them a smell check. The smell of sour milk would turn his stomach and he was hungry. Fifteen minutes later he called Cindy to breakfast.

She entered the dining room wearing his bathrobe belted at the waist. Her hair was damp and she had no makeup on, still he thought her beautiful. The dark green of the robe accentuated her hair. Lansdowne, not standing on formality, put her plate on the table and said to eat. It was hot. He could not carry two plates with one arm in a sling, so he went back for his from the stove.

Cindy Winters had a type of grace when she ate, making a crude breakfast look like a formal dinner.

He said all he had to drink was coffee, tea or water. She said coffee was okay. The way she balanced the heavy mug in her small hand made him think she was drinking from fine china. There was elegance when she used the paper towel in place of a napkin.

Nothing was said as they ate. After both had finished eating, she took the plates to the sink and returned with the coffee pot, refilling their cups.

"Could I ask a question, Mark?"

"Sure."

"What was that last night?"

"I don't know for sure, but after what happened I wasn't going to chance it. With you here I knew you'd be safe."

"Did you want me to stay, or just for my safety?" She took a sip of coffee.

He thought for a second before he said, "Both."

"And today?"

"Between the snow, and wanting a half-naked beautiful woman to spend the day with here, it was a no-brainer!"

"I like that."

"What's that?"

"A man honest about his animal urges is rare. Most want to play a game of wham, bam, thank you Ma'am and I'm outta here. Last night I was scared and after you took out the gun I was very much scared."

"I'm sorry. I didn't mean to scare you. I was thinking about your safety. If anything is going to eat you, it'll be me."

Cindy Winters' face went so red, her hair blended into the flush of her complexion. She smiled as she took another drink.

"Nothing like honesty."

"Yes, well…" He had not meant to say that, but it was too late.

"Clothes? You said there were clothes I could wear, or did you mean for me to stay in the robe until I leave?"

"Either way for me. Clothes are in the dresser and closet in the guest room. They should fit. Pick and wear what you like. You'll have to re-wear your underwear. I threw out my wife's."

Smiling, she said, "Seldom wear 'em, but thanks."

"What if you have to go to the hospital? You know the clean underwear thing mothers tell their children."

"Then they would know how far my bikini line goes!"

Shaking his head and chuckling he said, "Almost too much information too soon."

"You asked!"

"I suppose I did. The clothes are in the guest room."

"By the way, I want to change your dressing."

"My own personal nurse?"

Winters got up and stepped to Lansdowne's side, kissed his cheek and whispered, "For as long as you want me. No commitments." She walked down the hall to the guest room. She dropped the robe on the floor in the hall, tempting him.

She does have a nice ass, he thought.

Chapter 8

Lansdowne knew, or hoped, that dressing and makeup would take Cindy Winters some time. Today he needed to let Sheriff Benson know about the previous night. He may not have considered the problem as his, but Benson needed to be notified.

Calling the Sheriff's Department on the non-emergency number, the operator informed him Benson was not in the office, but would relay his message. He left his phone number, said it was important and that the Sheriff would want to know A.S.A.P. Then he hung up.

Just as he cradled the handset, the phone rang. That was quick, he thought. It was not Benson calling, but Warren Skruggs.

"Lonny is making your favorite fried chicken, mashed potatoes and peas too. We thought maybe at one or two…What's best?"

"Either time is fine. Tell her to make enough for four. Cindy stayed over last night."

"You ole dog, you."

"No, no. Nothing like your gutter mind is composing. I wasn't letting her leave last night. Like we thought…there are more. I think I saw one at the timberline. I definitely heard three more howling. Skruggsy, they were close. Too damn close."

"Didn't you say it wasn't your problem anymore?"

"I called Benson. He wasn't in the office. They said he'd call me later. We'll see."

"Anything I can do?"

"Nope, just bring the food. See ya when you get here. Later."

"Okay."

Fried chicken was his favorite for sure. Lansdowne thought back to the time Skruggs was grounded by his parents. Truth be told, Skruggs was always being grounded for the infraction of the day. Lansdowne found out he was again in trouble, so he bought a large bucket of take-out chicken with all the fixin's to go with it. Skruggs was to clean out the garage as part of his penance.

Lansdowne showed up with the food. He helped clean the garage, but not all of it right away. The two went to the attic and ate their feast. They spent the better part of two hours eating chicken, smoking cigarettes and talking about girls. When all of the chicken was gone, mostly, they cleaned the rest of the garage. Skruggs' parents could not believe how clean it appeared. They said he was no longer grounded. Neither of Skruggs' parents ever knew Lansdowne helped. He told Skruggs not to tell them. Maybe it would help regain good graces with his Mom and Dad. Skruggs got to go to a party that night. Lansdowne went back to work until well after the party was over.

The good old days? He chuckled and picked a cigarette from the pack. He walked outside to the patio, then fired it up. Standing there in the ankle deep snow, he looked at the tree line wondering if there were any tracks. There was no sense in looking. Lansdowne was not going hunting. The cold started to get to his wound. His shoulder was aching – borderline hurting.

None of the dogs were to be seen. The dark clouds gave way to lighter ones and the snow was now only flurries. It would stop altogether soon, but he doubted the sun would break through.

Cindy Winters opened the door, stuck her head out and said, "Mark, your phone is ringing."

He nodded his head, flipped the cigarette into the snow and returned to the house.

It was Benson.

"Mark, I don't have long. I have to leave for Jeff City, and with the snow the roads to Highway 63 will suck. So what's up?"

Lansdowne hesitated for a moment before he spoke. "Ralph, there are more of those things. I heard them last night howling."

There was silence at the other end of the phone.

"Are you sure? Conservation has had trackers out. They didn't find anything more. The tracking dogs didn't find anything either."

"The dogs didn't find your missing floaters then either, Ralph. I know what I heard. There are at least three, maybe four more animals."

"Deer season ended yesterday. Neither Christine McKay nor I got one incident report. Not one."

"Ralph, a bunch of hung-over guys shooting at tree branches and making enough noise to chase God out of the area, does not instill me with confidence because they saw nothing. Most would have missed Godzilla standing there. It wasn't dogs or coyotes. I damn sure know what I heard. You have it now, do as you please."

"Dammit Mark, I have to make sure. It's the cop in me. I do believe you. Have you told anyone?"

"Skruggs. He'll keep his mouth shut."

"That's all? Only him?"

"Did I stutter, Ralph? If you want people to know it's your place to tell them, not me. As I see it, with winter coming on there won't be many people out. The ranchers will lose some cattle, but maybe that will be all for now."

"What do you mean, for now?"

"Until these things are hunted down and killed, every last one, sooner or later more people are going to die."

"I'll talk to you later."

"Yeah, okay. Drive safely."

Cindy had cleared the dishwasher and put the dishes away. She reloaded the breakfast dishes in the machine and kept herself busy while he spoke on the phone. There was a touch of anger in his voice. She could not help but hear what was said. Giving him a few minutes, Cindy yelled, "I'm ready for your bandage."

A drawer opened and closed, and there was the sound of the chair moving away from the desk. At the doorway, Lansdowne appeared with a plastic smile on his face. She had a chair ready for him. Pointing to it, she told him to sit. Dutifully, he did. Winters helped him remove the sling and his shirt.

"I guess you heard." Lansdowne said.

"I couldn't help hearing. You think he believed you?"

"Yeah, he did. He just didn't want to admit it. One was bad enough but more, well, I guess it scares him. I shouldn't have gotten pissy, but I couldn't help it. I kept you out of it. I told him the only person who knew was Skruggs. No sense getting you involved."

"But I am involved. Should I be scared?"

"Everyone should be scared. Benson is keeping a lid on it for now. I'll bow to his judgment. It's his problem."

The bandage came off. She saw the wound was healing at a remarkable rate. It was weeks ahead of where it should be. Instead of a red color, it was white and healed. The skin was not wrinkled and pulling at the scar, but smooth.

"How does it feel? Hurt?"

"Actually, no. No pain, just sore is the best way to describe it. Why?"

"It is healing nicely, better than I've ever seen."

"That's good, right?"

"Yes, it's very good. Are you going to shower or do you want me to put a new dressing on it?"

"I'll shower. Skruggs and his wife will be over later. They're bringing lunch. Fried chicken. Hope you like fried chicken?"

She was awed that he would include her with his friends. "I love fried chicken."

"You look great in those clothes."

Cindy had picked an oversized black sweater with a loose oval neck. The sleeves were pulled up to her elbows. She found white sweat pants. The slacks were a bit too tight, but still looked good on her. She wore white ankle socks.

"Thank you. Your wife was smaller than me. Maybe I need to lose some weight?"

"From where? Your body looks fine. I need to go take a shower."

He was thinking a cold one was in order.

Chapter 9

Ralph Benson sat in his home office thinking about the conversation with Lansdowne. He knew Lansdowne was truthful. He also had a right to be angry. After all, Lansdowne was mauled and narrowly survived. Benson also knew he was correct, that something had to be done immediately or more people would die. The animals had developed a taste for human meat. By the time the two kids from Maple Hills went missing, the animal Lansdowne killed had been dead for several hours. There was still a chance they were grabbed by a pervert. There was no blood, nor were there any bodies found. The trackers and dogs had spent over a week looking. Lansdowne was also right about hunters flooding the area.

Benson was also honest when he said that no incidents or sightings were reported. Christine McKay said, "The deer left the county and left no forwarding address." She told him that there were no more than ten deer taken, that included bow and rifle season. McKay knew what was going on, but had no proof. Her department had spoon-fed her, what to say if asked. She did not like it…at all.

He had received a summons by fax to appear at the State Attorney's office at two o'clock that afternoon. The reason had to be important. Those guys in Jefferson City never work Sundays. The phone call he received after the faxed summons was short and to the point. "Be there and say nothing more about the attacks." He would be briefed when he arrived.

The hour and a half drive would most likely take three hours because of the snow, maybe more. It would have been a great day to just watch football and stay inside. Oh well, he thought.

Chapter 10

Moe liked to chase rabbits, not that he ever caught one. If he had he would not have known what to do with it. He just liked to chase them.

The four dogs wandered far in the fields that morning. They ran, chasing each other playing tag. Each one took a turn at being "it", even the new dog. At first he was not sure what to do but picked up on the game quickly, joining the other three.

The snow was not as deep in some places. Blowing winds had directed how deep the snow was in the fields. Where it was lighter, the dogs had better footing for running. The cold took its toll on the dogs fairly rapidly and they sought a place to lie down and warm up before returning home.

In the field, Moe heard movement in the grass. The hay was cut late and had not grown much. Watching, he saw what caused the sound. A lone rabbit sat cowering in an attempt to hide from the dogs. Though cold and tired from playing, Moe could not pass up the chance. It was an unwritten invitation that Moe saw as a challenge. Off he went at full speed toward the quick animal.

Waiting to see which way Moe would run, the rabbit sat in the brown snow covered grass. Once it was sure it had been spotted, the rabbit bolted from its hiding place. It ran in a zigzag pattern. Moe followed the rabbit's cuts to the right, then to the left.

A stand of trees in the field was straight ahead offering sanctuary to the rabbit. With a burst of speed fueled by fear, the small animal ran for the safe haven of cedar and pine trees. Moe had gained ground on the hare, not enough to catch it, but then that was not Moe's intention.

Moments after the cottontail entered the shelter of the trees, Moe heard the irrefutable scream of the hare. It so shocked Moe that he "Scoobie-Do'ed" to a stop before entering the dense vegetation within the stand of trees.

The dog could smell the blood and heard the snarls of a feeding animal. He also smelled the stench that he and the others followed with their master weeks before. He knew the beast would fight to protect the kill, but he also knew that it was invading territory claimed by him and the other dogs. That could not be, whatever it was must be chased off.

Moe cautiously entered into the undergrowth within the surrounding trees. The stink grew fouler the farther in he went. The snarls were louder. He saw the animal devouring its meal. The dark coat of fur, the large flash of teeth, was before Moe.

It noticed a different scent and stopped crunching the bones and flesh. Slowly, purposely, it turned its large square head looking at Moe with wide red eyes. It emitted a deep throaty growl.

Moe returned the growl. He had sized up the monster. It was big, almost as big as Curly, maybe bigger. Still Moe was no pussy and was not about to back down no matter how big the animal. This was his section of the world and he was damn sure going to protect it.

It continued its long growl, snarling back its lips to reveal the long sharp canines. So did Moe.

His teeth were not as long, but were just as sharp. The hair from Moe's neck to his tail stood on end. He crouched down with his back legs under his body, ready to spring in an attack. The time for barking to chase his adversary off was long past. This was the time to size up the opponent. Moe also knew, from the set of the other's body, that this fight was to the death. If it was not going to run away, neither would he.

The beast wanted to move his body so as to be head-to-head with Moe. It sized up Moe as well. He was smaller, with puny-sized teeth. He could never stand before the fury he could unleash, yet it did not back down nor run from his aggressive show of strength. The beast thought Moe stupid. He could not even catch the rabbit that he had done so easily before.

Yet the beast knew turning to face Moe would leave him open to attack, and as it was, he had no choice.

Moe waited. He knew the beast had to move. Yes, he was much larger, but Moe had to be quicker. After all, he did not chase rabbits to catch them.

The Mexican stand-off had to end. Both knew it was to be. The eyes of both animals were locked and which one blinked first was the loser.

Tension between the two animals had reached its crescendo. The beast misjudged Moe thinking he would not jump, that he was bluffing. The beast moved.

Moe sprang into action with such speed that it overwhelmed the larger animal. Before the beast could get head on, Moe had him on his back holding it down by the throat. Moe's head twisted and turned as his teeth sunk deeper into the windpipe, cutting off air. The larger animal gained its feet and flipped Moe from side to side, attempting to dislodge the teeth from his throat. Moe took a beating being clawed by the bigger animal. Still, he bit deeper and harder knowing he must, no matter how much pain was inflicted upon his body. The beast was getting weaker and knew it, and now for the first time knew something else – fear. He was losing the battle. Renewing his efforts, he clawed at the dog which held his throat, but now with all four of his feet. He knew he was inflicting deep wounds, yet the dogs teeth were getting tighter. No air entered the massive lungs. Fear gave the great beast one last frenzied burst of strength. It was not enough. It could taste blood in its mouth, rolling down the tongue and out the lips. Soon Moe's face was covered in his blood, matting his hair and blinding his eyes. The animal could no longer stand. It fell on top of Moe's ripped chest and stomach. The large fierce eyes were clouding with death.

The last thing it felt was Moe's teeth close completely together.

Chapter 11

With Lansdowne's shower finished and a new bandage on his shoulder, he and Cindy Winters sat on the couch sipping coffee. They sat waiting for the company of Warren and Lonny Skruggs, as well as the fried chicken dinner they would have in tow.

Lansdowne looked at the clock. It was one-fifteen and the dogs were not back. It was rare for them to be gone that long. The only one of the dogs that did like the cold and snow was Larry. Even so, by this length of time he wanted inside as much as the other two. He was not sure about the new guy, but since he had a short haired coat, guessed it would be much the same.

Cindy saw him look at the clock and then out at the door several times.

"You think something is wrong? The reason the dogs aren't back?"

"Naw, they're most likely okay. It's just they don't like cold, not much anyway. They'll be back soon, I'm sure."

From the snow covered road, the sound of Skruggs' Jeep came as he maneuvered the driveway. They heard Lonny's voice yelling at Skruggs. Something about if God had given him a brain…the rest was lost on the sound of Skruggs laughing and saying it would be okay.

Lansdowne opened the door and held it open. Walking the distance from the Jeep to the door was forty feet and she gave him hell every step. Skruggs laughed and shrugged his shoulders as he passed

Lansdowne. Lonny was red-faced with anger as she passed.

They both had pots and dishes in their hands. Lonny had one bowl that had gravy in it. The gravy was now on her black slacks.

Her face was blood red with anger. Lonny's blonde hair made her face look even more red, a stoplight red. It was a rare thing to see her angry, much less outright pissed. Warren Skruggs accomplished that feat.

Placing the pots and dishes on the stove and counter, Lonny took off her coat and gloves. She went into the guest room to place them on the bed. Lansdowne followed her, telling Lonny to find some slacks in the closet and change. He would put her gravy-covered pants in the washer.

Nodding her head okay, she said, "If I didn't love him, I'd kill him! No court would convict me! I sure hope he doesn't think he'll get laid tonight." She went into the closet.

Lansdowne took her by the shoulders and kissed her red cheek. "He's an asshole. Always has been, always will be." He turned to leave the room when she said, "Maybe he'll choke on a chicken bone."

"Honey, if we were both single I'd be the first to volunteer to lick it off your pants. Alas my dear, you are not."

"He keeps his crap up and you may get your chance."

"Right, well, I'll not hold my breath." They were both chuckling as he closed the door.

In Lansdowne's opinion, Warren Skruggs was a world class asshole, but did he ever love Lonny! From the very instant they met, he was lost to her. She was not the type of woman he had, as a rule, gone out with on a date, much less married. Skruggs had commitment problems. The key word was "had". The excuses all disappeared with Lonny. As far as Warren Skruggs was concerned, the sun rose and set because of her. She was the only woman he was ever completely faithful with in their entire relationship. Lansdowne knew Skruggs well enough to know that would never change. Lonny was smart and beautiful, with a great body. Skruggs often stated to Lansdowne privately that he wondered what she ever saw in him.

On days like the one they were having, Lonny wondered the same thing. She truly loved him as well. The proof was the fact in all the years of marriage she had never once tried to poison him – God knows he gave her justifiable cause on more than one occasion.

"What happened to piss her off?"

"I came in off the road into your driveway too quick. The gravy went all over her. She was holding it so it wouldn't spill. It may have been okay, but I laughed. You know me," Skruggs said while grinning.

"Yeah, I do. Anyone ever tell you that you're an asshole?"

"All the time pal, all the time."

"You are going to take your coat off?"

"I thought we'd go outside and have a cigarette."

"Sure, let me get my coat."

Cindy Winters sat on the couch saying nothing. She felt awkward with the momentary conflict which unveiled before her between Warren and Lonny. So she sat and sipped cold coffee until it was all over.

Lonny found a blue pair of pants. She washed the gravy stain out in the bathroom and set her slacks over the top of the shower door to dry.

The two women had met briefly at the hospital. So when Cindy heard Lonny's voice, which sounded calmer, she rose from her seat and went into the kitchen. She asked Lonny if she could help do something. Lonny stopped for a minute and looked at Cindy. Glenna would never have asked. She would have just jumped in to help. Lonny smiled her warmest smile and said, yes. This woman was not Glenna and Lonny realized she should not expect her to be like her.

As Lansdowne was putting on his leather coat, Lonny asked, "Where are my babies? They didn't greet me at the door."

"Must have heard you yelling at Skruggsy and they took off to lay low."

She laughed and started warming the food while Cindy set the table.

Lansdowne and Skruggs went out on the patio to smoke. Looking out into the fields, Lansdowne saw no sign of the dogs.

"They have been gone long?" Skruggs asked.

"Since early this morning, it's not like them."

"They'll come home cold, tired and hungry in a bit."

"I know," Lansdowne said, still worried.

Skruggs changed the subject, asking how Lansdowne liked his private duty nurse. He nodded, saying so far she was good. All the while he stared, where the night before he saw the eyes, the eyes that glowed with a murderous intent.

"Think it'll be back?"

"Yep."

"What do you want to do?"

"Nothing, it's not my problem."

"You keep saying that."

"Yep," said Lansdowne, but not in a very convincing voice. "Let's go back inside. My shoulder hurts."

The smell of food filled the house as it had not in a very long time. Bowls were full of piping hot food. Steam rose, carrying a mix of aromas throughout. Lansdowne's mouth watered as he handed Skruggs a bottle of white semi-dry wine to open. It had indeed been a very long time.

Food was passed around until everyone had a full plate. Skruggs poured wine in all the glasses and then raised his in a toast.

"Squid, you beat the odds again. You're alive and we are all truly glad you are," he said with the shit-eating grin.

"OOyeah," said Lansdowne.

"Semper fi, brother," said Skruggs.

They touched glasses, took a sip and then dove into their plates. Eating as politely as possible, Lansdowne shoveled it in as though he would not get enough, though there was more than plenty - especially the chicken. He and Lonny liked the dark meat, while Warren and Cindy liked white. Soon the mountain of mashed potatoes became only a memory, while the chicken bones piled high on Lansdowne's plate. The corn and peas disappeared equally as fast. It did not take long for the only remaining thing to be left was empty bowls.

Lonny cleared the table while Cindy served up coffee from the fresh pot she had earlier made. Lansdowne found an ashtray and after placing it on the table, lit a cigarette.

"That is a nasty habit," Cindy said as she placed his cup of coffee next to his right hand.

"He's a nasty man," said a grinning Skruggs.

"He hasn't proved that yet," Cindy retorted.

Lansdowne looked at Skruggs with a blank face, as close to embarrassed as Lansdowne could ever be. Skruggs laughed loudly. Lonny, who just kept rinsing the dishes said, "Give him time. He just got out of the hospital. Nasty pretty much describes him."

"Thanks, guys." Lansdowne said, jokingly sarcastic.

From the patio door came the sounds of the dogs barking. Lonny finished rinsing the plates and said that she would let them inside. She walked to the door while drying her hands and opened it letting the dogs enter.

"Damn Mark! Get in here now!"

Lansdowne and Skruggs moved in unison to the rec room. Larry and Curly were covered in blood. There was no Moe. There was no new brown dog.

Chapter 12

Benson sat in the outer office of Assistant Attorney General, William Jackson. What should have been a drive of an hour and a half, took about an hour longer. The snow packed roads caused him to drive slower and every mile soured his mood that much more. Sitting in the old wooden chair for forty-five minutes past his appointment time was doing little to improve his mood.

The clerk behind the desk was kind enough to get him a cup of coffee, but he knew she did not want to be in that office either. When he tried to make small talk about the snow with her, she responded with short curt answers. Her attitude gave the impression that she would rather have been thrown into a pit with hungry animals, than to be at her desk. After all, it was a Sunday.

Since small talk was out, he looked through the stack of magazines. Most were a year old with the mailing labels neatly cut off. He settled on the swimsuit addition of a Sports Illustrated that was well worn. It was not that he wanted to look at twenty year old supermodels wearing swim wear; he could not afford to buy one for his wife – even if it would fit her. It ran through his mind that maybe he should have been a brain surgeon.

It was another ten minutes of waiting before the phone on the desk rang. The clerk picked up the phone, listened for a moment and said only, "Yes Sir," and then hung up the phone. She asked the

Sheriff to follow her. Her voice indicated it was not a request.

She led him down the hall. The floor was tiled in white marble with a black border, which caused each step they took to echo. Normally, the halls bustled with people and the sounds of footsteps were intermingled with voices and drowned out. There was no one there that day walking the halls other than the clerk and Benson.

Stopping in front of one of the heavy oak doors lining the hall, the clerk turned the brass handle and opened it. The old, wavy frosted glass in the door announced it was a conference room. Benson entered the room, the clerk did not.

The room was painted a drab blue. The lighting did little to brighten it up. The three men sitting at the end of the dark finished wooden table had the venetian blinds closed on the only two windows, denying sunlight (not that there was much) into the room.

All three men were speaking until Benson entered. Their voices, speaking in soft tones, stopped until the door closed behind the Sheriff.

The stoic face on the tall dark haired man faded into a warm, welcoming smile. He extended his hand to Benson, who took and shook it. Ralph knew immediately that the man was Jackson. Only an attorney can offer a smile such as he wore. It was the same type of smile a soon-to-be ex-wife's divorce attorney has, just as he takes everything. Benson knew, for whatever reason he had been summoned, that he was about to be screwed.

Benson's guess was correct. The man introduced himself as Jackson (...just call me Bill). To his right side sat a man about fifty years of age, a squarely built man with black hair only starting to get grey at the temples. He was still tan at this time of the year. He was introduced as Earl Stafford from the Missouri Department of Conservation. Stafford shook hands with Benson. The Sheriff felt the strength in his grip.

On Jackson's left was a much younger man, possibly in his mid-thirties or just a tad younger. He sported blondish red hair and a darker beard. The man reminded Benson of Robert Redford in Jeremiah Johnson. Tall, lean and good-looking men that women liked. Jackson said he was Collin Reed of the U.S. Fish and Wildlife Service. Reed's hand was not as massive as Stafford's paw, but all the strength was the same.

Jackson started speaking, "Sheriff, we have a problem. It's the same one you have in Crawford."

Benson looked Jackson in the eyes and asked, "And that would be what, exactly?" I seem to have a lot of problems lately."

"You had several deaths in your county due to wild dogs."

"Nope, what Lansdowne killed was no dog."

"Speaking of Mister Lansdowne, what do you know about him?"

"Nice guy. Keeps to himself mostly since his wife died. Why?"

"It seems there is no record of him before he moved to Crawford County. He never existed."

"Maybe witness protection, although I

doubt it."

"Why?" Jackson asked.

"I said he was a nice guy, but I get the impression he's a nice guy only because he wants to be a nice guy. I don't get the feeling he would run from anyone. He certainly didn't run from that thing. So at the end of the day, I don't care who he was in the past. And for whatever it's worth, neither should you."

Benson was getting more irritable and his mood was visibly dark.

"You didn't call me here about Lansdowne just to talk out-of-school about him. Get to the point."

Jackson did not like the tone in the Sheriff's voice. He was not one to take orders, but rather to give them. He gave Benson the stare, the one a father gives his child when they are acting up. The look that silently says, "Anything more and your ass pays the price." Benson only returned the stare. The one that says, go for it.

Stafford broke the tension by interrupting and saying, "Ralph, the reason for this meeting is simply, you're right. It wasn't a wild dog. The best anyone can figure is that it is some type of wolf."

"I guessed as much. I don't know much about wolves but it did resemble one, or sort of. There wasn't much of its head left for identification. We went with the wild dog story for the public's sake."

"Lab results say it was a wolf. It was a wolf, not seen since the last ice age in America, or so the DNA says. It is called a Dire Wolf. It existed at the same time as the sabre tooth, the same time man first roamed the land. Most all we know about them comes from the bones that were found in the tar pits in California. Reed, here, is the real expert."

Collin Reed had been studying the Sheriff, his reactions, his body language. He deduced that the Sheriff had put some of the pieces together. Reed was not sure just how much.

Reed shook his head saying, "Not really." There are no real experts. That is not to say that science doesn't know much. We do. From the study of the bones, we know quite a bit. We know that they were big and being big, aggressive. We know from the teeth that they were strictly meat eaters, that they were opportunistic. When an animal became stuck in the tar pit they would try for an easy meal, only to become stuck themselves. The Dire Wolf most likely hunted in packs and was not that much different than today's largest wolf, the Grey. Physically, they were bigger with shorter legs than the modern wolf. They couldn't run as fast, but then neither could their prey. Dire Wolves died out somewhere around ten thousand years ago, although some were here in Missouri and Arkansas as recently as four thousand years prior."

"What you are saying is that they are big, mean bastards that can't catch a deer unless the deer is standing still. So it is now hunting an animal it can catch, man. And it has come home to the Ozark Mountains," Benson said, astonished.

Reed nodded and said, "That is about the size of it."

Benson wondered if it was too late for him to take up brain surgery.

Chapter 13

Before Lonny could close the door, the two dogs forced their way back to the outside. They were covered with snow, except from the muzzle and chest. Warm blood melted the snow that was there, only to freeze in its place.

Lansdowne, Skruggs, and Winters all rushed from the table into the room. The four people watched as Larry ran to the door, then stopped, turned and ran again in the other direction. He again stopped and turned his head, looking at Lansdowne. Curly was running back in the direction from which they had just come.

"Larry wants us to follow him," said Lansdowne, "Something is wrong."

"Larry, stay!" yelled Lansdowne.

Skruggs was donning his coat and gloves when Lansdowne told him to get the two ATV's, which were in the garage, ready. Without saying a word, Skruggs was on the run to the garage. Lansdowne went to the hidden gun safe and took out a shotgun (much like the other), and a converted AR-15. He loaded both weapons, put on an old foul weather coat and put extra ammunition in the waist pockets. He pulled on a pair of insulated boots, slung both weapons and ran to the door. He stopped just long enough to say, "Lonny, the magnum is in the top left-hand drawer of the desk. A box of ammo is in there as well. Both of you stay in the house! No matter what! We'll be back as soon as we can."

Running across the driveway through snow that had drifted to nearly knee deep, he could hear the ATV's both running. He gave the rifle to Skruggs, along with another fully loaded magazine and box of ammo. They placed the weapons in the rifle carrier and threw the crossbar to keep them in place. Skruggs wore a length of rope across his body diagonally. They looked at each other, nodded they were ready and drove out of the garage with Lansdowne in the lead. They circled the house and came around to the patio side, where Larry saw them and took off running following Curly.

Even if the dogs were not leading the way, it would not have been hard to trail where the dogs had run. The only tracks in the snow were from them.

The landscape was a carpet of white. Snow hid much of the golden-brown grass, which up to that morning had dominated the scene. Sunlight, as it was blocked by the cloud cover, would only be available for a short period of time. Other than the sound made by the engines of the two vehicles, all was quiet. No birds flew.

Neither man took notice of the peaceful setting that two lovers would have walked, as if they were the only two people in the world. They had no thoughts other than where the dogs led. Both had felt the urgency that Larry and Curly had projected. Moe, at least, must be in trouble somewhere in this white wonderland.

There was a knot in Lansdowne's stomach which seemed to grow the farther they rode. He ignored the pain in his shoulder caused by the cold. The ski coat he wore just seemed not to be enough.

The jarring ride across the fields was an added cause for his pain, yet the thought of Moe needing help blocked the thoughts of any discomfort he may have felt.

Curly was standing by a group of cedar trees waiting on the others to arrive. Larry was running, all out, to catch up with the four-wheelers. The stand of trees was on flat terrain so the two men cut the motors and coasted within ten feet of the edge, while moving the crossbar to clear the weapons. Their dismount from the vehicles was a smooth practiced maneuver, each man releasing the safeties on the weapons. They would enter the stand of trees together at the same time, but from different ends…one from one side, one from the other. If they needed to fire, whatever was in front of them would be in a crossfire situation.

The light of the day was slowly trading places with the coming night. Soon darkness would be wrapping her icy arms about the land. They would have to move quickly and quietly.

From within the dark of the trees, the men heard a growl. It was low and deep, from the throat. The odor of blood, stale with age, permeated the air. Snow had not been able to penetrate the cedar boughs as much as it did from outside the group of trees.

Before entering, Lansdowne had chambered a round in the shotgun. Now a few feet in, he relieved the safety, setting his finger on the trigger guard. Without thinking about it, he knew Skruggs would do the same.

The growling ceased and turned to a whining whimper as he approached. Peering through the limbs of the trees, Lansdowne saw the big brown dog standing over Moe, guarding him. Speaking low with a gentle tone, he told the dog all was well…that he was there now. Skruggs, entering from the other direction, stepped on a downed stick breaking it. The dog immediately went into a defensive posture. His hair, at the neck and down his back, stood on end. In the lessening light, his teeth gleamed as small daggers, with his lips curled back. The growl was menacing and came from deep inside. The dog's brown eyes were bright, shinning orbs staring at Skruggs' approach.

Lansdowne spoke again, talking low to calm the animal. He continued speaking and slowly moved forward toward the dog. Skruggs had the rifle pointed at the dog. Lansdowne knew his finger was set on the trigger, ready to fire. Still speaking, the dog calmed a bit, just long enough for him to reach out and with many strokes, pet the animal. The dog turned his head to look at Lansdowne and then returned to watch Skruggs.

The dog still growled, but the hair was relaxing, as the lips returned back over the teeth. Slowly, with caution, Skruggs again started his approach toward Lansdowne until reaching him. Skruggs spoke in the same manner as Lansdowne. Soon after, sensing Skruggs was no threat, he allowed him to completely enter where he stood guard.

Lansdowne turned his attention toward the ground. Moe was dead, his teeth still locked in a grip upon the damnable beast's stinking throat. Moe's chest had been dug open by massive paws in an attempt to loosen Moe's bite. Both animals lay in a pool of their own blood, mixed over both as well as under them.

As Lansdowne looked at Moe, a tear rolled down his face from the outside corner of one eye. Kneeling, he placed his hand on Moe's head and with a low, hoarse voice of sorrow, said, "I'm proud of you, old boy. So very proud of you, now go guard Glenna. Be with her."

The brown dog, no longer needing to guard Moe's body from predators, stood close to Lansdowne and rubbed his head on the man's leg. It seemed to Lansdowne and Skruggs that the dog was attempting to console him. Taking his hand and gently placing it on top of the brown dog's head he said, "You did well too. I guess you stay. You'll get a name later."

Lansdowne took his coat off and wrapped Moe in it. He had to cut away the beast's throat in order to move him away, so tight was yet the grip.

With a voice that also reflected the sorrow felt, Skruggs said, "I'll take Moe. You shouldn't carry him with your shoulder."

"I've got him!" Lansdowne snapped at his friend, not meaning to do so.

"Get that line you brought. We're taking that (motioning towards the beast), with us. Benson needs to see it. He said he believed me but I don't think that he did. Now he has to believe."

"Which do you want to take?" Skruggs asked.

A puzzled look set on Lansdowne's face. "What do you mean which one?"

"It looks like Larry and Curly got into the mix as well. There's another one where I came in and it doesn't look nearly as good."

"Really?" Lansdowne uttered with some amazement, "We'll take both. Drag the damn things."

He picked up Moe after putting the safety back on the weapon and after handing the gun to Skruggs, he carried Moe's body out.

The brown dog walked next to him.

Chapter 14

Driving home from the State Capitol, Benson mulled over in his mind all of the things that were said. So preoccupied was he that he never noticed that MODOT cleared the snow on both sides of Highway 63, the car accident that was on the northbound side, or that he was hungry. He just drove and thought.

On days like this he wished he had not quit smoking, because he really wanted a cigarette. What he really wanted was to wake up and find out all that had occurred was just a dream. Problem was, that it was no dream and that somehow he was going to have to deal with it. He had no idea how. That was up to Stafford and Reed. They were the experts. His job was to keep things quiet, not to let the media get wind of anything. To keep the public from finding out that these critters were roaming the area and planned to stay, would be tough. Someone was bound to see, or maybe even kill one. Lansdowne knew and he had killed one. The State had the body so he had no proof, but Benson knew he was not the sort to go public. Anyway, he was home recovering. Christine McKay suspected, but Stafford could quiet her. The detectives who processed Dave Malone's body and the den, he could order to secrecy. That pompous asshole, Jackson, would contact the other jurisdictions that helped and order them not to say anything, if he had not already done so.

No one knew how many of these things were out there or even how long they had been in the area.

Reed could only guess and that was based on studies of other modern day wolves. Reed got the assignment to help with the mess because he was a field biologist who studied wolves in their habitats. Wolves and their interactions in the environment were his specialty, but it was still guess work with these things. He said as much, all he had were educated guesses.

If the animals acted the same as other wolves, then they hunted in packs. There would be the alpha male and an alpha female. She could have a litter of up to eight pups per year and *if* half were female and *if* they could interbreed, then when the females were around six months old they could breed. There would be little wolves all over. Within a year or two it was possible to have two to four packs out making kills. Wolves in a pack are cunning hunters. They go for the easy kills. The young, sick, weak or old are first. Wolves are also opportunistic. If one sees an easy meal, well…

Reed had a lot of *If's*. He had nothing concrete until he was able to study them. Study them! Who the hell wanted them studied? Benson wanted them dead, every last one. For now though, he was overruled. Jackson, Stafford and Reed had not looked at the carnage in that den. They did not have to inform the next of kin. He did, and he took it personally.

Up ahead, Benson saw a gas station with an open convenience store. He decided to stop for a cup of coffee. The department vehicle that he drove still had a half tank of gas. That was more than enough to get back. Anyway, if he filled it he would have to pay out of his pocket and there was just no promise of ever getting the money back. The county was just too tight on money. This was only the first snow of the year. After the next one the road budget would be depleted. He had a shoestring budget, himself, to work on. The only redeeming factor was that none of the paychecks had bounced, not yet.

Benson drove into a parking space, turned off the engine and went inside for coffee. Behind the counter was an older woman speaking in whispers to a man, dressed in enough warm clothes to signal that he had walked to the store. Whatever they were speaking about, from their composure, was a serious matter. The man looked cold and gratefully sipped at the large coffee cup.

Benson was not in uniform, but the car was a marked vehicle. As the Sheriff poured himself a medium-sized cup full of hot coffee, the man and woman watched him, continuing to whisper.

"Are you a deputy here on the search?" asked the woman, as Benson approached the counter.

"No, what search?" The hair at the nape of his neck stood on end as his skin tingled.

The warmly-dressed man said, "We've been out in the woods all day searching for a little boy that went missing. Went outside to play in the snow and was gone. Must'a wandered out into the woods playing. We found nothing. This town is too little for someone not to have seen him walking around. Had to go into the woods and get lost. All there is to it. Snow wasn't heavy enough here for tracks to follow. Everyone's been looking, but can't see shit in the dark now. They called the search until first light. Maybe tomorrow we'll find him."

Benson pulled out some bills from his pocket to pay for the coffee. The woman waved him off saying, "Police don't pay for coffee here. It's company policy. Least we can do for you guys. Know you ain't supposed to take it, but you don't worry about it. We around here still respect the law."

Smiling, he thanked her, nodded to the man and left the store. Getting into his car, he noticed he had not turned his radio back on. Benson shut it off so as not to wear the battery down in the car. Cold weather takes a toll on batteries. He had no idea how long the meeting would take, so off it went. Benson was so deep in thought when he left that he never noticed the radio was quiet.

Turning on the radio, Benson checked in with the radio dispatcher. After acknowledging his call, the Sheriff told the dispatcher to use the scrambled channel. He switched his radio to that frequency and waited.

"Boss, a little boy is lost around Wellsburg. I sent three deputies there to help in the search. They just got back a few minutes ago. Morrison was one that went and he needs to talk to you. He said ASAP when you were available."

"I know about the kid. I just found out. Is Morrison there yet?"

"Yeah, I just flagged him into the radio room. Hang on…here he is now."

Benson listened to the scratches over the air waves as the dispatcher gave Morrison the headset.

"Sheriff," Morrison's boyish-sounding voice asked.

"Yeah, Ron, what do you need?"

"Boss, I was on the search today for the lost boy. I was in the woods walking from his house. I didn't say anything, but the stink that was in that den was all around out there."

"Good man. Keep it to yourself for now. We'll talk tomorrow. Tell the dispatcher that I'm going home."

"Yes sir. We're clear on the air."

"Clear." (Meaning that the conversation was acknowledged by both).

Benson was sweating, his hands shook (not that if someone had looked they would see it), but he felt it. They had increased their range, dammit, he thought. Wellsburg was thirty miles from Maple Hills.

Putting the microphone back in the slide on the dashboard, he set the coffee in the cup holder and went back into the store.

The man and woman stopped speaking when he reentered. He looked at the woman and said, "I need a pack of Marlboro and a cheap lighter."

Nodding her head, she took his money.

"Those you pay for."

Chapter 15

Cindy Winters made little out of what just transpired. Both Mark and Warren moved as one. Without speaking, each knew what the other was going to do, unspoken words passed between men. She stood slack-jawed, unable to speak. She would not have known what to say if she had found her voice.

Lonny took everything in stride. Things like this happened before and she knew as in the past, would happen again. Her life, since meeting Warren Skruggs, was one adventure after another. More often than not, that adventure included Mark Lansdowne. She knew the men were boyhood friends and had heard most of the stories about their growing up. There was next to nothing that surprised her when it came to what one would do for the other. There was much that was not talked about by the two and in all likelihood, never would be.

After the two men left to follow the dogs, Lonny returned to the kitchen to finish cleaning up. Cindy, not knowing what to say, followed her to help. Lonny knew Cindy wanted and needed something of an explanation. As soon as the dishwasher was loaded, soap added and started on its job of cleaning, Lonny turned to Cindy and said, "Why don't you get the coffee and we'll talk. I may not be able to explain everything, but what I can, I will. Just understand that it has taken most of my married life to learn about these two…and it is an ongoing thing."

Cindy smiled at Lonny. She really liked her. Lonny had immediately accepted her. Although Cindy did get along with most men, for her, women were harder to get to know. There might have been a self-confidence issue stemming from when she was a girl in grade school. She was, at that time, a skinny little red-haired girl. She was the only one in her class who did have red hair. She was also very quiet until she knew someone. Her best and only friend was a little blonde girl named Kaela, who never shut-up. The teachers in school would try to scold Kaela for talking in class, but they couldn't get a word in edgewise.

As friendship goes, they were perfect for each other and inseparable. The freshmen year of high school, Kaela and her family moved to Oregon and Cindy found herself on her own. By that time she had developed, what the boys called (behind her back), "perky little boobs". The rest of her body developed as well. (The boys all wondered if her pubic hair was the same color and as bright as the hair on her head). They all pooled their money and had fifty dollars for the first guy who could prove he found out. Word was that they gave the money to the class dork for safekeeping. The guys all knew he would not spend it, under threat of ass kicking. (The last heard after all the years, was that he was still holding the money).

Cindy Winters became very popular in high school. By graduation, she went out with most of all of the good looking guys, but she never opened her legs to them. She had plans for her future, which did not include a baby. Getting a B.S. degree in Biology was the important thing to her, not a swollen belly and breasts. Dirty diapers were not even on her to-do list. After graduation she found out about the bet and her self-esteem took a plunge. For a very long time afterward, men were in the same class as "worm-slime". In college she was asked out but remembering the bet, she declined most offers. The ones she did go out with were in a group with others and only in a very public place. Usually group study in the library was the extent. She never felt obligated to give a kiss goodnight to someone who walked her back to her dorm.

By her junior year, her attitude relaxed. Dating was fine now and since sex was part of her biology studies, she found petting and sometimes oral sex to be very enjoyable, but still not intercourse.

She met Kenneth Winters in her senior year. Cindy (who was Roberts at the time), fell head over heels for him. Shortly after graduation, they married. Everything went fine between them for several years. By the time of her thirtieth birthday, they found out she could not have children.

His attitude toward her changed. He was always sullen and in a bad mood, no matter how hard she tried to make him happy. After three more years they divorced.

Cindy went back to school and received a nursing degree. Now, after two years on a general floor, she was on the Intensive Care Unit working twelve hours a day. She lost herself in work. For all the time after the divorce she continued to wear her wedding ring, not in hopes of his change of heart, but so she would not be bothered by men. Just recently she took the ring off of her finger.

Again, her feelings changed after seeing Lansdowne. Why? She did not know, but decided to find out.

Now, she sat in his living room drinking coffee with his best friend's wife, while they were out with guns, doing God knows what.

Lonny was a good judge of people and somewhat empathetic. Cindy was upset and nervous about Mark and Warren leaving as abruptly as they did. Maybe the timing was off, but Cindy should know a few things about Lansdowne.

The large room was chilly. Cindy was, anyway, as she sat on the overstuffed blue couch facing Lonny. The sun had just completely set and as it did, the frame house cooled quickly. Lonny noticed goose bumps on Cindy's arms. Without saying anything, Lonny started a fire in the fireplace and within a few minutes the living room warmed. Watching the fire lash the logs with tongues of orange and yellows, was hypnotic. The warm room, the fire, and perhaps the wine, put Cindy at ease. Lonny saw her relaxed demeanor and felt she could talk some to her about Lansdowne.

She started the conversation by asking, "Do you want a heads up on him or do you just want to learn as you go?"

Cindy sat silently for a small time contemplating the question.

"I guess the best answer is, both. I want to know everything about him, but I know it's too soon. There are things he should tell me. I know there may be things of which he will never speak. Those are what I think he should say if he wants me to know.

Maybe it's too soon to know any more than I already do. I feel something that I haven't felt for a very long time. I'm not sure why I do. I only know I do have feelings for him. It's a mixture of feelings. The one thing above all right now, is that I feel safe when I'm around him. As much as I loved my ex, that was something that was missing in our relationship. Do you know what I mean?"

"Yes, I completely understand. Skruggs would die for me but he would rather live for me. Sometimes I want to kill him myself with some of the things that he does, but safe is the one thing I can be sure of, that and his love. I know he loves me completely, even if he does cause me to spill gravy all over myself."

Lonny smiled and Cindy laughed.

"Lansdowne was the same way with Glenna. He loved her."

"She has been gone, how long?"

"Almost a year and a half. Before her, he didn't care about much. The only person was Skruggs. The only person he ever trusted was Warren, until he met her. He changed after that. Mark never knew what a family was. He never had one. He never wanted one. Mark always said that Skruggs was all the family he needed."

"Her name was Glenna? I like that. Different."

"She was Scottish and tough as nails, yet gentle as a baby's skin. Glenna knew how to work him. If there was something she wanted, she got it. If there was something she wanted him to do, even if he didn't want to do it, he did. She would flap those long eyelashes, smile, kiss him and say, please. He was done. Glenna would never abuse him or use him. She realized Mark was Mark. He is the way he is and there was no changing him. I don't know of him ever telling her "no" about something, but if he did it was for a good reason. She knew that she could bring the subject up later if something changed."

"Mark doesn't believe in anything much. Ideals change. Politics change. Laws change. Mark does not. The only person other than Skruggs that he ever believed in was Glenna."

"Not even you?" Cindy asked somewhat surprised.

"I suppose that he does but not completely."

"Does that hurt?"

"No, that is Mark. He grew up with Warren. Each has almost died for the other. That being said, I think they still would if the need arose. No questions, no indecisions, they would just do it."

Cindy took a sip of her coffee and asked, "How does that make you feel?"

"In a strange way, good. I know either one would do it for me. That is what makes me feel safe. Mark knows I am now a part of what he can call family. He loves me in Lansdowne's own way."

"When he heard the howling last night, he made me stay here. Should I read something into that?"

Smiling, Lonny shrugged her shoulders saying, "Maybe yes and no. The no is that he thought for your safety as he might anyone's."

Cindy looked away from Lonny's eyes and dropped her head.

"The yes to your question is that there have only been two other women in this house since Glenna, myself and Janey Malone. Neither of us spent the night."

Cindy raised her head, her face was flushed and she was smiling.

Patrick Jones

Chapter 16

The silence of the night was broken by the sounds of the two ATV's returning. Beams of light emanating from the head lamps of the vehicles sliced the dark, pointing the way to the garage. Idling engines and garage doors swung open and signaled the two men's return. Half an hour later, the door of the house opened and Lansdowne and Skruggs made their appearance inside.

Warren carried both weapons. He took them and replaced them in the gun closet after unloading them, wiping both down with an oil rag.

Lansdowne was cold, frozen cold, close to Popsicle cold. He sat by the fireplace as Cindy put an afghan over him. Skruggs entered the room and asked, "What can I do, Mark?"

"Brandy. The good stuff, not that crap I feed you."

Lonny wanted to find out how to help. She got a drinking glass from the cabinet over the sink. Skruggs poured the glass a quarter full and Lonny gave it to Lansdowne. He gratefully accepted the glass and took a deep drink. It was smooth and did not burn on the decent from mouth to stomach. Within a minute, the feeling of warmth of the liquor wrapped around him as no blanket could.

Lansdowne knew it was nothing more than a myth that brandy warms, that it only feels warm. That was enough for him.

His shoulder hurt, not just from the cold but from carrying Moe to the ATV wrapped in his coat.

Taking another swig of the alcohol, he hoped it would help to dull the pain. It would have to suffice as it was the only thing available. The prescription for pain pills had not been filled yet. By the time he got home, Tim had closed the drugstore the day before. Tim Carter would go back to the store and fill it, if Lansdowne had called and asked. Lansdowne could have had it filled at the superstore in Sullivan, but he never gave the prescription a second thought until then. He would not have taken one along with the brandy, anyway.

Fifteen minutes after the first taste of brandy, the pins and needles of pain softened. The brandy helped, nullifying the pain in his shoulder from excruciating to a quiet roar.

Cindy waited to hear what had transpired after they left. Lonny knew Skruggs would fill her in on most, if not everything, after they left. From the conversation with Lonny, Cindy knew to be patient. If Lansdowne was to say anything at all it would be in his time, not hers. She had so many questions to ask him but she stayed mute.

Staring into the fire, mesmerized by the flames bouncing and skipping off of the logs, he thought about the last several hours events. Without moving his eyes he stated, "Moe is dead. I'm sorry, Lonny. I know he was your favorite. I put him in the shed. It's cold in there. The others are in the garage. I turned the heat on and gave them food and water. The guys will be okay until morning. I just wanted you to know about Moe."

Tears filled Lonny's eyes. She was partial to Moe, but her real sorrow was for Lansdowne. After

Glenna, they were all he had for comfort during the long hours. Moe was especially attuned to Lansdowne's moods. The weeks which passed so slowly for Lansdowne sitting in his chair, trying to think about what was to come, were made easier by the dogs. All that time, Moe seldom left the side of his chair. It was more than a loss of a dog; it was the loss of a friend. Lansdowne would be brooding over Moe for the foreseeable future.

Skruggs knew enough not to say a word – to anyone, just then. He walked across the room and refilled Lansdowne's glass. Tonight Lansdowne would get drunk and Skruggs would help him all he could to get him there. He would pass out and they would let him sleep on the couch. In the morning, he'd be pissed.

As Ricky Ricardo would say, "Someone has some 'splaining to do, Lucy."

Woe to whoever that someone was.

Chapter 17

Sometime during the night the sky cleared of thick, grey, doughy clouds, parting the way for the millions of diamond-like lights called stars, to shine through. They promised that a clear day for our star, the sun, would warm the calm still air. The mantle of snow cloaking the ground would be less than the previous day. The possibility existed that most of the snow could melt.

Ralph Benson did not care about the sky or the weather. If anything, another foot of snow on top of what was already on the ground would be fine by him, if someone asked. He spent a very restless night tossing and turning, waking his wife several times from her pill-induced sleep. She muttered something about him taking one of her sleeping pills and something else he could not make out. Her voice trailed off, back into the black abode from which he roused her.

All the events from Halloween, until that day, continued to run through his mind over and over again, sometimes in fast forward and other times in slow motion. He fought within himself as to what more he could have done. He felt responsible for the missing little boy from Wellsburg. He knew Jackson, from the State Attorney's office, would not care. He was only primping for a run at the Attorney General's seat later. Stafford seemed genuinely concerned. His body language and the inflection of his voice spoke to that. The kid, Reed, was hard to get a reading. He was too matter-of-fact. He gave history on the wolf, but nothing that would point him in a proactive direction. Benson wanted answers as how to wipe them out. Maybe it could have been done a month earlier but not likely anymore, especially now that the wolves had expanded their range. There will be more deaths. People appeared to be the food of choice.

For Benson, sleep had little to no chance and further attempts were futile. Sliding out of bed so as to not to wake his wife again, he started the coffee maker and then went to the hallway bathroom for toiletries. He had a hard time looking at himself in the mirror while shaving.

The hot water of the shower felt like thousands of hot needles stabbing his skin. Dressing in his uniform was a labor. As he was about to pin on the bright star, signifying that he was the Sheriff, he stopped. Rolling the badge around, studying each of the fine points radiating from the center, he had a passing thought that maybe he did not deserve to wear it. Shaking the thought from his mind, he knew it was tension and lack of sleep that allowed that thought. Benson went ahead and pinned it on his shirt.

He knew Jackson lost no sleep. Stafford most probably did. Reed? Benson did not know him well enough to venture a guess. He was inclined to think Reed slept well.

Stafford and Reed would be at his office at nine o'clock. Reed wanted to see the area where the deaths occurred, just to get a feel for the animals. They wanted to speak with Lansdowne. That could be a mistake. Benson had to warn them not to try and bullshit him. He would see through it as he would fine crystal. Lansdowne saw and heard everything. He may not act as though he did, but one of the few things he knew about Mark Lansdowne is that he missed nothing, and Ralph was certain of it.

Pouring his first cup of coffee, he looked at the clock. There were still five hours until Stafford and Reed would be at his office. Benson decided to have a couple cups of coffee at home and then go in early to work. He wanted to talk to Morrison about the day before and to explain why he was not to say anything. Benson thought he would attend roll call and talk to all of his people about the confidential nature of the matter.

He looked at the clock again. Less than five minutes had passed.

Mondays really suck, he thought.

Chapter 18

Skruggs and Lansdowne killed off a very expensive bottle of one hundred year old brandy. Ordinarily, Lansdowne would have drank just a small amount, savoring each sip as it rolled down his tongue to the back of his throat. That night though, after the third glass for each, the taste and quality of the drink was secondary to the alcohol buzz. Neither man was drunk, but that was only because the bottle's contents were emptied.

The group sat in front of the fire saying little. There was nothing really to talk about except how Moe had died and that was not a good subject for conversation. Not that night. Skruggs saw that the more Lansdowne drank, the more pissed off he got. Lansdowne set his jaw, with a penetrating gaze into the glowing embers of what was a roaring fire. The fire and brandy no longer warmed him. Instead, anger lit an internal fire and hate fanned the flames. Pain may still have been in his shoulder but he no longer felt it. All that mingled in his mind was the damnable hellhounds and how to destroy them, down to each and every pup. An Ahab-sized hate grew within his breast. These monsters were his white whale.

He could not have said how long Warren and Lonny were gone once he stirred from deep concentration, nor when Cindy fell asleep on the couch.

Lansdowne knew he must not give in to the rage. It would totally consume him as it had Ahab.

Blinding hate was Ahab's downfall. He was not going to let it be his.

Watching Cindy sleep helped calm him down. She was even more beautiful when she slept. Her breathing was soft and shallow. The allure of her breasts, rising and falling, was captivating. The curves of her body begged his caressing touch. He knew if he touched her, there would be no turning back.

After covering her with a blanket, he kissed her cheek ever so lightly so as to not wake her and went upstairs to bed.

Chapter 19

At the stroke of nine, Stafford and Reed stood in the hall outside Ralph Benson's office. He invited them in and motioned to the two chairs in front of his desk. Also present in the room was Deputy Ron Morrison. He stood at the right side of the desk, silent.

Reed eyed Morrison for several seconds and then shot his gaze to Benson. The look of disapproval was written on his face.

"What?" Benson inquired. He knew what was about to come out of Reed's mouth. Ralph was not in the mood to hear it.

"It was my understanding that all information was confidential. No others were to be brought in."

Ralph Benson's blood pressure was off the scale. His face was blood red. The veins in his neck bulged, almost enough to pop the button from behind the knot of his tie.

"You do not have all the information and while we're at it, let us get something clear from the get-go. I am, in fact, the Sheriff of this County. I was elected to this job, not some piss-assed attorney in Jeff City. Me! I will run this department as I see best, until either I am voted out of office, or I die. What is said or heard in this office IS confidential. All you know is second hand. The information this deputy has is first hand. He is a trained observer, not as a biologist but as a Police Officer. Now, take a damn step back, keep your mouth shut and listen. You will hear something that will help us find these animals. Do we understand?"

Reed was unaccustomed to someone speaking to him in such a tone. It both angered and embarrassed him. A half-assed Sheriff of a nothing-county had just verbally bitch slapped him. He stared at Benson with a hard piercing look, before it registered that he would need him and his help. When it finally did sink in, he took a breath and nodded.

Reed's nod for Ralph was not enough. He would demand he say it, "Do you understand?" It was a stern, yet direct, question.

"Yes, I understand." Reed stated, as he swallowed some pride. Earl Stafford was amused. Chuckling through a smile he said, "Give him a little rope, Ralph. The man was following his last order first. Let him have time to find out who is here to help him."

"Fair enough, Earl. So it is clear, in this county I give the orders. Too many people have already died. I don't want to lose one more, but the fact of the matter is that I most likely will. That doesn't sit well."

Collin Reed did understand. The Sheriff truly cared about these people, not for re-election purposes but that they were his friends, family and neighbors. He had a passion for his job, one that was long forgotten by his superiors, maybe by him as well.

"Sheriff Benson, I do very much apologize to you. You are right. I was not."

Stafford felt enough of a kinship with Benson to say, "Boy, you are in one foul mood today. You might try decaf." The electric tension evaporated and everyone smiled.

"I am. My deputy here can give insight as to why. You two know what happened up to yesterday, but there has been another incident. It took place in the town of Wellsburg while we were in our meeting. Deputy Morrison was there and will give us an oral report. Go ahead, Ronnie. The floor is yours."

Morrison spoke of the events in Wellsburg and the search for the child. He spoke about the size of the tracks in the snow and how the smell still lingered in the air. He recounted how he walked to one side of the tracks to help preserve them, until the light gave out. Possibly he would be able to continue to follow them today and hopefully find the child, yet his voice sounded less than confident. He knew what those animals were capable of doing and the type of deaths that they inflicted. Morrison also knew that there were more than the one that Lansdowne had killed. He did not voice that opinion. It was just that, an opinion which had no factual evidence to back it up. But he knew, after walking the tracks in Wellsburg and smelling the sick odor, that there were more.

Stafford admired the Deputy. He felt that Morrison had a "no quit" attitude. He thought the kid would be a Sheriff somewhere one day and it wasn't too far in the future.

Reed said nothing, asking no questions while Morrison spoke. He took every word in, evaluating as he listened. He also came to terms with the mindset of these people. They cared about each other. In all likelihood, people who never knew the family of the lost little boy were in the woods searching in the cold and snow all day. They would be out there again and again until they found him, if they found him. Reed was not from Missouri. He had no emotional ties to the people who lived, worked and died there. All he knew of the Ozark Hills was what he saw in the movie, "Shepard of the Hills." That was just a movie. He was a biologist, not an anthropologist…and he did have his orders, those that no one knew about. Locate and study. Take no offensive action or allow any. The animals were a new species and must be protected, whatever the cost. From what was said, the cost was high now – and climbing. It was already too high. He had his orders though.

Benson asked if there were questions of Morrison, otherwise he would allow him to join the search.

Stafford asked, "Will you make yourself available to answer questions later?"

"If Sheriff Benson so orders, then yes."

Stafford smiled, stuck out a huge paw of his right hand and shook Morrison's, while thanking him.

Reed remained silent and motionless, not extending his hand to the deputy. He was lost in thought, digesting what was said.

Morrison left the room followed by Benson, who patted his shoulder, thanked him and whispered to report to him, and only him. Ron nodded, turned and looked at Reed briefly before saying, "He's a smartass."

Ralph smiled and responded, "Yeah, well maybe. We have to go see Lansdowne."

Morrison grinned. "I wish I could be there."

"I wish I didn't have to be there, especially if his mouth overloads his ass. I'll have to stop it."

"Maybe he just slipped and fell. I'll write the report."

Benson smiled. The kid was a good cop. He was proud of him.

"Get going son, you're already late. Good luck."

"Thanks, boss. I'll let you know what happens."

Most of the November snowfalls do not stick around very long. As it was that day, the sun had pushed the clouds out of the way so that warm shining beams of light melted the snow. A good amount of snow would be gone by nightfall and the rest by the next day. The interstate and state highways were clear, but wet. It was the type of wet that drains windshield washer fluid quickly. The snow lasted longer on the gravel side roads.

Driving from the fairly new red brick building, that housed the County Jail and the Sheriff's Office, to Lansdowne's home took nearly forty-five minutes. As it was most days, the trek was uneventful.

Little was said during the drive. Stafford cursed about forgetting his sunglasses that morning. The guy had to live east of Steelville. Benson drove and chuckled about Stafford's plight. Reed sat in the back seat, saying nothing. With his sunglasses on, he could be sleeping. Ralph Benson did not care. He also did not like playing taxi.

Before leaving the office, Benson told Reed to watch his attitude with Lansdowne. He may have valuable information, not in the written reports. Alienating him was a mistake. Interview him, don't interrogate. That would be another mistake. Lansdowne would not suffer any crap thrown in his direction; just a word of warning.

The road to Lansdowne's home was scraped by the county road crew. Even though they rode in one of the Sheriff's department four-wheeled SUV's, Benson kept his speed at twenty mph.

Lansdowne's driveway was clear of snow, all the way to in front of his house. The Jeep, belonging to Skruggs, was parked there next to a blue Mustang convertible, which was owned by Cindy Winters. Benson parked behind the Mustang. The three got out of the SUV and walked the snow-cleared path to the front door. Benson knocked on the storm door, causing the dogs inside to bark madly at the men.

As he opened the door, Mark saw Benson and two other men. He raised a finger, denoting they should wait a moment while he let the dogs out of the other door. The dogs were hesitant to leave their master unprotected. Larry and Curly, who received baths in the tub earlier, were in a self-induced sentry mode. The brown dog followed their lead, being more vicious than the other two. Lansdowne calmed their fears and told them to stand down and to go outside. Larry and Curly understood the command and did so. The brown dog again took their lead and followed suit.

Closing the side door, Mark motioned the visitors to enter. Benson made introductions and Lansdowne shook their hands and led them to the living room, where Warren and Cindy were already seated.

Reed momentarily stood dazed, as he looked upon Cindy Winters. Just then, he could not remember any woman more beautiful. Stafford bumped his arm and Reed returned to the here and now. The day dream of her on his arm faded instantly at the nudge. No one seemed to take note that she took no notice of him.

Benson started the conversation by telling Mark their purpose, if he did not mind rehashing what happened during the attack. Reed broke in and asked if they could talk alone, just the four men. Lansdowne, in a calm easy voice but with eyes that penetrated to Reed's very soul, informed the three visitors that Skruggs already knew everything. Cindy was his nurse. Both had his confidence. That was the way it would be. They were staying in the room.

Reed started by asking if Lansdowne would relate his story from the beginning.

"It's not a story. I will relate the facts in their entirety as I remember."

He did, with few interruptions by anyone. When he was interrupted, the question asked was only to clarify a point. Reed asked most of the questions while making a few written notes. Stafford asked one or two questions, otherwise remained silent and studied the man speaking. He watched body language and eye contact. Stafford was sure Lansdowne spoke the truth.

Cindy busied herself by bringing coffee for all. Skruggs sat in the easy chair by the now cold fireplace, and studied the three men. He grinned most of the time, as usual. Reed cloaked his uneasy feeling of Skruggs.

An hour after their arrival and two cups of coffee later, Lansdowne was finished with his debriefing. Reed asked to keep everything confidential. Lansdowne looked at Benson with a raised eyebrow. Benson said the story was that Mark was attacked by a wild dog and that he had no doubts about Lansdowne.

The three men thanked him for his time and started to leave when Reed asked, "One last question. You are sure of your description of the animal that attacked you?"

Lansdowne had a smile pull at the corner of his mouth. Skruggs' grin went wide.

"Yeah, pretty sure. Maybe you should see for yourself. Follow me."

Lansdowne and Skruggs walked side by side to the garage, followed by the three officials.

Chapter 20

Reed stood dumbfounded at the sight of the two dead animals hanging by their back legs. His mouth was open but he uttered no words. Stafford was equally shocked. The beast Moe killed was fairly intact, while the other that Larry and Curly did in, was not. Benson was somewhat amused by the faces the two men wore.

"Where did you get these?" Reed asked.

Lansdowne spoke to the previous day's incident, about Moe and about getting them back to hang. Looking at the Sheriff he said, "Ralph, I told you that I heard them howl Saturday night."

Benson responded, "I never doubted your feelings. Not really. I guess I didn't want to admit to more of these damn things being around. Mark, I just wanted them to go away. Sorry if I hurt you feelings."

"You didn't hurt my feelings and there's nothing to apologize for. I kinda hoped the same thing, but I knew better when you said the one I capped was female. The bitch was dragging Granny back to the den for her pups, as they were yet too young to hunt. I hope you guys are working on a plan for a widespread eradication."

The three men said nothing, but continued to gawk at the two hanging animals.

Skruggs piped in with, "Eradication with extreme prejudice." He was no longer grinning.

Still not believing what his grey eyes saw, Reed asked, "Your dogs were able to do this?"

"Yes, but Moe paid the price," answered Mark.

"Tough little poodle if you ask me." Skruggs chimed in, grinning.

Benson knew better, but the other two did not until Lansdowne laughed. It was the first time he laughed in a long while, and yet so regretted losing Moe. It was almost as bad as losing Glenna in some ways.

"Can we see your dog's remains?" Earl inquired.

"Nope, we have already buried him. He's by my wife."

Stafford understood, but Reed did not.

"We really do need to see the dog," said Reed.

"I said no. Don't make me say it again."

Lansdowne's jaw was set and the depths of his cold green eyes echoed that Reed was close to hurting in ways he could not imagine.

"You're walking thin ice, pal. Don't be stupid." Skruggs, again, was not grinning.

Benson remembered about Lansdowne saying what could happen when Skruggs stopped smiling. Ralph thought quickly and asked if it was possible to have the dead beasts for further study. He did not know if either Stafford or Reed needed, or even wanted them. The look on Lansdowne's face told him Reed was about to suffer a great deal of pain if he persisted. Benson doubted that any, or all of the three, could take either Lansdowne or Skruggs into custody should they decide to resist. He did not think his gun would be of much use either. Ralph breathed a sigh of relief when Mark dropped his hard gaze from Reed's face and Skruggs once again grinned.

"Sure. Take them both, Ralph. They need to get on ice soon, or they'll stink worse than they do now. I kept them here because it was cold, but the temperature is rising…fast. I've got a few tarps to wrap them in."

Stafford saw what almost happened and said, "That'll work. We can take them now if Ralph has room in the back."

"I'll make room. Reed, come help me."

Collin Reed followed Benson to the rear of the SUV. Opening the back hatch, Benson started moving equipment as to accommodate the bodies.

Turning to Reed he said, "You nearly caused Lansdowne the pain of causing you a much greater pain."

"Just who the fuck is he? Why does he strike you with such awe?"

"I don't know who he is and I never want to find out. As for why I respect him, he did something no other human I know could have done. He killed one of those things up close and personal…and lived. In truth, you or I couldn't have done that. Now go over and help Earl and keep your mouth shut. Don't speak to either of them. I don't know Skruggs very well, but I judge him to be as bad as Mark, if not worse."

Reed kept his composure on the outside for the others to see, but inside he was beside himself. He was no pussy. He was from a tough neighborhood in South Philly. An ass-kicking street fight was nothing new to him (although he had not been in one since before he graduated college). Other than some hard looks, Lansdowne and Skruggs did not seem so tough to him.

By the time Collin Reed reached Stafford and the other two, the bodies were wrapped and taped in tarps. All that was needed was to cut them down and put them into the SUV. The tarps helped to block the putrid smell of the animals. Benson backed the vehicle to the garage doors where the wolves were hanging. One by one, they were lowered and placed inside the vehicle and then the rope was cut, releasing them.

Earl Stafford shook the hands of both men thanking them. Ralph told Mark that they would go to the coroner's office for autopsy and cold storage.

Skruggs laughed, saying he bet that would make the Coroner's day. Then he asked who would do the autopsy. Reed softly said he was a biologist and he would conduct it. That is what he did – study animals. His expertise was wolves in the wild.

"You intend to study these things? Not kill them?" Mark asked, astonished.

"That's right. They are an important new species. We have to study them. They can fill in the gaps in history we have only guessed about," Reed answered. "These animals disappeared, at the latest, six thousand years ago. We need to know why they did. DNA and other tests can only say so much. Field studies will answer more."

Lansdowne was becoming irritated with Reed's matter-of-fact and fuck-you attitude.

"Ralph…"

"Mark, there is nothing I can do – at least for now. I have orders from the Attorney General. My hands are tied, like I said, at least for now."

Mark Lansdowne nodded, "Okay, pal. It's not my problem. It's yours and I'll respect that decision, but only because it's you. I hope you all know what you're doing. You know more people are going to die if they are not hunted down."

Benson slid into the driver's seat. He picked up the pack of cigarettes he bought the day before, and lit one. Benson took a deep drag of the cigarette, exhaled the smoke and said, "Yeah. Yeah, I know. See ya." There was disgust, along with a small amount of defeat, in his voice.

Benson pulled out of the driveway and headed to the Coroner's Office in Steeleville.

Chapter 21

Skruggs was quietly pissed, but so was Lansdowne. Warren walked over to the small refrigerator that sat on the work bench and took out a couple cans of beer. Tossing one to Mark, he bummed a cigarette.

"Son of a gun."

"What? You want it back?"

Lansdowne looked at his friend who was laughing and said, "No, I don't want it back. Only you and God know where your mouth has been." Mark was laughing as well, but only momentarily. Then, he set his jaw again.

"I was just thinking what the science "shirt" said. He wants to study them in the wild."

"Pal, there's nothing you can do about it. You need to let it go," Skruggs advised.

"I know it's a load of crap and you're right, it's not my problem." Mark did not sound convincing to Skruggs or to himself.

Warren decided he should change the subject.

"You know that girl really likes you…maybe a lot."

"Yeah I know, but she could be a problem. She is everything most men could want, but I just don't think I'm ready for a relationship. I feel as though I'm cheating on Glenna," Mark said, as he turned the can up and drained half of it in one drink.

"There's no hurry Squid, just take your time. I loved Glenna too, but she's gone." There was nothing but sympathy in Warren's voice. His smiled faded as he remembered the pain his friend still felt.

"It just doesn't feel like she's gone. Everywhere I look I see some part of her."

"I do too Mike, I guess we always will."

"Too much thinking for one day, and remember to call me Mark. My shoulder is hurting and a pain pill is called for, the beer didn't help," he said as he drained off the rest of the can of beer. He dropped the cigarette into the empty can. He never filled the prescription for pain pills and if he had, would never take one after drinking the beer.

"I'm going inside, are you coming?"

"Nope, going home, later pal."

"By the way, next time bring your own cigarettes."

As Skruggs opened the car door, he said laughing, "I did but I left them in the car. It's cheaper to smoke yours."

Mark laughed too, saying as his friend was pulling onto the road, "You ARE such an asshole."

Cindy Winters just finished dusting the furniture in the living room when Mark entered the house. He was a tad stunned to see everything clean and straightened. The brown afghan was neatly folded over the back of the green couch, the floors were swept and the dishwasher was doing a load of dishes. The house looked as good, if not better, than after Janey cleaned. There was something wrong with Cindy cleaning his home, yet he welcomed the gesture. Cindy appeared comfortable as she went from item to item; dusting almost like it was her home.

Janey did a great job and she and Dave needed the money. She often said, when she and Dave retired they did not want to eat cat food. That was now something she no longer needed to worry about. They were both past that.

Anyway, Janey had great legs and in the summer looked exceptional in shorts and halter tops. Dave certainly was a lucky man. Mark hoped he knew just how lucky.

Cindy was bent over the coffee table dusting and revealed to Mark that she did not wear a bra as she worked. Shaking his head clear, he told her he needed to get a shower and then thanked her for cleaning. She responded by saying there was enough dirt for a pig pen and after his shower, to change his clothes. Next time, he was to take his boots off outside.

His eyes drifted back to the middle of her blouse. Her head still faced down but he saw she smiled, as he attempted to look without appearing to be looking. Turning, he walked down the hallway hoping enough hot water was left, but thinking maybe a cold shower would work as well. It was the second time in two days he had that thought.

While he showered with tepid water, his mind wandered to the events concerning the burial of Moe. Glenna's ashes were buried under the weeping redbud tree in the garden. She so loved that tree in the spring when it bloomed, so it only seemed right to bury Moe next to her.

Warren and Mark dug a four-foot deep hole a few feet away from the urn holding her ashes. Reverently, the two men placed the dog in the hole after first lining it with a heavy plastic tarp. Lansdowne petted Moe one last time and then wrapped the tarp around the animal, still inside the ski jacket. Warren gently poured several wheelbarrows full of gravel over the dead dog's body and then they replaced the earth over him. During the entire time neither man said a word, understanding that there were no words that needed to be said.

Shutting off the water in the shower, he toweled off and then looked into the mirror to comb his short-cropped hair. He saw the wound on his shoulder. It looked healed, but he knew under the skin it was not. There no longer was the sharp stabbing pain, but a constant dull throbbing if he stressed the muscles in his chest, as he had done while digging Moe's grave.

He briefly thought about having Tim, the Pharmacist, fill the script for the pain pills but decided against it. Reaching for the aspirin, he took several with a drink of water.

Cindy found enough edible items in the refrigerator to make a couple of sandwiches. The bread, being a bit stale, became toast. She cut the sandwiches diagonally, placed them on salad plates and set them on the dining room table. Mark seldom ate lunch at the table; usually it was over the kitchen sink.

She handed him a paper towel to use as a napkin and then asked if his sandwich was good. With the limited items in the refrigerator, it was the best she could do. He said it was the same way he made a sandwich, but it tasted better since she made it.

A smile, that caused her dimples to deepen the most he had yet to see, swept across her face. She was pleased he liked it. Doing a simple thing like making a sandwich for him and his liking it, made her happier than she had been for a long time.

Winters said, after lunch she needed to go home. He told her that he needed to run some errands, but how about dinner tonight? She deliberated and then said she had been at his house for three days already, that the neighbors might start talking.

He assured her his neighbors were much too far away to notice, unless of course, she was to parade about outside naked in only her high heels. Then, cars would be lined up along the road for miles with gawkers; otherwise he doubted anyone other than Skruggs knew where he lived.

Setting her gaze on his, she stated that if she were to dance naked it would be inside, for him only. She did not blush making the statement, but he did slightly.

Yep, he thought, it was too soon, much too soon.

Chapter 22

The stink inside the Sheriff's car was overpowering. Even with all of the windows rolled down, the stench was causing Reed to gag. Benson thought of the jar of Vicks he kept in the glove box, for the occasional dead body that was closed up in a house for a week. Stafford did not seem too bothered by the smell and Ralph figured he could live with the smell for a little longer. Reed looked close to the color green and if he puked in the car, then the rest of the trip would be intolerable. Benson suggested that Earl hand Reed the jar. Earl totally agreed, after hearing the hacking coming from the backseat and knowing the next time, Reed probably would vomit on the back of their necks.

Colin Reed gratefully accepted the offered jar, placing enough in his nostrils to block his sinuses for the next couple of weeks. If he thought about something else, it might help to take his mind off how bad his stomach felt.

As a field biologist, Reed was quietly excited by the two dead specimens. He wanted to cut into just one of the two and examine something that existed for thousands of years. He had so many questions and now he may have the answers. Reed saw all the crime scene photos taken when Lansdowne was attacked. They were excellent photos, but now he had bodies that explosive tipped ammunition had not blown apart. After Lansdowne finished, there was not enough left to really study in depth. Reed only needed one of the animals. The other should be sent to the main laboratory and then his notes could be compared with theirs. If he missed something, they would not. The University of Missouri had one of the top-notch veterinary schools in the entire country, but the drawback was that students did the autopsy. Certainly there were a great many promising future doctors there, but his central lab had the crème de la crème to work on this project. Once all was known about the wolves physically, then the next step was the field research.

That was Reed's field of expertise; watching and following their habits for weeks in the wild. Next to nothing was known of these once plentiful animals that roamed the land as the Native Americans slowly moved into the area. It was not known if the Dire Wolf was hunted to extinction or just went extinct, as did so many other animals during the last ice age. Up to then, bones were all he had to study. He wanted to know so many things about them. Were they lone hunters or did they hunt in packs? Did males do the hunting or did females assist? At what age did the pups learn to hunt and when did they go out alone? Did they mate for life, like modern wolves do? Reed had so many questions and the pile of bones from the one Lansdowne killed told him little to nothing. There was not much left to autopsy. Lansdowne did a remarkable job destroying it. The brain was in chunks, as well as most of the internal organs. Only by a miracle was the sex able to be determined. In a week or two Reed wanted to be in the field making notes. All he needed was to be pointed in their direction.

Thanksgiving was a few days away and he most likely would lose four days, unless he convinced whoever to keep the lab open for him. Most of this week would be lost too. Today is gone and tomorrow would entail packaging up the worst of the two and sending it off on Wednesday. Then he thought, would be the four day weekend.

Reed chuckled as he thought of the lab rat that got the job of opening the package. By the time the guy finished heaving his breakfast up, Reed would have his entire notes typed and ready for his paper on the matter. It should get him his PhD. Monster Quest on the History channel would have one less quest to go on when he finished. They could go back to Loch Ness and look for Nessie.

He decided after dinner that night he would definitely invest in his own jar of Vicks, or a respirator, or both.

By the time Ralph Benson rolled into the parking lot of the funeral home, that was also the County Coroner's Office, the Vicks worked it magic. Reed no longer felt like he wanted to void the wonderful and huge breakfast he ingested that morning.

After Benson backed up to the garage door that was used for the intake of bodies, all three exited the car in a more than timely manner. None of the three wanted to stay in the vehicle longer than absolutely necessary. Ralph rang the bell, notifying those on the inside of their presence, and waited.

David Potts was the County Coroner for the past twenty years and a popular and much liked figure in the community. Potts Funeral Home was one of a few dotted throughout the county. Dave not only sponsored sports teams for kids but the senior center as well. He buried a good many people in the county, whose relatives had little or no way of paying. He treated everyone with respect, whether living or dead, that entered the white-painted frame building which was surrounded by manicured lawns and flower gardens, blazing in colors. Mr. Potts believed that funerals were a way for the families to be able to come to terms with the loss of their loved one. He wanted to let people know that the place the departed went to was more beautiful than they could ever imagine.

When Dave saw Ralph standing in the garage, he hoped the visit was not connected with another body, but upon seeing the other two men he knew it was official. Benson brought him far too much business the past month.

Potts looked past the rear gate of the SUV into the back. Although he could see nothing through the plastic tarps, he certainly smelled it. Stafford asked if he had two body bags, but that they would not be returned. He would make sure the State reimbursed him for the use, as well as for the refrigerators that were needed for the length of time that he hoped would be no more than a week to ten days.

Potts smiled his soft caring smile then said he would get the bags and a gurney.

Reed felt uneasy around Potts and voiced his concern by saying, "That guy is freaky, like out of a horror flick."

Benson had taken enough of Reed's attitude that he could handle for one day. He looked Reed in the eyes, the same look he gave people he arrested for murder, before he said, "I've had about all of you I can take for one day. Remember asshole, before this is all over, he may be the man embalming you!"

Chapter 23

Cindy and Mark agreed to meet at Barkers that evening at seven o'clock, as he walked her to her car. She suggested that while he ran errands, he might stop by a grocery store and pick up a few things such as milk, bread and maybe some lunch meat.

He laughed, saying she missed the two jars of peanut butter and grape jelly. Cindy retorted that they still needed bread, unless he planned to smear it over her body and lick it off. Mark said he did not need peanut butter to do that.

Neither blushed, just a knowing smile passed between them.

Reaching for the handle of the driver's side door, Lansdowne saw paw prints on the hood and convertible top, that his dogs did not leave. The muddy prints were too large. He decided to lie to her rather than cause her concern at that time.

"The dogs must have played on your car before I put them up last night. Let me clean them off."

"Never mind, I'll run it through the car wash at the gas station before I go home. I'll see you at seven this evening then." She gave him a quick kiss fully on the lips, jumped in her car and was up the driveway and on the road headed east before Mark could say anymore.

Lansdowne toured around the garage and shed. There were more prints in the snow and mud and were from more than one animal. A faint scent remained, but to say it was from the two that hung in the shed overnight or the ones that left the prints, he could not say. He was stupid and angry when he dragged the dead ones up to his house the night before, leaving a trail right to his front door. The other animals must have followed the trail after Warren and Lonny left. He got drunk and passed out, so if the dogs did bark, he never heard. More than likely they would return. They were down by three. If they did come back, he vowed to reduce the size of the pack by a few more. Placing a call to "Benny the Bullet" was in order. He only had five rounds left of the explosive-tipped ones Benny loaded for him. Mark decided on asking for fifty more and another shotgun that could handle the rounds, then he'd run his errands.

His shoulder and chest started to ache. Lansdowne almost hoped they would return.

An hour or so later, Mark was at the Maple Hills Pharmacy owned by Tim Carter, Robert Carter's older brother. The place was a throwback to the type of place one saw in an old black and white movie. Tim was always behind the counter filling the scripts for the town's people, while his wife Kathy or one of the other women he employed, took care of insurance or waited the register. Tom tried to fill the emergencies as soon as he possibly could do so. Most were dropped off, being picked up at a later time. Many of Tim's clients were older persons that had watched him and his brother grow up. They talked about the times before the interstate and all the people from the city coming down to float their rivers. They never had the beer cans floating downstream back then, like they do now. Tim smiled his deep dimpled smile and just nodded his head in agreement. He was an easy-going, goodhearted man. He was also the best pistol shot in the county and had won the trophy every year he entered the competition during the Fourth of July events. He did not enter every year, feeling it was only right others win. He was not as good with a rifle, but Robert was and he won for as many years as did Tim for pistol shooting.

Tim had only three true loves in his life; his wife, the pharmacy, and pistol shooting.

Mark was met, upon entering the pharmacy, with gentle hugs and kisses on the cheek by the ladies working there. They all asked to hear what really happened to him and were the newspaper accounts true?

He told them he did not know what the papers said since he only looked at the comic section, but if the truth be told, he hoped he would never run into another pissed-off poodle ever again. Pulling away from the women, he handed Tim the prescription saying he'd be back later, but before Mark could leave the counter, the smile that usually graced Tim's face faded into a stern look. Tim asked Mark if he had a minute to talk. Guessing Tim already knew more about the incident, he said he would be in Barkers around seven and they could speak then. The smile returned to Tim's face and he told Mark he'd bring the medication with him.

Mark headed to the grocery store after leaving the pharmacy, hoping his visit would be less eventful…and indeed, it was anything but eventful. He hated grocery shopping. As a kid, he worked in Jim Martin's grocery store from the age of twelve until he graduated high school, and entered the service at eighteen years of age.

Luckily there was no one there that really knew him and if there were, they did not let him know. He was alone, strolling down the aisles looking for items that he, in all likelihood, would never use.

On one hand, Warren Skruggs spent hours cruising up and down the narrow aisles, examining each product and putting things in his cart that were found in his pantry a year or more later. On the other hand, Mark bought just what he needed and oft times found when unpacking, the main item that he went to the store for, he forgot to buy.

He was not much of a cook and anyone who ever ate his cooking knew that to be the gospel truth. Frying something, warming a can of veggies and instant potatoes were the limit of his culinary skills. During the summer he might barbeque something while drinking a beer or two and listening to a ballgame. Otherwise, it was sandwiches or he ate out.

Once he reached the aisle that housed the gelatin, he knew he had been there too long and it was time to go. His cart had the things he needed; the milk, bread, hotdogs, and a couple of frozen pizza pies, as well as enough pot pies to get him through until spring. He admitted to himself that Cindy was right about the bread being stale, since he bought it before the incident in the woods. Mark did not think

Cindy was going to take many meals at his house and if she did, she would eat what he ate.

The people in the store were always friendly and helpful, including the ladies at the checkout registers. The lanes moved fast and even though they might ask how one was doing, there was no time for an answer, other than fine.

Mark looked at his watch as he stood behind four people with full shopping carts.

He still wanted to get a nap and a shower before meeting Cindy at Barkers for dinner.

Chapter 24

The clock on the top of the Eastgate writing desk chimed to signify the half hour. It was five-thirty. The clock resembled a church and church yard, and chimed on the quarter hour. For the first time in a very long time, Mark really took notice of the clock and the man who made it for him and Glenna. Marveling at the ornate, hand planed walnut, he thought of Chuck Schwartz.

Chuck was a short robust man, who sported short cropped white hair from the time he and Mark first met in their youth. Although Chuck was over ten years Lansdowne's senior, they were instant friends.

There was little in the way of carpentry that Schwartz could not do. After doing two enlistments in the Air Force, Chuck worked at a variety of jobs, none that he had his heart into but they kept the wolf from the door. He was successful as a home remodeler and soon after had a thriving business. Still, he was not truly happy.

Lansdowne left for the service and after being gone for many years, came home to find out that Chuck was married to a woman he really loved and had just finished his internship as a doctor. He was selected by a local hospital to do his residency, thus staying in Saint Louis. Between marrying Rosemary and becoming a doctor, Mark never saw Chuck happier.

Finishing his residency, Chuck moved his family (he and Rosemary had a baby girl) to Springfield Missouri and opened a practice. Mark stayed in touch by letters, written mostly by Rosemary to him. At first he received a letter every other week, then once a month. The tone of the later letters was more somber, saying little. She no longer wrote of the work Chuck did, or how big their child, Penny (now ten years of age) had grown, or how she was doing in school. Mark took leave and went to see the Schwartz family, only to find out Chuck was diagnosed with an incurable cancer. At first Chuck attempted to work every day, but between the pills and the treatments at the hospital it became too much, both physically and mentally, until finally he sold his practice. On bad days all he could do was stay doped up enough until the pain eased. On good days though, he would be in his woodworking shop making cabinets and remodeling the kitchen or bath. Soon the large projects were too much, but still he worked in the shop keeping busy, making all sort of things for his wife and for others. One of the last projects he finished was the clock for Mark.

Chuck fought the cancer hard, never giving in to the depression or the pain. He fought harder than Rocky Balboa, but unlike Rocky, for Chuck there would be no rematch. He passed away in his sleep on Christmas morning with Rosemary holding him close. He just had his fortieth birthday a few days earlier.

Mark learned of his passing upon returning from an operation in a small country, God had forsaken and left to men.

Looking at the clock now made Lansdowne smile, thinking only of all the good times he and Chuck had together. The clock chimed that the time was forty-five past the hour and he was to meet Tim at Barkers shortly. Pushing away from the desk, he smiled once more, thinking to himself that there was no more getting drunk and chasing ducks around the pond at Clifton Park.

The brothers, Tim and Robert, sat at a side wall table facing the front door making small talk, when Lansdowne walked in and drug a chair to the table. Robert sipped a draft beer while Tim played with a bourbon and water. On the table, at the vacant spot held for Mark, was vodka on the rocks. As he picked up his drink, Tim pushed a bag containing his prescriptions in front of him, saying not to drink liquor if he took any pills. Mark nodded, taking a deep swallow of the cold liquid, feeling it burn going down his throat.

Robert smiled, asking how he was doing. Lansdowne retorted he was still alive. Tim said that it was a good thing. Shrugging his shoulders, Mark stated that it depended to whom they spoke to about it.

Tim's face took on a grim continence as he spoke, "Mark, a lot has happened around here lately and most folks don't buy the wild dog theory, and that includes us. Too many people are dead for it to be wild dogs. Dave and Janey are dead, as well as Myron Cox."

"Cox? When did that drunken son of a gun die?"

Robert broke in, "At Dana's house, Halloween morning. There was too much blood for him to still be alive and no one has seen him around. For a while the Sheriff thought I killed him, but a few days after your incident he told me I was no longer a suspect."

"Well for my part, it couldn't have happened to a nicer guy," Lansdowne said sarcastically. "So what is it you want from me?"

"The truth about what happened," said Tim. He shifted his body to face Lansdowne. Tim's steel blue eyes penetrated deep into Mark's cold green eyes for only a moment before he spoke.

"The truth and as far as I know, you've never lied to me or anyone else for that matter. We need to know what is going on. People are running scared, shooting almost any dog they see running around. Most aren't going out after dark. Almost all the people that come in here are carrying a gun in their belt...women too. People are really scared of what may be out there."

Lansdowne was silent for a moment, looking at his near empty glass before he spoke.

"Maybe they should be scared. I'm not sure just what it was exactly, that attacked me in the woods. There wasn't enough time for me to make a clear identification before it tried to make me its next meal. I don't remember very much before I passed out, except that it was big and hairy, with sharp teeth. Benson told me while I was in the hospital, that I pretty much destroyed the head with the shotgun blast but that it must have been a wild dog. Maybe he is lying to me and everyone else to avoid a panic. I really don't know about that, but I do believe it is possible there could be more of them. I don't know that as a fact. I'm guessing there are more. If I were you I would keep a gun handy, especially if you're alone walking at night."

"Do you really think there are more of them?" Robert asked.

"Like I said, I don't know for sure but just in case, have one handy. Just don't go around killing poodles. You could get sued for that, at least I think you can."

Robert waved to get Dora's attention and motioned for another round of drinks.

Dora wore a false smile and had ever since the Cox incident on her front porch, but now seeing Mark for the first time since what happened in the woods, her smile became genuine. After setting the drinks on the table, she gave Mark a kiss on the cheek and a small hug, thanking him for killing that thing. He told her, anytime, that he was glad to do it. Dora chuckled and said, "Yeah, I bet," as she picked up the empty glasses and placed them on the tray before returning to the bar.

Returning to their conversation, Tim said, "So…"

"So I don't know anything more than what I just said. You guys know as much as I do from just reading the paper. I played a small part in what took place. Benson has not told me anything more than what you've read."

Mark understood why Benson wanted to keep everything under wraps. If it wasn't kept quiet, anyone that had a firearm (which is nearly everyone in Crawford County), might go out on their own hunting trips, not killing any wolf but maybe getting killed by the wolves. Tim and Robert were smart enough to read between the lines of what Mark said.

He had not entirely lied to them, but had not told them all the truth.

The door opened and Cindy Winters walked in with all the grace of a queen, to where Mark sat with Tim and Robert.

Many times in a bar when the door opens all heads turn to see who entered, but seldom, if ever, does the noise level ever drop to a deafening silence. Men and women alike stopped their drinking and interactions to watch the splendid red-haired sprite. It was not like they all never saw a beautiful woman before, they all had, but on television or in a movie. This one though, was in their presence dressed in a blue gossamer blouse that shimmered, as the light in the room ricocheted from it, as she moved. The black slacks she wore embraced the muscles of her legs and the open-toed strap heels revealed the same red that was on her fingernails and lips. If that was not enough, her eyes shined as two highly polished pieces of walnut. Cindy Winters looked exquisite.

Slowly, coveted eyes of men and envious eyes of women returned to their drinks and conversations. Soon the sounds of the bar were back to normal.

The two brothers stood and each offered a hand as introductions were made. They excused themselves going up to the bar, while Mark led Cindy into the dining room.

Dora asked Robert who she was. Robert smiled and shrugged his shoulders.

"Well, Mark has a date, finally. It's about time he did. She is beautiful."

Someone at the end of the bar asked Tim who she was, but before he could answer that he only just met her, a thin, rugged-looking, sandy-haired man with something of a beard said, "She's his girlfriend. I met her this morning."

Neither Robert nor Tim ever saw the man before, so Robert bellied up to the bar next to the man and Tim flanked to the man's right.

"Are you a friend of Mark's?" Robert asked.

"No, not at all."

"I'm Robert Carter. I own the place, and you are?"

Feeling closed in and outnumbered, the man offered his hand and said, "I'm Collin Reed. It's nice to meet you."

Chapter 25

Her perfume, ever so softly, enveloped the area of their table. There was no mistaking the sweet floral fragrance. Lansdowne knew immediately before he hugged her, that she wore Poison. Of all the perfumes that Cindy might wear, she picked his favorite. It was the only one Glenna ever used, especially on her naked body just before making love with Mark. For him, it was a magical experience each time he and his wife made love. Mark mentally shook the memory from his mind.

The waitress, taking their drink order, walked as though her feet hurt. In fact they did, as well as her back. Her name was Edna, a woman in her early fifties that looked more like she was in her mid-sixties. Her hair was dyed unnaturally black and permed in tight curls. Edna also wore far too much makeup and it looked as though she put it on with a cement trowel. Her smile was warm and sincere.

Cindy asked for a glass of red wine, while Lansdowne asked for black coffee. They both chose porterhouse steaks and house salads. Edna thanked them and was off in a sore-footed flash, returning in moments with their drinks.

Cindy lifted the glass of chilled wine to her lips as though it contained the Blood of Christ. As she tasted the sweetness of the wine, Winters studied Mark.

In the hospital, he was just another patient. At his home, neither time nor opportunity presented itself. He dressed well. He was wearing a brown tweed sport coat over a black sweater; both looked to be tailored as did the black slacks. She never noticed the slight bulge under his left arm. He still wore a gold wedding band on his left hand and she thought it strange that he wore the black-banded watch on his right wrist. The face of the watch was a blue, with diamonds in place for the hours. His hands bore countless scars as did his body. She saw them during his hospital stay when she bathed him. His movements were smooth and easy, but deliberate. The perfectly trimmed beard hid the scars on his face, except the one by his right eye.

She asked about his day after she left. He spoke of going to the pharmacy and made a point of telling her about the grocery store. He left out about calling Benny because he did not feel she needed to know that.

Cindy very much wanted to ask him about Glenna, but before she was able to muster the courage, Edna appeared with the food. Cindy decided it was too soon to ask any questions about her.

Edna placed the steaks in front of them and asked if they needed anything else, like steak sauce. After hearing they were both fine, Edna said one of the things that most irritated Lansdowne. She said but one word, enjoy. Mark could never figure out if that was a request, an order, or a threat. It was a pet peeve but he knew better than to ask, otherwise he would be put in the same category as Skruggs…an asshole. The entire thought was a moot point.

The steaks were perfect and needed no help by use of steak sauce or, for those barbarians that completely smother a perfectly wonderful steak, catsup. Each bite made a person either wish to rush through, quickly chewing each bite in order to get to the next, or take time relishing each bite. Neither Mark nor Cindy rushed, but savored the taste.

The salad was crisp and cold, in opposition to the still sizzling steak on the platter. Regardless of what context Edna meant when she said "enjoy," they did. To make the dining experience even better, Edna did not come by within the customary ten minutes to ask if everything was good. That was another thing that irked Mark, as the server always came by and asked that stupid question when they had a mouth full of food, unable to answer. Even if it was terrible, what makes them think they would continue to eat bad food? They ate in silence.

Edna waited until they finished before making another appearance and only then did she ask if they enjoyed dinner. Lansdowne stated it was the best meal he had since lunch.

"What did you have for lunch, honey?"

"A sandwich in my home that I did not make," he said.

Cindy smiled and slightly blushed.

"That must have been a hell of a sandwich!"

"It truly was."

Mark and Cindy's eyes locked for a long moment, during which she blushed a bit more.

Edna interrupted by asking if he wanted more coffee and if Cindy wanted more wine. Lansdowne said he did, but Cindy asked for coffee instead of more wine.

As Edna left for the coffee, Robert sauntered into the room and asked how their dinner tasted.

Both told him it was wonderful. Mark stated Edna was no Janey, but she would work out and the new cook would certainly work.

Robert smiled and said he would give Mark's complements to his mother. He still had not found a cook of Dave's quality.

Bending over, Robert whispered in Mark's ear, asking to speak to him in private. The grim visage of Robert's face said it was important.

Mark excused himself to Cindy and the two men stepped out of ear shot.

"There's a guy at the bar sort of running his mouth about you. I don't think he much likes you. He says his name is Reed. You want me to walk him out the back door?"

"No, I think not. If he's not drunk, ask him to join my table. Ask don't insist. Let him decide and put his tab on my bill. Maybe he'll like me better."

Robert nodded and left the room as Mark reseated himself across from Cindy. The coffee came before Lansdowne spoke.

"We may have someone joining us for coffee."

"Oh?" Cindy raised an eyebrow.

"Yeah, that Reed guy who came to the house this morning. Robert got the impression that he doesn't like me. Maybe I can change his mind."

"Do you think?"

"Probably not, but I don't need another enemy."

"Somehow I don't think you have many enemies…alive at least."

"Who, me?" Mark feigned surprise.

"Yes, you!"

"No matter what you may have heard, I am a nice guy."

"I know. You are just nasty." Cindy was smiling a large smile.

"That's different. Anyway, you don't know that for sure yet."

"Yet," Cindy said in a soft sultry voice, "I hope to find out…soon."

Before Mark had to say it was too soon, Reed walked up, standing in a defensive posture between the two diners and asked, "You wanted to see me?"

Nonchalantly, Mark pointed to a chair and said, "Take it easy, I thought you might like to join us for a drink, that's all."

Toeing a chair from another table, Reed sat between Cindy and Mark, avoiding looking at Cindy. Reed saw how beautiful she was and he knew he would gawk. Not knowing if Lansdowne was a jealous man, he felt it was best to sit facing Mark.

Lansdowne waved Edna over and asked her to bring Reed a drink. She returned with a dark draft beer. Reed dug in his pocket for cash and was waved off by Lansdowne, who told Edna to place the beer on his check. Reed thanked him by raising the glass in a mock toast and taking a sip of the beer.

Reed worked up the courage to ask, "Something in particular you wanted to talk about or just talk?"

"Just talk. I thought it may just be good to get to know each other. I know what you say the reason is that you're here, but I was wondering what the real reason is."

"Are you saying I have an agenda?"

"That is exactly what I'm saying. I'm just curious as to what end."

"And do you have a hidden agenda after your injury, and what happened to your dog? Do you want payback?"

"Nope, it's not my problem, it's yours and Benson's. If Ralph needs my help I'll be glad to, otherwise the problem is yours. Moe took care of himself and as for me getting hurt that was my own fault. I got stupid."

If what Lansdowne was saying was to be believed, then he misjudged him. Reed felt Lansdowne was sincere and after what happened to him and then his dog, Reed would have been pissed too. Collin Reed decided to loosen up.

Cindy broke in by asking, "What exactly is your field?"

This was the first time Reed heard her speak. Her voice was as sweet and soft to his ears as her perfume was to his nose.

"I'm a field biologist with a specialty in Canidae; wolves to be exact. And what do you do?"

"I'm a nurse."

Turning toward Mark he said, "Your own private duty nurse."

"I've never thought of her in that context, but I keep her around because she makes a great sandwich from nothing and looks great doing it."

Cindy smiled, revealing a deep dimple that highlighted the red of her lips and the white of her teeth.

Turning to Mark, Cindy stated, "Excuse me Mister Reed. Mark, I need to go. The head nurse said I can work tomorrow and Wednesday to make up for the past two. I won't have any days off until Sunday night."

Mark looked at his watch. It was getting late. Edna was waiting to close out Mark's check so she could walk home on her sore feet. Mark excused himself and walked to the bar. He handed Edna a twenty dollar bill (which was the biggest tip she ever gotten) and told Dora he'd clear his check when he came back inside from walking Cindy to her car, and to give Reed another beer. Dora smiled and nodded, causing the light to highlight the blue of her eyes.

Returning to the table, Mark told Reed he'd be back in a few minutes, then moved the chair for Cindy. She told Reed goodnight and as they walked to the front door, Edna blew past them, pushing past the two in a hurry to get home.

Outside the air was almost cold and the stars winked at them. Mark was able to see that Cindy did not wear a bra under her sweater. They heard Edna's steps slap against the pavement until they disappeared in the distance. They were alone on the parking lot, as Cindy turned and gave Mark a kiss full on his lips, for what seemed like minutes. When they separated, she looked at him with walnut colored eyes, shining from the lights in the parking lot or maybe from the mass of stars twinkling billions of light years away.

Opening the car door for her, she slid onto the seat saying to him, "I'll call you tomorrow after work."

"I'll be waiting."

He kissed her again lightly. Cindy started her car, telling him goodnight.

"Goodnight baby. Drive carefully." He closed her car door and watched her car's tail lights until they were out of sight, as she headed down Main Street to the interstate.

Placing his hand on the bright brass handle of the door, the quiet of the night was broken by a loud howl that was undeniably one of a wolf that was close by…it was answered by several more.

The muscles in Lansdowne's jaw tightened as he thought, "My God. They're inside the town!"

Chapter 26

Lansdowne rushed back inside. There were still several people drinking at the bar. Seeing Robert standing at the end of the bar, Lansdowne waved for him to follow. Reed was sitting at the table waiting and upon seeing Mark's demeanor, stood up.

When the three men gathered at the table, Mark said, "They're in town. I just heard them." Turning to Reed, he said, "Are you sober? Can you fire a handgun if the need arises?"

"Well yeah, but I thought you didn't want any payback?"

"I don't! Edna just left on foot. The howling came from the same direction that she was walking."

Robert said, "I'm going too."

"I'd rather you stayed here and protect Dora and the rest. Don't let anyone go until we get back."

"Mark…."

"Please don't argue, Robert. Call 9-1-1 and get me some backup."

"Three are better than two," Robert was going to argue. He was not a pansy.

"You're right and if they show up here, you'll be on your own. You need to stay with Dora."

Robert did not like what Mark said but he knew it was right. The people at the bar had no weapons, should they be attacked. A couple of them would try to leave if it was just Dora there.

Robert asked, "Okay, you need another gun?"

"No, I've got the magnum and there's a 9 mm in the glove box. We should be good. Where does Edna live?"

"North of town about eight blocks, then one east."

"Okay, you call her and keep calling until you get her."

Robert said, "Good luck, guys."

Mark knew that time was short to find Edna and keep her alive. The two hurried out of Barkers to the truck.

Edna had no choice but to walk home. She could not afford a car and she had no one to get her. Her husband was dead, the daughter in St. Louis and a son in jail. She had no option but walk, and after hours of waiting tables her legs were heavy as lead. Edna thought it was not too bad. Since the few weeks of walking to and from work, she had lost fifteen pounds. The roll of fat, which hid her abdomen, was slowly receding. She could now look down and see her knees. That pleased her, but her feet hurt. Bad enough, she wanted to see a doctor. She just could not afford to go. The hot bath when she got home at night, just soaking until the water turned almost cold, helped. Edna thought about turning the temperature setting on the hot water heater up a few degrees, but she did not know how to do that, nor was she able to afford the increase in her electric bill. The job at Barkers was a Godsend. Soon she would catch-up with her bills.

She would think about the same things every night as she traveled the path down Main Street past the pharmacy, the grain mill and the Post Office.

Maple Hills Police patrolled the town streets at night – unless the officer on duty received a call. Edna felt safe. Maple Hills was a safe place for people to live. After ten-thirty at night, the residential neighborhoods were void of persons. They were lighted and good people live on those streets.

Walking as fast as her feet allowed, she heard what Edna thought was someone's coon dog howling. Damn thing would wake up the neighborhood. It was Monday night. Those that were not watching football were in bed. Her husband always watched football on Mondays before he died.

Edna heard another howling, that one was in front of her. The other came from behind. Turning the corner by the new doctor's office that she said was so nice and good, a pair of red eyes from down the street met hers. Somebody's dog is out running the street, she thought. She hoped it was friendly.

Lansdowne hit the button on his key chain, unlocking his truck. Mark jumped behind the wheel while Reed got in on the passenger's side.

"Have you ever fired a semi-automatic pistol?" Lansdowne asked.

"No. I've never had a reason."

Reaching under his tweed sports coat, Lansdowne handed Reed the revolver from the shoulder-rig. Collin's eyes went wide at the size of it.

"A forty-five?" he asked.

"No, a .357 on a .44 frame, but the load shames a .44. Dirty Harry would love it. If you fire, hold on to it!"

"Geez, what do you need that for?"

"Run-away rogue elephants and your wolves. If you shoot, don't miss. You may only have one chance. Trust me, I know. Don't hesitate thinking the sound of gun fire will make them run. It won't. It seems like it only pisses them off. Upside, they do die, just not very easily."

"Do you see her? The defroster isn't working fast."

"Yeah, she is turning the corner ahead. Open the glove box and hand me the weapon."

Reed released the catch and the door fell open, revealing the 9 mm. Taking the weapon out by the barrel, he handed it over to Mark.

"Do you always travel so heavily armed?"

"Yeah, ya never know when I'll meet a smartass field biologist that I want to shoot for talking and not watching."

Reed would have smiled at the comment, but he could now see Edna. She was a half block in front of their truck. A pair of red eyes was moving towards her at an incredible rate. She just walked towards them as if she had no care in the world.

"She walked right to it!" A startled Reed exclaimed.

"She thinks it is a neighborhood dog. She doesn't know about a Dire Wolf! Everybody has covered it up." Mark was angry.

The wolf was thirty feet in front of her, when under the light of the street lamp she saw it was not a dog. She screamed but no sound left her throat. Edna turned, dropping her purse containing her precious tips, and ran on her sore hurting feet as she had never run before. To her right, another of the beasts ran at her and then one closed quickly to her left. She knew she would be attacked. Edna knew true fear. Her eyes let tears roll, blocking her sight as she pee'd herself. There was going to be no outrunning them. Her chest hurt from the effort of running from them. A heart, not used for the type of movement she required, pounded like a drummer gone mad. Headlights were up ahead. Maybe she could make the vehicle. She dare not turn her head to see how close they were. If Edna knew, she might give up. She was slowing up anyway. Her body was giving out. Edna knew in that very minute that she was going to die, either from the beasts chasing her or from a heart that could not stand the fear.

The truck coming toward her stopped in the middle of the street. She thought it close enough to get to it. Edna could smell two foul odors. One was emanating from the animals giving chase. The other was from her, as she soiled herself.

Edna could hear the three animals breathing, as well as something resembling a growl. She'd never make the truck, she thought, and consigned herself to her fate. Oh, God! Please, oh God! The last bit of her adrenaline kicked in as she flew toward the stopped truck. This effort gained her an extra foot of distance between her and the three assailants. She heard three quick "pops" that she identified as gunfire. As she turned, she crashed directly into the hood of the truck.

Mark slammed on the brakes of the truck, forcing it to a dead stop. Throwing the gear shift, grabbing the weapon and exiting the vehicle, Mark released the safety, aimed and fired the rounds before Reed had his door half open.

The gunfire from Lansdowne's weapon surprised Reed, as he saw the three animals roll as they were struck in the head by the bullets.

Mark yelled, "Reed, take care of her!" He ran toward the downed wolves.

Collin dropped the magnum on the seat and rushed to give aid to Edna. She was shaking like a 7.3 on the Richter scale. Her breath was in short, shallow, labored gasps. He spoke to her softly and reassuringly, telling her it was alright. They were dead. Mark had killed them.

Edna looked with eyes of disbelief and gratitude together. She held his hand and gripped for him not to leave.

Three more gunshots broke the silent night air. Reed looked away from Edna for just a second, to see Mark firing one round into the heads of each of the three beasts, and then returned to them.

Lights inside houses came on, as well as porch lights. People filled the street. Some went to help Reed and some looked at the dead animals in the street.

The only Maple Hills police officer on duty pulled up, while the blue and white lights atop his car flashed streaking beams. Someone yelled for him to call the paramedics. As the officer ran to the front of the truck, he requested assistance over his miniature radio. An ambulance was requested code three.

Lansdowne reached Edna and knelt down next to her. He told her that they were all dead. She was safe. Help was minutes away.

The Maple Hills policemen reached for the weapon still in Mark's hand. Mark pulled it away saying, "Not tonight or any other, for that matter."

The look on Lansdowne's face gave the policeman more than enough reason for pause. He did not want to lock eyes with him again – ever!

Lansdowne turned his head and took a long unbroken look at Reed.

"Sorta looks like your secret is out," he said with a sarcastic tone, while reaching into his pocket for a cigarette and his Zippo.

Collin Reed, still holding Edna's hand, looked around at the gathering crowd and said, "Yeah, I think maybe you're right."

Chapter 27

Reed and Lansdowne spent until dawn sitting in, what Maple Hills Police Department called, an interview room. It was close to the size of a broom closet with only a table and two chairs. The walls were painted white and the bright lighting made the room that much brighter.

They were not under arrest but there were questions. Questions that Reed refused to answer and questions that Lansdowne referred to Reed. The officer taking statements convinced Mark to relinquish custody of his firearm. The 9 mm was the reason they were being held. When the officer attempted to run an NCIC (National Crime and Information Center) report on the weapon, he found no serial numbers to run. Not that the numbers were removed, it was simply manufactured without any. The officer had heard that certain government-issued weapons were made without numbers, but he had no idea which agencies had them. He was astute enough to know that if Lansdowne had it in his possession, he was not about to say why or how he came by it. He decided the Chief was coming in and he could ask about the gun.

Lansdowne suspected the gun was the reason they were still in the room the size of a sardine can. They were provided coffee and use of the men's room and were treated well by the officers on duty, but until questions were answered they were going nowhere.

Reed was unnerved by sitting in the police station, as well as the events of the night. He wanted to talk to Lansdowne, make conversation. Lansdowne quietly told him that if he was not going to reveal anything about the animals, to sit down and shut up. They may be in a small town interview room but there were, in all likelihood, cameras and sound activated recorders.

Reed tried once to pace but the room was not large enough. Lansdowne simply sat with hands folded, said nothing, and did not touch the coffee cup nor drink any. He had been careful not to use his hands, especially his fingers, as to leave prints.

Although there was not supposed to be a record of him left, and doubtless there was not, he could not be sure if he was still be on someone's watch list somewhere in the world. The mere chance was enough to warrant caution by him. The gun was going to have to be explained. He was going to make a phone call but not from the police station, nor from their phone lines.

Near five A.M., the Chief had them ushered to his office. He was young for the position of Chief of Police. He was a good-looking man, with dark hair swept straight back and a thin mustache that ended at the corners of his mouth. His keen dark eyes looked deeply into each of the two men's eyes. He watched body language, paying particular attention to the small things. Reed's actions told him that he was not accustomed to police detention. There was nothing observable about Lansdowne, as he offered nothing for the Chief to read.

Chief Lawrence Beegin's voice was deep when he spoke, as he thanked them for saving Edna's life. They did the community of Maple Hills a great service by killing the three wild dogs that attacked her.

Three wild dogs? If Beegin saw the bodies, he would know that they were not wild dogs. Lansdowne knew he saw them. Beegin would go to the scene before going to the office. It is standard operating procedure.

Someone got to him. The cover-up was secure for now. The town people that were there would read the story in the papers. Reed and Lansdowne's names would be withheld. The responding officer may even get the credit for the kills, which was fine by Mark.

Reed raised his eyebrows in surprise. He wondered if the Chief actually thought that the animals were wild dogs. These looked nothing like a feral dog. Feral dogs look like any other dog.

Mark asked the Chief if he had news on Edna's condition. Beegin said that she was in shock and that they were running tests on her heart. Preliminary diagnosis was that with a few days of rest and medication, she should be okay. Lansdowne suggested to the Chief that he mention to the doctors that they should look at her feet. She was complaining about them early in the evening. The Chief, who was looking at the officer's written report, smiled at what Mark said. He said he would run it by the doctors.

As the Chief read the report, his desk phone rang. Picking up the receiver, he just said, "Yes," listened for a few seconds and then punched a button on the console stating to the caller that he was Chief Beegin. Not a word was said by the Chief during the phone call that lasted no more than three or four minutes. He ended the phone call, by stating that he was glad to be of assistance and then cradled the phone.

Looking at Reed, the Chief told him he was free to go and then asked if he would mind giving him and Mark a few minutes alone. Reed nodded a nervous nod of relief, got out of the chair and waited outside the room.

Beegin's face had gone stern-looking during the brief telephone call. Now though, he was smiling.

"You, sir, have friends in high places."

"I wouldn't exactly call them friends."

"Maybe not, but this one certainly is. Your firearm will be returned when you leave and no mention of it will appear in the report, as neither will your name."

"Thanks, Chief."

"No, thank you. I very much meant what I said about Edna. She's a sweet lady who's had it rough. You saved her life tonight."

"Glad I could help."

"Me too."

"Maybe I should offer you a job?" The Chief jested.

"Thanks, but Benson has dibbs on me. I have a plastic Junior Deputy badge coming from him….sometime." Lansdowne said, smiling.

Mark stood, as did the Chief. The two men warmly shook hands and again, the Chief thanked him.

"You're welcome," was all Lansdowne said, then left to go home.

Chapter 28

Waiting outside the Maple Hills Police Station was Skruggs, leaning against the hood of Mark's pickup truck.

The morning air was biting cold and Lansdowne pulled up the collar of his sports coat. The sky was getting pink in the east with the rising sun, yet there were still stars in the west.

"Can't stay out of trouble, can you?" A grinning Skruggs asked.

"It seems that way. I want some coffee and a cigarette. I smoked my last one hours ago."

Reed invited himself by saying, "I'll buy."

"Looks like you've got a trainee, Squid."

"Thanks, just what I need."

Skruggs chuckled as he told Lansdowne, "By the way, you left your magnum on the seat. I put it under on the driver's side. Not like you to do that."

Mark reached across the seat and put the 9mm back in the glove box after unlocking the door. From under the seat, he took the revolver and replaced it in his shoulder holster.

"It was the kid. You drive, I'll follow."

Reed climbed into the passenger side of the truck as Mark started the cold engine. Luckily, there was no frost on the windshield. Backing out of the parking place, they followed Skruggs to the diner a few blocks away. The food was good there and the coffee hot. It was the only place open at that time of the morning.

The three men went inside together and found a table on the far corner. Soon many of the locals on their way to work would be in for breakfast or a coffee to go. The place would be full and finding a seat much less a table, would indeed be tough. The waitress, a woman in her mid-thirties, with brown hair and sleepy-blue eyes, took their order for coffee. She returned with three thick mugs filled with steaming hot coffee.

Asking if they were going to eat breakfast, Skruggs looked at Reed and asked, "You on expense account?"

"Yeah, why?"

"You said you'd buy." He pointed at Reed, "He gets the bill."

They ordered eggs, bacon and toast. The girl walked to place the order with the cook, a thin man with a thin mustache.

Lansdowne took a deep drink of the hot black liquid before asking Skruggs, "I know I'm going to be sorry for asking, but you found out how?"

"Apparently the Chief recognized your name from the incident in the woods. He called Benson who called me."

"And the call to the Chief from my friends in high places, as he put it?"

"I called," Skruggs eyed Reed who was taking in every word, "you know who." He said he'd take care of it, then went on to bitch me out for waking him. Friends, huh?"

"Yeah, he has always been one of the very few."

"True and he said something about missing equipment. You know about that?"

"Did you say it was all in your shed?"

"No, I didn't let him finish. I just hung up."

"Smart."

Skruggs smiled, "I thought so."

Reed had no idea what they were talking about. He asked if he could ask a question. Simultaneously, the two men said, "NO!" The food was placed, by order, in front of each man by the waitress, who then hurried to take another order. The diner was filling up. The next few hours she would be busy taking orders and just able in between to refill cups of coffee. She did make it past with the coffee pot once while they ate.

Once Lansdowne finished, he got a cigarette from Skruggs. After lighting it, he blew a cloud of smoke over the table just to see if it would bother Reed.

It did. He waved his hand in a brushing motion to move the smoke away. Reed coughed. Then Skruggs lit up and took a sip of the coffee. He raised his eyes toward Mark and smiled as he blew smoke in the top of the coffee cup. Reed coughed again, but said nothing. He did not finish his eggs, though.

"You guys know that torture has been outlawed by the President?"

"Must have missed that memo. Mark, you see it?"

"Nope." Lansdowne shifted his position and faced Reed. "Before you get Skruggsy excited about possibly waterboarding you, we have a few questions.

If you lie, we'll know. If you hold anything back, we'll know. Then I turn him loose on you."

Reed, for the first time since receiving this assignment, was not the person in control. He believed Mark when he said they would know. Skruggs was smiling a very ugly grin. Reed also believed that either man could be equally unpleasant, but that Skruggs would enjoy it.

"Okay, for my physical and mental well-being ask away."

"You have been given orders to study these things?" Skruggs asked.

"Yes."

"They must be of some importance other than just a new species of wolf? Correct?" Lansdowne asked.

"Maybe, but I honestly don't know about that. I am a field biologist. I spend my time in the woods watching and recording. If there is a high agenda, I'm not privy to it. My job was, by definition, to do my job. Field biology on this animal and compare it to other wolves."

"How long has the government known about their existence?"

"Just over a year and a half. At first, the sightings were thought to be what the cover story says – feral dogs. Someone, somewhere, got a damn good photograph of one and gave it to Conservation and eventually it worked its way up the chain."

"So, you really don't know anything about them?"

"Not really. All we really do know comes from fossils and educated guesswork."

"Okay, tell us about that. Pretend we know nothing about Dire Wolves or the fossil record. Don't explain it like we are fifth graders on a field trip, but also don't get too technical. I'd get bored and Mark would be lost."

"Skruggs…"

"I know, I'm an asshole."

"Right."

Collin Reed spent the next hour explaining everything he had told Ralph Benson on Sunday at the Capital Building. He omitted nothing. They listened to him, saying nothing. Except to clarify a point here and there, they remained silent. Neither man took notes but Reed could tell either man could repeat the conversations, perhaps word for word. If they asked a question, they would know if he spoke the truth; from his gestures, head and eye movements, and more. All the things a trained interviewer looks to see in a subject. While speaking, he knew beyond a doubt that these two men were observing him the same way he would observe an animal in the wild. The difference was that he knew they were observing.

Several cups of coffee and a half of a pack of cigarettes later, Reed finished his oral dissertation.

Mark Lansdowne leaned back in his chair and stared at the ceiling. Skruggs no longer grinned. He let out a long, low whistle and said, "Well, crap! And you want to go into the woods by yourself and study these things?"

"Yes, I do. Before I go, I have at least two, if not now five, I can autopsy. Doing that will tell me so much more. It will take years to learn about them. Seeing their interactions in the wild can explain if they are like other wolves or not. Breeding habits, number of pups in an average liter, monogamy between male and female. All the things we don't know, I can learn."

Reed was excited as he spoke. Again, he saw the papers, books, and the lectures in his mind.

He was more interested in what these beasts could do for him, rather than the information he would glean for science. What's more, it was evident to Skruggs and Lansdowne that this dreamy-eyed scientist was nothing more than a profiteer. Reed expanded about benefits to science, but thought of dollars and fame.

Collin Reed had not looked into the dead eye sockets of Janey Malone's face. He saw the fear in Edna's face the night before. Reed saw Edna's expression, screaming for life – for someone, anyone, to save her. When governments and politicians make policies or plan wars, they don't see the absolute fear in the eyes, in the minds, or written on the faces of the innocent. That is left for the grunts. They pray for God to have mercy, but in Lansdowne's and Skruggs' experience, in war God has little mercy even if He hears the prayers. Reed was one who was interested only in himself. If Mark had not killed the animals, he suspected Reed would have left them to their hunt.

Lansdowne said it was not his problem. The son-of-a-bitch Reed just made it his problem. The wolves, as much as he hated them, were only doing what they do to survive. This guy would let them and did not care. This man, Collin Reed, was not one of the innocent. He would report back that he had been interrogated, but told them nothing more than he did

Benson. Everything was still in place and he could proceed. Proceed to get more people killed.

"It sounds as though you're very excited to get on with your work. If for some reason we don't touch base for a while, good luck, and should there be something either of us can do to help, don't hesitate to ask." Reed was informed by Lansdowne.

"Skruggs will take you to your car. I'm headed home. Oh Skruggs, would you come by the shop on your way home? I can't seem to get the band saw blade to line up."

"Yeah sure, no problem."

Skruggs turned to Reed. "Thanks for breakfast. Pay the man."

Chapter 29

By the time Mark arrived home, the sun was above the top of the leafless trees. It was going to be another warm day. The rest of the snow would melt, leaving the ground muddy or soft. If the weather stayed as it was, Thanksgiving Day would be strange. That is, not that the events of the past month or so were not strange, to say the least they were.

Pulling the Chevy pickup into his customary parking spot at home and turning off the engine, Lansdowne grabbed the semi-automatic from the glove box to take inside and clean. That would be later after talking with Skruggs and stealing a few hours of sleep.

The dogs were dancing on their hind legs when he opened the door. They needed out – badly! It was more than twelve hours since they had a potty-break and the three were letting him know it was urgent three hours ago. Mark opened the patio door for them and they wasted no time getting outside.

He set the 9 mm on the desk after he ejected the clip and cleared the chamber.

Lansdowne heard the familiar footsteps coming over the flagstone walk, the door opening and Skruggs saying, "Band saw blade?" You couldn't come up with anything better?"

"No. It was enough."

Skruggs plopped himself in Lansdowne's leather chair. "That kid is going to get more people killed." It was a statement that did not need saying.

"Maybe, but what it seems is that someone is counting on the people of Crawford County to be stupid. That bullshit cover story can't hold water much longer, especially after last night. Enough people saw these things and know they were not dogs – feral or otherwise."

"Last night before dinner I lied, sort of, to Tim and Robert. I could see that they suspected as much. Now Robert knows for sure and Tim probably does by now. Everyone from the Cattlemen's Association goes in there, so by tomorrow most of the county will know."

"And that means what to us?" Skruggs asked lighting a cigarette.

"Right now I'm not sure about that. Reed supposedly can't do anything as far as an autopsy until Monday. Other than biomechanics of the animal, which from the fossil record he says he pretty much already knows, he may not find out much more. He seems to think that they arose again because of a long dormant gene. Maybe so, but I think not…and I think he's not that dumb."

"You think someone, for some reason, bioengineered and then released them here?"

"Yeah, I do Skruggsy. That puts us all in danger, making me a possible target. Someone may think I know more than I do or at least think we're smart enough, given ample time, to fit the pieces together."

"One problem."

"Huh?" asked Lansdowne.

"We're not that smart. Everything is guesswork up to now. The story about the gene thing is plausible. Unless we are going to start sticking our noses were they don't belong, it is plausible. Why would someone do it and who has the ability?"

"I can't answer that, brother. It is just strange that these things didn't exist around here for the past four, five, six-thousand years and in a place where there are no wolves. Now we have boo-coo of them."

"You really want to get that involved? They almost sent you home in a body bag a few weeks ago. I know losing Moe pissed you off. It did me too. But if what you suspect is true, then it's bigger than both of us."

"Losing Moe had something to do about the way I feel. After seeing Edna's face last night, Skruggsy, I can't leave it alone."

"We've seen those faces before."

"And neither of us have had a full night's dreamless sleep in years."

"We were not in a position to change things. It wasn't our job to change anything. Just carry out the objective and complete the mission."

"I know, but maybe this time I can. That little old antique lady shouldn't have died like that. Janey and Dave Malone never hurt anyone."

"She did have great legs, didn't she?" Skruggs said to lighten the tone of the conversation. In truth, Skruggs did not sleep much at night unless he took pills. Even so, most of the faces he saw in his dreams were the same ones Lansdowne saw in his.

"Who, Granny? I never saw them." Lansdowne teased, "Not my type."

"Now who's being an asshole?"

"Warren, if you don't want in, I understand. You have Lonny to think about. I don't have that anymore. Except for the short time Glenna and I had together, I guess I never did have anyone. So for me, it doesn't matter."

"That's cold, pal. Fuckin' ice. When have I ever said no? Never! I'm not about to start now."

Mark finally sat down on the couch. He was tired but his mind was running a mile a minute. Too many pictures flashed non-stop through his mind, giving him momentary pause to wonder if getting involved was the right thing to do. Suddenly he felt old beyond his years, as if he had lived many lifetimes. The dull ache in his shoulder and chest progressed past the throbbing point and was now a sharp pain. Taking out the little blue plastic bottle with the label from Maple Hills Pharmacy directing him to take a pill "when needed for pain", he opened it up and popped one down his throat. It stuck there. Rather than get a drink of water, he walked to the liquor cabinet and washed it down with vodka.

As he replaced the top on the vodka he said, "I'm sorry for what I said, pal. I know you're always there for me."

"No need to apologize. You're tired and you hurt. Get some rest. I'll come back later."

Mark sprawled out on the couch. As Skruggs was walking out the door he heard, "Thanks Warren. You're the only one who's never let me down."

"Go to sleep."

"Mike! Mike! Listen to me."

Lansdowne stirred from a dreamless sleep. He was still asleep and knew the voice he heard was not part of a dream.

"Yeah, honey, I hear you."

"Don't worry about the who and the why. You must just destroy them. You can. You must."

"Okay. I will. I'll kill everything."

"Not everything, you doh-doh head." He heard her giggle. "Just the beasts. You can do it."

"Yes I can, Glenna. I'm good at killing."

Her face was that of an angel and her voice was as soft as a cool gentle breeze, blowing in off of the ocean on a hot tropical day.

"Mike, there's one more thing. "That girl really likes you. She wants you."

"I don't know, baby. Not yet I don't. I still want you."

"No, Mike. You can't have me anymore. I'm not there."

Glenna's voice was fading away.

"I love you. Don't go. I don't want to go on."

"You must go on. You must kill all the beasts. It's up to you to do this, or more innocent people will die. I've got to go."

"Don't go! I love you!"

"I love you too Mike, but now it's time for you to love again - someone else."

"Will we talk again?" Tears flowed from Lansdowne's closed, sleeping eyes.

"No, I don't think we will. I... do...love... youuuu..."

"I will always love you. Stardust baby, until we're both stardust."

Mark awoke about noon from Benson pounding on the door. Sitting up with eyes that wanted more sleep, he could finally focus and see the Sheriff framed in the glass of the door. He waved Ralph in and then stood up.

Benson rushed through the door. Mark put up a hand to stop him from speaking, telling him to wait. He'd be right back. Lansdowne left the room to the bath, ran cold water in the sink and washed the sleep from his eyes and face. His mouth tasted like a litter box, so he used some mouthwash to gargle with. He still wore his sports coat and shoulder holster. Mark stripped them off, throwing them on the bed in the guestroom.

He returned to the rec room, but not before stopping to make some coffee for both of them.

Benson was sitting on the arm of the couch smiling, as Mark offered him a cup.

"What are you so damn smiley about?" Lansdowne was not yet fully awake. He sounded grumpy to Benson. Between the long night, a pain pill and the lack of sleep, he was grumpy.

"A little boy went lost outside Wellsburg Sunday. Ronny Morrison spent Sunday and yesterday looking for him. There were plenty of tracks of something hunting the kid."

"Yeah, so…"

"So, they found the kid almost at sunset yesterday. He was alive and thirty foot up a tree. He was half frozen, hungry and dehydrated. The bark on the tree was clawed off about six or seven foot up. The kid said the biggest, meanest dog with really big teeth chased him up the tree and wouldn't let him down. He slept up in the tree all night. The thing stayed at the bottom, just waiting. It only left when it heard all the noise from the people searching, calling out his name."

"The kid is okay?"

"Yeah, he's at the hospital in Rolla being checked out, but he'll be fine."

"That's good to hear," Lansdowne said, taking another drink of his coffee which was doing no good helping him to wake up.

"It gets a little better. Christine McKay went on the search. She was with Ronny when he found the kid. While Ron was getting the boy down, Chris went off following the tracks. Several minutes after the boy was down and had told his story, the searchers heard gunshots. Some stayed with the kid, while Ronny ran down trying to find Christine. He did, about seventy-five yards away. Little Christine was standing holding her grandfather's old "hog leg" when he got to her. She killed a male and a female. Ronny shot the six pups. Now most everyone in Phelps County knows about 'em."

The cobwebs were slowly slipping from Marks foggy brain when he said, "That's good news."

"Yeah, but there's bad too."

"Oh?"

"The male had a collar on with a radio receiver attached. Christine said she thought it was still working. You know what that means."

"Someone is monitoring their movements." Lansdowne's voice sounded disgusted.

So did Benson's when he said, "Yep."

Chapter 30

"Does Reed or Stafford know about the collar?"

"Reed didn't. Stafford only would know if McKay told him. Morrison told her not to say anything. He took the collar off and took out the batteries. I've got it now."

"Don't say anything to Reed. He has his own agenda. He's trying to play the people to whom he is supposed to report. As of now, he hasn't learned how to hide a lie within the truth. That makes him a conduit to the information about the wolves. There are too many unanswered questions. Who, why and how long have they been here? Reed doesn't know these answers. He thinks he was sent because of his being such an outstanding field biologist. Whoever really sent him was privy to that information, but he's foolish to believe what they tell him. Reed will do as he was told because he's idealistic, but he's also a climber. He'll tell them everything but after the fact, when it suits him. He doesn't know someone else is here already and I'm willing to bet, has been here for some time. He thinks they completely trust him to report back. Reed's arrogance is his shortfall. We may be able to use that."

Ralph peered long and hard into the half empty coffee cup, listening to every word.

"How can we use it?"

"Right now, I don't know. The who and why isn't really important just now. Odds are we'll never know those answers. What we do need to know is how to destroy them, all of them. Reed can give us that. I'm also willing to bet there are more of them wearing tracking collars. Leave Reed to me. He thinks he has won me over. You have the collar. If you can find what frequency is being used we can get the equipment to track them as well. We found one den and that was purely accidental. Unfortunately, there was only one there. We need to find where they moved. We may not get them all, but we can make a deep dent into their population."

"You're using the pronoun, we, a lot."

"I'm in. Completely in, but on my terms."

"Which are?"

"I'll let you know when the time's right. For now, all I ask is for you to trust me. I'm on your side in this mess. Too many people that I thought highly of are now dead."

"I thought you didn't want payback?"

"Yes, well, I lied. Can you find out about the frequency that the collar is using?"

"Maybe, I may have someone who can help but the tracking equipment is another story."

"Leave that to me." Lansdowne said with authority.

"You know we're going to step on some awful big toes. This may be a career-ender for me."

"Not if I have any say. I'm not under any orders. I don't take bad or illegal orders, not now or for a very long time. When the story comes out, I'll take the heat…and I'll make sure the story comes out."

Benson understood Lansdowne was going to protect him. He did not like it. The coffee cup was turning around and around in Ralph's thick hands.

"Mark, I don't want you to…"

Lansdowne cut him off, "You have everything to lose. I don't. I have nothing to lose. Anyway," Lansdowne smiled at his new good friend, "I don't lose. I will always complete the mission."

Benson placed the cup on the table and stood up to leave.

"Okay Mark, for now. I don't know what you're thinking and I feel safe in saying that I may not like it. I will trust you," Benson smiled, "and believe it or not I always have."

Mark returned the smile. "Thanks. See if you can find the frequency soon."

Reed arrived at his motel room in Cuba, Missouri after the ten minute drive from Maple Hills. The thought of calling his superior and apprising him of the incident from the previous evening, he decided was best done after some sleep. Too many things happened in the short time since he arrived and he wanted more of a clear mind than what he had presently. There were now five dead animals. The two in the coroner's freezers were his to autopsy. Those had intact brains. The other three could be sent back for his boss' people to study. Lansdowne had blown away the brains of the three in less than three seconds. No one shoots like that. Three shots, three kills, and in just three seconds? Maybe Benson was right to say that Lansdowne was not a man to be trifled with. He was well trained by someone. Lansdowne no longer was of any importance. He had offered help, but did not seem to want any further involvement. The Sheriff and Conservation Departments were under orders to keep a lid on everything. They knew next to nothing. All in all, he felt he had little to report. Maybe they hadn't found out about the two that the Coroner had on ice. In that case, his paper on the findings was almost as good as published. If they had, by the time they waded through the mess of the three animals, he would be finished and well into his field work. He would still tell them just what he wanted them to know, just enough to keep them happy.

He was asleep almost immediately after his head hit the pillow, with a big smile on his face.

Tim Carter opened the pharmacy late, while Robert Carter was up earlier than most days. The brothers sat together having coffee at a table in Barkers discussing what happened to Edna. Both men were a bit miffed at Mark, feeling he did not trust them with the truth. After an hour of coffee and Robert fixing them breakfast, they established to their satisfaction that maybe he had told the truth – just not all of it.

It was possible he did not know all the truth until that night. Robert left Barkers the night before, after hearing gunfire. By the time he got to the shooting location, people, police and paramedics were everywhere. He mingled in the crowd to get close enough for a look. Two had been downed with a gunshot through an eye, each. The other was dead from a single shot between the eyes. The brains of all three lay in pieces, swimming in blood puddles next to the bodies. What surprised Robert was the sheer size of the animals. The word "huge" was an understatement but it was the only one that fit. They stunk as if they slept in a Chicago slaughterhouse. Their canines were thick and long. Sabre tooth tiger, came into Robert's mind. All three were males with thick, grey and black matted coats. Robert would have liked to have gotten closer but he along with other Maple Hills residents were ushered away by the responding police officers.

"Tim, it was NOT a dog but I can't say it wasn't. It was just not any kind of dog breed I ever saw."

"Wolf maybe? Remember the black bear a couple of years ago?"

"Well, maybe. Those teeth were scary and the size of it was bigger than a wolf," Robert thought for a minute, then said, "Yeah, a wolf. Maybe a wolf. Damn big ones. Bigger than any wolf I ever saw at the Wolf Sanctuary in Eureka, or is it Fenton?"

"Eureka, Missouri. I think the Bird Sanctuary is in Fenton. Who cares? We're here and if they are that big we're in trouble. Everyone is in trouble. The papers reported they were wild dogs."

"Bullshit Tim, total spoon-fed bullshit." Robert was angry.

"Calm down, calm down there little brother. No one there last night is going to not believe what they saw. Most people aren't gullible, not around here. In St. Louis they just don't care."

"Only ones up there who would care would be the cops. It would just be something else on the streets to deal with, like they don't have enough on their plates."

"Quite so, but those things aren't in St. Louis." Tim retorted.

"So what do you want to do?"

"Let's see what the local law enforcement has to say about what they're doing. If its bullshit, as you say, we go from there."

Tim looked at his watch. The pharmacy should have opened twenty minutes ago. Getting up from the table, Tim told Robert that he was going to leave.

Robert stopped him by saying, "One other thing, you'd better hope and pray Lansdowne doesn't enter the pistol shooting contest this year."

"He's that good?" Tim Carter asked with a quizzical look.

"Yeah, he's that good. You'll lose for sure."

"Damn it. Now I have something else to think about today."

The brothers half-heartedly laughed.

Chapter 31

By Tuesday evening everyone in Maple Hills knew what had happened. No one who saw the animals dead in the street believed what they saw were feral dogs. Most of the town people were born and raised there. They knew there was a difference between wild dogs and wolves. Black bears came back into the area. Armadillos were working their way north. Wild pigs were now being sighted in the woods from time to time, so why not wolves? Why were the authorities lying to the public? Reporters from the local newspapers printed the dog story. That is what the officials told them. They had news releases ready by the time the reporters asked for interviews. The news articles reported what was said, but left it open for people to draw their own conclusions. When asked if the reporters could photograph the bodies, the Chief of Maple Hills informed them that the Missouri Conservation had seized them for further study and were already gone. That much was true.

The mayor of Maple Hills told the Chief, in a private meeting, to increase patrols for a while. Let the people see an increased police presence on the streets of town – until things quieted down. Cancel vacations and days off for the officers. Don't worry about the budget, they would find the money later. Both men knew the people expected action.

Women, who had last minute shopping for forgotten Thanksgiving items, were escorted by husbands, friends, and where there were small children, whole families. The town grocery store which was packed during the holidays anyway, was even more so.

No one walked the streets that Tuesday, nor would they on Wednesday. The stores in town would suffer. It was leading into the Christmas buying season and money for people to spend was tight enough. Bleak was the initial forecast before the invasion, but now it looked devastating.

Over dinner in many households in Maple Hills, the conversation was about the shooting. Decisions were made to keep children home on Wednesday, or the parents would just go into work late because of driving their kids to school. Everyone remembered the little boy and girl who disappeared Halloween night and were still missing.

Deer rifles that were just cleaned and put away until next season were brought back out and placed in a handy spot in homes. No one was panicking, just being careful.

Reed called his superiors earlier and reported to them. It was a short conference call and when it ended, all were satisfied with Reed's actions.

He felt happy with himself. All went as he planned and they knew little more than before. A few more days and he could really start working. After the autopsy he would be in the field. The toxicology would take a week or two, but he would get the results first. He could release them to his bosses later by saying he was in the field.

Rubbing the two day growth of beard, he decided a shower and shave were in order and then out to have a nice dinner. He heard Barkers had great steaks, but after last night Reed was not at all interested in returning to Maple Hills. Someone at the desk recommended a steak house twenty minutes or so west on the interstate. It was quiet with good food, a nice atmosphere, and everyone minded their own business. He doubted that anyone dining there would know him, so much the better. He could work on his laptop while he ate. Then, put it on a memory stick. That way, only he had all of the information.

Yes, he thought, stepping into the shower, so far it's good.

Earl Stafford spent the morning fitting the crew-cab pickup truck that Christine McKay used, with tarps and dry ice. The Maple Hills Police Chief was more than happy to see the dead bodies leave his custody. The animals were placed in the Street Department shed, which was immediately behind the Police Station. The Chief's budget did not include money for the thirty bags of ice used to keep the bodies cool, or for all of the cans of air freshener.

As the animals were transferred from the shed to the pickup, Stafford told the Chief that he would be reimbursed by the State for his expenses. The Chief explained that there was no such thing as petty cash in his department. The cost was his out-of-pocket expense. Earl knew the pay for any small town police officer was meager and payday was likely not until the end of the month. He told the Chief that he would attempt to expedite the reimbursement but that he could not promise anything. Stafford had a sincere appreciation for small town cops – or any cop, for that matter. They certainly did not do the job for the money or benefits. There were not many benefits, if there were any at all, and most had to work a second or third job to make ends meet. If he had the cash he would have taken care of it himself, but his payday was also the end of the month.

Ralph Benson called Stafford, asking him to run by the Sheriff's office. When Earl said he was on the way to Columbia with the bodies, Ralph said he would meet him at the truck stop on the interstate in Cuba. Thirty minutes later, Ralph was riding shotgun in the pickup. He started out by telling Earl they needed to stop in Wellsburg. There were a few more dead wolves there. Stafford raised an eyebrow, asking how many more? When Benson informed him as to the number, Earl glanced at Ralph and said, "Well, crap!" Then Benson dropped the bomb about the collar. This time Earl looked at Ralph as he took a deep breath, slowly exhaling. He knew everyone was being played, but by whom, he asked? Benson shrugged his shoulders and said he did not know, but they might soon. He explained to Earl his actions to find the frequency and maybe even the manufacturer. It did not appear to have been put together in a basement or garage. If it was manufactured, there were sales records. They would find out who bought it and when. As for why, he didn't care. It might be interesting to find out, but finding out why would not help destroy them. When would he tell them how long the wolves were out in the woods? That might tell them an approximate number, since they only have one litter per year. One hell of a lot of guesswork but it was all that they had to go on.

Stafford asked if Reed knew. Benson shook his head, saying he did not trust him. It was possible that he knew about the collar. If he did not, and found out, he would report it back. So far, the collar was not only their best, but their only lead. The possibility existed that the animal who wore the collar was the only one, unlikely but possible.

Earl said he did not trust Reed either. If Reed asked about the three bodies from Maple Hills, they agreed to tell him that they had been sent to the Conservation headquarters for prepping and forwarding, and they would not tell him about the others.

Benson said the Sheriff of the next county and the Chief of Wellsburg were both friends and that they could be trusted not to say anything. The only others that knew were Morrison, McKay and Lansdowne.

Earl understood about Morrison and McKay, but why Lansdowne?

Ralph looked out the windshield of the truck watching the telephone poles fly past. Stafford knew the people in Columbia at the School of Veterinary Medicine would do the autopsies and keep quiet about doing them. His people were sworn to silence but they were deputies, not hunters nor professional killers.

"Because when push comes to shove, we're going to need him and his pal Skruggs. And I have the feeling it will be soon. I just hope we are in time."

"Me too," said Earl as he pulled into the Wellsburg Police Station parking lot, "Me too."

Chapter 32

Tracking the movements of each of the four packs of wolves was becoming far more difficult. The lithium batteries in the radio collars were failing. One collar had stopped transmitting almost immediately after the animals were released. That was almost a year ago. Two were sending weak, but steady signals and the last one was working fine sending a strong signal, until last Monday. It just stopped. Even if the collar somehow came off the neck of the animal, it should still continue to send a signal. It would be at a constant location, if at all.

They did not like it when he reported the first was offline. He knew they definitely were not going to like hearing about this one either. There was nothing he could do about it. All that was left was to monitor the other two groups until their batteries failed, and from the strength of the signal, it would not take much longer. It may last a few weeks, maybe a month at best. Then he could go home.

The money was good. They paid for all of his expenses without question. Once the other two transmitters failed, he had no further purpose.

Tomorrow was Thanksgiving. He thought about taking the day off, finding someplace serving hot turkey dinners and watching football. No one would know. He could fake his daily report and tell them about the down collar next week. Mondays were when he emailed the weekly report, and he had sent the past report before he knew about the collar stopping. The tongue-lashing he received because of the first collar completely failing was unpleasant. He had no control over them. Since the other two were weak, he could say so was this one, and in his December report say it was the first of the three to fail. He would not be held responsible. They were aware of the batteries.

From the signals, it appeared the wolves had established territories and were maintaining them. None overlapped. By now, from the eight that were released, he guessed that there should be fifty or so, counting new litters. If any females were born in the first litters, those females could have their own litters by now and that would push the numbers up.

Still, he would have to stay until all transmitters were down.

He read the newspaper articles about the "wild dog" attacks. They said nothing. After living in the area for the better part of a year, he knew the people would soon figure out that they were not dogs, if they had not already. The people that he had contact with were intelligent individuals. If and when they found out for certain, he hoped to be long gone.

The crisp morning air was cold now and dawns no longer held their allure. It was time to leave. Soon, he hoped.

Sitting in the truck and driving the back roads was getting tiresome. The cup of tea he made in the motel room had cooled enough to drink. It was bitter and needed some sugar, but from months of sitting in the truck more hours than he liked, he was getting fat. The small amount of sugar would not have mattered too much, but he had to start somewhere.

Holding the Styrofoam cup in his left hand, he switched the radio receiver on with his right and turned the volume down. He wanted to hear the classical music station he found, drifting in and out on the vehicle radio, and enjoy his tea. The sun would be rising in a few minutes and he would start his day of monitoring – or trying to monitor.

He parked on the same old logging road every day for the past couple of weeks. The vehicle was far enough down the dirt road as not to be seen easily from the gravel road. He did not pick the spot, the wolves did, but it was nonetheless perfect for his purpose of concealment. There was not much traffic on the gravel road. Just the few people who lived along it and they were few indeed.

His cup of tea was empty about the time Mozart was finished. He pushed his canteen into the old military backpack and checked to make sure his book, with his field notes and pencil, was in it.

Pushing off of the seat after opening the door, he stood and stretched. The sun coming through the leafless trees blinded him, opening his eyes after the stretch. Reaching into the vehicle, he dragged the backpack across the seat with his left hand, grabbed the radio receiver with the other and moved the volume up halfway.

The signal was loud and strong, stronger than he had ever heard it before. He no longer needed the receiver to know where the wolf with the collar was located.

He smelled the strong musky odor that it used to mark its territory. Directly behind him came a low, throaty growl.

Turning his head to see if he had enough distance to launch himself back inside of the vehicle, the wolf jumped.

He did not have the needed distance.

Chapter 33

Wednesday morning, Earl Stafford sat in a chair waiting for Doctor James Lee, head of the School of Veterinary Medicine at the State University. The office was in the middle of the new, up to date laboratory. Having glass walls on all sides of the office meant Dr. Lee could see what was happening anywhere in the lab, at any time.

Earl remembered him as a bit of a gruff man who now neared sixty-five years of age, teaching for over thirty of those years with no intentions of retiring. Dr. Lee loved his work, the animals, but above all, his students. More than one student graduated only because of the interest he paid to their success. Dr. Lee silently felt if a student failed, it was because he, in some manner, failed the student. Over the years, there were disappointments with a few, the ones that had a true love and desire to help animals but not the ability to heal. He encouraged these men and women to work in other areas dealing with animals. He would help them to find where the student may be better suited. A letter from Dr. Lee was more than a recommendation. It was virtually a promise of a job. Stafford was one of those students.

It was not because, with a little more effort with the books, he was not adept and would not graduate. Earl believed that healing animals in the wild was as noble an effort as that of someone's pet. He would get upset when an older person brought in a grossly overweight dog or cat, and could not make them understand that they were killing the animal.

Looking at the old oak desk in front of him, Earl remembered the hours which probably added up in total, to days or even weeks. Dr. Lee would sit and talk to him; much like a father would speak to a son. Lee spoke like that with many of his students, but he knew there was something special inside Stafford.

Walking from the staircase, (consisting of four flights of steps he took every morning and evening instead of the elevator), Dr. Lee looked around the lab until his eyes settled on the man with the greying hair sitting before his desk.

The doctor's brown eyes smiled at the corners beneath the totally white bushy eyebrows, upon seeing Earl, who the doctor considered one of his greatest successes. The warm smile that spread over Stafford's face echoed the sentiments he felt for Dr. Lee.

Entering his office, dropping his old grey coat and leather brief case in a chair nearest to the door, he took the outstretched hand of Stafford. Earl noted that Lee's grip was still strong and firm. The face of his old mentor hadn't seemed to change, other than the white hair on his head which had thinned greatly since they last met. Small talk about families ensued for several minutes before Lee asked Earl the reason for the visit. He was sure it was not to wish him a Happy Thanksgiving.

Stafford was a man of purpose, so there was something of importance to the unscheduled interview. Earl's face took on a grim continence as he shut the door for privacy. The events of the past months were explained to Dr. Lee. The doctor sat listening to the fantastic story, analyzing each sentence. Earl told the professor everything he knew, from the beginning up to that moment. While relating the story, Stafford's voice would crack as he spoke of all those who died from the menace that was now plaguing the south central regions of Missouri. Lee saw the emotions revealing themselves, not only from Earl's voice but throughout his whole body. He watched hands folded in the Conservation Agent's lap shake slightly, as he progressed through the narrative. Dr. Lee knew Stafford could hide his emotions well, as a rule. Today they slipped out, ranging from sorrow to an angry man who wanted revenge on the animals who were wreaking havoc in his beloved woods.

When Earl finished his monologue, the two men sat silently motionless. Dr. Lee looked at Stafford as he ran through the fantastic story again in his mind, attempting to grasp the full implications. Once he felt he digested everything, the doctor asked Earl what he could do to help.

"I have several bodies of the things on ice. I would really like for you to dissect the best of the lot and help me find a way to destroy them."

Earl went on to explain that Reed would be there on the coming Monday to autopsy the bodies that were now held at the Crawford County Coroner's morgue. He needed the information, if any, before Reed. He went on to say Reed was not to be trusted and should not know about Lee's participation, if he decided to help.

"If what you say is all true and factual, which I have no doubt is, by New Year's we both may be looking for new jobs. Do you know how high up the food chain this goes?"

"Nope, but it must be high if they were able to get the Attorney General's office to go along. As far as jobs go, we can open a clinic. You and I could be a good team. Anyway, the wife's been on my butt about a vacation."

"Yes, mine as well," said Lee. "Of course I will help. Now, where are the bodies that I get to choose from? We need to start immediately."

"In the back of my truck."

The Wednesday before Thanksgiving went much as Thanksgiving Day did for Lansdowne, with the exception that on Thursday there were three football games on television. Thanksgiving Day morning, Skruggs called asking him to dinner. Lansdowne declined the invitation as he did the year before, thinking Warren and Lonnie knew that was going to be the case and without an explanation. Skruggs knew why and had expected the answer he received from Mark, but he asked anyway.

Most of Thursday, Lansdowne lost himself in the football games while drinking beer and eating microwave pizza for lunch. The day outside was moderately warm and partly sunny. Lansdowne took four thick rib eye steaks from the freezer early in the morning, setting them in the sink to thaw. At halftime of the Cowboy's game, he lit the grill and put the steaks on to cook. Since he liked medium rare and the dogs had not voiced a preference, they were all eating medium rare steaks by second half kickoff.

The dogs also enjoyed a can of beer each, with the steak. Lansdowne switched from beer to a medium sweet red wine. It was the one Glenna liked the best. She almost never drank alcohol, but she did like her glass of wine in the evening.

His mood started to become sullen and moody. He fought the feeling. Glenna told him that it was time to "cowboy-up" and go on. In life he refused her nothing, maybe it was time to do as she asked. It was no dream the other night. The least he could do was to try. That is what she wanted.

Lifting his glass in a toast, "I'll try. No promises my love. I will try," and he sipped the wine, tasting the mellow sweetness to deep down his throat.

After finishing the steak and letting the dogs out, he took his dish and rinsed it off in the sink. Opening the dishwasher, he saw it was full but could not remember if they were clean. Saying to himself, what the hell, he forced the dish into an already occupied spot, filled the washer with soap and turned it on.

Headlights of a car coming down his driveway flashed their beams of light through the windows. By the time he opened the door, a female figure with bright platinum blonde hair was attempting the journey down the flagstone walk, in boots with three inch stiletto heels. She looked more like she was dancing than walking. Lansdowne was mildly amused by the sight, but thought it best to turn on an outside light in order for her to see the path. Otherwise she would end up on her butt, or worse. The thought ran through his mind that if she did fall, he could offer to kiss her boo-boo. After all, Glenna said to try.

Continuing to chuckle, he opened the door for Amie. She smiled her smile that made the moon and stars, on a warm spring night, envious as she entered the house.

"Hey darlin'. How's my guy doin'?"

"Good, baby. Real good now. What brings you here? I didn't know you knew where the house was at."

"Didn't really. Benny came by work and asked if I would bring you something. He gave me directions from the interstate. There's a bag and a box on the backseat."

"Would you like some wine or brandy?" he asked, closing the door. As he turned, she surprised him by placing her ruby red lips on his cheek in a kiss. Amie's body felt warm against him and the kiss was soft, as soft as a feather moving over the hairs on an arm.

"Wine," she said, stepping away and sitting on the couch next to his chair. The bright red sweater was large and roomy. The black slacks were dressy, tight in the right places but not overly revealing. Mark turned off the television and the only light in the room then came from the "butt-ugly" lamp, casting shadows and highlights on her, yet smiling, face. Delicate hands accepted the glass of cool wine, which she raised to her lips and tasted the rich red liquid. She gave a nod of approval and smiled again, as if only for him.

Lansdowne thought he should say something to get the stupid "Skruggsy" grin off his face.

"If you're hungry I could fix you something," remembering he had only frozen pizzas and lunchmeat in the fridge.

"My God, no. I cooked today for Mom and my brothers. I couldn't touch anymore food. This wine is fine, thank you."

"Did Benny say what he sent?"

"He said I didn't need to know when I asked. If it wasn't for you, I wouldn't have done it. He was nervous, almost paranoid."

"I bet. He's always like that when he's asking someone to do something that will land them in prison for ten to fifteen years, should they get caught."

The smile left her face, "I'll have to thank him the next time I see him. May I ask you what I took the chance to bring?"

"Sure. Ammunition, and to be honest I don't know what else. Benny is always full of surprises."

"You ain't kidding! I'll know better the next time."

"There won't be a next time. I'll make sure. Let me go get it out of your car."

"Later. It's not eating anything or needs to be walked. Let's just sit and talk. Other than small talk as I cut your hair, we really don't know each other."

"Are you sure you want to know me?"

"Sure. Why not? You're not Jack the Ripper or a serial rapist. I like you. I always have."

"Okay," he said, refilling her glass of wine. "What do you want to know?"

"Well, for one thing, why you were Mike Linden and now you're Mark Lansdowne?"

"Not yet on that one. Maybe sometime down the road."

"Well, okay darlin' if not that, which is a biggy, why out here so far from everyone or anything? No neighbors for miles."

"I like to walk around naked and I don't want anyone to see me and laugh. Low self-esteem. No ego."

Amie laughed, almost choking on the drink of wine she was swallowing.

"No, really. Why?" she again asked.

"Really! You know the statue of David?"

She nodded and smiled.

"Well baby, I don't look anything like that. It's most embarrassing."

Her laugh was sweet and melodious. Her rich hazel eyes emanated lights. Amie was comfortable with him. She knew there were few, if any, questions he would, or could, answer. It didn't really matter to her. She was, for the first time in a very long time, comfortable sitting alone in a house with a man. Amie felt safe but she guessed most everyone felt safe around him. He just made people feel that way. Maybe not all people, just the ones who were easily hurt or harmed. Basically, somewhere deep in his soul, he was more than a good man. A bad and dangerous man, with a good heart. Someone she could easily care for deeply.

They sat for the next several hours talking more about her than him. She finished her third glass of wine, when she looked at the time on her watch. Amie said she needed to go. Lansdowne shook his head, telling her with three glasses of wine and the

late hour, she could stay in his guest room. She tried
to refuse his offer but he would not hear of it. She
would stay. That was all there was to it. She said she
had appointments starting at noon and she was
booked until New Year's Eve. Fine, he would wake
her early.

Amie knew he was right. A full stomach, a
long day, and three glasses of the best wine ever all
mixed together to do her in. Sleep sounded good.
Walking down the hall from the dining room, she
thought the house cozy and warm but needing a
woman's touch again. All of the house, but the guest
room, still stated that Glenna was there, a little bit
anyway.

Mark told her where to find nightshirts in the
dresser and kissed her on the forehead, goodnight.
They smiled at each other and then he left the room,
pulling the door closed behind him. Returning to the
rec room, he opened the patio door and called the
dogs back. Brownie went by the fire to lay down,
Curly by the small couch, and he put Larry outside
the guest room door, only telling him to protect and
stay. Mark listened for a brief moment for movement
in the guestroom and upon hearing none, went to the
front door, pulled on a jacket and went to Amie's car.

The bag was green, but rigid. It resembled a
duffle bag in length and had a handle strap in the
middle for balanced carrying. The box was of wood
and was padlocked. By the smell, it contained the
ammunition, a lot of it. The box fully measured a
foot and a half wide by two feet long. He carried
both into the long unused woodshop and put them on
the bench. Popping the lock with a crowbar, he saw

the shotgun shells along with boxes of cartridges for his magnum, and some that were completely new to him. He found fifty rounds of those, along with a note that read:

These will only work in the weapon that's in the bag. Will open a hole in two inch armor. Have fun.

Opening the bag, he found two boxes of similar length. One box was twice as thick as the other. Looking inside both, he smiled.

"Looky, what I've got here!" he said, and then closed the box, locked the shop door and returned to the house for a nightcap.

Chapter 34

The patient count during the holiday season in most hospitals is lower than at any other time of the year. So it was that fact that enabled Cindy Winters to have Thanksgiving dinner with her family in Perryville, Missouri. In the several years of working at the hospital, Cindy was lucky enough to draw either Thanksgiving or Christmas Day off work. She loved the holiday season, especially at home with her family. It was so "Currier and Ives," or maybe "Norman Rockwell," to her. Life on her family's farm was hard, hot work most of the year tending fields, laying in hay for winter feed and all the rest of the things it takes to run a family farm. From the start of rifle season for deer until after the first of the year, things on the farm slowed down. Daylight was shorter, which meant the work day was shorter. When Cindy was young, that meant instead of all the chores she did in the spring and summer, that she was able to relax some, giving her time to do other fun things. If there was an early freeze the large pond was perfect for ice-skating. Wood that was cut, split, and stored, was burned in the fireplace all winter, warming the entire first floor of the house.

Sometimes she so missed her family and the farm. She missed her uncle Ed most of all. He was her favorite – excepting her mother and father, of course. Ed was a mellow sort of guy, made even mellower by the beer and liquor he consumed daily. He was famous in certain circles of Perry County for his ability to out drink any three men in a row, before passing out. Nowadays his drinking lessened with a few health problems, but not by much. Ed was always happy, or so it seemed. The advice he gave to Cindy as she grew up was sometimes back-woodsy, but was always sound. She would tell him things that she would never tell her father, or her mother for that matter. Ed would never tattle on her if she did something wrong but always convinced her to tell her parents.

After finding out she could not have children and her eventual divorce, she talked to Ed for hours on end. He listened saying little or nothing until she finished opening her soul. Then whatever he said always made things better. Maybe not right away, but eventually. Ed loved his liquor, but he loved his niece more than anything on earth. Cindy loved him as much as her father.

So on the Wednesday before Thanksgiving when she was told by the head nurse that she had the holiday off, Cindy made her famous (within her family) rum cake. It was Ed's favorite, made by his favorite, and only, niece.

Cindy thought of inviting Lansdowne to go home with her but it was far too soon for something like that. They were possibly friends, but not more. Certainly not lovers. He did not seem to be ready for that either. He still wore his gold wedding band. Mark was sure to be lonely and now with Moe dead…Lonny and Warren would invite him to dinner, or so she hoped. She was not quite certain how to think about Mark. Cindy thought maybe if the opportunity presented itself, she might talk to Ed about him.

The drive to the Lester Roberts' farm took about two hours. Taking State Highway 185 South was longer than taking the interstates, but it was a nice day and the State Park was a nice diversion to what she would have otherwise seen on the interstate. The hills and curves of the state highway were relaxing as was the lower speed limit. Although the sun had been out and the temperatures were warm, there were still patches of snow in the woods. The road was clear and that was the main thing. The drive was quiet and pleasant through each of the three counties that 185 ran through. Once reaching Interstate 55 South to Perry County, she would be home with her family, whom she considered to be the best people in the world.

It was close to noon when she pulled up the long gravel road that led to the two-story frame house. Nothing had changed. If anything had, it was nothing of note. She drove past the house, parking in front of the house next to her Uncle Ed's old black Ford pickup. Getting out of her car, the stale smell of beer emanating from empty cans in the back of the pickup made her smile. Cindy did not like the taste of beer but loved the smell of it. It was a smell that reminded her of summer barbeques, swimming in the pond on hot days and fishing with her father and Uncle Ed. Beer was a staple at the Roberts' home. If the refrigerator in the tractor shed was empty, the one in the barn was not. Lester always said, "As long as there is food on the table, there'll be beer in the barn."

Opening the front door, the aromas of roasted turkey and fresh baked pies filled the air. Each aroma fought with the other, to see which could escape to the outside world first. Cindy loved these scents more than she loved the beer. Her mother greeted her from the kitchen, where she was putting the finishing touches on her deviled eggs. Cindy laughed to herself, as she thought of how much the pollution levels would rise the next day in Perry County, because of the deviled eggs and beer consumed by both Lester and Ed. That was a smell neither she, nor anyone else, loved. She could hear her mother at two in the morning, yelling at Lester to go to the barn and fart. Lester would just laugh and say something about that much gas being a fire hazard, not covered by farm insurance if the barn burned down. Then he would fart again and would laugh even harder. Her mom would eventually be forced downstairs to sleep on the couch.

From the kitchen, Cindy heard an unfamiliar female voice asking what else she could do to help. She immediately knew it must be a new lady friend of Ed's. Ed was married twice previously. The first almost ended at the reception, when Ed and Lester were found drinking beer from the cooler in the trunk of Lester's car. The bride was Baptist. The second marriage was annulled, because after two months they had never consummated the marriage. Ed kept passing out before they could. (He said drunk was the only way he could stand to see her naked).

Setting the cake on the side bar with all of the other desserts, and hanging her coat and purse on the coat rack that her father made before she was born, Cindy entered the living room. In front of the television, Lester and Ed sat watching the football game and hardly gave her notice until the quarter ended. Then hugs and kisses were exchanged. Ed whispered in Cindy's ear that he wanted to speak with her outside. Grabbing his almost full can of beer, he snatched his coat and accompanied Cindy to the front porch.

He was quiet for a bit, taking several drinks from the can. It was as though Ed did not know where to start. Finally he looked at Cindy and blurted out, "I invited Kenneth to dinner."

Cindy looked as if she had been slapped with a wet sock containing a bar of soap. "Why?" Was all that she could muster.

Ed wanted to pace and wished he had not invited her ex-husband. "Honey, you know I love you like you were my daughter. I always have but you know that. He came to me about a month ago just wanting to talk, nothing else. Kenneth said he was wrong about everything. He still loves you…never stopped. He said he tried but couldn't do it. Out of all the times we talked, this was the most sincere I've seen him. He's wanted to talk to you but didn't think you would."

"You got that right!" Cindy was red with anger, not toward Ed but toward Kenneth. "After all he's done, he thinks he can just act like nothing has changed! He still loves me? Sure he does!"

"Cin-Cin, I think he does, but he wants to say things that maybe should have been said before. He just didn't know his own mind. You gotta listen to what he has to say, if only to let him get it out. He's different somehow. After hearing what he had to say to me, I gave it a lot of thought. Baby, you know I've messed my life up and never found a woman I ever really cared about. There were a few barmaids but that's been about it. There's never been anybody I wanted to live my life with. You know that too. I don't apologize for my life, but some things I wish I could have changed. Give him the chance to say he is sorry. He means it."

Cindy took a deep breath and held it. She knew Ed would never have asked Kenneth to dinner if he thought Kenneth was lying. Ed only meant well and it would not be such a hardship to be civil and listen.

"Uncle Ed, you never have to apologize to me for your life. I love you as much as Daddy. I always have. Okay, I'll listen to him for you and because you asked. Do mom and dad know?"

"Yeah, I had him talk to them first to make sure your dad wouldn't kill him over the dinner table, or your mother poisons him."

They both had tears in their eyes.

"Let's go back inside. My beer's gone and I want to see how bad the Lions are losing."

"Okay you old softy," she said smiling at Ed, but dreading what was to come later. Just then a car was parking in the driveway next to hers.

Chapter 35

The lab was to be empty from Wednesday evening until Sunday night, when the cleaning crew returned. But the lab was not empty. Dr. Lee and a group of hand-picked students were hard at work. They listened as the good doctor outlined the job saying how secret it was, not to be discussed even between them until later, if ever. They had until Sunday morning to complete the project. That meant complete analysis of the body, organs, blood and other fluids as well as the disposal of all. There was to be no trace. The records of the instruments used were to be wiped clean, meaning time and dates along with the findings were to be back dated; hard drives were to be wiped clean. Then he simply said that human lives hung in the balance. There could be no mistakes. No one would ever know how many lives they were about to save, but if just one was saved that person owed their existence to all of them. The clock was ticking toward Sunday.

Dr. Lee's excitement spilled over to the students. What they were about to participate in was clandestine, so "James Bond-ish," (actually more like "Q").

Lee led the group over to a metal examination table to a sheet covering a body, an animal's body. Once all were gathered, he pulled off the sheet revealing to them something that had not existed for six or more thousand years. The wide-eyed students gasped with awe upon their first viewing. Dr. Lee gave them their moment, for the seriousness of their duties to sink into their student minds. All of them understood that this was not an animal, but a true monster that was unleashed into the world of modern man. Their job was to find a way to end it. It was up to them to find a way to send this thing back into extinction.

As almost a side note, they were told about Reed's coming activities. He was, of course, not to be made aware of the incidents from the next few days and they were to give him full cooperation if asked for any. Reed would probably do the autopsy unassisted, but any lab work was to be brought to Lee prior to being run. If Reed wanted to use the MRI or CAT scan, he was to be referred to Lee. He would stall Reed and take the flack, if any, for stalling.

His clear excited eyes swept from face to face. No one protested. Everyone was in agreement as what to do and what was expected of them. To make sure, Dr. Lee asked, "Are we all together on this?" Each nodded yes.

"Okay, as the "Duke" says, we're burning daylight. Let's get going."

The group started to disburse when Lee said, "One other thing, thank you all."

Chapter 36

Lansdowne's cell phone rang. The sun was out, shining its warm golden light upon the earth. It was going to be a very cold day though. He was sitting on the deck watching sunrise, having his first cup of coffee and cigarette of the day and thinking about everything. His involvement with Cindy would have to wait. He just was not ready to move on to the next level in a relationship. His eyes moved over to where Moe and Glenna's ashes were buried. Moe was gone. Mark's eyes moved to the creek and he remembered how excited and happy she was watching the cold water running through patches of snow on the rocks. It was the time of the ice storm when the ice hung on the trees. Then the sun broke through the light grey clouds, long enough to cause a misty fog and changing the world into an enchanted land, short of fairies and dragons. There were still no fairies but he had dragons of a sort. He knew soon he was to play the role of Saint George, the dragon slayer. He was not interested in answering his phone but did anyway.

It was Benson. He asked Mark if he had any plans for the next several hours. Mark informed Ralph of his house guest and said he would be home until she left. Benson said he had something to show him and would be by a little later. Lansdowne said okay and closed the flip lid to his phone.

Amie came out of the house with freshly brushed platinum blonde hair and sleepy hazel eyes, toting coffee in a heavy mug. She was wearing

Glenna's long, heavy brown camel-hair coat. It was a touch small on her, yet it looked good. Sitting in a chair next to Mark, she took a sip of her coffee. The way she balanced the mug in her delicate fingers made him think she was drinking from fine china. Seeing his pack of Pall Mall's, she asked if she could have one. Pulling one from the pack, he gave it to her and lit it. He said he did not know she smoked. Amie answered him by saying, only in the morning after consuming too much wine, or after sex. The wine, of course, last night was the culprit.

Mark smiled at the comment.

"I bet the garden is beautiful in the spring," Amie said.

"It was once. Maybe this spring I'll clean it up. Glenna was the gardener. My job was to dig holes and plant. She did everything else." He took another sip of coffee and crushed his cigarette out.

"Sorry Mark."

"For what? You didn't say or do anything wrong. Fact is, the garden was beautiful and I let it go to hell. She'd be ashamed and pissed at me about it. She worked too hard for me to let it go to weeds. Like I said, kiddo, maybe this spring."

"Okay. After my coffee, I'm going to go."

"You don't have to go."

"Yeah, darlin'. I do. Got work, remember?"

"Want me to make you breakfast? It's about the only meal I do that doesn't gag someone."

"No, the coffee is fine. Can I take a rain check though?"

"Anytime, and as often as you want."

She smiled a smile that caused the rising sun envy.

"Okay darlin', it's a date."

They sat together thinking. Her, of the future possibilities with him. Mark sat wondering how he was going to be able to track down and kill all the wolves.

Cindy awoke naked in her own bed next to her naked ex-husband. The sunlight had slipped through the half-open blinds, gently coming to rest on her closed sleeping eyes, waking her. She did not want to get out of bed or to move away from Ken's warm strong body. It may be a mistake, she thought, but she had fallen in love with him all over again. Cindy thought of making love with him again after the years of having not. His touch was as it was the first time, firm but gentle. She loved the way he kissed her neck. Goose bumps rose on her arms the way they did when he kissed and caressed her. His fingertips had not lost their touch as they stroked the length of her waiting body. She knew she had not fallen in love with him again. Cindy had never *stopped* loving him. There was a pang of despair in her stomach. What if he was lying and didn't love her? No, she would have known. He was not good at telling a lie. When he lied to her in the past, she always knew. Ken was sincere. They would have to start slowly, although last night was not starting slowly.

He turned in bed to face her. "I love you, Cindy." She looked long and deeply into his brown eyes. She hesitated and then said, "I love you too.

More than you can ever know, I love you." At that instant, she made up her mind to tell Mark. They made love all morning and most of the afternoon.

Benson did not know how to feel. He had another body, rather parts of one. The body was fed on. The fleshy parts of his legs and back were eaten. His internal organs were gone. What was left of the body was lying in a pool of its own blood that was not soaking into the clay. All in all, it was a gruesome sight that made the Sheriff sick. The upside was that a radio receiver and handwritten notes were found along with the victim's identification card. The vehicle was rented. It was the first break into finding out who and why. That made Benson's stomach stop producing acid.

After calling Lansdowne, Benson tried to get Stafford but could not. He stayed onsite until his detectives arrived. He told them when they were finished processing the scene, the things that he wanted. Who rented the vehicle and how it was paid for? Check every hotel, motel and bed and breakfast. Get into his room and process it as a crime scene. Benson wanted to know everything about the victim. Seize everything in the room. Bag and tag. Get a uniform if they needed help. Morrison was already deeply involved. Use him first and then go from there. He told them he'd be on the radio or cell phone. Benson left, taking the receiver and book of field notes with him.

The anger had built inside Benson, now he felt he might be able to direct his anger.

"This shit ends now!"
The detectives agreed. Enough was enough.

Reed was only getting twenty-five dollars a day food allowance so breakfast was at McDonalds. It was closest to his hotel and as cheap as he could go. Sitting and eating his sausage and egg biscuit and trying to drink coffee that was much too hot, he thought today would be a good one to gather his notes and start his book. He daydreamed about the possibility of movie rights. Who did he want to play his character? Johnny Depp? He was the right age and women loved him. He shook the thought from his mind, smiling. He had to write the book first. After the autopsies on Monday, he could dream more.

Amie stood by the driver's side of her car looking over the gingerbread house. In some ways it was large, but not in others. Flower gardens of all types surrounded the structure, painted in pastel colors. It was a fairy tale house, one she knew she could be comfortable living within. But it was Glenna's fairy tale house and always would be hers. She would always haunt the house. Something of her would always be there. As easy as it would be for her to love Mark, he would never love her as he had, and still did, Glenna. What they had was a fairy tale love and they lived happily ever after – as long as it lasted.

Lansdowne walked up to her to say good-bye. She turned from looking at the house and gave him a kiss lightly on the lips. Amie wanted to pull him close and hold him to her. She did not want to leave, yet she could not stay.

Pushing him back a little, she said, "Thanks for making me stay last night."

He surprised her by saying, "You're welcome to stay as often and as long as you want."

"Really?"

"Yes, really. You are a friend and always have been one. I don't have so many friends that I want to lose even one."

"Then I will be back, darlin'." She kissed him again as she did before, then got in her car and left. He held up is hand waving good-bye until the car was gone from view.

Walking toward the house, he heard a car pulling into his driveway. He wondered what Amie had forgotten and had returned for? Instead, it was the Sheriff's car with Benson at the wheel. For some reason, he forgot Ralph was coming by to talk. Mark saw Benson was excited by the look on his face. Mark was not sure he was ready for any excitement.

"Mark, we have another body."

"Who?"

"Don't know yet, but he had these with him." He held the notebook and receiver out for Lansdowne to see. "We can track them with this and his notes. By tomorrow morning we should know who he is and who he worked for."

"Maybe. I'll bet you won't…not by tomorrow. If someone released these things, then you can be sure they took enough effort not to be found, just in case something like this happened. But it doesn't matter as to who or why. You have the most important thing in your hands. I'll call Skruggs and get him here."

"Why? Do we need him?"

"Yes, we need him. We need him to tell us how many bands are programmed into it and if there are sub-bands within a band, for multiple real time tracking. Did the collar have a GPS chip as well?"

"I don't know. Never thought about that."

"If it does, then the body you've got was not the only one watching and that means satellite time. Does the receiver have a GPS chip? You don't know. Skruggs can take that box and answer all of those questions and more. He's not just a pretty face."

"I don't think he's so pretty."

"If you've ever been up to your ass in bad guys trying to kill you and he shows up, trust me, you'd think he was beautiful. Now, do I call him or not?"

"You trust him and I guess that's going to have to be good enough. I just don't know him."

"A hard man to know. Sometimes, I'm not sure I always do. What I do know, in short, is that he will kill without hesitation and knows more than we do about the electronics."

"Call him, please. No hesitation?"

"None whatsoever." Lansdowne said matter-of-factly.

Benson and Lansdowne studied the notes made by the wolves' last victim. They were very good and complete. The notes held the answers, as Lansdowne said, to most questions.

The releases were six in number at night starting back in late May. One male and one female were released together within a specified territory. The last release was in the first week of July. Crawford County was picked for a great variety of reasons. Freeway accessibility and the condition of the state roads were all good. They were well kept, as were the county roads. Sparseness of indigenous population, food and water sources as well as breeding dens, were prime factors. The forests and the terrain were much the same as when the Dire Wolf became extinct.

Franklin and Jefferson Counties were rejected because of population growth and future loss of terrain. Washington and Dent Counties were not considered, mainly because of proximity to a freeway. If all went well, the wolves would migrate there anyway and by then packs would be established. Within five years of the first release date, the animals would have large territories and a substantial population. At least enough that hunting them to extinction would be hard, if not impossible, as was done early in the last century to the Grey Wolf.

Unfortunately, the male from the first release died. He was struck by a pickup truck as it was attempting to cross a state road. The man monitoring the wolves was able to retrieve and dispose of the body. The female of the second release met a similar fate within hours. She must have still been groggy from the sedation. The male's collar was found close to her body. He was an exceptionally large animal and without the radio beacon, could no longer be tracked. He hoped the female from the first release and the male from the second would hook up. After the release of the first two pairs, it was decided to release anymore onto the old logging road no longer in use. It was felt that perhaps life expectancy of the animals would be longer than previously demonstrated.

While Ralph and Mark continued to read the handwritten notes, Skruggs worked slowly and methodically on the radio receiver, testing and checking every chip and circuit. Warren almost looked comical – nerdish is a closer description – wearing the magnifying glasses. Lansdowne's dining room had been transformed into a Radio Shack, with all the equipment Skruggs brought. It paid off. After two hours of scrutiny, he found everything out that there was to find. Getting up from the table, he walked into the den where Ralph and Mark were working. Lansdowne reached into his shirt pocket, took out a pack of cigarettes and lit one of them. Benson and Lansdowne looked at Skruggs and waited for him to speak.

"Well, I found out all that there is to find." He directed the question to Benson by asking, "Where is the collar?"

"In my office safe."

"The batteries are out?"

"Yeah. Why?"

"Leave it that way. There is more than likely a GPS chip in it. The chip works like the one in your cell phone. If it has power it can be located, not just by that box but by satellite – just like a cell phone. The GPS was used to find the collar in a general area and the radio frequency for a more direct and closer location."

"We thought as much," said Benson.

"There's more. A secondary chip, integrated for finding a secondary GPS signal, should have been implanted in the animal. However, a second GPS will not be found in the collar. It's more likely been surgically implanted. In the first one that Mark killed, was one found?"

"Nothing was said about one."

"That makes sense," Lansdowne interjected. "The notes say the first male was killed, as was the second female. The implants took place only after they died. It was so that if the collar came off, they could still be tracked."

"Yeah, but not necessarily by your victim today. I'm fairly sure it was for a close relay through a Com Sat. In other words, the radio receiver would pick up the exact location on one chip and then boost the signal of the second. Then it would be picked up by a cell phone satellite, bypassing a cell tower so that no record was made. It was no amateur but no CIA, or other agency either."

"Can we find out who is getting the information? Can we reverse track?" Benson wanted to know.

"Ralph, we can find out who it is, but right now it's more important to be able to find a way to tap into the second chip, find all of the wolves and kill them," Mark said.

"We can do that. Like I said, it is not ultra-sophisticated. Actually, we can do both or we know who can.

"How soon can we start?" Benson wanted to know.

"Depends on some things but by Monday if it goes right. Mark, I need your computer and I have to use the secure phone."

"Upstairs. Use the land line. It was swept just before my hospital stay, so it should still be clean. Foxtrot X-ray was the scramble mode and Greystroke Delta was the verification code. Call sign – Star One."

Benson stared at the two and wondered just who the hell are they, or were they? Calls from Washington, guns with no imprinted serial numbers, scrambled phone lines, were starting to bother him. While Skruggs left to go use the computer, Benson said to Mark, "I never heard any of that."

"Doesn't matter. After the call it will all change. I trust you enough to forget things you may see and hear."

"I just don't want a visit at home by guys in black suits, with silencers on their guns."

"That's movie crap. If it does happen, call me after they leave. I'll take care of it."

"I'll be dead."

"Maybe your wife and dog too, but I'll complain anyway."

"Oh, thanks."

"No problem," Mark said chuckling, "Let's get back to the notes. There may be more useful intel."

Chapter 37

Cindy Winters, sitting in the restaurant across the table from her ex-husband Ken, was sore, very sore. She had not had sex over the past several years, long before her divorce. Still, she was enjoying the pain more than she did from her honeymoon. Having an orgasm an hour was something she did not know was possible for her. Ken had to be sore as well, but the continuous smile on his lips hid it if he was. No one in the world would, or could have, detected their joyful plight.

Dinner was wonderful. They ate, laughed and talked about things they never could before. Everything seemed new and fresh between them. Cindy was in love again. Truly in love.

By the end of dinner, she decided to tell Lansdowne. Cindy spoke about Mark to Ken and he knew she was truthful when she told him nothing had happened between them. Tonight she would tell Lansdowne it was over.

She slid the extra key to her home across the table. He told her he would go home and get some clothes and meet her there later. Tomorrow they could go to St. Louis, to the Zoo or anywhere she wanted. With stars in her eyes, she said they could decide later – if either of them could walk. They both laughed, looking forward to more intimacy later that night.

Ken drove her back to her car. He asked if she could wait to tell him later. No, she said. She wanted it out of the way. No disruptions. They were starting over and he would understand. Mark was a nice guy and someone she would like Ken to meet.

He felt a tinge of jealousy but said maybe.

Kissing her delicately, he told her to hurry back. Cindy said it should not take long. They kissed again, this time more deeply. He watched her get into her Mustang and drive off.

He felt he had been stupid and such a jerk about things. They had lost all of this time together. Ken hoped he could make it up to her.

A smile again reached his mouth. Good ole Uncle Ed.

He owed him big time.

Benson was gone nearly an hour before Skruggs walked back into the den. Lansdowne was still reading the leather covered book of field notes, made by the last victim. The man's notes were meticulous. Not only geographic locations on each pack, but information about general health injuries, litters of pups, numbers and more. Things were noted on stalking habits, color of the newborn, mating, and growth. He had even started naming them. The guy was beginning to think of them as pets. Growth rates were of particular interest to Lansdowne. Astonishingly, by four months they would hunt either as individuals or with the pack. Luckily, thought Lansdowne, the animals did have trouble producing offspring. The male and female of groups one and two were unaccounted for and had not been seen, so nothing was known if they had pups. Group five had a new litter, but he was unable to check on them because of the search for the Wellsburg child. He thought about joining the search but felt it could be awkward, especially with the need for the radio monitor. Since the collar was offline, it did not much matter. He would wait until things cooled off and locate them by the GPS in the collar, if it was still working.

Skruggs got out the vodka and made each a drink. It was early evening and Warren was hungry. He had said as much to Mark, who agreed he was hungry as well. They decided to call Lonny and have her meet them at Barkers for dinner.

Lansdowne got up from his chair and put ice in their drinks from the freezer. The drink went down fast and tasted good enough for a second quick one before leaving.

Skruggs told him the receiver was going to be monitored and back-traced to the source. They were also able to read, from the last week, the different location codes. They would continue to send a signal blocking the true signal, but imitating it so they could use the monitor to search. Lansdowne filled him in on what he learned from the field notes. Warren smiled his big ugly smile. "No walk in the park, but better than searching blind."

Mark called to dogs inside the house. Curly was first, followed by Larry, then the big brown guy.

"You named him yet?"

"Nope. I was waiting to see if an owner ever showed up. Doesn't look that way. I'll give it some thought later. By the way, I want to show you what Benny sent us. Interestingly different. They're in the shop."

"Anything from Benny is usually of interest. Especially to ATF. I heard Benny was dead – again."

"I resurrected him and got the charges dropped so he could come out of hiding. I think we may be glad I did."

"It won't last. Before long, that little 'Jew boy' will be in shit again."

"And I'll resurrect him – again. He's a good guy with bad habits."

"Yeah Mark, they all go "boom"! But you're right, a good guy."

They went to the shop and Warren saw what Benny sent by way of the beautiful Amie, then climbed into Mark's pickup truck and went to meet Lonny for dinner.

Lansdowne and Skruggs were gone an hour when Cindy Winters pulled into the driveway. The first thing she noticed was his pickup was gone from the accustomed parking spot, but Skruggs' Jeep was there. The next thing was that she had to pee and was wishing she had gone earlier. It was not yet urgent, but she hoped Lansdowne would get home soon. All she could do was to wait for him to return.

Leaving the engine running for heat, Cindy cracked the windows on both sides an inch or so and then turned out the lights. The air was crisp and clear, as was the sky. The stars, shedding their pinpoints of light, lit the night. She often pitied people who lived in cities. They could never see just how many stars were really in the sky because of the lights. The mercury vapor lights lit the streets but blocked the stars. Most city people really would not notice anyway. They always were too busy to look up. With the soft music from the car radio and all that had gone on in her life, Cindy, sitting and waiting for Mark's return, could have been very contented if only she didn't have to pee. It was getting harder to hold it. She was now squeezing her legs tight and rocking in the car seat. It was too far to drive back to the all night gas station in Maple Hills. She'd never get there in time. Cindy was not sure if the dogs would let her in, or for that matter if the doors were locked. The hedge of forsythia bushes, although naked of leaves, would give her privacy. After all, she was a country girl and it would not be the first time she went in the woods. She decided she would try the house first. Nature was no longer calling, it was screaming. She shut off the engine and walked to the house.

Walking through the gravel and over the flagstone walk was something Cindy had not given any thought about, as her high heels impeded the pace she needed to set.

The dogs were at the door growling and barking and hitting the glass in the door with their heads as they jumped on the door. Almost at the door, she knew they were not going to let her into the house. Cindy was going to have to settle for the bushes.

As she was about to turn and walk back, the gentle wind changed directions and carried on it the smell of rotting meat. It was rancid, harsh, and getting closer, not far away from where she stood. The smell permeated the area causing her to gag.

Turning her head she saw, slowly moving from the dark, two large red eyes in a head as big as a horse. The animal moved cautiously into the light, stalking its intended meal. The great canines the animal touted slashed the air as it continued toward her.

Cindy thought quickly. Trying for the door could be a huge mistake should it be locked. It would have her. If it was not locked, the dogs did not seem that they would let her enter. The best bet was her car. Slipping from her shoes slowly, she estimated the distance between the advancing beast and the Mustang. Cindy would either make it to the car or be killed. There was no third option, but she was not going to die without trying.

The fear that momentarily gripped her and almost froze her in place, was replaced with the urge for flight. As soon as Cindy broke into a run for her car, the quiver in her legs was gone. Her long strong legs moved with a speed she did not know possible. However, as she ran so did the beast. It was a race that coming in second must not be the result – for her.

She heard the three dogs, each in a frenzy, hit the door with even more force. The glass was cracking but had not yet broken. Suddenly, the monstrosity stopped to face the dogs. Seeing their plight and feeling confident that it would not be attacked from the rear again, it turned its attention toward Winters.

The wolf's brief stop was all Cindy needed to reach the car. She was inside fumbling to turn the key she left in the ignition, when the beast projected itself through the air, striking and shattering the passenger's side window. Her right hand found the key and turned the engine on.

Sweat rolled down her face, getting into her eyes and blinding her. She tried to clear her eyes by rubbing her left arm across them, while reaching for the gear shift. Pulling the shift back, she stepped on the accelerator only to find she hit neutral.

The animal hit the glass again projecting its massive bulk against it, but this time the glass gave way allowing its head and one leg through. Cindy could smell and hear its hot rancid breath. The knife-like teeth were only inches from her, attempting to slash and cut. It pushed its other leg through, soon it would reach her. Cindy screamed a scream that echoed through the valley. She found the door handle and was outside the car, slamming it shut just as the wolf forced the rest of its bulk into the car, trapping it inside. A frustrated growl was emitted from the beast, as Cindy ran toward the door of the house. The gravel and rock tore at her bare feet, leaving bloody foot prints from her sprint. Reaching the storm door, she pulled it open, turned the door handle and pushed. The dogs let her inside to the safety of the house, but Brownie had pushed his body past her to the outside, leaving Larry and Curly to guard the bleeding, shaken and crying woman. She was safe. For the first time in her life, she felt completely safe. Cindy crawled further into the room, away from the door. Seeing the light switch at the side of the door, she found her knees, and then her feet, enough to make the switch. Light flooded the walk and driveway.

The wolf turned itself around in the car and was out of the window to pursue, what it thought was, an easy quarry. Only it was met by something it had never encountered, some other animal not in fear of it, Brownie. Even though it was over a third larger than the dog, Brownie did not back down. Instead, he showed the wolf his own fangs, crouched his front legs down readying for the soon oncoming attack. The wolf growled louder than Cindy's scream; Brownie's was low and throaty. It tried to circle around the dog looking for an opening and in an attempt to intimidate him. Brownie would not have any of it. As the wolf circled looking for the offensive opportunity, Brownie, still crouching, moved his back legs to keep each face to face. This would be no standoff. One would die. The wolf's size gave him cause to feel he would be victorious. He continued to growl and showed the puny dog his great sharp canines, looking like swords flashing in the light. Brownie only waited.

When the wolf had worked himself into the killing frenzy, he jumped to attack the smaller dog. Brownie waited until it was airborne, then he jumped as well, but not as high. As he did, his jaws clamped closed on the soft belly of the beast, and with a twist of his head, ripped open the stomach. The piece of flesh came away from the underside of the wolf in Brownie's fanged jaws. The beast let out a howl of pain, like none ever heard by human ears. Brownie dropped the hairy tissue from his mouth and quickly turned to meet the pain-crazed beast. The wound was fatal. Blood spewed from the hole. Although Brownie could see the wolf's intestines hanging out, he paid them no heed. The wolf was still alive and a formidable foe, more so now than before. It sensed it would die, but the brown dog would also. Again the wolf wanted to circle but was losing strength from the blood loss. Its back legs were almost too weak for it to even stand under its own weight. Still, Brownie waited for the wolf to make its final mistake. The beast could wait no longer. It again jumped, trying to put all of his mass upon the dog. When he landed, Brownie was not there waiting. Instead, he rolled to the side out of the way and then sprang, hitting the animal in the side with the top of his head. Cindy, inside the house, heard the ribs of the wolf crack. The sound was sickening. The wolf rolled over twice again, howling in pain.

It fought to stand. Breathing was sharp, shallow and painful. No longer could it focus its eyes. The dog was a blurry shadow that still stood crouching, waiting. The wolf worked up one last lunge toward the dog's direction. This time Brownie let him meet. Then, as the four inch fangs attempted to seat themselves in the dog, they missed. They missed because Brownie had it by the throat. His teeth sunk deep into the flesh like a vice. With a sudden wrench of his head, the wolf's flesh and windpipe left its body, while leaving it lying on the ground making a gurgling sound. The great red eyes, which just minutes before glowed with hate and pain, now clouded over with death. It made one last try to raise its head, before the long dark sleep overtook him.

Cindy remembered the desk drawer where Mark kept the revolver. After getting the weapon, she pushed past the two dogs who were her self-appointed guardians. She cocked the hammer, pointed the magnum at the animals head and squeezed the trigger. The sound was a deafening roar that caused her to slip and nearly fall from the blood on the bottom of her feet, which was mixed with the pool of blood from the wolf all over the ground.

Lansdowne, about to pull into his driveway, saw the light which he knew he had not turned on and heard the gunshot. In front of the house he saw Cindy's car, Brownie, and Cindy standing with his gun over the body of one of the wolves.

Skruggs and Lonny stopped short behind Mark's pickup. All advanced toward Cindy, as they left the vehicles with firearms in hand. They surveyed the carnage, not believing what they saw.

Brownie lay wagging his tail as Mark walked past, stepping over the dead body. Reaching to take the weapon from her, Cindy jerked, not realizing he was there. Cindy at first did not want to give the weapon up but reluctantly did so. She stared with the faraway look one has the first time they kill someone. It was the look of disbelief and shock.

Slowly, she turned to him and with a nervous giggle said, "I stopped to go pee."

Cindy Winters turned her head and threw up. Then she fainted.

Chapter 38

Lansdowne carried Cindy into the guest room, followed by Lonny and the brown dog. He gently put her on the bed, while Lonny filled a bowl with warm water and found a washcloth. By the time Lonny came in, Mark had Cindy's clothes off and in a plastic bag and had covered her with a sheet. There was nothing more he could do, so he left the room, as Lonny washed Cindy's face to clear the blood splatter from the coup de grâce. The brown dog lay on the floor by the bed.

Mark joined Warren to look at the wreckage, that a short time before was a monster someone had unleashed.

"That new dog did this," Skruggs stated. He had closely examined the body prior to Mark's appearance.

"Yeah, must have. I never expected this. He's good."

"Yes, he is. You thought of a name yet?"

"Not yet. It didn't seem important. Maybe later. After we're finished."

"We goin' hunting?"

"Yep, and this time it's not men."

"When?"

"Soon. Real soon. I've tried to keep this from feeling personal. I can't any longer. These things are indiscriminate killers and they have to go. Receiver or not, we know where to start."

"You think they're back at that rock face?"

"Probably. We can go find out."

"When?"

"Tomorrow works for me. What about you?"

"Semper Fi brother, Semper Fi."

The two men locked eyes, smiling. This was not the first hunt they were on together. They also were cold killers. The difference is they had technology and things that went "boom". If it was a game, the wolves had the score in their favor. It was time for a comeback.

Except it was no game.

"What do you want to do with this?" Skruggs asked, indicating the body.

"We'll get the gas and burn it."

Cindy woke up when the warm water touched her face. She saw Lonny sitting on the side of the bed with the washcloth in her hands and the water in the bowl was red. Realizing that everything which had transpired was not a nightmare, that it had really happened, Cindy burst into tears. She cried so hard that her body shook violently and her breathing racked when she tried to speak.

Lonny held her, telling her it was over and that she was uninjured. The beast was dead. Lonny, speaking as a mother would to her child that just woke screaming and crying about the monster under the bed, soothed and comforted Cindy. After a long while, Cindy was able to speak. She explained to Lonny why she was even at Mark's house that night. She wanted to call her ex-husband and have him get her. Lonny got her some of Glenna's clothes and said she should get dressed first. Then she would call and give him directions. Cindy said she wanted to tell Mark. Lonny smiled and said she would tell him. Not to worry, he of all people would understand and be happy for her. Cindy nervously smiled as she pulled on the sweater, saying okay, that Lonny knew him best.

Point of fact, Lonny knew just about everything about Lansdowne. Skruggs told her of his childhood. He was rejected almost from the time of birth, until he met Glenna. Glenna was the only one who was ever able to get through his defensive perimeter successfully, and yet even then, she in all likelihood never knew everything. Ever since Glenna's death, Lonny saw that defiance go back into place. There would never be another Glenna and Mark would never look. Skruggs was the same way, but different. Skruggs would eat a bullet and join Lonny in death. It wasn't that Mark was in anyway stronger than Warren, it was just that when Mark met death, he would do so killing. Warren knew that. Lonny knew that. Cindy did not need to know that.

Skruggs pulled the animal's body to the trash heap, dowsed it with close to two gallons of fuel and then at a safe distance, ignited it. There was a loud "whoosh," and then flames shot up ten feet high, lighting up the night sky. With all of the tree limbs on the pile that Lansdowne pruned from the trees, the fire would burn long and hot. Warren loved blowing things up and burning others down. He loved doing it ever since he had his first chemistry set. In high school, chemistry class was a big disappointment. Nothing exploded. The United States Marine Corps changed all that. He learned that household cleaners were not just for cleaning anymore. The enemy used them in place of C4 in IED's. He excelled in every class offered. When something needed to be destroyed in totality, Warren Skruggs was the man to call.

Lansdowne had the hose out washing the blood away. He did not want Cindy to walk out of the house and see it. She would have enough problems over what happened. There was no sense, in his mind, compounding it.

Lonny came outside to talk to Mark. Pulling on her coat, she asked where Warren was at, before she saw the flames. She told Mark, in a very straight forward manner, of her conversation with Cindy. When she finished, he nodded his head and all that he said was, "Okay." Lonny turned and went back inside.

Mark just finished hosing the walk when Kenneth Winter's car entered the driveway and parked. Ken walked up to Lansdowne and looked at him for a minute before sticking out his hand, introduced himself and thanked him for taking care of Cindy. Lansdowne shook his hand, stating she was in the house and to go inside.

Skruggs walked up as Mark was rolling up the hose.

"I think now is a good time to break out the weapons Benny sent. Have you looked at the tree line?"

"No, but I can smell them. Let's walk over and unpack what Benny sent. It's a good time to test them out. How many?"

"Looks like five, maybe six. There's one further back in the woods. I only saw his eyes, but he is a huge monster."

"They're all monsters. The upside is, they're coming to us."

"Yeah, but it can't be all of them. No such luck."

After getting into the shop, they quickly unpacked the new weapons. They were modified .30-06 semi-automatics. The rifles were cut down and fitted with pistol grips and a flip arm for shoulder firing, with a folding bi-pod fix on the underside of the barrel. A night vision scope was on top. There were four, ten-shot clips which they quickly loaded with the ammunition Benny sent. What was amazing was that he fixed what appeared to be a silencer, some six inches in length, at the end of each of the extra heavy barrels.

They filled their pockets with ten extra rounds each and then hurried to the house. Lansdowne ignored Kenneth, who was holding Cindy. They sat on the couch in the den. He walked to the desk and picked up the magnum, giving it to Lonny.

"There are five rounds in this. More in the desk. Let's hope you don't need them."

Lonny gripped the weapon, feeling the balance and weight. "Where are they?"

Warren, who had turned out all of the lights, was looking through the scope. "Tree line, Squid. Same as before, five with one holding back. These scopes make us even with their night vision. How you want to do this?"

"Up close and personal. Needless to say, terminal prejudice applies."

"No shit! I was hoping for harsh language at best. Boy, you are pissed." Skruggs was smiling.

Kenneth got up and said, "You got an extra gun? I'm going too."

Mark, not looking at him, said, "No, you're not. You are staying here with your wife."

"I'm not scared. Those goddam things nearly killed Cindy. I'm going."

"Want me to shoot him in the leg?" Skruggs asked.

"It's a thought, but no." Mark turned to Ken, "Pal, I've got too many faces I have to deal with. I don't want another. You've got a wonderful woman there. Stay with her. Love her. Don't screw up again. You're getting a second chance. Take it and make the best of it. Skruggs and I stand a good chance of coming back. If we have to look out for you, we cut the odds down and you'll probably get killed."

"I can shoot. I'm good. I want to go," demanded Kenneth.

Skruggs said, "I still say I shoot him."

"Blood is hard on the carpet."

Cindy, who was quiet during the verbal exchange said, "I'll clean it up!"

Kenneth looked at her, stunned.

"Ken, no one doubts your courage, but they are professionals. If you got one of them killed saving you, I'd kill you myself. Now shut up and sit down, or I'll put one through your leg." Lonny turned to Skruggs, "I love you. Now go and hurry back. You know how horny I get when you smell like gun oil."

"I thought it was the cheap after shave that did it?" Skruggs blew her a kiss.

"Enough of this crap. Let's go kill something," Mark said smiling. He too, blew her a kiss and said, "I love you too, sis. Keep the dogs quiet."

The two men moved through the door and disappeared into the night, much like the spectrum of a bad dream. They made their way to the edge of the pond and waited. The wolves were advancing, but still too close to the trees that would offer them protection once the shooting started. Skruggs was to Lansdowne's right. Those were his, the three on the right. He set the scope's hairlines on the head of the wolf closest to the trees. It would be first. Lansdowne could not make out the wolf which was still in the forest. There was only a flash of eyes, then nothing. The trees blocked any reasonable shot. The other two were another matter. Soon the five would be dead. That was a given.

They knew Benny had sighted the scopes in already. Both were using the flip-stock. Safeties were off. They just waited for the few more yards needed. The wolves did not give it to them. They stopped frozen, sniffing the air. The fire was dying down and with it, the scent of their dead comrade was no longer in the wind, causing them to advance further. The wolf that was closest, slowly, warily, took a step back. They sensed something wrong.

Lansdowne fired. The silencer did its job. The bullet left the weapon as quietly as one could expect, but when it hit the animal it exploded causing the head to disappear, flipping the wolf several times. Skruggs' weapon had the same effect. Before they could turn and make the trees, they were dead.

The pair of eyes in the woods stared directly at Lansdowne and then moved out of sight, back into the woods.

"We got the five. Damn Benny…did you know about these rounds?"

"I suspected." Then Mark said, "I never had a shot at the sixth. He was smart. He lay back waiting to see what would happen. He's a leader. That one acted as though he could rationally think."

"You want to go after him?"

"No. All the night vision we have now are the scopes. We'd be fresh meat."

"My thoughts but I wanted to make sure. You want to check the bodies?"

"Nope. Let them lay until morning. Anyway, you have to go get laid. Gun oil, huh?"

"I never knew, Squid."

Skruggs took the lead back to the house. They stood back to back so each had a 180 degree range for cover fire, should it be needed. As Skruggs touched the handle of the door, he stopped dead in his steps. The area all around vibrated from the wolf howl, so loud it was. The very earth seemed to bounce under their feet. It was answered a dozen times or more, all seemingly close by.

Lansdowne and Skruggs looked at each other as if questioning what they were hearing.

"Looks like they're coming to us," said Lansdowne.

"Well, crap!   Looks like I don't get laid tonight!"

December

Chapter 1

To say Dr. Lee and his crack team of student scientists were tired as the sun rose on Saturday morning, was a misstatement of the fact. They were beat and that was an understatement, but they were all finished. All of the autopsies were completed. All of the blood and chemistry tests were finished. The only thing left was for Dr. Lee to read the results while everyone else did the cleanup.

Bodies were cremated. All of the hematology and chemistry equipment were recalibrated and all results deleted. In some instances hard drives were wiped clean, in others they were replaced. By ten o'clock in the morning everything, with the exception of the DNA, was done.

Dr. Lee sat in his office satisfied with his students. The impossible was done by these young people, faster than he thought could be accomplished. All testing was run twice. Tissue samples were looked at and compared under a microscope by several people, and then by Lee himself.

They all complained at first about the horrid smell. A couple almost lost their lunches, but soon they all became accustomed to it. The air processors in the building's ventilation units now had the laboratory back to a disinfectant smell. Other than the smell clinging on clothes and bodies, no trace of what went on was noticeable. Before anyone left, they were instructed to shower and change into the extra set of clothes they were told to bring with them. Afterward, they were all asked to return. Dr. Lee had a few parting words for them. They all performed their duties admirably without one word of complaint, other than the smell. Lee was going to tell them they all were receiving A's for the semester. He felt each one earned the grade. He was quite proud of them, as proud as any father could be of his children.

Sitting in his office, he went over all of the test results. That was the first time he had time to look at each. Everything was within a normal range for a wolf, as far as hemostasis went. There was nothing in the results that Stafford could use as a weapon against them.

Lee too, was tired. He rubbed his eyes lightly so as to refocus on the small printed numbers. The drink of coffee was thick in his mouth. He cleaned his eyeglasses and started over with the blood results. Lee was, very shortly, glad that he did. A wide smile crossed his face. Digging through the papers of the first results, he found the one he wanted. Looking at the piece of paper that resembled a cash register tape, the smile on his face grew larger. Placing the two together, he stapled them together and went on reading. He was wide awake with excitement. He was even more excited after he went through everything. There was so much to read and interpret.

Dr. Lee was almost giddy when he reached for his phone to call Earl Stafford.

Reed rose with the sun shining through the crack where the two metal curtains met. The day before, he outlined the chapters of the proposed book and daydreamed of just how smart he would look when he told the world of academics of his discovery. In two more days, Reed could dive into the beasts, on his terms. All of the assets at the State Veterinary College would be available for him, exclusively. His reports would be short and almost complete, almost. He would, of course, save the best for himself and then report those parts when he no longer needed to hold them back. He was satisfied with himself, his intelligence, his cunning and above all, his ambition.

Upon waking that Saturday morning, he was bored and restless. He still had two days to burn. Until the animal carcasses were picked up and delivered, he had nothing to do. Perhaps a stroll through the woods to see and get a feel for the area where the wolves hunted, would be in order. Reed felt he would be safe enough, after all, he was a field researcher and in his mind, a damn good one. Regardless, it would be another chapter in his book.

He made up his mind. He would go and explore right after a big breakfast.

There was no way for Lansdowne or Skruggs to tell how many of the beasts were outside during the night. The wolves stayed back in the dark beyond the tree line so as not to be visible for a clean shot, only furtive flashes of movement. Their growls were heard. The pack wanted to rush forward to take revenge, but the large alpha male held the vicious group in check.

Lansdowne, in a strange way, admired the alpha wolf. That one is smart, he thought, the most dangerous. He could think and analyze. He sent the others to test him and Skruggs, to see if there was an opening; could they defend against numbers? The animal was akin to a general sending in his troops to find a weakness in their defenses, to see if overwhelming numbers were the answer. The squad failed only because the numbers were weak. It was not a mistake that the alpha male would make again. He let Lansdowne know as much, by the amount of beasts responding to his howls.

Yes, they would be back again and again until Lansdowne and Skruggs tired. The animal would do what Santa Anna did at the Alamo, wave after wave, probing and testing until they broke through. One or two would try during daylight, maybe. The main assaults would happen in darkness, when Lansdowne relaxed.

The wolf did not really know his enemy. He had learned a few things but not enough. True, the wolves killed, but they did so for food. Lansdowne and Skruggs were professionally trained killers who did so calmly, with no emotion. As with the wolves, it was who they were. The difference was that Lansdowne and Skruggs knew what the animals would do. They also knew that they had to take the fight to them. Waiting for the enemy to make a move was mindless, stupid. Warren and Mark knew that the animals could launch an offense, but what about a defense? They would have to find out.

As the sun broke over the horizon, the two men had finished discussing a plan of action.

Cindy Winters and Kenneth were asleep on the leather couch. They sat holding each other tightly as they slept. Lonny took a towel and pan of water, washing the blood from the coat of the brown dog.

After dumping the water from the pan into the toilet and scrubbing her hands, Lonny sat in Mark's favorite chair falling fast asleep. Curly and Larry lay in front of the patio doors emitting low growls deep from their throats most of the night. The brown dog slept in front of the fire. For all the prior havoc, it was a quiet, almost peaceful scene. Mark smiled at them. They knew as long as he and Warren were alive that all was secure. That is why they did what they did. That is why they trained for those days, hoping it would only be training, never needing to know it would not be at some point. They endured all of the hardships so that people could sleep safely and in peace with the knowledge that people like he and Skruggs were out there, somewhere, making their world safer if only for a little while. Should one or both die in whatever action, the government would say that it never took place. There would be others to replace them as they had replaced ones who went before them. They watched friends die, sometimes for no useful purpose. Lansdowne, and he knew Skruggs too, died a little bit with each one yet none of them died alone. Each took many of the enemy with them. They fought until the blood no longer flowed in their veins. No flags were presented to families. No medals awarded for valor. They simply became another face in Lansdowne's dreams asking why, to which he could never answer them adequately.

Mark knew what he and Warren would soon do was not just to make the people of Maple Hills or Crawford County safer. For him it was payback for all of the new faces that came into his dreams. The feelings that he had, he should not have. They could get him killed. He had them anyway. It was like before Glenna, he had nothing to lose, but not before he wiped out the terror menacing everyone.

Looking at Skruggs' half-closed eyes which were asleep yet awake, he asked if Warren wanted to keep watch or make breakfast.

"I'll fight alongside of you, I'll die alongside of you, but I'll be damned if I eat your cooking, Squid."

Earl Stafford was sitting at the kitchen table eating eggs and sausage gravy over toast when his home phone rang. This Saturday morning he did not want to hear about killer wolves, or for that matter any other problems. What he did want was to eat breakfast in peace. Outside looked to be a fine day. Maybe he could enjoy it, if he just ignored the phone and did not answer it.

After ringing ten or twelve times, it stopped. Earl continued to shovel the food into his mouth, thinking that by not answering the phone whoever called would call and bother someone else. The quiet did not last. A few minutes later, the ringing started again.

"Are you going to answer the phone?" asked Earl's wife, Nancy. The ringing was becoming annoying.

"Nope," was all he said as he took another bite.

"Dammit Earl," she said, as she pushed away from the table and answered the wall phone next to him.

Picking up the receiver, she said hello, listened for a moment and then handed it to Earl saying, "It's Dr. Lee."

Taking the phone, Earl said hello to his old mentor and then listened. Earl started smiling and the longer he listened, the larger the smile grew.

Nancy, who returned to her place at the table, could not help but see the grin spread slowly across his mouth and eyes. The conversation, on Lee's part, took several minutes. Earl ended it by saying to thank everyone for him and that he would see Dr. Lee again soon. He returned the phone to its cradle and entered into deep thought.

The smile never left his face.

Benson sat behind his desk doing catch-up on paper work. There had been far too much time spent on the wolf thing, to his way of thinking. He was far behind on the everyday mundane, yet important, things it took to run the Sheriff's Office and Jail. He still needed to finish his budget to present to the County Board. That meeting was in eight days. This would be the first year he might be late with the figures. Might hell, he thought, he would be late!

Benson hated pushing paper. Sitting behind his desk with mounds of papers to read and sign, he longed for the days of being just a cop; catching bad guys was so much fun for him. His age was one thing and retirement wasn't too far in the future. Then he and his wife could take some time together. Ralph glanced at her picture on his desk. She was, to him, just as beautiful as the day they met.

He shook his head to clear the thoughts. Retirement was still two re-elections away and unless he finished the paperwork, the County Board might retire him early.

As he reached for the papers telling him how overcrowded the jail was, especially since the last meth bust, his private line rang. Picking up the phone, he barked a hello and waited for the caller to reply. It was Earl Stafford who gave him the information he received from Dr. Lee.

Benson could not help but smile at the news.

"Is he sure? Absolutely sure?"

"I have never known him to be wrong. Lee checks and rechecks everything. He wouldn't have called if he wasn't sure, what you guys call, "beyond a reasonable doubt".

"That's something, but we still have the immediate problem, Earl."

"True, and we only have a few days before Reed finds everything out. At best, a week to ten days."

"Can you get your people together for a hunt?"

"Done. What about Lansdowne?"

"I'll call him," Ralph said, "He should know."

Chapter 2

Breakfast was all but finished in the Lansdowne house when the phone rang. Mark answered it and said nothing…just listened. Benson was telling him of Lee's findings.

"You know of course, this changes nothing," Mark said. He went on to tell Ralph about what happened the previous night.

"For whatever reason, you've really got them pissed off at you, Mark."

"Seems that way but like I said, it changes nothing," Mark said.

"Yeah, I know pal. You be careful for now. Stafford and I are putting a war party together."

"When?"

"Next few days. You in?"

"I'll let you know," and he hung up.

"What's up?" Warren inquired.

"Sort of good news, I suppose. Long term anyway. Stafford's friend in Columbia tested the animals I shot in town the other day. Seems they have no way to fight infection. A cold will kill them. They have no way to produce antibodies. What's more is, they can't reproduce after the second or third generation. They are a laboratory hybrid. They can't produce sperm in the males and the females have no usable eggs. Only the first generation is viable. In other words, given enough time they'll all die out and become extinct again."

"Given enough time," said Warren.

"Yeah, given enough time. In the meantime, there seems to be enough of the damn things around to reduce the present population of Maple Hills. Benson and Stafford are putting people together for an all-out hunt."

"Which means what? We wait? It's your war, Squid. Either way I'm with you."

"No, I don't wait. They brought it to us last night. They aren't going to wait. The leader is smart. He is going to keep trying. Last night he was feeling us out, finding our weaknesses. He was overconfident. He won't make the same mistake. Not twice."

"You're givin' the bastard a lot of credit," Lonny injected into the conversation.

"I'd rather plan for the worst and hope for the best. I want to catch him off guard. There is only one place to find him relaxing."

"His den," Warren said.

"Right!" We can't wait. It's today or not at all. We'll let Ralph and Earl do the mop-up. We don't need the radio receiver. They will."

"You think they are back at the rock face?"

"Yep, or at least I hope so."

Kenneth sat quietly listening to the two men while he held Cindy's hand. Taking a deep breath, he said, "I'm going with you."

Cindy's mouth fell open and she squeezed his hand firmly. The feeling of fear from the prior night returned to the pit of her stomach. Her eyes welled with tears. She tried to speak but no words left her throat.

Lansdowne felt a smile pull at the corner of his mouth. He admired the man's want to get payback.

"No. You and Cindy are leaving. You lost something, but you found it again. Most don't get a second chance. Don't be stupid and waste it. Take her away to someplace safe for both of you."

"I can shoot!" He protested.

"Look, we went through this once. I have had enough of body bags in my life! Take your time in life, and live. Cindy is a wonderfully beautiful person and she wants you alive. If you truly love her, get her out of here. Have a life with her. I'll get us even with the animals. You're not a coward. You're untrained. It's going to take more than shooting to end this...and I'm not sure even then that we can put an end to it. Now take her, marry her and make babies."

Kenneth knew Lansdowne spoke the truth. It was going to take more than being a good shot during deer season.

The color returned to Kenneth's hand as Cindy relaxed her grip. For a moment she thought Mark may have said Ken could go with him and Skruggs. Everyone heard Cindy sigh a breath of relief.

Lonny giggled at the sound. She knew no matter how much Kenneth may have wanted to go, Warren and Mark would never allow it. They would spend more time trying to keep him alive, than hunting. Lonny had lived through too many of their Op's. She silently worried about each time they left but knew they would always return. The only time

Lansdowne wasn't with Skruggs, Mark almost didn't come back. She and Warren had only been married a short time. Mark did not want married men, regardless of who they were, on his team. Sometimes being married would cause them to hesitate. That could cause everyone on the team to get killed. He also had a hard time with widow's wanting to know why their husbands had to die. Telling a mother or father about how it was a tragic training accident wasn't any easier, but they always bought the story. He was never sure what a married man would tell his wife in those intimate moments when she asked questions. The one and only time that Warren did not go, Mark spent a year in rehab along with two others on the team. The rest were dead. Mark was the only one of the three returned to full duty. Even then, it took another six months to get back into fighting shape. Warren was with him each and every day, pushing him harder than anyone else would have done.

Warren told Lonny he knew Mark would be okay physically, but he wasn't sure about mentally ever being able to command a team.

The "powers that be" were not sure either. They gave him two or three more missions to find out if he could take command pressures again. Lansdowne had no say about who went with him. Skruggs was there each time, alongside. After several missions, Lansdowne had had enough and retired. Warren put in his papers shortly afterward, but both knew they would never truly be retired. They would always be contract agents doing whatever, whenever they were told. Those times were few and far in between. For their services they were kept on the payroll, the one that cost the American taxpayer five-hundred dollars for a hammer. Their homes were bought and paid for and Michael Linden was given a new identity. Mark Lansdowne. Skruggs refused, saying he couldn't afford to change the monograms on his bath towels, and Lonny was happy with who she was sleeping with.

"How soon you want to go, Squid?" Warren asked.

"After we get Cindy and Kenneth out of here safely. I think now is a good time."

Lansdowne opened the outside door after he and Skruggs picked up their weapons. Mark heard Cindy choke back the vomit when she saw the place where the beast died.

Mark went out first, closely followed by Cindy with Ken pressed tightly into Cindy's back. Lastly was Skruggs walking at a backward angle to cover the rear.

As they were almost to the car Cindy yelled, "Dammit Ken!" Mark stopped suddenly and looked at her quizzically.

"He's got a hard-on in my back!"

"I can't help it!"

Lansdowne rolled his eyes and Skruggs cracked-up laughing.

"So much for leaving quietly," Mark said.

"I really couldn't help it," Ken protested.

"Shut up and keep going, needle-dick," said Skruggs.

"What he has in my back is no needle!" Cindy half yelled.

Skruggs was almost laughing out loud.

Getting to the car, Ken broke away running to the driver's side and started it. Cindy stopped short of opening the door, turned and looked deeply into Lansdowne's eyes.

"Mark…I just…"

"Some other time. Right now, just go. Ken, drive like you never have before. Keep going until you're far away. Understand?"

He saw Ken nod, as he pushed Cindy into the car and slammed the door.

"GO NOW!" Mark yelled.

The tires spit gravel as Ken reversed out of the driveway.

"You let one hell of a woman get away, Mark."

"Maybe, but it wouldn't have worked. You know how I feel about redheads."

"Yeah, and she fit the bill. Warm and breathing."

"And you need gun oil."

"Like the man said, a little dab will do ya'… Skruggs said laughing.

"You need to find out if it's true. You missed your shot last night with Lonny."

"She's not going anywhere. Let's get back inside. I'm getting a hard-on."

"No one can tell, speaking of needle-dicks."

The back and forth banter ended as they made the door and went into the house.

"What now? Asked Lonny.

"You two go home. Skruggsy, you get geared up. We'll go when you get back. Two hours enough time?"

"Should be, unless I handle gun oil."

Lonny shot him a look and said, "Fat chance, buster. That was a last night thing. He'll be back in a couple of hours."

Walking the two out to the Jeep, Skruggs asked, "What are you going to do until I get back?"

"I'm going to skin a wolf or two. See ya in a couple hours."

Chapter 3

Reed found out where Dora Cox and Robert Carter were living and parked his car on a little used utility road, not far from their house. From there, he could start his venture into the forest of leafless trees. He pulled his back pack from the back seat, slung it on one shoulder and then started his walk.

Where the sun had not been, the leaves of the undergrowth still had frost on them. Still, the dried leaves crunched under his steps. He tried to be silent but there was no possibility of that happening. No matter how hard he tried, each step announced his approach. The original den was about a mile or so from where he parked and having no other information where the wolves were, he felt that place was as good as any to start – if he found it.

As he walked, the squirrels scampered along the tree branches high from the ground, mainly in the oak trees where there were still leaves. There were an abundance of acorns on the ground, yet the squirrels were content to look for them in the trees. Birds stayed up high as well, chirping their songs, more like they were scolding Reed for his invasion than singing to him.

The musty smell of decaying vegetation filled his nose. There was blue sky above that he saw in flashes. The sun was beginning to warm the air enough that the jacket he wore was becoming uncomfortable. It was too much trouble to carry it and the backpack, so he continued to sweat. His flannel shirt was starting to get wet and stick to his skin.

Early Decembers in Missouri can change in an instant, as Reed was finding out. The morning when he started out was sunny, but cool. Now it was warming up. His living in the northern United States taught him Decembers were cold and snowy most of the time. He was too far into the bush for turning around and shedding the heavy jacket. He would just live with the heat.

He wasn't sure what direction he was heading. The compass was in the pack so he consulted it, finding he was headed northeast. Northwest was the direction he wanted, or so that is what Benson's police report said. Reed was angry with himself as he shoved the instrument back into the compartment in the pack, not pulling the zipper completely closed. He had estimated that he walked over a mile in the wrong direction.

A drink of water was what he wanted. Looking in the backpack, he did not find the bottle he bought just that morning. He tore the bag open, looking in each zipped section and feeling for it. It was not there. The quart bottle of water must still be on the front seat with the contour map of the county. He had no choice but to go back to the car. Reed turned and started walking back.

Reed was frustrated with himself for wasting the last hour and a half. It was tough going with no trail to follow, no water and no map. Still, it was early. Sunset was around five, so he had time to go back and start again. He wanted a look at the rock face cave. That was a whole chapter, maybe two, of his upcoming book. He decided to leave out the part of forgetting his water and the map.

As he walked, he looked for signs that he left going into the woods but he saw none. He was sure he was headed back in the right direction. Then, he thought he was going in the right direction when he started out. There was only one thing to do. Look at the compass. That is why he had it.

Unslinging the pack again, he went to open the compartment. The zipper was back all the way open and there was no compass. Reed was no longer frustrated or angry, he was frantic. He was lost. There was no sign of his passing, no trail, and now no way to find the direction to his car. Nothing looked familiar, but then he was watching more for tracks and a game trail than for landmarks. The sun had warmed the ground enough that his footprints, which were in the frosty leaves, were gone.

Reed looked at his watch. The time had just passed 10:30. He was out walking longer than he realized. Backtracking to find the compass was his only bet. He knew that the road was not far away, but without the compass it was doubtful that he would find it anytime soon.

Through the top branches of the trees, the sun was no longer shining. It was blocked by fluffy white and grey clouds. No longer was the sky blue. The winds were moving the clouds quickly and they were getting darker. Weather was coming in. He thought for a minute. The weather this time of the year usually comes from the north or the west, especially if there are snow clouds. Reed smiled at his ingenuity and knowledge of weather. Northwest was the direction he walked, so he just had to follow the clouds and eventually the road would appear.

The leaves in the oak trees rustled as the breeze became a cold wind. Reed continued to walk, picking up his pace as he headed in the direction that he thought would take him back. He silently cursed himself for being overconfident and stupid.

The sky was becoming dark with heavy clouds. The wind started blowing hard, as raindrops the size of quarters fell from the clouds, out of the southwest.

Chapter 4

While sitting at his desk waiting for Skruggs to return, he looked out the window, past the patio and pond, to the forest. His green eyes watched for any activity as he thought about all that had happened, bringing him to this point in time. Faces of those who had died whizzed through his mind. Pushing the faces away, he thought about his new friendship with Benson and his almost love affair with Cindy. He decided he was glad it did not go to the next step. Mark would never have loved her, not like she deserved. A relationship with her would have ended badly. He was glad she and Kenneth would give it another try.

Lansdowne never really noticed the sunny sky slip away, to dark ominous clouds that spoke to the wrath of the heavens opening, and dropping a heavy cold rain. His thoughts moved to the monstrous fiend with the great burning red eyes. No matter what else happened that day, the animal had to be among the body count or it was all for naught. Cut off the head and the body dies. Regardless of how many other of the beasts died that day, that one - the leader, was the main goal. Benson and Stafford could tend to the mop-up of whatever Skruggs and he did not kill that day.

The sound of a vehicle pulling into the driveway caused Mark to break his train of thought. The cigarette in his fingers had burned down to them. He crushed it out in the green marble ashtray that Glenna had bought as a room accent that he was never to use, except as a paperweight. He thought that maybe when everything was over he would consider quitting. Wasn't it Mark Twain who said, "Quitting tobacco was easy – he had done it a thousand times." Maybe he would.

At first, Larry and Curly growled at the sound of the Jeep's engine, and then went to whining and a dance upon seeing Skruggs walking to the door. The brown dog, laying in front of the fire, opened an eye, shifted position and then went back to sleep. The actions of the other two dogs signified that there was no danger.

Mark momentarily studied the dog. His body was covered with scars. A few new ones from the other night but most were old from past battles. The brown dog was much like him. There were a lot of scars. Too many.

Skruggs opened the storm door and walked into the house, pushing past the two excited dogs who welcomed him. He was dressed like Lansdowne in green camouflage battle dress. Warren carried a black duffle bag that appeared heavy.

"You ready?" Warren asked. He was grinning.

"Yep. You fully outfitted, or you need something?"

"We are going to the den? The rocks face, right?"

"That's our best bet. It's close to here and the only place that really affords them protection."

"There IS only one way in or out?"

"I guess. The last time I was there, I didn't really spend time studying it. Anyway, I hope so. Why?"

"I brought something to close it up and we don't have to get too close." Skruggs was really grinning.

"What?"

"The Mark–14. I think twelve rounds are enough, don't you?"

Mark shook his head. The Mark–14 was a six shot, 40mm grenade launcher and only used by SOCOM (Special Operations Command). Skruggs never ceased to amaze Mark at what he could steal.

Smiling, Lansdowne said, "That should do the trick. You know Skruggsy, one day they are going to want all of the stuff you've stolen back?"

"I know, but by then I'll be too old to use it, or dead. Either way, it doesn't matter. What about you?"

"I thought we'd use Beowulf. Not the range of the M-16, but the .50 caliber packs the punch."

"And just where did you get them?"

"The same place you got the Mark-14."

"Well, maybe we can be roomies at Leavenworth."

"Maybe. Let's go and wreak some havoc on the canid population. Okay, Cisco?" Mark asked.

"Okay, Poncho!"

The two men donned rolling packs of ammo as well as their weapons, which was what they hoped would result in mass destruction of the biologically altered wolves.

As they walked out of the door and headed toward the woods, the sky started spitting large raindrops. The wind picked up, causing the falling water to sting their faces. Soon the temperature would start falling. If the animals were denning in the cave, this would be the chance to get the whole pack.

Chapter 5

Reed was very upset with himself. He was wet, he was cold, and most of all – lost. If he had guessed correctly, he should have hit the road by then... but he hadn't guessed correctly. The rain was coming down harder, making walking more difficult and seeing where he was going was almost impossible. The wind had shifted and was no longer at his back, but in his face. Keeping his head down, watching where he stepped was the best he could do. He could slip on a rock hidden under the forest's blanket of leaves or trip over a tree root. He spent nearly as much time on the ground and getting up, as he did walking.

Raising his head to look, he saw the woods giving way to a grassy field. Perhaps he could see farther than ten feet in front of where he walked, he thought.

There was no place in the forest to take shelter. Maybe he could see something from above the grass.

The grass was taller than he thought and even though the rain bent it over, the whipping wind righted it again. He had little choice. Stay where he was and wait out the rain, or go through the grass. Hopefully, it would be shorter and he may possibly see a house or a barn. There were no other possibilities. Going on was to him, the only logical option.

Now he could see the sky. It was heavy with dark storm clouds all the way to the horizon, or what he could see over the grass when the wind would slack.

Struggling through the grass was a labor equal to any of the twelve Hercules performed. The grass tangled under his feet, causing him to fall even more than he did in the woods. The ground turned to mud with the rain and with each upright step he took, he heard a sucking sound as he pulled his feet up for his next step.

He was silently cursing himself for his stupidity and arrogance, thinking he could do this all alone. No one even knew where he was going. So no one was going to sound an alarm when he was not seen. All he knew now is that he had to find shelter, especially before nightfall. The immediate prospects were not looking much in his favor.

After what seemed to be hours, he found a game trail. He could still not see above the grass but at least it was a start. The rain washed away any tracks. Judging from the width of the trail and the ground, it was well used. Deer, probably. He could walk the trail to his right, which would in all likelihood take him back into the woods where he would be lost again. He could also go to his left through the grass and see if it came out near something of salvation. He went to the left with the wind again at his back, as was the rain.

Had he gone straight he would have been a half a mile from Dora Cox's home, where he had left the car.

Again, he made the wrong choice.

Chapter 6

The wind blew its icy cold breath through the branches of the trees that surrounded Skruggs and Lansdowne. As the trees bent, they gave the eerie impression of tall monsters with multiple arms, reaching to grab the two men up. The men never noticed, as their single minded purpose was to make the den and end the murderous rampage plaguing Crawford County.

Mark and Warren both welcomed the wind and rain. The rain dropped in torrents, making their trek harder but covering the sounds of their passing. The wind, blowing between the hills to each side, masked their human scent.

On the left was the hill that held the rock face and cave. To the right, the hill gently rose to a lofty height that overlooked the clearing and cave. Each of them hoped the pack would again be using the cave. It only made sense that they would do so. No one had been there since that day, just over a month prior.

As they came within half of a mile of the target area, they climbed the hill to the right of the game trail. They would have an elevated position from which to fight. If the animals were taking refuge in the cave, Lansdowne would keep them pinned inside until Skruggs fired the grenades. The Mark-14 held six in a rotating cylinder and fired as quickly as he could pull the trigger.

That was the plan. It wasn't the best but under the circumstances, it was the only workable one.

Reaching the top of the hill, the wind carried on it the stench that billowed from the cave. The smell was fresh and strong, not old and stagnant. They were using the cave, but were they there then?

After taking off his pack and reaching inside, he found the small field glasses that Lansdowne had tucked away. His pale green eyes observed the cave. At first he saw nothing, but then a movement from within the cave caught his attention.

They were there - inside the cave.

With the rain it was hard to count. At least four, probably more, were in the cave.

Lansdowne turned a bearded, grim face toward Skruggs. He took his two fingers and pointed at his eyes, then put up four fingers. Warren said nothing, he nodded his understanding. Then he pointed at a place he would take position. Mark agreed, by giving the grinning Skruggs a half-smile. Taking the bag with him, Skruggs moved ten yards to Lansdowne's right and several down the hill. Once in place, Warren took the short-barreled grenade launcher from the bag, twisting the cylinder counter-clockwise. It turned silently and smoothly. Once cocked, he loaded it with six rounds and sighted it for the mouth of the cave. Each round would be on a flat trajectory. For a brief instant, Skruggs thought how unfair it was to fire on them. Then, he thought how cold and wet he was just then and pushed the thought from his mind. This group was the wolves that were doing all of the killing in the area. Fair or not, they had to go.

Mark had no thoughts about fairness. To him there was no right or wrong. It simply had to be done or more people would die. He was indifferent about killing man or animal. There were no faces in his sleep, until he met Glenna. She gave him what he never had all of his life – a conscience. When she died she took everything with her, except that. For him, this action was nothing more than payback.

Locking the butt of his weapon into his shoulder, both men heard the grass rustling from clumsy steps, toward the hollow.

They both saw Reed break through into the clearing.

They were not the only ones who heard him.

Chapter 7

Reed was not concerned with being quiet. Being lost was a large concern and his clothes were totally wet. With the wind blowing as hard as it was and with the temperature dropping, he knew he was in trouble. He was starting to shiver; it is the body's way of trying to stay warm. It wasn't working. If he did not find some type of shelter shortly, he would pay a high price indeed, for his arrogance. To be lost in the woods was bad enough, but following a game trail through grass standing taller than him, was moronic. He, at this point, had little choice but to keep going.

He had kept his eyes on the trail. When he looked up, the stinging rain beat his eyes and face. Covering his eyes with his hands, he saw two rising hills with trees to either side. That meant that he was leaving the grass soon and that the trail led back into the forest.

Forming coherent thought was becoming harder and his body was racked with almost uncontrollable shaking. Well, at least there would not be any ticks, he thought, and he started laughing and then abruptly stopped. It wasn't funny. Reed was losing what wits he had left. Then, he actually knew how much trouble he was in. He did not know how long he had been gone but it was not long. Each step was an effort and his breathing was short and shallow. He was slipping in the dirt of the trail and the matted grass kept tripping him. Reed had not been properly prepared for this venture into the woods.

That is when he stumbled through the high grass into a clearing. There was a cave on his right. The entire hill was rock, covered with scrub trees. The clearing was circled by more grass, with another game trail in front of him. Although the cave was not warm and inviting, it was shelter from the weather. There was only one thing to do, enter the cave and hope there were no other occupants presently in residence.

Taking a couple of steps in the direction of the cave, the smell of rotting meat filled his nostrils causing him to gag.

Reed's mind did not immediately recognize the overpowering smell. His eyes did not see the paw tracks that covered the ground in front of his path to the cave. Not until he heard growling, did he see a dozen pair of gleaming red eyes glaring at him. He stopped dead in his tracks. His heart beat fast and hard in his chest. Reed realized just where he had entered. His stomach was more than upset as he was about to lose control of his bowels and his bladder.

Several sets of eyes turned into large snarling faces, with fangs only rivaled by the long extinct saber-toothed tiger. Hunger forced them out of the cave into the most disagreeable weather. They may get wet, but their bellies would be full to help fuel warmth upon returning to the cave.

He now knew what any prey animal feels, knowing its demise is imminent. Reed was shaking, not from the cold but from absolute terror. Tears filled his eyes. He wanted to scream but could not. His legs were frozen with fear. Any movement was completely out of the question. The only thing that he could do was to wait for the certain death that was now just a few yards away. His only hope was that they would kill him before they fed on his body.

The one closest to Reed, the biggest, raised its head opening his growling, yawning mouth. He showed his huge shining teeth in an attempt to cause enough fear that Reed would not break and run. The beasts were overconfident of their kill. Reed could not move, even though his mind ordered his legs to do so. He knew from years of field study on grey wolves, the next step the animal took would be for the kill.

Almost simultaneously, Reed heard a crack and then the wolf's head exploded, causing him to be showered in bits of blood and brains. The other two wolves, shocked by what happened, turned their attention from Reed to the direction of the crack. The next one went down, as its head exploded as well. The last turned to run for the protection of the cave. It never made it.

It was struck in the back of the head, causing it to do an unwilling somersault. Reed saw its brains and eyes fly from its head. The last lay on the ground twisting and turning, in the throes of death. Its body had not yet realized there was no head to direct it.

Reed heard a man's voice yell, "Down and cover, asshole!" He knew the voice and the chuckle, just as the cave exploded at the front. Mud, grass and rock flew everywhere. He did not have to think about falling – the concussion knocked him down. Reed covered his head, pushing it down into the freezing mud. There were several more explosions. Each one picked him off the ground, only to slam him back down. He felt someone's hands grabbing his arm and the back of his jacket. Looking up, he saw Mark Lansdowne.

"Get up and run! Skruggs has more ammunition!"

Lansdowne half dragged the stunned biologist, as they ran through the grass into the woods at the bottom of the hill. Mark threw Reed on the ground and then fell on top of him, covering him from the next three concurrent blasts. The rain that fell was mixed with dirt and rock fragments, which barraged Mark's back and legs.

The blasts stopped. Mark again grabbed Reed, pulling him from the ground, "Run! He's reloading!"

Where before Reed could not command his legs to move because of cold and terror, he found no problem now. He moved up the incline with relative ease. Mark's grim face spurred him on.

Upon reaching the crest of the hill, Reed saw a camouflaged figure he knew to be Skruggs.

"You want me to level that hill to the ground?" Skruggs asked Lansdowne.

"How many rounds have you got left?"

"Six. Why?"

"See the ledge about twenty feet up? If you can hit it there, it should collapse the inside as well."

"And just where did you get your geology degree?"

"Missouri School of Science and Technology."

"Bullshit. They wouldn't let you on campus." Skruggs retorted.

"Will you do what you do best? Blow up the goddamn hill!"

"My pleasure." Skruggs was grinning a happy grin, as he did truly love blowing things up.

The first round hit ten feet high.

"You missed."

"Shut up, Squid. It's not an exact science."

Skruggs fired again, and again he missed.

"You want me to give that thing to Reed, here?" Mark asked.

"Bite me."

The next four rounds found their mark. The entire top of the hill collapsed into itself. If anything was alive after Skruggs closed the front of the cave, it was not now.

"Are you happy now? You know the U.S. Geological Survey is going to have to change the topographical map of the area."

"Let's get back. Reed is almost frozen."

"You think we got 'em all?"

"All of them that were in the cave? Yes. Stafford and Benson can take care of the rest. I don't think anyone else in the area is going to become a meal. By the time another pack figures out this territory is open, hopefully they'll all be dead and just a bad memory. Right, Reed?"

Reed looked into Lansdowne's green eyes wanting to thank him and Skruggs for saving his life. Most of what Lansdowne said was true. All Reed could muster to say was one word.

"Hopefully."

Chapter 8

The rain eased immensely. Dark threatening clouds still hung low in the sky, with the promise of more of the same punishing downpour to come. When it did, it would be in the nature of a freezing rain. Temperatures were in the mid-30's. For now though, it was just cold and wet.

Lansdowne and Skruggs fought hard to retain footing, as the men half carried Reed. His ability to walk was greatly diminished because of the weather and fear. Reed's body began to shake again, so much so that Mark took off his camo blouse and put it over Reed's shoulders. He was soaked as well, and his shoulder and chest hurt but Lansdowne ignored it. There was nothing that could be done about it.

Skruggs knew Lansdowne was in pain. His eyes were watery and the moisture on his brow was sweat, not rain. He felt for his friend. Warren thought of the time Mark had carried him miles through some of the most God-awful terrain, to where a helicopter waited to extract them back to the world. Both men took hits from enemy fire, but Warren got the worst of it. Mark did not allow Warren to die. Each time he started to pass out, Lansdowne would stick a finger in a bullet hole causing pain enough for Skruggs to retain consciousness.

Even carrying Reed, the time it took to get back seemed shorter than the walk out. Still, they paid due diligence, taking nothing at face value. There could be more of the animals lying in wait, taking advantage of the thick woods for cover. They saw everything, but luck was on their side. There was nothing sinister to see. For then at least, all was quiet.

Soon the woods gave way to expose the fields by Lansdowne's home. The two men broke into a trot, half carrying, half dragging Reed. He was now shaking and jerking so badly that the two could hardly hold on to him.

At the patio door, they stripped Reed of his wet clothes, then took him inside. Mark went to the bathroom closet and got dry towels. He stopped in the guest room long enough to grab up a couple of wool blankets.

Warren had laid Reed on the couch. Reed balled himself up into a fetal position, in an unconscious act to retain what warmth his body had left. They dried him and covered him with the blankets. Reed's lips and fingertips had gone blue. He was going to need more medical attention than they could render. Lansdowne called for an ambulance, while Skruggs stowed their gear in the guest room and snatched a couple more blankets for Reed.

Mark told Warren to change out of his wet clothes and that he would stay with Reed until his return. There were large trash bags in the laundry room to place the clothes into.

Skruggs was back in a short period of time. He had a towel and was drying his hair, when he asked how Reed was doing.

Shaking his head, Lansdowne said the ambulance was on the way. Reed was still in spasms under the blankets. Hypothermia, as well as shock, was taking its toll on Reed's body. There was nothing more they could do for him.

Mark got out of his wet clothes, toweled off and was dressed just as the ambulance pulled up to the door. He ordered the dogs outside. The rain had stopped for the moment.

The two EMT's came into the house and went immediately to work. Reed's shaking limited them as to how much aid they could render. One EMT asked questions, while the other got the gurney. Skruggs told them he must have been caught in the rain for some time, and left it at that. They wasted no time in transporting Reed to the hospital in Sullivan.

As the ambulance was leaving, Ralph Benson pulled into the driveway. He was on his way home when he heard the call for the ambulance and recognized the address.

Ralph met Skruggs at the door as Warren was carrying his equipment to his car. Warren smiled at Benson. For the first time, it was a warm sincere smile. Skruggs had grown to like Benson enough to trust him – to a point.

"It was Reed. We found him wandering in the rain. Mark's making coffee. Go on in, I'll be back in a minute, Ralph." That was the first time Skruggs called Benson by his first name.

Ralph was outwardly calm and cool, but the palms of his hands were sweating. He had grown to like Skruggs, as well. Warren and Mark were cut from the same mold. Benson was relieved that the ambulance was not for either man.

Nodding, he stepped past Skruggs and went into the house. Mark, upon seeing Ralph, smiled and took another cup from the cupboard. After asking Ralph if he was off-duty and Benson acknowledging that he was, Mark poured some brandy in each of the three cups before filling them with very strong black coffee.

"It's a damn cold day, Ralph. This will bring us up to room temperature."

Skruggs came back into the house, as Mark handed Ralph the coffee. The three went into the living room and sat. They all took a deep pull of the coffee. Mark lit a cigarette, filled his lungs with smoke and slowly exhaled. Skruggs grabbed the pack and lit one as well. He offered one to Benson, who shook his head.

After a short period of quiet Mark spoke. He related to Ralph all that had happened. Benson listened to every word, taking the events in. When Mark was finished, again there was quiet. Finally, Ralph told them of his and Stafford's plans to hunt down the rest. He had recruited the best shots and the most level-headed people in the county. People he could trust. Tim and Robert Carter, his deputy Ron Morrison and a couple of others Lansdowne did not know. Ralph went on to say that Earl had four or five agents from around the state. They would start Monday and go out until they were wiped out. Hesitantly, he asked Mark and Warren if they wanted to go as well. Both men said no. Warren said with the group that he chose, Ralph would not need them.

Ralph was hoping they would go, but after hearing about their day understood the refusal.

Warren suggested they all get together for dinner that night at Barkers, wives included. Mark said it sounded like a good idea. Seven would be a good time. Then he said Ralph should invite Earl and his wife, as well.

They all rose and Mark walked Warren and Ralph to the door. Warren walked to his Jeep and yelled back that he'd see them that night. Ralph stopped at the door. Turning, he asked Mark if he thought he had killed all the wolves. Benson studied Lansdowne's face for any deception, but found none when Mark answered, "Yeah, we got 'em all."

Lansdowne in fact, lied.

Chapter 9

By seven-thirty that evening, Stafford, Benson and Skruggs were at the bar at Barkers having drinks with their wives. At seven forty-five, Lansdowne was still not there. Warren called on his cell phone attempting to reach Mark, but each time only got his voicemail. Warren's stomach growled and it wasn't from hunger. Instinctively, Warren knew what Mark was doing, where he was and why.

Quickly, quietly, he told Benson and Stafford what he thought. Turning to Lonny, he said he was going to Mark's house. She saw the concern on his face. The last time she saw that face was when Mark's team was wiped out. They didn't know if Mark was still alive or not. Skruggs was allowed to take in a rescue team. Lansdowne was found alive, but just barely. He sat in front of all of his team members, out of ammunition. Mark was gravely wounded, waiting on the next wave of the enemy, with only a knife. Around him were the dead, all of Mark's team but for two and the bodies of enemies.

Lonny knew that nothing she could say or do would stop Warren. He kissed her cheek and then left, followed in a calm hurry by Benson and Stafford. Outside, he jumped into his Jeep and drove as a man possessed by a demon. Benson and Stafford were in the Sheriff's car trying to catch up to Skruggs.

Dora Cox saw the three leave in a hurry. She took Lonny and the other women fresh drinks and asked if something was wrong. Lonny knew one way or the other, all would be out, if not the next morning, by Monday, whether Lansdowne lived or died that night. There were tears in her eyes. She loved Mark. She and Warren were Mark's only family. Lonny broke the pledge of silence and told all to Dora and the other two women. Dora called Robert over, who listened as well. Shortly he went to his brother Tim, told him what Lonny said and then left heading to Lansdowne's.

Mark sat on the big rock on the forest side of the pond; the one Glenna always sat on. The rain moved out and the sky was clear, stars were twinkling as a full moon rose to obscure their light. It was cold out. The temperature was in the mid-thirties, but the wind had left with the rain. Soon the moon would be high in the sky, lighting the field in front of where Mark sat.

He didn't know how he knew that the alpha male was not in the cave. He just did. Just as he knew that the anger would well up in the beast so much so, that it would have to take vengeance. The animal continued to test him. Lansdowne guessed he killed the wolf's mate that Halloween afternoon. He reasoned that was why one tried to kill Cindy. Maybe he was giving the beast too much credit but, in Lansdowne's mind, it worked. He also felt it would be outraged that the pack was killed off and the den destroyed. Maybe his new mate was in it. Mark hoped so. That would piss it off that much more. The fervor would be too much for the beast.

The moon's bright light cast a long shadow of Lansdowne out into the field, as he stood. Though there was no wind, a smell of death announced the approach of Mark's nemesis. No sound was heard as it drew near, through the woods. The vegetation was wet but it was not cold enough for it to freeze. It didn't matter they both knew each would be there. The wolf bearing down, on what it believed to be its quarry, and Lansdowne waiting for its appearance.

Lansdowne first saw the saucer-sized eyes, red with madness, at the edge of the woods. Ever so slowly the head, large enough to hold eyes that big, emerged from the darkness of the forest into the lighted field. Light gleamed off of the dagger-like fangs. It stopped for a moment and sniffed the air, satisfied that there was no trap. All that waited for it was the puny man. The man was all dark. Even his hands and face, the wolf thought, if it actually thought and reasoned. No matter, he could see him. It was his scent, but he could smell no fear coming from the man.

Throwing his head back, he opened his mouth wide and roared a sound that was not wolf-like. After he finished, the animal again sniffed the air. Still there was no smell of fear in the air coming from the man. This aggravated the wolf more. It roared again, even louder. There was no reaction by Mark, as he stood waiting.

Cautiously, the wolf continued forward. Now, most of its body was visible. Huge muscles rippled under the dark coat of hair. Lansdowne had grossly misjudged the size of his adversary. It was fully six feet long, weighing probably three hundred pounds or more.

The beast seemed confused as it came to a full stop, again smelling the air. Lansdowne did not break and run like all the others. There was another roar of maddening anger. Its open mouth reminded Lansdowne of a manhole. The beast was so frustrated by Lansdowne's lack of fear, it wanted to break and run at him to chase him down and rip the man apart. Yet the animal slowly stepped towards Lansdowne, stalking him.

The wolf was closing the distance between the two.

Lansdowne smiled. It was not a becoming smile, but one that signified that death was to follow. There was no anger, hate or any other emotion. The only certainty was that no matter what else happened that night, the beast would die. It would lead no more packs to kill and turn people into meals.

It was ten yards away.

Skruggs, Benson and Stafford arrived at the same time. They had no more exited their vehicles than Robert and Tim Carter were there. The five men ran to the top of the deck. Robert had a .270 Winchester and was shouldering it, when Skruggs told him to stand fast and not to fire.

"Mark wouldn't be out there if he didn't have a plan. You fire and you could kill him."

"That goddam thing could kill him!" Robert said, just short of yelling.

Skruggs turned and smiled, "Maybe, but I don't think that's his plan. Just watch."

The distance between the two combatants was five yards. Lansdowne knew the desire for the wolf to kill him would be uncontrollable. Any moment…any moment, he thought. No sooner had the words left Lansdowne's mind, than the animal pounced.

As it did, its entire chest and under-belly were revealed. Without hesitation and in a single move, Lansdowne fell to one knee, picked up the shotgun and fired. The round found its mark, striking the wolf in the chest. Then there was the sound of an explosion as the explosive tip struck. Fur, blood, and internal organs, all flew out the back of the abomination. Before Lansdowne could rack another round into the chamber, the wild beast, who did not yet know it was just ticks from death, struck with its full momentum sinking fangs deep into his chest. Both flew backward into the pond.

Four of the five men stood in utter disbelief at what they had just witnessed. Skruggs had a look of misgiving.

"I don't think that was part of the plan!"

They all broke and ran from the deck to the pond. Skruggs ran to the house, turning on the floodlights and then returned to the pond to search.

Five men stood around the perimeter of the pond, watching the water for any sign of movement. Time did not seem to pass. Eyes strained looking for anything, but the water remained still. Almost imperceptibly, a small wake moved from the middle of the black water to the bank of the pond. Suddenly, the wolf's head broke the water, then rolled over the ground, stopping at Tim's feet. Mark's head surfaced. There was blood running from his nose and mouth.

Earl and Warren extended an arm each and pulled him from the icy water.

Skruggs half smiled and said, "When in trouble, head to water." The others looked puzzled. "Rebreather, there are no air bubbles." Warren told them.

Lansdowne rolled to his hands and knees desperately attempting to catch his breath. They watched, as blood pouring from his face pooled below.

Warren rolled his friend onto his back. One of the wolf's fangs stabbed through the rebreather unit, into his chest.

"I think I may have screwed up good this time." Mark said as he gasped for air.

"Not damn hardly, you son of a bitch. You don't get to die. You don't have time," Skruggs screamed at Mark as he closed his eyes.

The last thing Warren heard Mark say, as he threw him over his shoulder and ran, was a weak one word.

Glenna.

Epilogue

February snows can be the worst. Snow covered the ground in a solid white blanket and the cold kept it there. And it was cold. So cold that the dogs went outside, did their business and came back into the warmth. Most folks forgot what it was like to feel sunlight on their faces. The cloud cover was locked in place and forecasts said the cold would linger a while longer.

Lansdowne never knew that Christmas and New Year's had come and gone. He never cared much about the holidays, until Glenna. They were days others spent with family. She was the only family he ever really had. There was Warren and Lonny, but they both had mothers and fathers, brothers and sisters to spend holidays with. So he did not care that the holidays passed by, since he was in a dreamless sleep most of the time. What he did remember was foggy and then only bits and pieces.

Warren filled in most of the rest but not everything.

That night, Benson got him to the hospital in the back of his car, with red lights flashing and the siren screaming. Skruggs carried him into the emergency room. The crew in ER cut off his clothes and equipment, and then prepped him for surgery as they rolled him to the operating room. The same tech, who tried to take his wedding ring off the last time, took tape and wrapped it over the ring. For some reason known only to Mark and Skruggs, he was wearing his dog tags.

Eight hours of surgery with several different surgeons later, he was again in ICU. The prognosis was grim, to say the least. One lung was punctured and his heart had been nicked. The doctor said there was grave concern. Mark's chances of living were slim to none. The rebreather unit had helped take most of the fangs, otherwise it would have been an autopsy rather than surgery. Some of the chemicals from the unit leaked, but luckily onto his body and not inside. He had a nasty burn from it but that was the least of the things to worry about. If Mark lived, he would be in a weakened state and may never fully recover all of his strength. The damage from the first attack and now this, was extensive. It would take time for him to heal; months or possibly years.

Waiting and watching went from days to weeks. After several weeks, he finally opened his eyes to see Cindy Winters standing over him. During his time in the ICU, he was her exclusive patient. Although she remarried Kenneth, she still had deep feelings for Mark.

As soon as he could stand and take a few steps, he signed himself out of the hospital, but not without a fight from the doctors. They lost. He said, if he was to die it would be in his home.

Upon arriving home, the dogs met him outside the door, dancing in circles on their hind legs, happy that Mark was home. The den was full of flowers and balloons from Maple Hill's residents, most of whom he had never met. The fifth grade classes from the Middle School made Lansdowne get well cards. The sixth grade made a banner (that Skruggs let them hang) saying, "Thank you for not letting the Big Bad

Wolf do a Goldilocks on us." Mark smiled a weak smile and called them smart-asses.

Mothers of the children baked pies and cakes, enough for a few bake sales. The kitchen counters and the dining room tables were full of sweets. Mark didn't eat any of them, but the dogs all gained a great amount of weight.

Collin Reed stopped by the house. He thanked Mark and Warren for saving his life that day. Reed related that he, Benson and Stafford had spoken. He told them everything he knew, which wasn't much more than they already knew. He offered his hand to Mark and Warren. To his surprise and relief, they both warmly shook it.

Ralph and Earl both heard Mark was home. They had a lot to tell him. After seeing his condition, they decided to make the story short. Two days after the incident with the alpha wolf, Benson led one hunting party while Stafford commanded the other. The radio receivers led them to most of the packs. Those they dealt with fairly quickly. The Carter brothers killed the most, followed by Ron Morrison and Christine McKay who, by the way, got engaged the end of the second day. Stafford and his group of trackers from around the state, found what they thought were, all the rest. After three weeks, there were no more to find. They were still looking for the who and why, so far no luck. Whoever controlled Reed, the other man, and the rest of the operation, closed down. The FBI took over the looking. They had no luck as of yet, either. The newspapers ran the story but Mark and Warren's names were never used. The local reporters knew most of the truth, but had no evidence for verification. When reporters from outside attempted to find out, the people of Crawford and Franklin counties gave them a very cold response. More like icy…simply said: Go Home. Mark and Warren were one of them now.

Warren called Amie to cut Mark's hair. A few days later she was there. She was shocked to see how weak he was. Mark didn't even laugh when she tickled his upper lip, trimming his beard. Amie left that day with tears in her eyes, wondering if he would soon be seeing Glenna. She didn't tell him Benny blew himself up before Christmas, making some new type of explosive.

One day while Skruggs was making sure Mark took his medicine, a man knocked at the door. He was vile smelling and nasty looking. The man said he heard the story of how a big brown dog killed a wolf. One of his dogs ran away and he thought it might be his. The dog was a champion dog pit fighter and he wanted it back. Mark wrote him a check for a thousand dollars and told the man the dog was retired. The man was about to protest, saying the dog would make him more than the check, but after seeing the grin on Warren's face and the magnum in Mark's hand, took the check and left.

Mark decided to call the dog, Buttkus. He hoped that neither the dog, nor the former football player would be offended. The dog did not seem to mind. He still laid on the bricks in front of the fire, while Larry and Curly were on the couches that flanked Mark's chair.

Late one evening, Mark switched on the

"butt-ugly" lamp. The pain pills he took earlier were starting to take effect, as a wave of relief washed over his body. Thumbing the remote to the stereo, the sweet sound of Claire de Lune played. His green eyes fell upon the well-worn copy of Dante, that he had placed on the table next to his chair so long ago. He picked it up to read, but soon it slipped from his fingers into his lap, as his eyes closed for sleep.

Tonight he would no longer have ghosts haunting his sleep.

Granny Barton, Dave and Janey Malone and the rest, convinced the specters to accept his apology and no longer haunt him.

Glenna stood a post watching over his sleep, as she had every night since her death and would do so the rest of Lansdowne's life.

Stay tuned for further adventures of Mike Linden.

**Please visit the website:
http://www.thelindenchronicles.com**

Made in the USA
Charleston, SC
30 March 2012